"Terah Shelton Harris's daring debut is nothing short of astonishing. To write a novel that has the capacity to uplift you while it tears your heart to shreds is a balancing act few can achieve, but Harris does with ease and endless empathy. We are brought face-to-face with the most difficult questions—of family, forgiveness, and how to make a way forward—but if we can muster the courage of characters like Sara and Jacob, we will find answers that sustain us for years to come. The best writers are brave writers, and Harris has proven herself among those ranks."

—Mateo Askaripour, *New York Times* bestselling author of *Black Buck*

"Every once in a while, a book comes along that touches the reader at the very core. *One Summer in Savannah* is that book. Terah Shelton Harris's provocative debut is beautifully written, absorbing, and brimming with emotion and insight. A poignant, touching, and timely novel that asks the question: What does it mean to truly forgive? This is unequivocally a best book of 2023."

—Rochelle B. Weinstein, *USA Today* bestselling author of *This Is Not How It Ends*

"An unforgettable portrayal of familial tragedy, bravery, and redemption. Harris delivers a powerful, heartrending debut about what it means to forgive the unforgivable."

—Kim Michele Richardson, *New York Times* bestselling author of *The Book Woman's Daughter*

"Terah Shelton Harris blew me away with *One Summer in Savannah*. The grace and ease of her storytelling is a thing to behold. This book, put simply, is a masterclass, a lyrical meditation on trauma, forgiveness, compassion, and love. Harris is definitely a writer to watch!"

—Catherine Adel West, author of *The Two Lives of Sara*

"A poignant and nuanced exploration of forgiveness when stakes are high and outcomes uncertain. In this beautifully written debut, Harris grants us entry into the hearts of two wounded characters for whom running away from family secrets has offered no real escape. This layered story of love and courage reminds us that sometimes the way forward requires looking back."

—Kelly Mustian, author of *The Girls in the Stilt House*

"A gorgeously written, tender examination of love, loss, and the heart-wracking journey toward forgiveness and self-discovery. Terah's elegant prose draws you into the intricately woven lives and nuance of emotions she explores through unforgettable characters. A gentle reminder of the self-healing power of forgiveness."

—Lọlá Ákínmádé Åkerström, international bestselling author of *In Every Mirror She's Black*

"*One Summer in Savannah* is a powerful and thought-provoking novel. Terah Shelton Harris beautifully explores courage, strength, and the power we can derive from all that surrounds us: in the words of a poem, in those we love, in ourselves. Sara's journey in moving past her torments, finding love, and finding peace for herself is equal parts inspiring and enchanting."

—Shauna Robinson, author of *The Banned Bookshop of Maggie Banks*

"Steeped in poetry, place, and compassion, Terah Shelton Harris's moving debut novel, *One Summer in Savannah*, will turn readers' hearts inside out as her characters navigate the vagaries of forgiveness and the boundaries and boundlessness of love."

—Julie Carrick Dalton, author of *The Last Beekeeper*

One Summer in Savannah

A Novel

Terah Shelton Harris

sourcebooks
landmark

Published by Sourcebooks Landmark, an imprint of Sourcebooks
P.O. Box 4410, Naperville, Illinois 60567-4410
(630) 961-3900
sourcebooks.com

Library of Congress Cataloging-in-Publication Data

Names: Harris, Terah Shelton, author.
Title: One summer in Savannah : a novel / Terah Shelton Harris.
Description: Naperville, Illinois : Sourcebooks Landmark, [2023]
Identifiers: LCCN 2022050978 (print) | LCCN 2022050979
(ebook) | (trade paperback) | (hardcover) | (epub)
Subjects: LCGFT: Fiction. | Novels.
Classification: LCC PS3608.A7832845 O54 2023 (print) | LCC PS3608.A7832845
(ebook) | DDC 813/.6--dc23/eng/20221128
LC record available at https://lccn.loc.gov/2022050978
LC ebook record available at https://lccn.loc.gov/2022050979

Printed and bound in the United States of America.
VP 10 9 8 7 6 5 4 3 2

For Leir
I love you.
I miss you, Alice.

Forgiveness is giving up the hope
that the past could be any different.
—Oprah Winfrey

The weak can never forgive.
Forgiveness is the attribute of the strong.
—Mahatma Gandhi

AUTHOR'S NOTE

Dear Reader,

Thank you for picking up a copy of *One Summer in Savannah*. It is such an honor to share this story with you. In writing this novel, my goal was to challenge readers on the definition of forgiveness and what it truly means to forgive. To do that, I tackled a difficult topic rarely covered in fiction.

One Summer in Savannah is a story about a woman who conceives a child after a sexual assault. While the assault is not detailed on the page, it's mentioned in various pieces of dialogue throughout the book. The overall topic was difficult for me to write, and I understand it could be triggering to read. If you find pieces of yourself in parts of Sara's story, please feel free to step away and come back when you feel comfortable; that's okay. If you choose not to return, that's okay too. More than anything, I want you to be safe.

One Summer in Savannah is a work of fiction, but portions of Sara's story are not. There's a person in this world who lives Sara's story every day, and the decisions she made, the decisions Sara makes, in this story belong to them and them alone.

Sara is not the only character grappling with the idea of forgiveness. Jacob also struggles with the idea of forgiving his brother who committed such a heinous act. There's a line in the book that says, "forgiveness…is like a door. You can open yourself up to it or close yourself off from it at any time." Forgiveness can be a powerful tool. It can loosen the knots we often tie ourselves. It can bandage up wounds, large and small. It can heal traumas, visible and invisible. But withholding forgiveness can also cause more harm than good. It can tighten its grip on you and keep you bound to the person who hurt you.

The choices Sara and other characters make are not easy, and it's perfectly acceptable that you may or may not agree with them. But I challenge you to define forgiveness for yourself. Because forgiveness is for you, and you deserve to be free.

With Love,
Terah Shelton Harris

SARA

———

IT'S DIFFICULT TO PINPOINT the moment I started loving my daughter. I wish it were when she fluttered inside me for the first time. Or when I cradled her tiny body seconds after birth. The truth is, my love for her started much later, when the reality of her conception had faded enough for me to see only her, when I realized that she, like me, was a survivor.

Probably, though, there was no *one* moment but an aggregation of moments, many of them happening because of her vulnerability: when she suffered through her first bout with colic, during her fussiness over cutting three teeth simultaneously—moments when a maternal mixture of emotions and hormones hummed through me, signaling that it was normal for me to love her and reminding me over and over again that having her was well worth the emotional cost.

I study her now, playing down in the water. Her long hair catches in the breeze, whipping sandy strands across her golden face, her unafraid green eyes watching, waiting for the next wave. These features—his features—are all I remember about her father. And yet, what I didn't know about him I see in her, like a window into a stranger's soul. Her drawings always resemble, a bit too perfectly, her intended goal. A dog. A tree. A house. Her proficiency for mathematics, in algebra, in trigonometry, in calculus. Talent you're born with, not taught. I often wonder if she doesn't eat fish because he didn't or if she loves to swim because he did. One thing is for sure: she is all him and none of me. And that single thought terrifies me.

"Mom!" Alana yells, pulling me from my thoughts. "How long was I under that time?"

I close my notebook, its lined pages almost blank, and glance at my watch. "Fifty-two seconds."

She twists her full lips and churns her arms to control herself in the strong current of Howard Cove. "I can do better."

Alana possesses the intensity of someone far beyond her eight years. She is already stronger, more determined, more driven than I was when I had her at eighteen, like she is living her life at a faster clip than everyone else.

"One more time, and then we have to go."

"Aww...Mom," Alana says, her shoulders collapsing with the weight of disappointment. The water moves her a bit, and she makes herself straighten up and tread again. "Can't we stay just a little while longer?"

I don't want this day to end either. Just after nine, Alana had leaped into my bed, sending a wave of sheets billowing into the air. She settled against me, her right forearm propped against my thigh, her left hand moving steadily, her finger drawing something on my knee, probably another clock. I wrote two lines of a poem, the fingers of my other hand entwined in her unbrushed hair, my mind churning for a third line. We clung to each other like that, the bed strewn with books, transfixed in the rhythm of our everyday life, surrounded by silence, until Alana's stomach, or maybe it was mine, growled, a deep bellow. We looked at each other and laughed. Alana glanced at the yellow watch (her fifth one this year) strapped to her tiny wrist. Five past noon. Had we forgotten to eat breakfast? Again?

It was my idea to come to Jasper Beach. As I sliced avocado for our turkey sandwiches, I pointed out to Alana, who was masterfully mustard-smiley-facing the bread, that the entire house glowed with the return of the prodigal sun. Down East winters are frigid and brutal, biting to the bone. It had been an exceptionally long winter, with record-low temperatures and record-high snowfall. So when the early summer sun beckons, heating the water to a tolerable temperature, you heed its call.

Now, the afternoon sun gathers at the break of the horizon, and an ashen blanket of clouds looms overhead. A sharp wind whistles around my ears and whips against the gravel beach below. That's the thing with Maine: Don't like the weather? Wait five minutes.

"It's getting late, and I want to get home before the rain." I stand, my left hand saluting the setting sun. "Ready. Set. Go."

Alana wipes her nose, inhales deeply, and dunks back

underwater as I gather our things, which is no small task. I'm prepared—overprepared—for everything. Into our monstrous bag, I stuff a pair of goggles, two beach towels, sunscreen, empty bottles of water, a fully stocked first-aid kit, a book I knew Alana wouldn't have time to read, a second bag of chips we hadn't opened, a safety whistle, and hand sanitizer. I hook the small, pink life jacket over my arm, chuckling to myself for bringing it along since Alana can swim now; she has been able to for two years. But when I start packing our beach bag, somehow, it ends up in there.

I acknowledge the smothering grip I maintain on Alana. Being a mother is a lesson in impossible love. I know I need to let go. That I will have to. And I have. I no longer tote extra clothes, a rain jacket, bug spray, blankets, and garlic powder (for jellyfish stings) on these beach trips. But I can never be too careful when it comes to Alana. Her safety.

I collapse the umbrella, grab a dry towel, and walk to the water's edge. Jasper Beach is a rarity. Heaps of ruddy-brown stones stretch its entire length, from the sedimentary cliffs closer to Old Radar Hill to the caves at the far end. Under each of my steps, rhyolite stones crunch, their polished surfaces rubbed smooth by the sea. As the waves skulk to the shore and recede again, the beach hisses.

Alana pops out of the water, gasping for air, and I dutifully look at my watch.

"How long was that?" she asks, wading out of the water, running her fingers through her hair.

I open the towel and engulf her. "Fifty-nine seconds. Good job."

"I knew…I could do it!" she says, her voice muffled by the towel. "Next time, I'm going to go for a whole minute."

"I know you will, honey."

I bend down to her level and dry her body. It's red and blotchy from the May sun. I find the sunscreen in the bag and squeeze a dollop in my hand.

"Wait. I thought we were leaving. Why are you putting more sunscreen on me?"

I lather my hands and rub her shoulders and on down to her fingers. "Because I don't want you to burn on the way to the car. Remember how bad that burn hurt last summer?"

Alana crosses her skinny arms and shifts her bony hips with the proclivity of a teenage girl. "It didn't hurt that bad."

"Well, I don't want you to hurt at all." I finish and dab a bit on the tip of her nose.

"Mom!" She wipes it off.

I stand as she slips her feet into her flip-flops, and I hand her her bag, a pair of hot-pink sunglasses as she checks her watch again. She smiles and adjusts it around her wrist, clearly pleased the second hand is still steady on its journey around the dial. I wonder how long before this one starts ticking backward or stops altogether.

"Could my dad wear a watch?" Alana asks. "Or did they always break like mine do?"

After eight years, she increasingly wants to know more

about him. Her interest always starts with a question. Sometimes it's pure silliness: "Did my dad watch reruns of *Gilligan's Island* when he was a kid?" Today: her perplexing fascination with time.

I swallow hard to ease the constriction in my throat, a move imperceptible to her eye, and respond. "I'm not sure." My voice pitches up on the final syllable. I never know the answers to her questions. Since she's filled with all sorts of mysteries I attribute to her father, maybe, just as watches strangely malfunction around her wrist, the same happens to him too. But when I answer her, I look the interested-and-thoughtful part as best I can. We've been on this seesaw for almost a year now, and I don't know how long it will continue.

"Why don't you ever swim with me?" Alana asks as we slog to the car.

I am grateful that her tender age often means she doesn't dwell on questions or the answers for too long.

"Well, today, I wanted to write," I say.

As a girl, I had been happiest in the water, floating among the reeds, the water lapping over my body, the sky in its vastness above me. The air tasting like salt and sunshine, like freedom. Back then, it didn't cost much to be free, just a strawberry Charms Blow Pop and the belief you could conquer the world.

"Can we come back next Saturday?"

"We'll see."

"Hold on," she says, stopping and foraging through her

bag. When she finds her yellow notebook, she flips to the page with *MOM* written across the top.

"See your page? It's almost blank. If we come back next weekend, then you can swim," she says, her emerald eyes dancing. "It could be an LT task, Mom."

Alana has built her life around time. The minutes it takes to brush her teeth. The seconds she can hold her breath. The hours to finish a drawing. But it is the missing time, time spent sleeping, at school, or doing chores—what she deems her lost time—that she obsesses over the most. What could she accomplish in the eight hours she sleeps, she often wonders. Her Lost Time notebook lists things she feels she misses during Lost Time. Activities like putting together a five-thousand-piece puzzle (eight hours) and memorizing the dance routine to "Thriller" (two hours) fill the pages.

"We'll see."

But again her mind is already moving ahead. She's focused on more reminders in her notebook, like the one that causes her to start bouncing as she walks. "My Google project! What about the Google Science Fair? Can I do it? Pleeeaaassseee! I'm finally old enough."

I hold my smile, hoping it doesn't look nearly as lopsided as it feels, while my mind churns and a flutter of panic knifes my heart. Talk of the Google Science Fair started when she read an article about one of the finalists. Six at the time, Alana had been two years too young to participate, a reprieve I know is now up. Still, I hadn't expected this quite so soon. I thought I had at least another month until the applications opened.

I sift through various responses I had planned for this moment, fully aware none will be adequate, and decide on the noncommittal choice: "We'll see."

Alana's steps slow. "You never say yes. You never let me do anything."

Her words slap me, hard. Suddenly, I am aware of myself, exposed, as someone I don't recognize.

I clear my throat and keep my voice level. "What about today?"

"It was your idea." Alana kicks the sand with each delayed step. Her head is tucked, her arms dangling, her bag trailing behind her.

My mind whirs with the complications her participation in the Google Science Fair would introduce. Winners' and finalists' names, pictures, and projects are published online and circulated for the world to see.

No, I have to focus on salvaging the rest of our good day. Such a day is not to be wasted.

"Well…I thought I would let you pick where we eat, but since everything is my idea…" I sigh playfully. "I guess we'll just eat at home."

In a blink, her expression changes again, from disappointment to jubilation. "Can we go to McDonald's?" she yells. Her voice carries across the water, disturbing a flock of seagulls. "Please! Please! Please!"

I smile wide.

"Yessss! Thank you! Thank you! Thank you!"

"Are you sure you wouldn't prefer fish chowder from Helen's?" I tease.

As Alana bounces and rattles off her order ("I want a cheeseburger. No, I had that last time. A caramel frappé! A big one!"), I inhale and exhale deeply, loosening the knot in my chest, feeling slightly relieved that I avoided this hurdle. For now.

"Mom," Alana says a few steps behind me as we reach the parking lot. "Wait for me."

"You're the one moving like a turtle."

"Nuh-uh."

"Oh no?" I say, securing the heavy bag up on my arm. "What if I beat you to the car?"

She smiles, revealing a row of slightly crooked and spaced-out teeth whose future behind a string of braces is all but certain, before darting the remaining feet to the car. Her long legs quickly outpace mine; her laughter fades in the distance between us.

———

In the booth, even as Alana smacks on her chicken nuggets and fries dipped in a concoction of mayo and ketchup, her large caramel frappé at her fingertips, she doodles in her notebook, stopping only to check her watch. She blackens the lines of what looks like a box with buttons and levers, her tongue protruding from the side of her mouth, a cute quirk she's had since she was four. Underneath the box, a string of numbers and mathematical equations stretches the width of the notebook and continues for several lines.

Before, an afternoon at the beach and a trip to McDonald's would have been enough to fill her for days. Such treats are rare, indeed, and not expected. I could replay the day for her, keeping the outing at the forefront of her mind until the next time. I am a master of distraction.

But as she grows older, my distractions don't transmit their old potency and dilute far sooner than desired. Her ability to focus after a camera flash is improving. It's only a matter of time before she sees right through me, through all of this.

The noise level crescendos and plummets as families flood in and out. Restless kids bark their orders before scurrying off to the play area. Two girls from Alana's class stop and say hello. As always, I wish they would invite her to join them. They never do, and I know she would not accept anyway. Alana hates school and displays an even deeper aversion to the kids, especially the girls, in her class. But it doesn't stop me from hoping that she can be a normal eight-year-old who watches cartoons, listens to One Direction, and engages with humans, not just ideas. After acknowledging her, the girls move on, arm in arm, giggling, unbeknownst to Alana, who barely lifts her head to look at them, let alone speak. I utter apologetic hellos to their parents as they navigate to clear tables, balancing trays of french fries and Big Macs around darting kids.

Not that I try to join the adults either. Like my daughter, I am lost in my own mind. The welt from Alana's "you never let me do anything" still smarts. I am just as aware of my prohibitions as she is. No, we aren't going to visit Grandpa and Sylvia. No, you can't have a Facebook or Instagram account. No, you may not meet your grandmother.

There's so much I will one day have to tell her about the basis of these *nos*, the origin. It's a harsh truth to face, about me, her, and him. She will ask about him again. And not simple questions. She'll ask how we met or why he isn't here or why I never talk about him. What do you say to your daughter who is half the DNA of a person who causes your heart the daily battle of forgiveness versus vengeance?

This cowardice embarrasses and shames me. I know I shouldn't be afraid of my past, but I am.

Until that day, I do need a win, and not a temporary one. I need to say yes, and not to a large, caffeinated coffee drink. A *yes* to make up for all the *nos*. A *yes* to buy me time to become brave enough to tell her the truth.

I gulp, pushing down the unease that chokes my dry throat, and force the words out. "Is that your project?"

She nods as she slurps the last of her drink.

"What's it about?"

"Interconnectedness of all things and the realization that instantaneous travel…"

I barely hear her; in my distracted mind, her voice trails off as if someone has turned down the volume. My heart pounds and aches all at once at my decision. Everything in me signals that flight instinct that has served me well, that warns me not to make this choice. And yet, when she finishes speaking, I say, "Okay, you can enter the fair."

Alana stares at me, her mouth agape. "Really?"

I nod several times and force a smile, my fingers pumping my straw in and out of my empty cup.

Alana's eyes widen, and her smile broadens before she leaps out of her chair and hurls herself into my arms. Her classmates stare, then snicker at Alana's overt sign of affection. A current of heat runs through my body. I hold her, kissing her still-damp head and inhaling the scent of her, all coconut oil and salt water, and remind myself that this, this is all that matters. Then, she fist-pumps the sky, and she's peppering me with a barrage of questions: Can we submit her idea tonight? How long do I think the entire process will take? Do I think she can win? To all I answer: we'll see.

As we gather and pitch our trash, Alana begging for a second frappé before returning her focus to her project, I finally feel layers of tension dissipate, my slumped shoulders lifting. I have done it. I have bought myself time in having to answer the truly difficult questions.

Time. It is the word that echoes in my head as Alana settles into the front seat while shadows grow deeper around us. The rain stayed away till now, and the air snaps with an ominous feeling. Flashes of light pulse, and in return, a rippling wave of thunder roars. *Time.* How much time?

"Mom," Alana says, stifling a yawn as I start the car. Before I turn onto Rogue Bluff Road and hit U.S. Highway 1 back to Lubec, she will be asleep. "Can you recite a poem?"

"Which one would you like?"

"The one about the tiger."

"Tyger Tyger, burning bright
In the forests of the night;
What immortal hand or eye,
Could frame thy fearful symmetry?"

I've been reciting poetry to Alana since her birth. For me as a child, bedtime stories consisted not of tales from Dr. Seuss or Walt Disney but of the poems of Frost, Tennyson, and Brooks. I am the daughter of a gentle but capricious father with an unapologetic love of poetry. He sees the world through a prism of language, blending into magical lines and stanzas. That sounds rather beautiful, but if I'm being honest, this "love" of his can be as alienating, even as destructive, as it is astounding.

But I'm not dwelling on my father right now. Poetry has become as much my and Alana's realm as it is his. Speaking the words of the prolific Blake makes me consider my own dry spell. Two decent poems in six months? Definitely not okay for a poet who is supposed to be finishing her second collection.

When I wrote my first collection, inspiration pumped through me. Poetry was an outlet for everything I couldn't say to those I needed to say things to. I didn't expect to be published or garner enough royalties to put a modest down payment on our house and supplement my measly teaching salary—but I did. Nearly unheard of these days. But with the high school's abrupt closure and writing becoming my sole income, my reason for writing became less of an outlet and more of a necessity, and the words dried up.

I follow the winding, lonely Highway 1 out of Machiasport toward Lubec, population 1,652 and shrinking, the eastern-most town in the continental United States, four hours from an airport, and our home for the past four years. At night, there isn't much on the road. The occasional headlight pierces the black-stained sky; an abandoned building or sporadic house rises from the dead earth. In twelve hours, it'll be a different place. Under the morning sun lie green meadows spangled with purple lupines vying for attention against the sprawling horizon and sporadic views of the gray-blue waters of the Bay of Fundy.

There, host to some of the highest tides in the world, I'm home. I grew up along the high tides and salt marshes of Georgia's lower coastal plain. *"The tides are in our veins, we still mirror the stars,"* my father often quoted. Every day, the tide rolls out, new water rolls in, with no memory of yesterday, a fitting refuge.

I glance at Alana; her chin rests on her chest, her seat belt cutting into her sun-kissed cheek. I contemplate repositioning her, when the shrill ring of my cell phone breaks my thoughts. Eyes still on the road, I rummage through my purse. The options of who can be calling are limited to the fingers on one hand. The word *Dad* illuminates my display screen when I finally hold my phone up.

"Hi, Dad. I was just thinking about you."

I know his response will not be a typical greeting.

I was nine years old when my father started incorporating poetry into his speech. He finds peace in poetry, spending hours every day studying the artistry of it in all its forms, styles, and rhetoric. It brings a fresh sense of life to communicating, he once told me when he still spoke in prose. After my mother died in a car accident when I was five, words became difficult for him, and he spoke less and less. Eventually, other people's words became his way entirely.

I wait for his mellifluous, basso profundo voice, which resonates with confidence and only hints at his Georgia roots. Everyone close to Dad gets their own special greeting. Mine? A Sara Teasdale:

I thought of you and how you love this beauty,
And walking up the long beach all alone
I heard the waves breaking in measured thunder
As you and I once heard their monotone.

But instead:

"Sara, it's Sylvia."

Sylvia and my father have been companions, neighbors, and coworkers in his bookstore for over twenty years. As a child, I secretly hoped that they would get married, but their quirks (my father's speech and Sylvia's refusal to share either her house or his) prohibit it. Sylvia is also a confidant of mine, but she is not someone who calls me from Dad's phone. Hearing her voice—hushed, serious but calm, loving, all at once—I'm taken back in time. It's the same tone she used to coax me out of bed after I learned of my pregnancy nearly nine years ago. Her voice pushes at those old memories, another reminder that my wounds have resisted healing after all this time.

"It's your father, hon." I count the number of breaths I take before she continues. Three. "He…he…had a heart attack."

I grip the phone tighter. "Is he…"

"He's stable."

"What happened?"

"He's been under a lot of pressure at work."

"Pressure…?" My father runs a tiny bookstore, Poetry & Prose, and while I'm sure it offers its own kind of challenges, I don't understand—

"The Barnes & Noble closed a few months ago," Sylvia says, interrupting my thoughts, "so he's been rearranging the store, moving whole sections around. Redecorating. Expanding, really. We're the only bookstore left now."

Sylvia continues, her voice shaky with the effort of holding back tears. "I've been begging him to let Jacob help him, but you know your father."

I picture him, boxes in his arms, with an unapologetic tilt of his head, his deep-set eyes bright with pride and surrounded by thin, rectangle frames that rest low on the bridge of his prominent nose, saying:

"Be wise as thou art cruel; do not press
My tongue-tied patience with too much disdain;
Lest sorrow lend me words and words express
The manner of my pity-wanting pain."

My mind, seconds before stagnant from the shock, snaps to with questions: Why didn't he tell me about the expansion? How is he paying for it? Who is Jacob? The weight of Sylvia's tears keeps these questions tamped down in my throat, leaving room only for the pertinent one.

"Where's he now?"

"They just wheeled him into surgery."

A piercing siren squeals through the phone. I envision her pacing outside the hospital's emergency room, her gray locs shaking as she moves, her black reading glasses perched on top of her head.

The siren fades, and I hear her say, "You need to come home."

I stare at the road, trying to construct the memories of a place I called home for eighteen years. The intoxicating sweet smells of magnolia blossoms that perfume the South. Lazy Sunday afternoons on Dad's porch, curled up with a good book, a glass of sweet tea within arm's reach. The coiling strands of kudzu vines that blanket everything. A place I swore I would never return to.

"Sara, did you hear me?" Sylvia asks. She draws a long breath, like a smoker taking a drag. "Your father needs you."

I want to remind her, of all people, why I left in the first place. That even my ill father can't make me step foot back in Savannah.

But all I say is "I'll leave in the morning."

JACOB

———

MY BOAT LURCHES, ITS motion propelling me forward, then rocking me back. Though I can hear the soft whirr of the trolling motor, the boat remains stuck. I am doing something wrong. Again.

The engine growls, louder this time, as I try once more to start it. The rumble echoes across the water like a skipping stone and sends a pair of seagulls retreating into the sky.

"You're gonna flood it," a man wearing a blue baseball hat in the next boat slip yells. "Take it easy."

His friend laughs in concert. Another man walking along the dock holding a knot of fishing nets stops to also watch my folly. From their exaggerated movements, my mind tricks me into hearing *tourist* delivered with disgust along the afternoon breeze.

In some ways, I am a tourist. Though only an hour south, Hird Island, where I've been for two months, seems like an entire continent away from where I grew up in Savannah.

Culturally, they can't be more different, and Hird Island offers the quietness and peace I crave. The isolation too. There are no stores or post offices. There are only two ways on and off the island, by boat or by single-engine aircraft.

The local in the baseball hat ambles toward me as if he hasn't made up his mind if he wants to come closer. "Do yew need he'p?" he calls when he's still a good ten-foot pole away, his accent a topography of dropped consonants and stretched vowels.

I wave him away before he reaches my boat. "I have a PhD in astrophysics from Columbia University. Surely I can deduce my own shortcomings."

The man raises his hands in concession and walks away, shaking his head in mockery.

"In addition to an MPhil in astrophysics, an MA in astronomy, and a BA in physics—from Harvard," I mutter under my breath as my fingers clumsily flip through the manual, desperate to recover the answer.

What did it say about engine flooding? Hold the throttle? Lift the throttle? Is that on page thirteen or page fourteen? Hearing laughter again, I clench my jaw and turn away from the locals. I would rather sleep on this boat than ask for their help.

Another boat slows against the current of the river and pulls into the slip next to mine. Locke, a short man, stout through the barrel of his body, stands on the bow and drops the anchor, sending it crashing into the water. He gives it a tug, setting it into the muck on the bottom of the river, and ties it off at the bow. Even new residents know his name because he makes sure they do, as soon as they arrive. Newcomers to the island aren't welcome until Locke, the unofficial king of the water, approves them. But I'm not a newcomer. I've known Locke my entire life.

"How are you adjusting?" he asks, grabbing a second rope and jumping down to the dock where he ties the boat to a metal cleat. On his way up the shore, he stops at my boat, his thumbs hooked in his pockets.

"There's a term in physics, *entanglement*. It's when two subatomic particles interact. They can separate, but no matter how far apart they get, they are always connected." I stretch my six-foot, three-inch frame to the full extent, satisfied with my answer.

Locke opens his mouth to speak, but after a pause, he laughs energetically, his aging ponytail, striated with gray, bouncing.

I laugh too, a strained chuckle that catches in the back of my throat, not because what I said was funny but because I want to mask my frustration. It seems impossible to analyze a question and then contemplate an evidence-based response all while someone is watching, waiting for a reply. I find the entire practice tiresome and impossible to assimilate.

"I'll take it that you are doing well." Locke nods as if to reinforce his conclusion.

This statement is an excellent illustration of Locke's

ability to find solutions to my social problem. He knows I don't belong but persists in his attempts to ensure I do. I would have been satisfied with our relationship for this reason alone, but he has proved to be more philosophical than the typical boat-loving local, a characteristic that probably helped solidify his friendship with my dad.

"I don't breathe well on land," he had told me when we reconnected two months ago, as we bobbed on the water in our respective boats, mine flooded for the first time. "The water's rhythm is a vital factor to my inner peace."

I understood. I'm more comfortable in the stars than I am on Earth, where I feel as if I'm stumbling about with my shoes on the wrong feet. I was safe in the stars. Safe from her face. Safe from Daniel's, my family's, the truth's light. "'*A calmness that always dissolved far sooner for most*,' my father used to say," I replied.

Locke stared at me. "Why are *you* out here?"

And I knew that he was not asking why I was on this boat right then but why I'd moved to the island at all.

Something in his eyes, something empathetic, made me open up to him.

"I'm chasing something." I sighed. "Someone."

He nodded. "Ah. The White Rabbit."

"I'm no Alice."

"And yet you're following something to see where it goes. Hmm…"

I masked my fear with a nervous chortle. "Yeah."

"I once chased the White Rabbit," he said, looking past me. "Stumbled through Wonderland."

Not caring if I won his favor but already knowing it'd be smart of me to, I accepted his game.

"What happens if I catch it? The White Rabbit?"

His eyes burned into mine. "Different outcome for everyone. The only way to find out is to go down the rabbit hole."

He studied me, searching for something affirming in my eyes. When he found it, he extended his hand, then quickly pulled me into a hug, welcoming me back to the island. He rattled off some rules: Side-to-side and Mediterranean mooring of vessels were not allowed. Quiet hours were to be observed between 10:00 p.m. and 6:00 a.m. A nickname he gave me, Doc, soon followed, the makings of a new friendship.

Now, I try again to answer his question, this time with a lie I hope is obvious only to me. "I am doing well, yes. Today I'm going to work on cleaning up the land."

He takes visual inventory of the newly purchased yard equipment in my boat. "That property has been vacant for years. You're gonna have a hell of a job on your hands."

"I have all the tools I need."

He looks at me, squinting in the bright sun. "So, what are you waiting for?"

I turn and look in the direction of the locals. They've all moved on except the man untangling the knot of fishing nets, who watches me with a look of amusement.

"It is likely I have flooded the engine," I say in a lowered tone.

"Again?"

"Again."

"Don't pay him any mind," Locke says as his eyes follow mine. "A real fisherman would never allow his nets to knot."

"Excellent observation," I say, finding Locke's assessment both satisfying and noteworthy.

"Can I help?"

"I'm perfectly capable of figuring this out," I say, reaching for my manual. "I have my manual right here."

"A manual?"

"Of course."

"You learned how to drive a boat by reading a book? I remember your father teaching you."

"He did, but I needed some refreshing. And I don't believe we can accurately refer to it as a book. This is a handbook, or a booklet, if you will. But," I say as he squints this time, I can tell, not at the sun, "yes, I learned how to operate a boat by reading a manual."

"Boats are like women, Doc. They are unpredictable. You can't figure either of them out by reading a book...um... manual." His laugh is a cheerful hoot. "Move the shift lever back to neutral, hold only the throttle button, and move the throttle lever forward just a little."

I do as he says, and the engine turns over immediately.

His face relaxes, his version of a smile. "Keep the engine at about 1,000 to 1,400 rpm for a minute or two to warm it up.

After that, lower the idle throttle down completely, and then back the boat up."

"Thank you," I say, committing these instructions to memory.

"You know…you could try renaming her," he says, gently running his hand across the bow, almost petting it. "*Ocean Breeze* is a horrible name for a boat."

"I read that it's bad luck to rename a boat."

He flicks his hand. "No matter what happens to a boat, people blame the name. If you need a new sparkplug in ten years…it's because you renamed it. Bird shits on it? It's the name. What's gonna happen is gonna happen. New vinyl on the side isn't gonna make a damn bit of difference in that."

"What do you name a boat?"

"A name that means something to you."

I glance over his shoulder at his boat's name. *Lucy Belle*. His daughter.

Again, he follows my eyes. "I was never one of those guys who name their boats after their wives. Hell…they come and go. But Lucy will always be my daughter."

A name—*her* name—pushes to mind, almost willing me to speak it.

I don't.

When Locke shuffles his feet, I thank him for his help and advice, back the boat out of the slip, and pull away, leaving a gentle wake and the locals' mocking applause behind me.

The marina narrows into a fine thread of pale-blue horizon, pressed between the light sky and the calm sea, until it is submerged completely.

My eyelids lower as I draw in a long, deep breath, inhaling through my nose for a few beats and exhaling through my mouth, measured and deliberate, as my shoulders ease.

Hird Island is a three-square-mile finger of land that seemingly belongs to both the land and the sea. Fed by a maze of twisty waterways that wash into Doboy Sound, on the east side a thick marsh protects the island from the Atlantic Ocean, which stretches unbroken all the way to Africa. Live oaks shield the mainland, nearly ten miles to the west, with a dense canopy of branches, roots snaking along the ground like lava tubes and stretching as far below as the branches above.

On the final turn, my inherited house, flanked by two live oaks that clog the sunlight, emerges into view. I acquired the house unseen—well, unseen with my adult eyes. It is nothing special, a gray-washed cottage with royal-blue doors hoisted on wooden stilts above a yard choked with weeds, its paint fading and flaking and the lace curtains in the windows yellowing with age.

Weather-beaten and neglected, it's the least exciting, the least picturesque, and the least noteworthy of all the places I've lived. And yet, every morning I wake here, where there's nothing but light and water and stars and time, of all the places I've lived, it's the only one that feels like home. It's not much, but it allows me to be here, present, and that's enough for now.

Time stops or reverses itself for no one. As an astrophysicist, I understand time and its demands better than anyone. But comprehension is different from truth.

—

I ease into one of my inherited rattan chairs on the screened porch. My muscles ache after hours of work in a yard that has fallen into such a state of disrepair. I cut the grass, which was at least a foot in some spots. I pulled weeds that had run amok and wrapped themselves around flowers and sprouted up along the house. Even as the sun beat down, I took comfort in the work, the act of doing something that serves no practical purpose other than doing.

After a long shower, my body craves sleep, but my nightly routine beckons. I engulf myself in Whitman, Yeats, and Dunbar anguishing over language I can't fully comprehend, tamping down my desire for literal certainty with every stanza I read. There's not much embellishment in me. Just facts. And yet, I press on, feeling the words pulling at me. She calls me to do this, to follow the instruction of my other new friend, the bookstore owner. I sit on the porch, watching the way tall grass sways with the grace of a dancer. Soon, the sun will retire, and casually, the night sky will be electrified with balls of light millions of light-years away, sweeping to the limits of eyesight. I am amazed by their brightness and endurance every time I look up at them.

Tonight, also, I wait for her. In the beginning, she visited frequently, first on Poker Flat in Alaska, and now here, curling up in an Adirondack chair, barefoot, her knees tucked to her chest, her favorite sitting position. She always wears yellow, her dress is always flowing. Some nights, we talk. Others, we stare silently at the night sky. Just after nightfall Orion sets along with the Pleiades, her favorite constellation. Soon, Orion and the Pleiades will be gone, disappearing into the southern hemisphere for the summer. Her visits are more sporadic now, and soon, I suspect, she'll be gone too.

There are too many unknown unknowns in the stars, Daniel once said. As Wylers, that idea encourages, inspires us. We come alive at night. The moon, our sun. As children, we stayed up too late, our eyes glued to our telescope, trying to spot ever-more-distant stars and planets. My father nicknamed us Castor and Pollux, two of the brightest stars in the Gemini constellation, inseparable, distant twins. Our story is one that could be told in those stars. While the brothers appear close, they are actually light-years apart.

As we grew older, our interests splintered, Daniel's toward biology, mine staying in astronomy. Despite his diminished interest in that subject, he encouraged me to peek into far corners of galaxies and stitch together the story of the universe. Could he have had any inkling that doing so would eventually provide me with an outlet to forget him? But the universe no longer provides me with a viable diversion.

I miss my brother.

I hear a boat, its motor humming in a steady rhythm, before I see it. My property is tucked into a cove at the southern tip of the island, so visitors to it are only intentional. As the boat approaches, familiar markings emerge: a red stripe wrapped around the hull with an accompanying red bimini top. I check my watch. Why would Locke be coming here this late? A figure who is not Locke, in white with contrasting black hair, is sitting in the boat. The distorted image smooths into focus: Birdie.

Something flares inside me. I will the energy back where it came from, smoldering in my chest, and stand up to meet the boat.

I descend the stairs that trail from the porch to the boat dock and catch the rope Locke throws. Birdie is seated for arrival, her hands clasped in her lap, until the boat draws to a complete stop. She stands, shaky, uncertain within the boat's perpetual movement.

"What are you doing here?" I ask, stepping onto the boat.

She takes my hand. "I wanted to surprise you."

"If I knew you were coming, I could have picked you up from the marina."

"I was going to call, but Locke offered to bring me."

Locke stands on the bow, his hands relaxed by his side. "No trouble at all, Doc," he says before I can thank him.

"Care to join us for a drink?" Birdie asks Locke.

His eyes search mine. After I have lived on the island for two months with no visitors, he understands that Birdie's visit is unusual and possibly not good. Determining that I'm okay, he says, "No, thank you. I need to get back." He swats at a gnat. "The missus is waiting, and you know we can't have that."

"Thank you, Locke," Birdie says. "Send my regards to Hilda."

I untie his line, and he pulls off, the boat puttering into the increasing darkness.

Her arrival came so fast that I didn't have time until this moment to think about seeing her for the first time in over eight years.

"Hi, Birdie."

"David."

I blanch at the use of my given name. "Jacob, please," I remind her.

"Then I would like to be addressed as Mom or Mother."

"Okay…Mother."

She shakes her head in disapproval.

We both wait out the silence.

"Talkative as ever, I see."

I shrug. "Processing."

Bernadette "Birdie" Ross graduated from Yale with double degrees in biology and chemistry. However, she never worked for a wage outside our home nor had any inclination to do so. Instead, Birdie dedicated her life to helping advance my father's medical career and raising her children to follow their parents' scientific footsteps. Later, when tragedy threatened her family, she remained resolute in her commitment to us. By any means necessary.

This included making use of her naturally cold heart, iced further after Daniel's trial. Those closest to her were always strangers to her inner thoughts. As a result, I can't recall her ever offering a motherly touch or if I ever longed for it.

Until now.

I look at her, her face fuller than I remember, and I'm suddenly homesick for something I've never had, the sensation of warmth that envelops you, a feeling that can only come from a mother's love.

I open my arms, choosing to believe that, for some, time and space do indeed heal old wounds. As I slip my arms around her, drawing her close, she freezes, her arms locked to her sides. Releasing her and glaring into her brown eyes, a hue I did not inherit, I see the same hurt, unchanged and ever present, that resided in them all those years ago.

She fidgets, straightening her white tunic, finger-combing her hair, and adjusting her purse up on her arm. Her lips pinch tight. I absorb her rejection, which hurts more than I expected, and search her eyes for a trace of maternal love, but they are as empty and wanting as the gnats flying around us.

"I stopped by a few times, but Marsha said you were out. And I wanted to get settled before I invited you here."

She looks up at my father's old fishing cottage.

"It always felt like home," I say, and I register something— surprise?—flit across her face.

Another memory pushes to the surface. Daniel and me sitting on this dock, fishing poles in hand, feet swinging in contentment, drenched from an impromptu dip. Dad nearby whispering instructions to our eager—

I cap the memory, saving it until later.

"It's so far away from everything," Birdie says.

"That's the point."

"You were always more of a loner," she says, swatting her hands across her face at a swarm of gnats. "Not like your brother."

I came home to make amends. To pick up the pieces of my shattered family and glue them back together. With pieces missing, and two lost forever, the task will not be easy. Disgrace crept into our family and altered our dynamics so much that our previous life seems like it happened to other people. Individuals once bound by blood and love morphed into strangers barely strung together by misfortune and circumstance. We are a broken family of five, divided by two, remainder of one.

Based on my mother's and my awkward hug, no one would blame me for being pessimistic. But optimism hangs nearby like a halo. I have to try. Our family matters. Once, we *were*.

"Would you like to come up?" I ask.

Once we reach the porch, she immediately steps to my telescope, Reggie. "Your father wanted to study astronomy. He used to say that astronomy confronts us with some of the biggest and most challenging problems about the nature of ourselves."

"There are questions we may never solve, no matter how much we want to," I say, repeating one of his lines.

"He said he didn't have the luxury of solving all of life's scientific questions, just individual ones."

In her smile at the memory of her husband, in wrinkles around her eyes and down her cheeks, signs of wisdom reveal themselves. I realize she has entered a new season of her life.

She eases into one of the Adirondack chairs—*her* chair. Tiny drops of sweat dot her upper lip. "Let's sit out here. I could never breathe in there after—"

"Can I get you anything?" I interrupt.

She waves a hand and picks up a newspaper. The humid air stings with unspoken words that, no matter how frequently she fans that paper, hang in the air like smoke.

"I want you to go see your brother," she says finally, without looking at me.

"What?"

"You need to go see your brother, David."

I stiffen, once again, at her use of my former name, and at her request. "Not yet."

"Why not?"

"I haven't seen him in eight years."

"That wasn't his choice."

"He never wanted to see me."

She finally looks at me. "Why do you think that is?"

I lower my head beneath her glare, owning what she's accusing me of. "I'm sorry. I can't."

"You don't get to say 'I can't.' Not after what you did. You betrayed him. *You* did this."

"*I* did this?"

"You ruined him. You destroyed our family. The least you could do is go see him."

Her words hit the same nerve now as they did when she said them almost nine years ago. That was one of those moments in life that never goes away. That sticks with you. Becomes you. "Did you come all the way out here to talk about him?"

"He needs his brother."

"Daniel seems to be doing just fine," I say. "I read about his project in the *Times*."

"You need him too."

The truth of her words slaps me across the face. But I'm not ready for it to root there. "He sent you, didn't he?" I stand quickly. "You've got to stop doing that. Fighting his battles."

"I don't fight his battles."

I glare at her. "C'mon, Birdie. You destroyed that girl on his behalf." The strength of my voice surprises me.

Birdie smiles, matter-of-factly, as if my comment isn't worth consideration. "I did what I had to do to save him."

I never shared her blind optimism about Daniel's innocence. "Daniel has never needed to be saved. Not then and certainly not now."

"He has cancer."

I stare at her, first unmoving; then I drop back into my chair. It squeaks and groans under my weight.

"It's more advanced than they thought. If he wasn't…they would have caught it sooner…" she says, her voice trailing off.

I run my hand across my mouth and collapse slightly, my elbows pressing into my thighs, my hands clasped together close to my mouth, like a person in prayer. "Are they sure it's cancer?"

I already know they are. Cancer is rarely a mistake.

She pinches the bridge of her nose. "Will you please go see him?"

I am back up again, walking to the porch railing. I grip it tightly. The first of the evening stars glisten in deep violet. The river is still like a mirror, and a thin piece of moon reflects in it.

"Dammit, why can't you just listen to me, David?" she says. "I'm asking you to do this for me."

Her forehead creases, her eyes narrow, an expression I haven't seen in so many years. It's the expression she wore daily during the trial.

I draw in a deep breath to center myself in the peace of my surroundings. Daniel is the reason for every phone call or email from Birdie over the years. It is for Daniel that she risked everything, her husband, her sanity. Saving Daniel became her purpose.

And then I know. The full reason for Birdie's visit. I know it in my racing heart, the knowledge of it coursing through my veins, before the words leave her lips.

"He's dying."

SARA

———

THE PLANE DIPS AND lurches and I clutch the armrests. *Please don't let us crash. Please don't let us crash.* I've never flown before. The escape to the Northeast came via four wheels, my old red Dodge Daytona. I know Alana's mind, next to me, whirs not with lament but with opportunity. She has spent the three-hour flight pressed against the window, seemingly oblivious to the turbulence as she watches the earth and clouds below, and adding, then crossing off tasks from her list: *Meet an airline pilot. Sit in a window seat. Use the bathroom at thirty thousand feet.*

She was saddened by the news of her grandfather's heart attack. Alana has seen her grandfather in person only a handful of times and none since she started walking. But today's technology makes it possible to hold a place in someone's life without physically being in it. Had Alana been born when I was, my father and Sylvia would have only heard her voice over the phone and received an occasional school picture. Because of video calling, he and Sylvia have watched her grow up and gotten into her heart and mind from thousands of miles away, as if they were always next door.

But Alana is a kid, so she is also intoxicated by this trip: new people, colorful experiences, modern conveniences. Rural, remote Maine living is the only home she's known. But our tiny town at the end of the world has gotten too small for her. Like most children, she covets what she sees on television. Mostly, what she has dubbed her three *M*s: movie theaters, malls, and McDonald's. She is growing up, becoming a person I don't understand anymore (if I ever did), and as is true of the past twenty-four hours, I stand powerless to stop it.

I envision our trip to be a short one: check on Dad and leave the minute he has received a clean bill of health. Heart attacks are not automatic death sentences. People recover and continue to live highly active lives after them. Dad has always been in great shape and should be back on his feet running the bookstore soon, I tell myself. How I see this trip mostly is a break in the seven long years since we've seen each other and time to reconnect. I will never again let a calendar year turn over before I see him.

Our plane lands, and we disembark. Alana bounces slightly ahead, her head whipping from side to side as we move through the airport, mesmerized by the fast-food offerings and retail stores, turning and pointing to the Brookstone and begging for a latte at Starbucks. Her eyes widen when we approach the long escalator that will take us to the underground train system.

"This is so cool!" she says as we descend and again, louder, as the train zips us to the baggage claim area.

Since tourists are a phenomenon in our part of Maine, Alana has rarely met a stranger, an observation made painfully clear when, turning from filling out the paperwork for our rental car, I see her a good distance from me engrossed in a conversation with a man.

"Alana!" I call, but the bustle and noise of the airport swallows my voice.

I call her again, moving toward her. This time my voice reaches her ears. She waves happily, unaware of the danger of strangers. She shows no fear.

"Mr. Lopez was electrocuted and can't wear a watch!" Her high-pitched voice trails off into an elated giggle.

As I approach, I smile and mumble a weak apology to Mr. Lopez, a grandfatherly figure with a bushel of gray hair. "Alana, don't walk off from me."

"*Ella no ha sido ningún problema, señora.*"

I look at Alana for translation.

"He says I've been no problem."

"*Siempre me he preguntado por qué dejé de ser capaz de llevar un reloj, pero tu hija me estaba explicando que el impulso eléctrico en mi cuerpo debió haber sido alterado cuando fui electrocutado en el trabajo hace veinte años.*"

"Mom, Mr. Lopez got *electrocuted* at work."

Even I am distracted by this comment.

Mr. Lopez blushes, and he chuckles. "*Hace veinte*

años," he says, palms up, as though to tamp down Alana's incredulity.

"A long time ago. Twenty years ago. But anyway, I was explaining to him that the electrical pulse in his body must have been altered when that happened. That's why he messes up watches too."

"*Ella es una niña muy inteligente.*"

My high school Spanish allows me to translate that line.

"Thank you," I say, taking Alana's hand and returning to the rental car counter. "Say goodbye to Mr. Lopez."

"Bye!"

After we pick up our car, we are off on the three-and-a-half-hour drive to Savannah.

"Alana, you can't run off and talk to strangers like that," I say once I'm outside of Atlanta and the sprawling lanes of traffic have dwindled to two. "This isn't Lubec."

"I just wanted to know if he could wear a watch," she mumbles, looking somberly at her yellow watch, which stopped on the plane and has since begun ticking backward.

"I understand that, honey, but not everyone is going to be nice to you like Mr. Lopez."

She removes her watch and shoves it into her backpack.

"When we're here, I need you to extra listen to me, okay? I'm going to be taking care of Grandpa, and I don't want to have to worry about you too."

"Okay," she mutters.

I make a mental note to buy her another watch at the first opportunity to make it up to her. Her sixth one this year.

"No talking to strangers, especially telling them stuff you know. And definitely no speaking in other languages." That becomes a memorable feature of a girl her age. "Remember the rules."

———

Two hours into our drive, the rain beats against the glass like tiny pebbles, slowly at first, then all at once. I turn on the headlights and the windshield wipers, smearing the gushing water across the glass. It's all so familiar, like being reintroduced to my own palm. By the time we arrive in Savannah, the rain will be gone, replaced by the waning hours of a burning sun. I seem to live in places with dramatic swings of weather.

I suppose I knew that eventually I would have to come back and face my past. But that level of awareness had never been where I could reach it. An invisible boundary has separated the girl who fled from here eight years ago and the woman I am today. With great care, I confined that girl, her memories, and the crimes committed against her. And now the moment I've avoided has come around. With one phone call, suddenly, I'm back in that other country, which is burning bright as the morning sun.

I was a vibrant teenager before it all. Nice at times. Moody at other times. I smiled at people and meant it. Looked them in the eye when I spoke to them. I laughed. At everything. Tyler Robson's corny jokes in homeroom. ABC's TGIF sitcom lineup. I befriended the least popular and stood up to bullies. I valued holidays, Valentine's Day in particular, as a way to celebrate individuals and relationships. I saved my money from working at the bookstore and bought everyone in my classes a Valentine. I personalized each one, with my signature and a little heart above the last *a* in my name.

Being back in Savannah plants me, firmly, into the middle of those memories, that time, being that girl again. But that's not who I am anymore. In Maine, the pain is as distant as a star. Trauma doesn't punch a clock, but you can set your watch by it. It works overtime most of the time. But it can be smothered like a whisper in a storm. That's what I do by living in Maine.

I turn on the radio to drown out my thoughts. "This spring is on track to be one of the wettest ever for Georgia. So far from March through May, we've had 18.13 inches of rain, making it the seventh wettest on record. Expect afternoon showers the rest of the week."

My grip on the steering wheel is sweaty, tight knuckled. Inside, however, I am eerily calm as my foot slowly presses down on the accelerator to bring us just above the speed limit. I'm so calm that it scares me, like it's not really me driving, not really me in the car, like I'm operating on autopilot.

I drive straight to the hospital, remembering every turn down the streets lined with historic buildings and the smell of the paper mill at the end of town. Try as I may, there are certain things I just can't forget. Like the street Dad has called home for fifty years. Or the park with a basketball hoop without a net where we girls played hopscotch. Or the hospital where they took Mom, even though there was no hope.

Once we're parked and out of the car, it doesn't take long to find Sylvia. She's in the waiting room, reading a book, her glasses precarious at the tip of her nose. Despite the room being packed with other readers, and texters, a shroud of silence hovers as if speaking or moving could negatively affect the outcome of loved ones. I approach, and Sylvia looks up from her book and stands. Even since our last video call, there are a few more lines around her eyes, and her locs seem longer and grayer, almost white. My eyes fill with tears as we finish closing the gap with outstretched arms. She swallows me in a hug that neither of us releases right away. We cry silently, swaying back and forth like a pendulum. Being in her arms, inhaling her sweet scent of honeydew, I realize how much I missed her.

Alana burrows her way between our legs. Sylvia stoops to Alana's level to see a child she has loved from afar but rarely seen in person. "My God. Hey, ladybug," she says, studying Alana hungrily. "You've gotten so big."

She stands and gives me a long once-over. "Still beautiful." She touches my rain-and-tear-soaked heart-shaped face. I shift my wet braid, my typical hairstyle, over my shoulder, knowing that I haven't changed much since I left. Same doe-shaped eyes the color of fine gold, wide and open. Same black hair, longer and straight. "And wet." She huffs, but the sound seems forced, unnatural. "This rain is horrible. It has rained every day here for almost a month."

"How are you?" I ask. "Did you get any sleep?"

"Not much." She wipes her eyes with a ball of tissues clutched tightly in her hand. "I wanted to be here."

"Can we see Grandpa?" Alana interrupts.

Sylvia starts to speak, then stops, then begins again. Her eyebrows collapse into a Y, an undeniable question. "Why... um...why...don't you...go to the house and...and dry off? Come back in the morning."

I give her an incredulous stare. "I need to see him now."

She looks past me, over my shoulder and down the hallway. "Let's find the doctor, first. To explain everything. I think you should speak with him before you see Hosea."

I open my mouth to speak, but Sylvia retrieves some change from her purse and says quickly, "Alana, there's a vending machine just down the hall. Would you go get me a Diet Coke?"

Again I start to speak, but Sylvia speaks first, whispering, "She's okay here."

I watch as Alana takes the change and disappears around the corner.

"Have a seat, Sara," Sylvia says, her voice so soft I can barely make out the words. "There's something I need to tell you."

I comply and watch her take a quiet breath.

"Hosea didn't have a heart attack." Her lip quivers. "He has a brain aneurysm."

The silent room quiets even further as the world melts away. My vision blurs, and my ears ring with that one word, replaying louder and louder. *Aneurysm. Aneurysm. Aneurysm.*

"What? No. No," I say, shaking my head emphatically with every *no*. "He had a heart attack. He's going to be fine."

Her eyes fill again. "He didn't want you to know. Not until…"

Her voice trails off as if she doesn't have the words to finish.

"Until what?" I snap. What follows this question will be everything, my linchpin. What follows these words will mean everything.

"The end."

I look at her and blink, feeling light-headed at the weight of her words.

"I'm sorry, Sara," Sylvia continues, wrapping her hand in mine. Her voice cracks. "The doctors have given him six months."

I stand abruptly and back away from her. "You said he had a heart attack. Why would you tell me he had a heart attack? Why didn't he tell me? Why didn't *you* tell me?"

Sylvia stands. "He didn't want you to worry." Her quiet voice doesn't soften my anger. "He didn't want you back here until absolutely necessary."

"Wait…how long has he known about this?"

"They discovered it a while ago."

"I'm going to see him," I say, my voice loud and demanding. "What room is he in?"

"Sara…" She stops, looking wilted. "You need to prepare yourself."

"What room is he in?" My heart thumps wildly.

Sylvia sighs. "312."

As soon as Alana returns, holding a Diet Coke, I am moving toward the elevator. Twisting around, I point and say, "Stay with Sylvia until I come back."

I float like a ghost to Dad's room, unseeing and feeling unseen by others in the hallways. A dry-erase board outside the room has *speech impediment* written in hard red letters. The room glistens clean in the moon- and streetlight from the large window. Everything, from the pale-brown laminate tables to the polished white tile floors, smells sterile, as if just scrubbed.

Longing and guilt wash over me as I see my father lying in bed, an IV attached to his arm. His eyes are closed; his chest moves up and down. A once stout face sags like it is melting. Tears burn in my eyes. This is not my father. My father is a proud man, shoulders erect, head up, a brawny man. A man who dons four-piece suits, flamboyant bow ties, and pocket watches. The man before me with tubes, dressed in a paper gown that swallows him, is not my father.

I tiptoe across the room and slide into the chair next to the bed, careful not to wake him. I stare out the window, watching the way the tiny raindrops slide down the glass, collecting rogue drops along the way, amassing in size, before disappearing.

Against my will, my mind casts back and snags on a memory from that night. I've been here twice before. First, for Mom. Then…the next time I don't remember getting to the hospital. But Dad and I ended up in a room similar to this one. Our positions reversed. I remember my eyes blinking open in alarm. From my place in the bed, I glanced around the blurry room to see the silhouette of Dad sitting in a chair staring out the window. A gentle rain tapped against the glass. Everything hurt, and I released a moan that brought him back. I waited for his words with the hope that maybe, just maybe, what he said would help all of it make sense. I waited for something that would never come. Not that night or the following. What do you say to your daughter who has learned just how hard and cruel the world could be?

"This is thy hour O Soul, thy free flight into the wordless…"

At the sounds of Whitman, I turn and see Dad looking at me. His eyes sag with fatigue. On the surface, Whitman's poem depicts a night spent in silent reflection. Underneath this facade lies a metaphor for death. Unlike some poems that paint death as a horrible experience, this poem sees it as the simple ending of a day. Whitman was making death sound peaceful. I take Dad's hand into mine. It's bone dry. "Don't try to talk."

His voice is low and scratchy, but he continues.

"Away from books, away from art, the day erased, the lesson done..."

"You are not alone. I'm here."

"Thee fully forth emerging, silent, gazing, pondering the themes thou lovest best,
Night, sleep, death and the stars."

"Please don't talk like that," I say, my voice wavering.

Dad shifts his slumped position to an upright one. He takes my hand and squeezes it.

"I missed you too," I say, kissing his hand, wetting it slightly with my tears.

I stare at him, searching for more words. Finally, I choose bluntness: "Why didn't you tell me?"

"Till at length the burden seems
Greater than our strength can bear,
Heavy as the weight of dreams,
Pressing on us everywhere."

"I could have handled it." Usually, I answer him in kind, with poetry. But I am not in the mood to indulge.

He squeezes my hand again, weakly, this time in acknowledgment and as an attempt to control me, I know. He's always had a way of doing that. Growing up with a father who doesn't speak normally, I became attuned to all his distinct techniques of communicating that don't involve speech, like a scrunch of his nose when he doesn't like something. A nod for yes *and* no. A firm pat on the shoulder for confirmation. A wink for a quick show of affection. A throat clearing for attention or an act of anger. Or, in this case, a tight squeeze of the hand to silence.

"Were you not going to tell me?" The tears stream down my face, and I don't wipe them away. "So, you are ready to die?"

He turns his head away from me.

"Talk to me, please. Just this once."

I know he won't. But it hasn't stopped me from asking over the years.

Poems that convey his precise feelings and exact thoughts are his second nature now, a perk of his advanced study. As a child, I was left to decipher his poems and translate them into what I considered "actual" words and feelings. It is only now that I understand and interpret the poems clearly and immediately. I still feel like a stranger to his truest thoughts, and it's what he doesn't say that wounds me more than he will ever know.

"Alana's here," I say, finally wiping away a tear. "She wants to see you. What am I supposed to tell her?"

"I have walked and prayed for this young child an hour,
And heard the sea-wind scream upon the tower,
And under the arches of the bridge, and scream
In the elms above the flooded stream;

Imagining in excited reverie
That the future years had come
Dancing to a frenzied drum,
Out of the murderous innocence of the sea."

"She will be fine, but what about me?"

The door pushes open, and Sylvia and Alana enter.

Alana takes inventory of the room, releases Sylvia's hand, and walks over to the bed. Without hesitation, she climbs on the foot of the bed. Dad looks at her and says,

"Come to the pane, draw the curtain apart,
There she is passing, the girl of my heart;
See where she walks like a queen in the street,
Weather-defying, calm, placid and sweet.
Tripping along with impetuous grace,
Joy of her life beaming out of her face,
Tresses all truant-like, curl upon curl,
Wind-blown and rosy, my little March girl."

Everyone close to Dad gets their own special greeting. This is hers.

To it, Alana is always supposed to reply, as she does so now:

"The Mountain sat upon the Plain
In his tremendous Chair—

His observation omnifold,
His inquest everywhere."

If Dad's altered appearance startles her, I can't tell. They sit and talk. Her in prose. Him in poetry. Her intelligence affords her the ability to decipher his poetry at this tender age, but she has not yet mastered the ability to speak to him solely in poetry, and my heart sinks at the realization that there no longer is the time for her to learn.

JACOB

———

ACCORDING TO BIRDIE, DANIEL wakes every day at 4:00 a.m., an hour before the mandatory wake-up call. He knows his space well, his hands instinctively reaching and finding his Bible before he's even opened his eyes. In the filtered light, he reads a few chapters, the pages yellowed and arid as dried flowers. He prays, always the same prayer, always the same way, the life of mundane routine. He thanks God for his life, for being the Lord of Second Chances, and for the health of his family. He begs God to forgive him of his sins and offer peace for the people he's hurt. He closes his Bible, minutes before roll call, and thinks about the day's purpose, imagining ways he might help others.

He has, by her account, lived the life of a world-class do-gooder. That's how he's survived the last seven-and-a-half years. Days marked by the number of people he's touched, helped. Not by scratching lines on walls. But by believing every step toward good is one more away from his bad one.

But he's no fool. He knows nothing he does or ever will do will erase the fact that he's a convicted rapist.

Yet he tries anyway.

To see him now, shuffling into the visitor's room, handcuffed and shackled, a surgical mask dangling from around his neck, it seems unfair to only refer to him as a rapist. We're not all permanently branded with the name of our biggest mistake. Some sins, of course, are less egregious, more understood, easily forgiven. Lying? We've all told a lie. Adultery? Beg for forgiveness and promise never to do it again. Rape? That's all most need to know. Forever a rapist. That's his fate. He gave up his rights to any mention of forgiveness.

Despite his good behavior, Daniel is still considered dangerous. But standing erect, dressed in the standard-issue prison uniform—a stark-white shirt and pants, trimmed with a navy-blue stripe—his face relaxed into a lazy smile, he looks as peaceful as any free man you're likely to meet. "A walking angel," a journalist once wrote about him.

The visitor's room, a low-slung space decorated with beige-painted walls and fluorescent lights that cast puddles onto the polished floors, buzzes into a crescendo as more prisoners march in. Symmetrical rows of metal tables and chairs fill as inmates sit across from their loved ones. Positioned at the far end of the room sits a wall of bulletproof glass, divided by plastic partitions.

Daniel flexes his fingers and massages his wrists to ease the cramped muscles. At the sight of me, he tilts his head back to acknowledge me, the move slight. In prison, exhibit too much emotion and you're considered weak or soft. All these years in prison taught him this, and as he walks to my table, although he looks neither to the left nor to the right, he remains in a state of awareness. His mind has always operated this way, gathering and feasting on the tiniest particulars. I watch as his eyes silently catalog the tables of girlfriends with too much makeup and mothers with too many gray hairs.

His relaxed face tightens as he reaches me. I stand and smooth out my shirt, tugging on it from the bottom. The temperature in the room hovers above seventy-four degrees as sweat stains begin to flower in the armpits of my blue button-down shirt. We hug. Two quick pats on the back. Even though it's been eight years since I've seen him, the hug is a reflex. But it is not one of love or admiration; it's an allowance. We sit and in the same moment instinctively clasp our hands, outstretched, in front of us. He smiles as I move my hands to my lap, annoyed at the similarities of identical twinhood.

"I see you're still trying to hide who you are."

"I see you're still trying to buy your way into heaven," I say, indicating the visitor and prisoner at the closest table whose eyes continuously slide to him in admiration. If we were somewhere else, they'd be asking for a photo with him.

He doesn't take the bait but, rather, keeps his eyes tightly locked on me, appraising. Staring back at him now is no longer like looking into a mirror, as it once was. I don't remember a time when I was ever aware of the differences between us. We have tawny hair, fair skin that glows the ruddiness of a sunset, and green eyes that burn in the dark. Our looks are a rarity, a byproduct of our biracial heritage. Up close now, I can see what prison has done to him, and the toll the cancer has taken. The malign yellow in his eyes has dulled the brightness that once resonated there. His skin has a rubbery texture, like the surface of a balloon. As an identical twin, I knew only the world of dualism. Now, it seems, he's a different version of me, of what we used to be.

"Look at you. You look good,"—his eyes dart to my name badge, then shift back to me—"Jacob. Birdie said you were trying to rejoin the world. Trying to look…normal." He leans in. "We aren't—normal. We never were. And we never will be.

"I get the look," he continues. "What I don't understand is the name change. From David, the king of the Jews, to Jacob, the father of the twelve tribes of Israel. The symbolism abounds."

"I would have taken any name to disassociate myself from you."

"God has forgiven me. When will you?"

I lean back in my seat, the metal chair shrieking against the tile floor, and rub both hands against my thighs. It's a question I've often pondered. He committed the crime, and yet our entire family was convicted and sentenced to a fate we'll never escape.

No one ever wonders what happens to a criminal's family after sentencing. The criminal goes to jail. Justice is served. Few mourn for the family. Criminality is the criminal's fault, something they have done deliberately and with choice. It is also the parents' fault; proper rearing and a sound moral education could have prevented such a crime from happening. And siblings are guilty by association. But Daniel does not come from a broken home or have a previous criminal record. And when the dust settled, he drew a ten-year sentence, which we all got to serve right along with him while struggling to forgive both him and ourselves.

And now he's dying, a particularly cruel mechanism of nature.

"Are you asking for my forgiveness?" I ask.

"Someone once said that forgiveness is an act of the will, and the will can function regardless of the temperature of the heart."

"Forgiveness takes more strength than anger."

"You have strength in you. More than you know. Always have."

"I think you've exceeded your analysis of me today."

He concedes, raising his hands, palms up, in defeat.

I cross my arms. "If your God has offered you his forgiveness, why do you seek mine?"

"Ah…" He exhales and peers toward the ceiling. "I see science has made you soft on God."

"Science has taught me to believe in things that can be derived rationally through logic. I have no interest in a God that has to be believed in."

"God is not a theory. Science can't disprove his existence."

"You talk a lot about your God and forgiveness. But I wonder… When you're alone in your cell in the still moments, when it's just you and your thoughts, I wonder if you've forgiven yourself."

He retreats, patting his pants pocket and retrieving a pack of cigarettes and matches. He pushes one into his mouth, cups his hands around the flame of the match, and sucks in smoke so deeply his cheeks collapse.

It is the last of his vices from his former life. The alcohol, of course, went first, although I hear prison produces pretty good hooch. Women had to go too. Everything that was left has been transformed into the man before me. A new man. And I realize I don't really know this man, my brother, at all anymore.

He's always offered himself as a puzzle. People struggle to grasp, to comprehend, things about him, especially his level of brilliance. As a kid, before we were homeschooled, he routinely corrected teachers' sub-par education and taught math class while Mrs. Lattimore graded papers. At age twelve, he created an innovative flashlight that harvested heat emitted from the human hand so he could read in bed at night. At sixteen, after our grandmother died of breast cancer, he mourned by retreating to his room for the summer, emerging with a computer program that detected patterns in test results that identified breast cancer. Daniel is that man who intimidates the hell out of you, not because he is the smartest man in the room but because he may be one of the smartest men in the world.

"Birdie says she'll do the NBC interview," I say, breaking the silence.

"And you?" he asks, his eyes hopeful like a child's.

I shake my head, the move almost faint.

He blows a cloud of smoke away from me and immediately takes another long draw on the cigarette, his knee pumping assiduously, a soft, rapid rhythm. "I'm doing great work."

In one of Birdie's emails, she told me of his plan to transform as many lives as he could during his decade in prison. I wondered which was more delusional: his efforts to develop a plan that would reform the prison system or his belief that his good works would make anyone forget—or forgive—what he did.

The truth is I was the delusional one. Six months after that email, he saved a female prison guard who was being attacked by an inmate. A reporter wrote about it in our local newspaper. A year later, he started a program that teaches inmates to read and write at a college level and guarantees that graduates of the program can score a 700 on the SAT, the minimum score needed to attend Harvard. All but two have scored 700. There was another local newspaper write-up, which was picked up by the *Atlanta Journal-Constitution* and the *Chicago Tribune*. He was making a name, a positive name for himself. And fans as well. Letters of encouragement and care packages arrived along with sporadic calls for a drastic reduction of his sentence. Since then, he's been addicted to helping others. It's his good fight, he says. His purpose.

His latest good deed, Sustainability in Prisons Project, is what he's most known for. His program brings science and nature into prison and reduces the environmental, economic, and human costs of prisons by inspiring and informing sustainable practices. A prison garden served as his first project and last year resulted in over thirty-five thousand pounds of fresh vegetables, fruit, and herbs for the prison. His composting program, which manages food and other organic wastes, has saved the prison $30,000 per year at a time when prison costs are rising. This made national news with a feature in the *New York Times* and landed him a jailhouse interview with NBC News. Ahead of the interview scheduled to air a few weeks before his parole hearing, a petition, circulated by his fans, requested his immediate release. I knew all of this because Birdie made sure I did.

"Tell me something: How much weight do you think *she* would give your good works?"

Daniel deflates. "The Lord tests us through various trials, and how we react to those trials defines us. 1 Peter 4:12 teaches us, 'Do not be surprised at the painful trial you are suffering, as though something strange were happening to you. But rejoice that you participate in the sufferings of Christ, so that you may be overjoyed when his glory is revealed.'"

"Have you asked for her forgiveness? Do you think you should ask for her forgiveness?"

"I've thought about it," he says. Smoke holding deep in his lungs, he takes the cigarette from his mouth and looks at it, flicking the ash with his middle finger. In his gray exhalation: "But I think it will hurt her anew."

"Do you ever think about her?"

"Every day," he says. "But I can't focus on the pain I've caused. I can't erase it. I can acknowledge the good I *can* do and live every day as if it were my last. Proverbs 27:1 says, 'Do not boast about tomorrow, for you do not know what a day may bring.'"

"'Let someone else praise you, and not your own mouth; an outsider, and not your own lips.'"

He smiles at the Scripture. "Ah…Proverbs 27:2. So you do believe in its existence? In heaven?"

"I was being ironical. Because isn't that what inmates do? Commit crimes and find 'God' in here?" I gesture around the room, believing that if there were a God, he sure wouldn't be found among the criminals within these walls. Surely, he had enough to do without trying to rehabilitate those who cannot be rehabilitated.

"Heaven is real. God is real. When will you accept that?"

"When you accept that composting banana peels won't change anything. That it doesn't change what you did."

His face freezes with the intake of breath, and then he lets it go. "Why do you mock my work? You either believe I regret my crime or you don't," he says. His body stills, almost statuesque, his voice calm, barely above a whisper.

"Do you? Regret your crime? Because according to Birdie, it never happened."

"I'm in here, aren't I?"

"What happened that night? What *really* happened?"

I hold my breath as he gives me a pained look that tells me he's not ready.

I pivot. "How do you think what happened has affected Sara, her life?"

His expression clouds at the mention of her name, and I wonder if he's heard it, spoken it, since the trial.

"That which doesn't kill us makes us stronger. I pray that she's been able to move on and live a fulfilling life, despite the past."

"Wouldn't that be lucky for you."

"You were always the emotional one." He wags his finger. "Always interested in the feelings of others. Not afraid to express your own feelings. Your name change symbolizes that you are not motivated by power, status, or fame but by love."

"And you were always the stubborn one. Analyzing me when I dared to show my feelings. Displaying little to no empathy or compassion for others."

He pinches the butt of the cigarette between the tips of his thumb and index finger and inhales, like it's a joint. The mud-yellow nicotine stains on his fingers showcase the dirt also permanently embedded in the pores around his splintered nails. His hands are calloused, his knuckles scarred from long hours in the dirt of the prison garden. One knuckle is swollen and raw, and there's a deep, fresh gouge along the back of his hand where blood had dried to a crusty, yellowish scab. He takes one last inhale and drops the butt into the ashtray.

"Why are you here? After eight years, I can't imagine a walk down memory lane is what you have in mind."

I deadpan, "You know why."

He retreats. His facial features pull down. "When did Birdie finally tell you?"

"Last week."

He leans in. "Look, you don't owe me anything. I understand if you choose not to do it."

"Shouldn't you be wearing that? And not smoking?"

He instinctively looks at the mask and smiles. "A few germs won't kill me. By His stripes I'm healed."

"He hasn't healed you yet."

He starts to laugh. It turns into a rattling cough, wet and phlegmy, that continues long enough to redden his face and water his eyes. He lifts the surgical mask over his nose, leaving visible only his weakened eyes.

Despite my resolution to forgive him, his action, even after all of these years, still cuts into my mind like splinters of bone, and it remains difficult to think of him without thinking of his crime and how it devastated our family. And yet, at the sight of his weakened state, something eases inside me, like the air from a deflating balloon, and part of the anger I had twenty minutes ago lessens. I could see my brother again, the one who encouraged me to question and chase the biggest questions in astronomy: What is the universe made of? What came before the big bang? I cross and uncross my arms, then rub my hands together, at this sign of weakness. Unable to make sense of what I'm feeling, I release it and say abruptly:

"I was finally able to oversee NASA's Ground-to-Rocket

Electrodynamics-Electrons Correlative Experiment. I finally connected with Aurora."

His face softens under the mask; his cheekbones sink.

"The mission's objective was to understand what causes the swirls seen in very active auroras. By launching disposable probes into a northern lights display in Alaska, we hoped to learn more about the heating and expanding of Earth's thermosphere during the aurora."

"How many probes?" he asks, leaning forward.

"Six."

"Where in Alaska?"

"Poker Flat. It's about thirty miles north of Fairbanks."

"When?"

"February."

He huffs. "I'm sure the weather was not optimal."

"The conditions weren't exactly ideal, but after five days, the weather broke."

"And?"

"After months of planning and testing, and after careful monitoring of activity the day of, the order was given to launch. The rocket ascended to an altitude of 220 miles and recorded data as the video and still cameras took pictures from the ground," I say.

"How long was the flight?"

"Ten minutes fifteen seconds."

"And?"

"And she was pretty consistent with what we've known.

Auroras run on an eleven-year cycle, corresponding to the activity level on the solar surface. The low ebb of that cycle, which is measured by the number of sunspots and accompanying solar flares, reached its solar minimum a few years ago and has been decreasing again."

He shifts away from the table. "That's it? You've been chasing the aurora borealis since we were kids. You connect with her, and all you have to say is she's pretty consistent with what we've known? You sound like a scientist."

"I am a scientist."

"You used to talk about the aurora borealis as if she were a woman. Your Aurora. Her beauty, her colors, her lines and curves, her seduction and allure. And now you speak about her technically and matter-of-factly, as if she didn't have a purpose in the universe."

I fell in love with the scientific phenomenon the aurora borealis after a ski trip to Tromsö, Norway, when I was fourteen. Daniel, Dad, and I chased her every night for a week. Finally, on the last night, she revealed herself to us, like a mirage in the desert. The black sky, dotted with stars of all shapes and brightness, lit up with rods of shimmering green light, pink ripples. She captivated us all but no one more than me. Dad whispered in my ear, "If you love the heavenly aurora, wait until you find your earthly one." Ever since, I've been fascinated by the idea that a phenomenon of such extraordinary beauty and grace could be replicated in human form.

It reminds me of the Yeats poem:

I will find out where she has gone,
And kiss her lips and take her hands;
And walk among long dappled grass,
And pluck till time and times are done,
The silver apples of the moon,
The golden apples of the sun.

"I thought you didn't see much purpose to looking behind the universe. Too many unknown unknowns," I say.

"I've always believed something more exists and that things happen within it. And we are among the things that happen. But not you. You've always looked up and thought, why not?"

"Who's mocking whom now?"

He lifts his hands in a defensive, don't-shoot pose again.

I cross my arms again. "I'm fine."

He hesitates, waiting for more. As my twin, he *knows* there's more. He understands me in all my moods, and I understand him. But as the guard announces that visiting time is almost over, he knows we're not at the place of sharing deep emotions.

"What now?"

"I don't know. There's still years of data to analyze. I've also been offered a teaching…"

Daniel slices the air with his hand and huffs a deep groan. "Hell no. We're not…teachers. Any hack with a PhD can… teach." He says the word as if he doesn't like the taste of it on his tongue. "We're scientists. We're discoverers. Pioneers. Remember what Dad told us."

"It is up to us to give reason and purpose to events that would otherwise be meaningless and arbitrary," we repeat in unison.

After an eight-year absence, I barely know my brother anymore. There's a certain unbridgeable distance between us. Things will never be the same. No getting back to who we have been. But we could have a fresh start.

Something flares inside me again. Talking seems to cool my anxious mind. Unsure of what to do and unwilling to let the feeling escape, I open my mouth again.

"I'm living in Dad's old fishing cottage. I've been renovating it. Slowly. Cleared the land last week."

"*You?* Clearing the land?" he says with one eyebrow lifted. "An astrophysicist with a leaf blower. This I want to see."

"Dad taught us well."

"Yeah…" His voice trails off as his eyes flutter with memories.

More words bubble inside, so I continue. "I bought a boat that I keep flooding. On my first day, I hit the dock right where…she…would backflip into the water," I say, trying to breathe out the pressure that presses down inside. "She loved it out there. She never wanted to leave. I think I moved into the cottage not for me or to remember Dad but for her. Like she's still here, swimming around that dock."

His eyes brighten at the memory and the memory I capped when Birdie visited, the memory with us on the dock with Dad, and with her, fishing, plays in my head like an old film.

"Still can't say her name, can you?"

I shake my head. "There are so many unnamed women between us. I wonder when we'll both be able to say their names."

Daniel scoots his chair closer and leans toward me. "I see *her*," he says weakly, looking bereaved. And I know which *her* he is referring to. "Everywhere."

"I see her too," I whisper. "Almost every night. She's the one who told me it was time to come home."

In science, uniformitarianism is the idea that things change relatively slowly. Today is not very different from yesterday, which is not very different from the day before. If we understand today, we understand most of yesterday, and so on. The present is the key to the past.

In order to understand the past, I need to be present.

In order to be present, I need to forgive him.

I need him to forgive me too.

"I'll be back next week."

Daniel stands quietly as a guard approaches and chains him.

"Being normal is never a mistake. It means you are evolving," he says. "It's nice to see that one of us is capable of that."

I watch as he shuffles back to the metal door through which he came. He stops suddenly and turns back to me. "It was good to see you, Jacob."

SARA

———

THE SADNESS ABOUT DAD comes again and again, each time a slash across the heart. As the days pass and my new life roots, the pain comes less in crashing waves and more in stabs, quick and painful. When I don't actively hurt, the ache evident with each blink, breath, and step, I flop about the days, both clumsily and controlled, like a marionette, moving and operating at the control and the mercy of a puppeteer. If Alana needs me, I help her; if Dad does, I help him, but I don't really understand or feel any of it.

I settled Alana into my father's unused guest room, lined to the ceiling with bookshelves and stacks of rare books. Alana's eyes lit up, and she immediately began cataloging the collection, running her tiny finger across the books' antiquated spines. Before I finished making the bed and flinging open the curtains, she had already plucked one from its place on the shelf and begun reading it. I settled Dad into his room, after thoroughly scrubbing it and the house as if a single germ or dust particle could cause his aneurysm to burst. Through all of this, I plaster a smile on my face, pretending that if I keep moving, keep weathering the sadness, everything will be fine. I'm versed in the art of pretending.

But I can't escape the truth: my father is dying. *Will* die. Soon.

His neurologist, Dr. Mundy, explained to me that Dad has a small aneurysm on the carotid artery, and because of its location, deep in the circle of Willis at the base of the brain, and its star shape, it's inoperable. When (not if) it ruptures, which the doctor calculates could be between three and six months, Dad has no chance of surviving. Dr. Mundy followed the news with the offhand advice: "Let him live his life as normal."

The idea of mortality affects everyone differently. Rarely are we privy to the moment of our death. Most of the time, death sneaks up on us like a sneeze. My father knows that he will die soon. And yet, a week after he's returned home from the hospital, I find him in the bookstore working, in preparation of the reopening in just under a month, pushing entire sets of rolling shelves around, as if nothing has happened at all.

I suppose the bookstore offers him a respite from reality. It always has.

Standing in the second home of my youth, completely gutted and renovated, I'm amazed by how much nothing about its heart and soul has changed. Timbered ceilings and wide plank floors still dominate the space. The iron-framed windows still bathe the room with soft, natural light. Otis Redding still coos in the background. Dad always plays Otis after he closes the bookstore for the night. Real music with real lyrics, he once told me.

From the back room, I watch him, my head spinning with thoughts, as he shifts and rearranges books, rotating the new-release shelf and placing the older books in the sale section. Alana helps, calling out the names of the to-be-rotated books. As I see them in tandem, my heart fills, the love pressing against my chest.

Their connection was instant. Love at first sight. This morning, I awoke to the sweet sound of Alana's laughter tumbling throughout the house, like a piece of paper caught in a breeze. I found them in the kitchen, the sunlight pouring through the window and the aroma of bacon wafting in the air. Dad was reciting Carroll's "Jabberwocky," complete with silly faces and hand gestures as nonsensical as the poem itself.

"And, as in uffish thought he stood,
The Jabberwock, with eyes of flame,
Came whiffling through the tulgey wood,
And burbled as it came!"

Alana listened with rapt attention as Dad spoke in a deep, throaty voice. I mouthed the words, remembering when he first recited them to me.

As I watch them, a suffocating wave of remorse floods me for not being here for my father and for keeping him and his granddaughter apart all these years. I thought I knew nothing of guilt. Its paralyzing grip or clashing shame. I have never regretted or felt guilty for leaving home. It seemed like the only way. Now I don't know that it was.

Dad finishes the poem, and it is Alana's turn. She attempts to mimic him, his low tone, his comical movements. Dad's hearty laugh, the one he lets loose then, is always infectious to all in earshot.

Remember this, I think. *Remember him as he is now.* The crescent dimple between his brows. The tenor of his voice. The love in his dark-brown eyes.

Now, in the bookstore, the last of the full moon creeps behind dark clouds that hover on the horizon, dimming the light, as a stiff breeze pushes against the windows. I step reluctantly in from the back room, feeling like an intruder.

"It's getting late. How about we call it quits for tonight?"

Dad empties a box and reaches for another.

"The woods are lovely, dark, and deep,
But I have promises to keep,
And miles to go before I sleep,
And miles to go before I sleep."

"Yeah, Mom," Alana chimes in. "We have miles to go before we sleep."

I give a half smile and start to protest but stop myself and decide to give them more time. That's all I have left to give him, them.

———

The decision came quick: go to the grocery store and pick up a few things for Pizza Friday. We made homemade pizzas every Friday when I was a kid, and we are all eager to continue the family tradition and introduce it to Alana. Alana and I have been confined to Dad's and Sylvia's houses and the bookstore, our version of a safety net, and as soon as the automatic doors of the store crack open, I know it's too soon to be out in this town.

Walking into the store, I feel on display like the barrels of oranges, apples, and bananas. I do not look anyone in the eye as I place assorted cheeses, pepperoni and sausage, and onions and bell peppers in the basket. I want nothing more than to get out, but the anxiety I'm feeling causes me to forget all that I need to buy, and I find myself walking laps around the store, plucking cans of tomatoes from the shelf but forgetting the tomato paste sitting right next to them. When my basket is finally full, I head to the checkout line. I'm almost there when I hear my name from behind me.

"Sara?"

I turn and see a woman with long, brown hair, a long nose, and a long face looking at me inquisitively. I blink, and her childhood face pops into my mind. Abby. Her features have always looked stretched, and now time has exaggerated that. She is pregnant. By the looks of it, four or five months, the cute stage before the swollen ankles and cheeks.

"I thought that was you. Hi!" She walks me into an awkward hug, my arms locked at my sides, the basket's metal handles cutting into my flesh.

She appraises me from head to toe, her hand propped on her hip. "You look exactly the same."

She doesn't. The beginnings of crow's-feet line her eyes. Her long lines are heavier now, her once lean body filled in with maturity, and I suspect that the child she's carrying has at least one or two siblings. She's too made-up for the grocery store, her red-lipsticked mouth bold and catching, camouflage.

Caught in her silent review, I don't know what to do and glance toward her basket. That breaks her stare. "I promised myself I wouldn't gain as much weight with this one, but…" Her basket overflows with packages of Oreos, a jar of honey, and a gallon of Blue Bell ice cream. "I've had the weirdest cravings. I want honey on everything."

Cheetos and strawberry yogurt. That's what I craved when I was pregnant with Alana. I would plunge a Cheeto and spoon it out topped with a flat swoop of strawberry yogurt. I can't stand to eat either today.

"What about you? Any kids?"

I look into her basket again; a white frost has begun coating the sides of her ice cream. Before I can answer, she's speaking again. "Of course you don't have any kids. Look at your figure." She puts both hands on my waist and turns me like a key. "You always had such a cute shape." I remember her teenage days of Diet Coke and Ritz cracker diets.

"You have to tell me your secret." She runs her hand counterclockwise around her stomach. "This is my last one. I'm losing this weight forever."

"Kyle…you're needed at the customer service desk. Kyle…customer service desk, please," the PA system bleats.

She steps closer to me. "So…how does it feel to be home?" Her tone drops an octave.

I want to make myself invisible. Teleport myself away. Even just drop my basket and run. "It's okay," I say with the understanding that I'm not having this conversation just with Abby in the middle of the grocery store. That I'm having this conversation with every person from high school she's still in touch with. What I say, soon enough, will be known by everyone. I must choose my words carefully. "Dad's sick."

She ducks her head somberly. "We were all so surprised when you left. No one knew where you went. Rumor was that Birdie ran you out of town. Everyone was asking me, and I told them you needed a fresh start," she says, her head tilted proudly.

"Yeah…I did," I say, liking the way "fresh start" sounded. It wasn't far from the truth.

"Where have you been? Inquiring minds want to know."

"Here and there."

"I wish I would have done that. Travel. Before I started having babies. I'm so jealous."

Anyone else would have pressured me for a better answer about myself, but she can't help boomeranging the conversation back to her. I tell her that Dad is waiting for dinner. I'm almost free when she touches my arm, her touch surprisingly cold.

"Look, I hope you aren't upset that I didn't reach out. Daddy was the Wylers' banker. He didn't think that we should get involved. You understand, right?" She nods as if enforcing the thought.

Her family's opinion was the popular one at the time. Everyone claimed they didn't want to take a side. But they did. Sales at the bookstore dropped 40 percent during the trial. My closest friends since kindergarten, including Abby, stopped calling and hanging out with me. Side-eye glances and constant chatter accompanied me down the halls and in the cafeteria. No one believed what I accused him of.

I force a smile. "Of course." I see the checkout counter, the cashier finishing up with a customer, hear the sliding of the automatic doors opening and closing in a steady rotation. I can get out the door in less than five minutes, away from her, back to the safety of the bookstore.

"Because we really don't know what happened," she says, her voice a loud whisper.

"Excuse me?" I am amazed at the stillness of her face, the ease as she utters such a comment.

"I said, we don't know what really happened," she repeats.

A woman with a full shopping cart brushes past me to the available cashier and begins unloading her haul. Another customer lines up behind her.

In the early years, I rehearsed monologues of what I would say if I ever encountered someone from my past. I would be brave, my head lifted, shoulders rolled back. I would proudly tell them about Alana, my choice. I never planned on returning home, but these monologues, along with my poetry, served as therapy, an avenue to say everything I never got to say to the people who hurt me the most.

As I stand in front of Abby now, my skin crawls with anger but also with sad resignation that collapses my shoulders. This is who I am here. How people here will always see me. No poems or monologues could have prepared me for how others perceive me, continue to perceive me.

"How can you say that? You were there."

"I was there, but I wasn't *in* the room."

A foggy memory flashes, of Abby stumbling out the door with Tommy, her eyes droopy and red-rimmed. "No, you were not in the room. Because you left me."

She freezes, her attention dropping to the floor, absorbing the accusation I wield at her.

"And *I* know what happened. *I* was in the room," I say.

Now she stares at me still in disbelief, her hand pressed to her chest.

I start to walk away but not before saying, "Your ice cream is melting."

—————

Dad and Alana are still at it when I return from dropping off the groceries at home. I watch them again, reluctant to interrupt. My anger from the grocery store has finally dissolved but is still heavy on my mind.

"He's pretty stubborn," Sylvia says, coming up behind me. "So is she."

Tears well in my eyes. I haven't spoken to Sylvia much since I returned. I guess I'm still angry at her and my father for lying to me and completely blindsiding me with the news. And yet, as she stands beside me, her warmth pressing against me, I feel relief that she's here. That I'm not alone.

"It's time we talk," Sylvia whispers as Dad looks over. "I'll make us some tea."

I follow her to the back room, which doubles as a storage area and break room. The confined space features the same wide plank floors and exposed wooden beams as the front, without the natural light. Like most of the bookstore, the space is a city of boxes, stacked like skyscrapers, some packed with new and old books, others broken down.

As Sylvia pours the water into the kettle, she tells me about her latest project, a summer day camp for underprivileged children. Sylvia believes in the dreams and imaginations of children, cultivating their desires (and her own) with a steady stream of projects and field trips that could one day augment the people they become. Her heart is as expansive as the sky and her attentiveness to their futures heartwarming and inspiring. She tells me that some of the less fortunate children in her day camp will have never had the opportunity to leave Chatham County, and the kids are excited about an upcoming field trip to Fernbank Science Center in Atlanta. Maybe Alana could tag along, she says; it is only sort of a question.

"Normally, I would worry about throwing a new child into the mix this late into the session. Cliques have already formed, and a shier kid would feel left out. But I'm not worried about Alana. It will only be a matter of time before she lowers that notebook and interacts with someone. I hope it's Brixton." She carefully pours the hot water into two mugs and plops in tea bags to steep. "He's already full of the ways of the world and empty of the things kids should never be. He's only ten and has watched his alcoholic father beat up his mother and watched her take him back. These camps offer him an escape. Even if it's only temporary. He's gifted, not like Alana, but close. He took a liking to physics and math early on and attends a private school outside of Savannah."

She hands me a mug and settles on the couch next to me. "This could be good for Alana. She would really enjoy it," she says, continuing to talk, not noticing I haven't. "It's in Atlanta. She'll be safe. She'll be with me and a bunch of other smart kids."

I mumble a noncommittal "We'll see," which she barely hears.

"I'm so tired of looking at boxes." My eyes follow hers across the room. She takes a tiny sip of tea. "But the renovation is almost over."

I nod, indicating I'm processing even though I'm not. "How is he paying for all of this?" Outside of keeping the doors open and providing a modest salary for him and Sylvia, the bookstore has always been more of a labor of love than a financial gold mine.

"I don't know."

"Are you not handling the invoices anymore?"

"I haven't seen any invoices. All deliveries have been paid in full."

"Has he hired anyone else?"

For as long as I can remember, my father and Sylvia have manned the bookstore, working eight hours per day, six days a week. As a teenager, I often helped after school and on weekends, filling in for Sylvia while she tended to her projects. But with the store's recent expansion and the buzz it is creating, I can't imagine how the two of them will handle the influx of traffic.

"Two college kids but only temporarily."

I look around the area again. "Can we call them? Oh, is one of them,"—I snap my fingers—"what's his name? You mentioned him when you were at the hospital. Have them help out this week?" The invoices may be a mystery, but I could at least solve our obvious lack of people power.

Sylvia shakes her head as she takes another sip. "Oh no. Jacob doesn't work here. He recently moved to Savannah. All I know is every time he comes in, he wants a book on boats. I've only been here once when he's been here, but your dad said he comes around with some regularity. They seem to have hit it off."

"Really? How?"

Sylvia shrugs. "I don't know. I've driven by at night, and Jacob's truck is parked outside."

It's too much to contemplate, and my mind, normally up for the challenge, stops wanting to ask questions. I stare into my cup.

"How are you holding up, honey?"

I shrug, holding my shoulders at the apex, then releasing them. It's a gesture a child would make when they don't know the answer to a question or how to feel about something.

"I'm sorry I didn't tell you the truth. He thought it would be easier if you didn't know."

Anger is easier to handle than grief, and I allow a little to seep out from the crack of my resolve. "*You* didn't think I had the right to know that my father had an inoperable brain aneurysm? That he could die at any moment? How is that easier for me?"

She exhales, wraps her fingers tighter around her cup, and tries again. "I'm sorry. I now wish I had handled things differently... I really do."

"What if he died and I didn't get to say goodbye? You would have robbed me of my closure. And I need closure, Sylvia. You know that."

Her face crumbles with genuine sympathy that softens me. Sylvia has been the closest to a mother I've ever known, moving in with us for a short period of time after my mother died. She's been present for all of my milestones, both celebratory and unsung: birthdays, graduations, and, later, the tears.

"I know. But this hasn't been easy for me either."

Looking into her wet eyes, for the first time I acknowledge

someone else's grief other than my own. I take her hand into mine, letting go of any lingering resentment. "I know. I know."

"What are you going to do?"

"I don't know," I say. "I honestly don't know *what* I'm going to do."

"We'll figure something out."

I place my untouched tea on a box in front of us. "We can stay for maybe another week or so. That should be long enough to hire someone to oversee the bookstore if you don't want to take over. Is there anyone else close enough to Dad to help?" Thoughts and words come quick. "I have money from my 401k that I can use to hire a private nurse to look after him. While I'm still here, I can start to clean out the house and prepare to sell it. Do you know of any good real estate agents…?"

Her eyes lock on to mine; her hand pulls away. "You're leaving?"

Her interruption breaks my flow, and I blurt, "I can't stay here. I just ran into Abby from high school, and it was awful."

"Abby." Sylvia snorts. "I remember that girl. She desperately wanted to be anybody other than herself. Absolutely no self-worth. Such a shame. I would have hoped she'd outgrow that, but some never do."

"Well…she just confirmed that I will always be the girl who accused a Wyler of rape. I can't go back to being that girl."

She takes a deep breath and says, "You can't leave him."

I stare at her, processing her words, the last thing I expected to hear from her. "What?"

"You have to stay." She sniffles. "Until the end."

I give her an incredulous stare. "You know it's not that easy."

She is silent for a moment. "And what will you do? Go back to Maine?"

"Yes," I say, my voice cracking around the edges. "Yes, we'll go back to Maine."

"And then what? Continue to keep Alana hidden from the rest of the world?"

Wounded by her words, I stand so abruptly I brush the box, sloshing tea on the floor. "That's not fair. I'm not hiding her. I'm protecting her."

"From who?"

I shoot her a glare. "You know who."

Sylvia sighs, and when she speaks again, her voice is level. "Sara...they are long gone. Birdie still lives in Savannah, but she hasn't been seen much since her daughter died, and Tom committed suicide. She's somewhat of a recluse now."

"What about the brother? David?"

"I heard he went to Harvard after the trial and hasn't been back. He's an astronomer or an astronaut or something."

"What if someone recognizes Alana?"

"How can they? No one knew you were pregnant when you left."

"She looks just like him."

"Honey...that was eight years ago. So much has happened to that family. No one has seen or talked about them in years."

The Wylers were one of the wealthiest and most influential

families in Savannah. Progressive too. Their interracial marriage was one of the first in the city. Their house in Ardsley Park was the biggest and brightest at Christmas, and their three perfect children were beautiful and smart, almost geniuses. It's hard to imagine a Savannah without their presence and influence.

I shake my head, refusing to allow her statement to root. "I can't take that risk. No one can know about her. No one."

"You leaving is not about your father or Alana. It's about you. You're scared."

I furrow my brow. "Excuse me?"

"You're scared, Sara."

"How can you say that to me?" I say, realizing the crystal-clear clarity of her words. "Of course I'm scared! If they find out about her, that awful woman will try to take her from me."

"Or maybe they have moved on."

I snort, a loud, ugly sound. "I doubt it. I sent her son to prison. She would sue me for custody just to spite me, and she would win because of a mysterious large donation that would magically appear."

"Alana is…special. She doesn't deserve to be hidden away or sheltered. You cannot continue to hide her gift."

"I'm doing the best I can!"

"Really?"

I cross my arms. "I can't lose her, Sylvia. They can't do to her what they did to me. I won't let them make her feel less than."

"You have got to introduce Alana to the world. She has no friends. No social skills. She doesn't know how to be a kid.

You said it yourself that she didn't have any friends in Maine. All she does here is work on math equations. She doesn't watch TV. She doesn't listen to music. She's too comfortable hanging out with adults and not with kids."

"And that's my fault? She has no friends because of me? She doesn't know how to be a kid because of me?"

Sylvia steadies herself, aware of what I'm accusing her of. "Listen, I get that this is unprecedented. But a lot of time has passed. It's time for you to stop hiding and move on with your life and allow Alana to start hers."

"We have a life in Maine. A home."

She snaps, finally, frustration rising from nowhere. "This is your home. *'The tides are in our veins, we still mirror the stars.'*"

"This isn't my home anymore," I say flatly.

Sylvia pauses, considering her next words. "Think about your father. These are his last days. Alana deserves to know… to really know her grandfather. She deserves to know who she is. And you need to make your peace with what happened. Think about that before you make any decisions, okay?"

There are no easy decisions. But I take comfort in the certainty of one as Sylvia stands and heads to the door. We're leaving. Just as soon as I figure out how.

"For what it's worth," Sylvia says. "I haven't seen Hosea this happy in a long time. If he died today, he would die a happy man."

Sadness wafts in again, another quick slash to the heart.

JACOB

———

"DR. WYLER," A NURSE, a slim woman with close-cropped hair and honest brown eyes, says as she tightens the tube around my arm. "Are you okay?"

I nod my head and look at my arm. The vein she targeted plumps to the surface. "There it is," she says, touching it gently with two fingers for good measure.

She flashes a quick, flat smile at me before picking up the needle. I'm not sure why she smiles at me. Maybe it's because she knows this is the first of many pricks, shots, and probes Daniel and I will receive over the next three months. This blood test is the last of a series of tests, beginning with imaging tests, including a chest X-ray and a CT scan, and a physical examination that I've had today. Maybe her look is one of sympathy and comfort or one of understanding or guilt. I'm not sure.

I watch as she inserts the needle into my vein. Blood streams into the small vial, filling it in seconds.

"That's it," she says, pulling out the needle and placing a cotton ball on my arm.

"That's it?" I echo.

"Yup. Hang tight. The doctor will be in to explain everything in a sec."

She packs up her supplies, taking my blood with her. She doesn't look at me again.

She closes the door, leaving me alone in the blue room with the "Keep Calm I'm the Doctor" poster. White cabinets with glass doors house gauze and clamps and scissors. A brown leather chair and a stool huddle against the wall awaiting their purpose: they're there for the patient's spouse or parent, the doctor. Lofty responsibilities for furniture.

My family once had a purpose. *It is up to us to give reason and purpose to events that would otherwise be meaningless and arbitrary.*

We were The Wylers. That's how people referred to us, as if the *The* were capitalized too. As if we were always one entity. But we were never The Wylers. We were always Tom, Birdie, Daniel, David, and Naomi.

In life, we were blessed with a full, heaping share of everything that people admired and envied. We were rich (old money on Dad's side of the family, money that he couldn't give away fast enough). We were good-looking (our heritage creating skin the color of wet sand and bold green eyes). We were smart (with IQs that far exceeded those of anyone we would ever encounter). Those were the labels and characterizations placed on us. We found it odd that people cared about us, envied us, in such a way. We weren't perfect. No family is.

Footsteps ricochet across the tile hallway outside the door before it swings open. Dr. Bennett, a stout man with thinning hair and an impish, middle-aged face, enters and swings the stool in front of me. He studies my chart without saying hello. His facial features are a mask of contemplation over these long seconds.

He inhales deeply. "Okay, David…"

"Jacob, please." I interrupt.

His eyes dart to my chart again. Presumably to make sure he did, in fact, say the correct name.

"Jacob is my middle name, and that's what I go by."

Dr. Bennett does not react. "Do you have any questions about the procedure?"

"It's pretty straightforward, right? You take some of my bone marrow and give it to Daniel."

"Sort of. But first we will do bloodwork on your sample. This is just a precaution. Since you are your brother's identical twin, we already know you will be a match for him. We just want to make sure there are no surprises."

"What sort of surprises?"

"Testing blood samples at this stage is routine. We want to make sure donors are the best possible matches. In your case, we know you are, but we can never be too careful."

"What's the probability of success?"

Dr. Bennett pats my knee twice with my chart and stands. "I wouldn't normally say this. As a doctor, we can't promise favorable outcomes, but in this case I would say excellent."

I ignore the way my heart eases, the pressure lifting like birds taking flight, and focus on moving off the table and retrieving my clothes.

"Your brother is pretty lucky," Dr. Bennett says, washing his hands at the small sink.

"Excuse me?"

"Daniel is pretty lucky," he says, his eyes meeting mine.

I lift my eyebrows at the ease with which he considers Daniel to be lucky. I say the word again inside my mind... *lucky* as if to conjure a new meaning, then wonder how much, if anything, he knows about Daniel's crime, and if he knew, whether it makes a difference to him.

"How's that?"

"Most people have to wait months, even years, for a perfect match. Very few people have identical twins, so very few with leukemia do find that match. You two have the exact same immune composition, so there is no risk his body will reject your bone marrow." Dr. Bennett's hand rests on the door handle. "Your bone marrow will save your brother's life."

I am aware of the pressure building, once again, in my chest and fight back my gnawing doubt and anger. Who am I to deny Daniel a second chance at life?

Especially when I still grieve another death.

———

Naomi died on a Tuesday. That useless bit of trivia, the day of the week, is frozen solid in my memory, yet I've forgotten the sound of her voice. I know it was a Tuesday because that was trash day, and it was my chore to roll the bin to the curb. Just as the police arrived to tell us that Naomi had died in an early morning car crash, a garbage truck inched toward our house, a crescendo of roaring as the engine blasted. Daniel and I, eighteen on our next birthday, lurked on the second-floor landing, listening. The garbage truck arrived at our house, the mechanical arm lifting a garbage can just as one of the officers told my father and Birdie that Naomi was dead. The lowering of the arm punctuated my father's cries. A deep bellow that reverberated around the foyer. Birdie didn't cry then or at the funeral. She didn't cry when my father, still devastated by the loss of his daughter and faced with Daniel's sentencing, died by suicide one year later.

At fifteen, Naomi was everything already. All by herself. Precocious with a bewitching smile, she ruled our house since the day she was born. She was the best of all of us, the perfect balance of everything good in us. Passionate like Dad. Motivated like Daniel. Curious like me. I was the least talented, therefore the least favorite, of my parents' children, but I was Naomi's favorite, the one she preferred to curl up next to during thunderstorms, before she realized how complex and exhilarating they could be. She was a kind soul, and her loss left me without the one person who comforted me with her affection and understanding.

It takes a million years for a star to die. A fraction of a second for its core to collapse. Hours for the shock wave to reach the surface. And then, months for it to brighten for the world to see, and years for it to fade away. We had fifteen years with Naomi, but it took seconds for the truck to swerve across the road and take her from us. The shock wave of her death gripped us and ripped us apart, slowly, like paper, and exposed the huge crack already in our foundation. Naomi's death provided the catalyst that swallowed us whole. We didn't talk about what happened to her. We didn't show emotion. We didn't know how. We pressed on. Or thought we had. Until Daniel raped Sara. Until Dad killed himself. Until our entire world was turned upside down.

———

After I'm finished at the doctor's, I find myself pulled to a familiar place from my childhood. The Fernbank Science Center hums with a steady cadence of footsteps. Groups of students on field trips snake disjointedly throughout the lobby. A dull buzz of laughing and talking hangs in the air.

At first, I follow the throng of kids with tapered jeans and colorful sneakers, their ears plugged with white earbuds, expertly noting the exhibits while snapping up incoming texts and social media notifications on their cell phones. I have no destination in mind. No exhibit I want to see. I just want to be here. After spending the morning being poked and prodded, I want to be someplace safe. Where life makes sense.

Naomi, Daniel, and I spent many summer afternoons here, at Fernbank, learning, studying, our parents keen on turning us into the next great scientists. *It is up to us to give reason and purpose to events that would otherwise be meaningless and arbitrary.* A boy with silver-framed glasses and a mop top of curls pulls his friends over to the *Apollo 6* space capsule. His eyes are full of joy as he points at several different features. My heart swells. Such eager, fresh minds waiting, wanting to be fed. Daniel insists that we are not teachers, but it's where I find my heart wanting to go.

Lately, more than I ever have, I've been listening to my heart. To Naomi.

She had been gone for twelve years when I saw her on Poker Flat Research Range in Alaska.

That night, I was packing up my truck for the twenty-minute drive back to my apartment in Fairbanks when I saw something, out of the corner of my eye, in the dim light, a figure wearing a yellow spaghetti-strap dress standing in the ink-black field of Chatanika River valley.

A hush floated in the air as snowflakes collected across the flat terrain. In the far distance, trees, thin and bare, twisted up from the cold ground, their branches laden with the weight of freshly fallen snow. My feet crunched the thick blanket of snow as I walked out to where the figure stood. Part of me thought I was hallucinating. It had been a long week, preparing for the launch of the probes, and sleep had eluded me. But a larger part compelled me to check on this very real person.

"What are you doing out here? Are you okay?" I asked once I was within hearing distance. The figure turned slowly, and the face morphed into Naomi's. I blinked twice as my mind comprehended what I was seeing. When she died, I lost the ability to conjure her face, to say her name out loud, the syllables lodged in my throat. Looking at her there in Alaska, her long, sandy hair in loose waves down her back, I recognized everything, the Cassiopeia group of freckles just below her right eye, the crescent moon–shaped crease from her dimple, and it scared me a little. Finally, my mouth caught up to my eyes, and I whispered, "How?"

She stepped closer, seemingly unaffected by the snow collecting on her bare shoulders and cold under her feet, and placed her hand on my cheek. She always did that, cupped my face, the only form of physical affection I received from a family member, and smiled. I leaned into her hand, the warmth it provided then and now. In the wattage of her eyes, I was seventeen again, and everything I had bottled up since we lost her shattered like broken glass. "There's so much I want to tell you," I said.

We walked across the field, and I told her about Daniel and the trial, Dad and his suicide, and Birdie and her quest to save Daniel. She listened as she always did, quietly and keenly.

When I finished, I felt lighter, unburdened, somehow, as if I had shed pounds of invisible weight I didn't know I carried.

Naomi stopped walking and looked southeast over the dark field. "Home." Her voice didn't sound quite like hers, but it was also not unfamiliar.

It took me a moment, and then I understood. Four thousand miles in that direction lay Savannah. "That's not my home anymore."

The light from her countenance diminished in an instant. She looked back at me with a sparkle in her eyes and said, "Sara."

"Sara?" I repeated, stunned by the utterance of a name I'd never forgotten but hadn't spoken in years. "What about her?"

Naomi didn't answer. She smiled and continued gliding across the field as the snow fell like confetti.

"Should I try to find her? What are you telling me to do?"

She didn't look back, and I didn't follow her. I watched as her yellow dress faded away and the thick night swallowed her whole.

That night, a sixth sense awoke in me, an ache for the family I had walked away from. I didn't believe in the existence of ghosts. But Naomi had come back. And the thought made me homesick for a mother I had tried to forget and a brother I had abandoned. So, I decided to go home. I would face what I ran from. I would reunite with my remaining family and understand the incident that had destroyed us.

Now, I realize I'm thinking of Naomi because once again, she's standing before me. But not exactly. Just someone...who looks so much like her.

I hadn't noticed the little girl at first. Then the boys darted off to another exhibit, breaking in such a way that opened sight to her, like the parting of the Red Sea. Her movements are peculiar. She busies herself at the golden ratio exhibit, staring; then she's back to the bench where she sits to doodle something in a notebook, and back to the exhibit again. She repeats this practice several times, each time her face crumpling into a deeper pout, her gaze trained on the floor as if the answer she seeks resides there.

She is trying to make sense of what she is seeing. The exhibit, "Mathematica: A World of Numbers and Beyond," features the mysterious principle that appears in nature, architecture, and mathematics and that has baffled mathematicians for centuries. The idea is to engage visitors in the golden ratio and provide an opportunity for everyone to enjoy the wonder of mathematics as well as the beauty of the post-modern design. But something about the golden ratio equation seems to bother, almost annoy, her. I watch, a little awed, as she once again tracks back to the bench and squats, using the bench as a desk, furiously writing in her notebook, her nose wiggling as she writes, her tongue slightly protruding from the corner of her mouth.

My face burns with remembrance at this gesture. I look away from the girl as the memory plays in my mind like an old home movie. Naomi, Daniel, and I are at the kitchen table, our books and homework a buffet before us, Birdie hovering, teeming with answers to questions we had yet to ask. Naomi, a ball of concentration, is engrossed in her physics homework, her tongue lodged at the corner of her mouth, tilting her head ever so slightly to one side. "I can't help it," she always said to Daniel and me when we ruthlessly mock the quirk. "It helps me think."

The gesture isn't the only one my sister and this stranger share. She is left-handed like Naomi and writes with the pencil perfectly perpendicular to the paper. Her hair is the same hue as Naomi's, the color of wheat just before the harvest.

I find myself continuing to stare at this little girl who could be my dead sister when a tiny voice brings me back to myself.

"Excuse me? Do you work here?" The little girl's question surprises me. I must have watched her walk toward me, but I don't remember that. Now, her green eyes cut through me like a knife, ripping something apart, a sadness I've kept locked away from the world.

I instinctively look down at my brown blazer and green polo shirt for an indication that my dress would warrant such a question. "Uh, no," I say. There is a wobbliness to this entire circumstance, and I feel unsteady.

"Can you keep a secret?" she whispers, giggling, revealing a set of white, slightly crooked teeth.

I look around as if the answer is written on the wall or floor, for one last verification that I am the intended recipient of her question. To my right, a group of kids of all ages and sizes, whom I assume she's with, huddles at the next display case a few feet away. I blink in astonishment as I recognize the woman with gray dreadlocks, Sylvia, from Savannah.

"It's wrong," the girl says, breaking my trance, not looking at me but at the exhibit, searchingly.

"What's wrong?" I ask, my voice gentle.

But the little girl isn't through asking questions. "Can you wear a watch?" she says, turning toward me.

At the same time, we both look at the black Omega Speedmaster Professional chronograph watch on my wrist.

"Cool!" she says, not waiting for my answer. She drops to her knees like a rag doll and begins riffling through her green backpack, dumping and flipping out its contents all over the floor. A yellow notebook skids under a bench.

She doesn't notice it and produces a tiny, nondescript yellow watch from her backpack. "Here's mine," she says with a hint of sadness. "It stopped working on the plane."

I bend down and take the watch in my hand. Its second hand jerks backward, not forward.

Her sadness is palpable yet her acceptance of the loss of her watch is unwavering, and I feel the pull to console her, this stranger, as if I've known her my whole life, as if it's my job to absolve her. "I'm sorry about your watch," I say softly. "Maybe I can fix it."

She brightens, all her facial features lifting. "Really?"

"I can try," I say.

She twists her lips in contemplation. "What if you can't fix it?"

"I'll tell you what," I say, removing my watch from my wrist. "How about I give you my watch until I fix yours."

Fixing her watch will be easy. But I know I will never see this little girl again to return it to her. Giving her my watch, on the day when Naomi's spirit radiates as strong as if she stands next to me, comforts me like a hug.

The little girl smiles at me, moon-eyed and unblinking, a look that pains me, like looking at the sun. She even smells like Naomi, sweet and powdery, a scent that wafts in my nose as she tries to wrap my watch around her tiny wrist.

"I'm Jacob."

"I'm Alana," she says, not looking at me but at the watch. "But I'm not supposed to be talking to strangers."

I laugh. Of everything I miss about Naomi—her intuitiveness, her curiosity, her wildness—this, her blatant honesty, is what I miss the most. And here it all is, manifested, in this stranger.

"Well...you know my name, and I know your name, so we are not strangers anymore."

She attempts to balance my watch on her tiny wrist to tighten it, her tongue once again protruding from her mouth. I look at the exhibit to escape this sight and remember our initial interaction. "Alana...you said it's wrong. What's wrong?"

"The exhibit," she says, pulling the watch strap to the tightest hole. It's still not enough. Crafted from a single block of black zirconium oxide ceramic, the face of the watch swings under her wrist. She tries to adjust it a few times before giving up.

I look at the equation and smile at the innocence of a child. At least the exhibit intrigued her enough for advanced thought, unlike most of the kids who never broke stride to read it.

"The exhibit is not wrong. But it is quite hard."

She frowns in contemplation. "Yes, it is. See," she says, finding her notebook under the bench. "There should be plus signs, not minus signs."

I take the notebook from her hand. A chain of equations covers the entire page. I stop studying the equations and look at her, amazed. She can't be more than ten years old. And yet, she has attempted to work out the equation, evident by problems scribbled across the page. I turn back to the notebook. The equation carries on for four pages before it concludes.

I quickly look at the golden ratio equation in the exhibit, back at her notebook, and at the equation once again, vexed at what I know to be true but cannot believe.

"Is it waterproof?" she asks, tapping on the face of my watch. "Does it ever stop while you are wearing it?"

My mind snaps with questions. Who is this little girl? Did she correctly identify a problem with the golden ratio exhibit? I open my mouth to speak, and I hear from across the room, "Alana!" The little girl snaps to attention and begins refilling her backpack with its contents. The group she's with shuffles down the hall and out the door. She runs to rejoin them, her ponytail bouncing behind her.

I stand, her notebook and watch in my hand, speechless.

SARA

————

A FEW DAYS LATER, Sylvia finds me on the front porch, a cup of coffee on the table, my legs pulled into my chest, a knot of tissues balled in my hand. As a teenager, I would spend hours on this porch, just like this, writing poems or reading. I adjust my position in my chair when Sylvia nears and look up at her with wet eyes pleading—*please don't*.

"I didn't come to convince you to stay." She lowers herself into the seat next to me, immediately suffocated by the sadness in my eyes. At seven in the morning, the humidity has already thickened the air, and her upper lip is damp with sweat.

Sylvia pulls herself straighter in her chair, and a line crosses her smooth forehead. "Sara…I don't want to push, but I am worried about something else. I haven't seen you writing. Have you stopped? Alana also told me that you don't swim anymore. Why?"

More time passes before I speak, and Sylvia allows it. Finally, I sigh and begin. "We were at the beach. I was floating in the water, in a tube...I think it was orange or yellow... just watching the sky. I remember the sky. It was so blue. Like a new color blue. I had just stuck a strawberry Charms Blow Pop into my mouth. I sat there floating, sucking on that sucker. When I looked up, I saw Rachel and Abby talking to some guys. They were always flirting with guys at the beach. Later, they waded out to me and told me that the Wyler twins were having a party at their mansion that night and asked if I wanted to go. I didn't, but they did. They were curious about the Wylers. Everyone was. But it had been such a great day so I said, sure. I guess I associate water with that night. It was the last time I remember being completely free."

"You have to stop punishing yourself for what happened."

"I'm not punishing myself. I'm being cautious." I pause. "I do want to let her go," I say, because of course what we're talking about is Alana. "I do. You know...I have this recurring dream. Except...it's not really a dream because I always have it when I'm dozing, right before I fall asleep or right as I'm waking. More of a blending of a dream and a daydream. Alana and I are in a hallway. A long hallway except it doesn't lead anywhere. It looks like it goes on and on. It's white, pale white. We both see something, but I don't know what. And I look down at her and she looks up at me for confirmation of something. I'm holding her hand and...I just let go."

"Where is she going?"

"I don't know. She just walks away from me. And all I know is that I'm not afraid."

"You can do that. We can do that. Let me help you."

"How?"

"You've already started by letting her come with me to the science center. She had a great time. And…" Sylvia stops. "You can stay."

I'm still not convinced and close my eyes for a long moment. What kind of daughter would leave her dying father? I think about that constantly, the idea replaying over and over in my mind. I never have an answer. Already I have watched the calendar days wither and May slowly fade into June. Maybe Sylvia is right. Maybe Daniel's family has, indeed, moved on. That should create a sense of ease within my soul. It does…but it is replaced with another weight. Who am I if Alana's safety isn't at the forefront of my mind? With that constant known ruling my every decision, the safeguards I firmly put into place, crumbling before me. What does that mean for me now?

"Alana needs this, Sara. You need this. Stay."

I consider this for a second and nod as bravely as I can.

A wall of silence lifts before a car pulls in front of Sylvia's house and a boy climbs out. Sylvia waves at the passing car as the boy runs across the street to us. She greets him and he mumbles a weak hello, his eyes fixated on the porch, a Rubik's Cube in his hand. He's adorable, with black curly hair and glasses. He's wearing a pair of khaki shorts and a black Star Wars shirt. And there's something about the way he twirls the Rubik's Cube around his knuckles that gives me the impression that he carries it less to solve it and more as a security blanket.

"Sara…this is Brixton. Brixton, can you say hi to Miss Sara?" Sylvia stands to the left of him, her hand on his shoulder to ground him as if he may lift off.

"Hello," he says, still not looking at me.

Just then, Alana bursts through the door and stands an equal distance from him. He lifts his eyes to her. They met last week at Fernbank and yet they don't speak, just study each other before Brixton begins solving the Rubik's Cube, his eyes darting in concentration as he moves the pieces around. As soon as he begins, Alana's eyes travel over to him, and she watches, appraisingly, as he moves the slides into proper color placement. He finishes and resets it, the noise a crunching sound like grinding rocks.

"You could have solved it in two less moves," Alana says.

"No, I couldn't," Brixton says, pushing his glasses up his nose.

Alana looks at me as if for confirmation, and my heart aches that she doesn't feel encouraged to exhibit her abilities, a condition I caused. I nod a bit too enthusiastically, probably, but I want her to understand that there's no shame in her intelligence, despite my reluctance.

She reduces the space between them and stands there, arms folded, her hip slightly protruding. Brixton peers up at her. In response, Alana presents her hand, and he drops the Rubik's Cube into it and watches as Alana turns and twists the slides into place, counting each move she makes. When she finishes, she extends the cube back to Brixton.

Brixton's eyes grow behind his glasses. "How did you do that?"

Alana shrugs. "I don't know. I've never done it before."

Hours later, to my amusement, they've become fast friends, with Alana re-creating her moves, even reducing the number by one, and Brixton offering up his own wonderment, a physics equation, which Alana eagerly accepts.

———

On the morning of the grand reopening of the bookstore, I hear the house inch to life from my bed. The groans from the old hardwood floors as Dad leaves his bedroom and the crunches of the stairs as he descends to the kitchen. A screech from the screen door as Sylvia's short commute from across the street ends in the foyer and a staccato slam as the front door closes. It's become Alana's habit to wake early, and now her giggle and high-pitched chatter echo upstairs. A chorus of clangs and bangs from cabinet doors and pots.

Downstairs, I stop in the doorway of the kitchen. Morning sun fills the room, lighting the cabinets and floors with gold. Laughter and conversations bathe me in togetherness. I'm the only person missing, and I don't mind. It gives me time. Time to remind myself to make the most of this, despite my push to get back to my normal. Time to watch him live.

"Grandpa made pancakes," Alana announces as I enter the kitchen. From her place at the table in the corner, she cuts her pancakes into perfect squares and dips them one by one into a separate container of syrup. As always, next to her, a page of math equations, a series of expressions the length of the page. Across the table, Sylvia is reading the *Savannah Morning News*, "Light of the Coastal Empire and Lowcountry."

"Good morning," I say to the room before kissing Dad, who stands at the stove flipping pancakes, and taking a mug from the cabinet and sitting down. Alana also gets a smooch on the cheek, though she squirms when I go to deliver it.

Dad remains as spry as I've ever seen him. Sylvia says that it is because we are there. It pains me to believe that she may be right. He's still handsome despite it all, more salt in his hair than pepper. His gaunt figure is hidden underneath pressed khakis and a dapper brown tweed sport coat with a red-and-navy plaid lining and a navy polka-dot bow tie.

"What are you working on, honey?" I ask, looking over to Alana.

"Just some math," she says, her sharpened pink pencil perpendicular to the paper. "Brixton says that these problems are impossible to solve. But I told him they aren't."

I steal a look at Sylvia and open my mouth to voice my concern about someone else knowing about Alana's gift. She seems to know I would look to her, because she lowers her newspaper and gives me a reassuring look before stabbing one of her own pancake squares and shoving it in her mouth. I swallow my concern along with a gulp of coffee.

"Where's he getting these?" I ask, reaching for the plate of pancakes.

Alana doesn't look up. "The internet."

She scrambles a series of numbers and lines across a single sheet and flips the page over, stacking it back with the rest.

"Where's your LT notebook?"

She sighs, a heavy breath that slightly lifts the edge of the paper. "I lost it."

Sylvia stands and places her plate and Georgia on My Mind mug in the sink. "We called the museum's lost and found, and no one has turned it in yet."

"It'll turn up," I say. It's not the first time she's lost one of her LT notebooks.

Alana shrugs. "It's okay. I remember everything," she says, continuing to solve the equations, pencil alternating with fork. "I just don't want to write it all down again." She stretches this sentence like a rubber band.

Dad joins us at the table and starts piling his pancakes on a plate. Sylvia is now looking over her final to-do list for the reopening.

"I can't believe we pulled this off," she says. "And in just a few short weeks. Unbelievable."

I can't believe it myself. After Dad's seizure, I oversaw the renovation with Sylvia, in charge of managing the deliveries and ordering books. She showed me the renovation plans organized in a neat binder. Every detail was considered. From the color of the bookshelves to the LED light bulbs in the new lighting fixtures to the kind of receipt paper the printer would spit out. Such preparation required time and thought. And I wonder how long it took Dad to plan it all.

The clock in the front hall strikes nine. *"Allons! the road is before us!"* Dad says, clapping once.

"I need to run home and grab a few things and stop at Party City to pick up the balloons," Sylvia announces. "I can take Alana with me if you want to get dressed and meet us there."

I thank her and kiss Alana goodbye. Dad stands, putting the rest of the dishes in the sink. As Sylvia walks by, he takes her face into his hand, just below her chin, and touches her nose. It is all he offers, has ever offered, the height of his affection.

She holds still and smiles wide, her eyes fixed on him, and touches his face, her whole hand on the side of his cheek. The entire display lasts seconds. And yet, I find myself still thinking about it as I pull back the shower curtain later that morning.

They are still in love, despite it all, the rapidly upcoming conclusion of their courtship. Maybe it is because of the opening, the fulfillment and completion of something, but I am acutely aware, more than I ever have been, of their affection. It is nice to behold, and part of me aches for my own touch on the nose.

There have been two men since my assault. Owen and Todd. Both varying degrees of seriousness. I didn't know what sex was like prior. I was a virgin before the rape, and it warped my understanding of what sex could be and how it should feel. Owen, an English graduate assistant at Brown, was my first sexual experience two years after the assault. Sex with Owen was awkward, mostly because I just wanted to get it over with. Afterward, I fled his apartment somewhat numb to the experience. I didn't enjoy it; his touch felt stiff, his kisses flat, but I was happy to have cleared that obstacle. I never told him about my assault or why I left in such a hurry. I told him I needed space, and he gave me all the space I needed. I never heard from him again and moved to Lubec soon after.

Todd was safe in every definition of the word. He lived in Machias, a neighboring town to Lubec. Close enough to visit but far enough away to maintain a healthy distance. Unlike with Owen, sex with Todd didn't feel like an accomplishment. He was older, patient, and understanding when I told him of my assault. With Todd, I realized how enjoyable the experience could be, an exploration into what I liked, and I learned to rebuild my idea of what sex should be. The arm's length I kept him at prevented anything from developing between us despite his affections and wishes. Despite this, I remained hopeful that my future wouldn't be entirely sexless and that my past would not be a third wheel in my relationships.

After my shower, I put on a navy slip dress and a light blue cardigan. Blame the sugar from the syrup, but the haze that has followed me since my arrival seems to lift as I flat-iron my hair and apply makeup, my mood turning jovial as I drive to the bookstore.

For the grand opening, Dad has opted for a simple

unveiling, no press, just a few of his loyal customers and us. Sylvia and Alana tied a few royal-blue and white balloons on the sign out front and in various places around the bookstore.

A few minutes before ten, Dad clears his throat. Sylvia, standing across the room, mouths, "Yeats."

"Whitman," I mouth. "Always Whitman."

My father dismisses the notion of favorites, but if his personality could be matched with that of a poet, it would be Walt Whitman's. He's partial to Yeats, Donne, and Bryon, but he often quotes Whitman, becoming a fan in college after reading *Leaves of Grass*. Whitman was a man of the people; Dad would say, if he spoke, that Whitman understood people, their motivations, their lives.

Dad begins Whitman's "Song of the Open Road."

"I am larger, better than I thought,
I did not know I held so much goodness.
All seems beautiful to me,
I can repeat over to men and women You have done such
good to me I would do the same to you,
I will recruit for myself and you as I go,
I will scatter myself among men and women as I go,
I will toss a new gladness and roughness among them,
Whoever denies me it shall not trouble me,
Whoever accepts me he or she shall be blessed and shall
bless me."

Claps and cheers fill the store, which has transformed from a dark, outdated space to a bright, modern bookstore, complete with open, sleek lounge seating and dedicated shelf space for small and independent presses, natural lighting, outward-facing books, and not a magazine in sight. Poetry will still be the focus, but other genres finally have a place alongside what Dad considers the "highest form of literature." Sylvia and Alana hold a blue ribbon, and Dad cuts it. He doesn't speak again, but his face glows with happiness as he unlocks the door and lets in the first official customers of the day. It is what he always wanted. A dream realized. A dream that surely will be short-lived. From across the bookstore, Sylvia knows it too as both happy and sad tears flood our eyes.

———

Thirty minutes before closing, a woman in jeans and a white blouse approaches me. "Can you help me?" she asks. "There's this poem that I heard once, and I don't know who wrote it."

"Do you remember any of the lines?" I ask. "Though I'm not as good as my father." It has become somewhat of a tradition to try to stump my father. No one ever has.

She twists her lips in contemplation and blushes a faint pink. "Love is more thicker?"

I smile.

"love is more thicker than forget
more thinner than recall
more seldom than a wave is wet
more frequent than to fail

it is most mad and moonly
and less it shall unbe
than all the sea which only
is deeper than the sea"

I continue reciting the verse as a deeper voice begins to accompany mine. I follow the voice toward a man standing nearby, his face shielded by a Braves baseball hat.

"love is less always than to win
less never than alive
less bigger than the least begin
less littler than forgive

it is most sane and sunly
and more it cannot die
than all the sky which only
is higher than the sky"

I can tell the poem means something to him in all the ways that poetry, if you let it, gives context and meaning to life. When we finish, his head snaps back as he scans the bookstore, suddenly aware of himself. His hand moves to the brim of his hat, pulling it down even farther on his head.

There's an awkward beat of silence before the woman finally speaks. "That's it. Thank you," the woman says to the man and then at me.

The man bows his head and moves deeper into the stacks.

"Do you have that somewhere?" the woman asks.

"We do," I say, walking over to the poetry section and retrieving the book for her. She pays and leaves the store, the bell above the door clanging cheerily as she disappears into the quiet night street.

Much like his clothing, a white button-down shirt sharply cuffed to his elbows with one tail tucked into khaki cargo shorts, the man is casual in his perusal of the store, nothing holding his attention for too long. I watch as he runs his fingertips across the top of a bookcase and then his hand along the royal-blue velvet wingback couch until he notices the last customer leaving, and he moves toward the door as if to follow.

"I'm not the only E. E. Cummings fan, I see," I call out to him, tidying Sylvia's magnetic poetry display, which became disarrayed during the rush of the day. I'm not sure why I speak to him, especially since he seems to be embarrassed, and as he is the last customer of the day, any idle small talk will delay closing. But something about him intrigues me. There are not many people who can recite poetry from memory.

He stops at the door, a statue for a moment, his hand

almost on the door handle. His presence overwhelms the doorway, leaving just a fist of space above him. "Yeah," he says, not turning around. "You could say that."

"Lifelong or recent?"

He's still frozen at the door, hidden by a shadow, his back to me. "Recent."

"He makes me cry in my notebook."

He turns half his body, his head quirked in curiosity. "You're a poet?"

I throw a dismissive hand. "Sometimes. Lately, I'm more of a poser."

He steps out of the shadow and stands with his body weight evenly distributed, his hands buried in his pockets. "Published?"

I nod. "One collection."

He moves another step closer. "What's your collection about?"

"Mermaids."

He considers this, tilting his head. "Mermaids?"

"Yes."

He releases a nervous chuckle, a cough really. "You wrote a poetry collection about mermaids?"

"Oh yeah, sure. They are fascinating creatures. Their calls. Their tails. Their mating rituals."

A full laugh, a wild one that I don't expect, rumbles from the pit of my stomach and out in a breathless giggle.

"I'm sorry," I say, gasping for air. "I don't know why I said that."

The curve of a smile grows, cracking the stoic face he held, and he breaks into a staccato chuckle, our laughter merging and bouncing around the bookstore like a ball.

I don't remember the last time I laughed this hard, this long. As the tickle subsides, my body eases into a state of contentment, relaxation. Blood rushes to my head, and a cooling sensation calms me as the tension dissolves. It feels good to surrender to a force beyond my control.

I open my eyes to him. The brim of his hat shields details of his face, but from the sharp curve of his jaw, I can tell he is handsome. My body, my heart, still buzzing from the laughter, race at this realization. My reaction startles me, and I knock a pile of magnets from Sylvia's poetry display onto the floor. They stick to each other in clumps, arranging themselves into undecipherable word soup.

At the same time, he and I sink to the floor. I feel his eyes watching me, radiating an unexpected warmth in me as we both scoop up the magnets.

"I'm sorry," I say, trying to separate the magnets. "Once they're together, they're hard to separate."

"Don't apologize," he says. "It's just attraction."

"Excuse me?"

He blushes. "Not attraction...I mean...attraction, but not that attraction. Not that I don't think..." He gives up and holds up two of the magnets, the words *always* and *more*, together. "Energy is needed to create movement. The magnetic field that surrounds magnets contains stored energy. Whenever there's stored energy in an object, like a magnet, it will be pushed in that direction. Bringing magnets closer together decreases the stored energy in the magnetic field and they are forced together," he says, pushing the magnets together. "That's attraction."

"Oh," I say, in lieu of something profound, marveling at how he can make something like magnets sound so...so... what? Captivating. "That's interesting."

He stands quickly with a trace of annoyance and frustration. "I'm sorry."

"Don't apologize," I say, joining him upright. My college physics comes to mind. "I'm more of a particle person."

He smiles. "Actually, particles work somewhat similarly to magnets. They can be light-years separated, but as long as they were entangled at one time, and nothing has interfered with them in the interim, changing something about one particle affects the other one instantly. They are connected, even at other ends of the universe, intimately connected, across time and space."

His every syllable flirts with me. My stomach drops and my entire body tingles as I become more aware of him and my body's reaction to him. I nod, somber at the buzz shooting through me. "Poetry and science. You are quite the renaissance man."

"I'm a poser too," he whispers.

We share another laugh. This one shorter and intimate. There's something familiar, even comforting about him. We hold each other's gaze. Seconds stretch before we speak again. In that space, I don't move. He doesn't either.

"Can I help you with something?" I say finally, clearing my

voice to steady it against the unexplained emotions rippling through me. I'm nervous, and I don't know why. "I doubt that you came in to help me pick up magnets and explain the interconnectedness of particles."

"No…I…just wanted to see the new place."

"What do you think?" I ask, gesturing around the bookstore. "What you expected to see?"

"Not at all," he says, not looking away from me.

"Oh yeah? In a good way, I hope."

He nods an imperceptible confirmation.

I point to a stack of books, looking for an escape, hoping he cannot sense my uneasiness. "I'm going to shelve those," I say, picking them up. "Feel free to look around. Let me know if I can help you with anything."

I take a few steps backward before turning but spin around to him. "I'm sorry. I never got your name."

"Jacob!" Alana yells, appearing from the back room.

"You're Jacob?" I ask. "*The* Jacob?"

He doesn't answer. Instead, he braces himself for Alana, who is running at him full speed. As she reaches him, his face radiates with excitement like he's known her all his life. I don't have time to wonder how Alana knows him. I don't have time to wonder why he's so happy to see her before his wide, toothy smile slowly dissipates, and as he kneels to her level, his hand slowly removes his hat.

The brim had concealed his green eyes and sandy hair. If it had not, I would have recognized him immediately.

Glints of brown specks sparkle in his eyes, the same ones I see in Alana's, as he pieces together what I already know.

Alana could be his daughter or sister. Or niece.

I feel the air leave my body.

JACOB

———

"ALANA," SARA SAYS BEFORE I can speak. "Go get your stuff. We're leaving."

The little girl, rattled at the forcefulness of Sara's request, jumps. "But…"

"Go!"

We watch her disappear into the back room. Sara turns to me, her eyes narrowed, hands balled into tight fists. "Why did you come here?"

I hold my hands low. "I told you. To look at the place."

"Well…you saw it. Now go."

"Sara…"

She scrunches her brows. "How do you know who I am?"

"How could I forget you?"

She digests this information, unsure of something in my tone.

I continue. "Your father talks about you all the time."

"Yeah…I heard you've been bothering him…"

"I thought of you and how you love this beauty,
And walking up the long beach all alone,
I heard the waves breaking in measured thunder
As you and I once heard their monotone."

At the sound of the familiar lines, the confusion on her face abates, and something gentle, almost remorseful, fills its space.

I inch closer, slowly. "He never told me about her. I'm... so sorry."

The softness in my tone again surprises her but doesn't lessen her anger.

She snaps back. "How does Alana know you?"

Her tone is sharp; her eyes flash with worry. I hold still, my arms locked to my side, aware that any sudden movements or gestures could enhance her fear.

"I met her at Fernbank."

"I thought you moved away."

"I did, but I moved back a few months ago."

All at once, her shoulders collapse a little. "I should have never come back here," she says. She touches her fingertips to her mouth briefly, but she recovers and darts around me so fast a stack of bookmarks sails to the floor. She walks to the door and swings it open. "You have to leave."

The street is empty and silent, except for the faint chorus of raindrops tapping on the pavement. A crisp wind blows, cooling the sweat on my brow.

I meet her at the door, hat in hand, eager to comply. "May I talk to her?"

"No!" Her voice severs the thin air, and the sharp punch in her tone vibrates every muscle of my body.

I pause for a moment, stunned by the force of her voice. "Why?"

Sara looks to the back room where Alana is and lowers her voice to a loud whisper. "She doesn't know anything about what happened. I have to protect her."

"From whom?"

"You, your family. Him!"

The mention of Daniel causes the muscles in my face to pull tight and my jaw to tense.

Following her cue, I drop my tone to a gentle whisper. "You don't have to protect her from me," I say, making a clear distinction. I approach her again slowly, hands out and open. "You can trust me."

She holds my eye, a glimmer of hope dancing inside, and for a moment, I think she may believe me or, at least, want to believe me. But there's no way she will trust anyone in my family. Not after what we did to her. Her eyes flood. She jerks her head away so I won't notice the tears. "Please just go."

She rolls her shoulders back, determined to remain strong against the confusion, hurt, and anger I see, all at once, in her expression. I'm the reason for her warring emotions.

Every part of me demands I reach out to her, apologize for

everything. But I know she's not in a place to receive it. Not at this time—if ever.

I open my wallet and pull out a business card. "Here's my number. If you ever want to talk."

She wipes a falling tear, looks at the card and then back at me. I pin the card to the community announcement bulletin board next to a card for a plumber that says, "We'll Repair What Your Husband Fixed!"

I sigh, a deep frustrated breath, and leave but not before saying, "I'm not my brother."

———

I suppose, on some level, I had been looking for her. Not actively, of course. But I thought of her daily and hoped our paths would cross again. Her disappearance was the root of many questions over the years. Where did she go? Why did she leave? None of the town's rumors trying to answer those questions were ever positive. Some people said she was a call girl in New York City. Another rumor involved an affair with a married man.

The rumors died off and were replaced by the next big scandal, but every now and then someone would mention her and the trial. Even I lingered when I heard her name. But the truth is always simpler than fiction. At least in Sara's case. She left Savannah, had a baby, and published a collection of poems. Not quite the life of a Jezebel.

Sara had a child. Daniel's child. The veins in my knuckles bulge as I grip the steering wheel tight, my hands shaking. A haze clouds my thoughts as I sit in my truck, sifting through the knowledge of what I had just learned, baffled at the ripple effects of Daniel's crime. And I'm angry. Angry for Sara. Angry that such a brilliant child was produced under such circumstances. A child that Sara had to carry, along with the stigma of conceiving a child from rape, alone. And of all places, here, in this place where judgments grow as thick as kudzu. That's why she moved away. Who wouldn't under those circumstances?

It all makes sense now. No wonder Alana reminded me of Naomi, acted like Naomi, embodied her characteristics. No wonder she exhibited the math proficiency to correctly identify an error in the *Mathematica* exhibit. She is one of us. A Wyler. Birdie would be proud. For eight years, Alana has graced this world and we never knew, couldn't know. Because knowing would subject her to what my family put Sara through. Sara understood that. Understood it all too well. She left because she knew the consequences of staying and reliving the torment of my family.

When I arrived at the bookstore earlier that evening, I recognized Sara immediately. Those eyes. I'll never forget those brown eyes. The same ones puddled with tears during the trial. I tried to leave today. The second I realized who she was, I wanted to flee, but my feet would not comply with my mind. I wanted to see her, see if the weight of what happened still hung on her shoulders, see if she had picked up the pieces of her shattered life. I watched as she worked with customers, smiling, laughing, and discreetly looked away when she looked in my direction. Why did I stay afterward? Because she drew me to her in all the ways I never expected.

Just like her father had.

I didn't mean to recite the poem. And I still don't know why I did. I started visiting Hosea the day I moved back to Savannah. I came home to make amends and not just with my family. Walking into the bookstore, a bead of sweat misting my brow, from the humidity or the reality of a decision made on Poker Flat in Alaska, I don't know, I introduced myself, extending my hand to him. Immediately, he recognized me, and I prepared for a jab to the face or a one-way trip to the curb. I told him about why I came home and my goals. He didn't speak, of course, and relaxed his rubbery face into a calm one, the wrinkles stretching across his forehead smoothing straight. After disappearing into the back room and returning with three poetry books, he says,

"Oh me! Oh life! of the questions of these recurring,
Of the endless trains of the faithless, of cities fill'd with the
   foolish,"

He continues, staring at me.

"The question, O me! so sad, recurring—What good amid these,
   O me, O life?

Answer.

That you are here—that life exists and identity,

That the powerful play goes on, and you may contribute a verse."

I'm not sure when, or if, he ever forgave me for what happened to Sara, but over the next two months, we met every night, after closing. He was the teacher and I the student. I listened as he recited poem after poem from memory. I didn't understand at first. I'm a scientist, an astrophysicist. A man of facts, not embellishment. So, I studied, every night. I read every book Hosea provided. And it was in the words of Whitman, Yeats, and others that I discovered the scope of my journey and what I had to do. I learned that poems are as much about facts as anything else in the world.

———

The day after Poetry & Prose's reopening, the prison visitor's room swarms with activity. I glance at the prisoner at the table to my right. He clasps and unclasps his hands, positioning them in and out of his lap while he waits. Every few seconds, he cranes his neck, scanning the crowd for a familiar face. He's young. Too young, I think. Too young to have made a choice that landed him here. Young enough, however, for atonement and a new life after he completes his sentence.

Daniel left a life on the table when he went to prison, a decade of discoveries in science and medicine unfulfilled. He would have, no doubt, finished medical school and immediately begun advancing the field that has always captivated him. He earned a bachelor's degree while in prison, though it currently serves no purpose for him other than a piece of paper to look at. Daniel's intelligence has always far exceeded what others taught him. But he's not the same eighteen-year-old kid who made that horrible mistake all those years ago, and once he's released, I have no doubt he will start on the next chapter of his life.

The gray metal door opens, and Daniel inches toward me, his steps slowed by the chains on his ankles. With his every step, the knot in my chest tightens. It's too soon, I think. Too soon to face him after the reappearance of Sara and the discovery of Alana. Twenty-four hours later, I still haven't grasped the notion of Alana's existence or considered the implications to my family or to Sara. Their presence introduces a wider dimension on my road to amendment and forgiveness. And I have no intention of telling him about them. Not yet. If ever.

Blinking into the darkness on Poker Flat in Alaska, I had made a silent promise to Naomi, one I intend on keeping.

"I didn't expect to see you back so soon," he says, as one of the guards, Kevin, a tall, dark-haired man with a graying goatee, unchains him. "To what do I owe this pleasure?"

He looks better than the last time I saw him. His face is flushed with color, and the yellowing jaundice seems less prevalent.

"I told you I would be back," I say, thinking back to that first visit. So much has changed since then.

"You did," he says.

"I meant it," I say. "And I'm going to keep coming back."

"You don't owe me anything, Dav—" Daniel says, sucking the word back in. "Jacob. I appreciate what you're doing. But you don't have to come here. See me."

He leans back and draws a deep breath that catches in his throat and transforms into a moist cough that lasts about a minute.

"I do."

Daniel doesn't ask why, and I do not volunteer. Some things are better left unsaid.

"How's your evaluation going? Dr. Bennett said that you needed to be ruled eligible to receive a transplant."

He turns his head and takes inventory of the room before answering. "Yeah..." he says, his leg pumping like a piston. "No more cigarettes."

As a kid, he had a habit of doing that. Disconnecting from a topic that didn't interest him, letting his mind drift. The topic of his health doesn't interest him.

I know what does, though.

As kids, we didn't watch cartoons or ride bikes in the street. Those familiar childhood activities served no place in the Wyler household. We bonded over possibilities and theories. Talked and debated for hours about Einstein's and Newton's scientific discoveries. After my last visit, I knew we needed a bridge, a safe place to trudge as we figured out this new relationship. Very recently, I had discovered just the thing.

"I could use your help with something," I say, tapping my fingertips across Alana's notebook.

Daniel perks up and rubs his hands together. "Something you've been working on?"

"Not exactly," I say, sliding the notebook across the steel table. I debated whether to bring her notebook, which has baffled me since left in my care. I needed someone to help me make sense of it, of her abilities, and confirm what I already believe to be true. Why not the smartest person I know?

He opens it, scans the first page, and flips to the second page.

"This is the Navier-Stokes equation," he says, looking sharply up at me.

The Navier-Stokes equation is one of the Millennium Problems, seven of the most intriguing unsolved mathematical problems in the world. As an incentive, the Clay Mathematics Institute in Massachusetts has offered a $1 million prize to anyone who successfully solves one. These problems could unlock the secrets to how the universe works. Only one of the Millennium Problems, the Poincare Conjecture, has ever been solved since the competition was introduced in 2000.

He flips through more of the pages, a bit more eagerly.

"What do you think?" I know what he thinks.

"Where did you get this?"

"A student of mine," I lie, breathing heavily, feeling the rise and fall of my chest.

"You are really going to do the teaching thing?"

I lean back in my chair and cross my arms. "What do you think?"

He closes the notebook and nods approvingly. "I think this is solid work," he says. "An excellent start."

"What if I told you that was the work of an eight-year-old."

He shakes his head. "No way. The handwriting looks childlike, but there's some advanced mathematics and applications here." He taps the notebook with his forefinger. "This is the work of a genius."

His last sentence sounds like a declarative one, but based on Daniel's stare, he expects an answer.

"She is," I say, swallowing hard. I'm hit with pride and melancholy that our DNA could produce such a wonderful being.

"She? A *girl* genius? An eight-year-old girl genius?"

Your daughter, I fight the urge to say, ignoring his sexist implication.

Daniel runs his palms in a circular motion around his head. He's rarely impressed by others. His advanced intelligence prevents him from appreciating the accomplishments of others because he assumes that knowledge comes as easily to them as it comes to him. But as he flips through the pages of Alana's notebook once more, an eight-year-old girl attempting to solve the Navier-Stokes equation impresses him.

"Could she solve it?" I ask, knowing the answer.

"She needs more study. Her math is lacking in certain areas. She's probably only had a public school education. But with a little instruction…" His voice trails off. "You could really help her."

"Me?" I say, shaking my head. "This is beyond my skill set."

"You've always underestimated yourself. When we were kids and even now."

"I'm flattered that you have that much confidence in me, but we're talking about a Millennium Problem. Not help with her high school calculus homework."

"Your job is not to solve it but to teach her what she's missing. She's a Mozart. He looked at a piano, and he could play," he says, his tone clear, so matter-of-fact. "But he had to be introduced to a piano. Take her to her instrument. She'll do the rest."

"I thought we didn't teach?"

He pulls his mouth into a straight line. "This is different. Much different."

"I don't know," I say, more to myself than to him. If only he knew the complications. Sara refused my request to simply speak to Alana. Tutoring her to solve one of the hardest equations in the history of the world would be out of the question.

"We are just beginning to understand the unfathomable. As we advance and our technology grows, we are answering questions left and right and asking new ones we've never thought to ask. Solving this equation moves us one step closer to answering those questions before we even ask them."

Daniel leans in. "This," he says, jabbing his finger against

Alana's notebook once again, "is what Dad meant about giving reason and purpose to events that would otherwise be meaningless and arbitrary. What if you had a hand in shaping those events?"

———

It's past midnight, and I can't sleep. The full moon beams like a spotlight in the cloudless night sky as I sink into a chair on the porch. A hushed breeze rattles the live oak leaves and ruffles the Spanish moss that hangs like spiderwebs as two seagulls squawk constantly, diminishing in the distance.

It is all too much. All of it. Sara's return. Alana. Her genius. Her similarities to Naomi. Not to mention Daniel's diagnosis and the bone marrow transplant. I stare out onto the black waters, the shine from the moon coming in and out of focus. These unscheduled events have clouded my ability to concentrate, think, see things clearly. The more I seek to reason and process the events of the past few days, the more my head spins. The answers are not as obvious as they've always been, and for a fleeting second, I question my judgment to come home. How did I become the bearer of this burden?

I've been taught that every scientific problem has a solution. It can be reasoned and solved. But making decisions in a pressured environment when things are beyond my control overwhelms me and shuts down my ability to think. That's why I moved away after Daniel's trial, to rid myself of him and all that chased him. That's a hard heart, especially for your brother. I could not solve the problem of losing him. I couldn't bring my father or sister back.

It comes to a point of making choices. I made a choice when I came home and leaving is not one of them.

I need time.

It reminds me of another poem Hosea recited to me.

Let us, then, be up and doing,
With a heart for any fate;
Still achieving, still pursuing,
Learn to labor and to wait.

Longfellow advised the importance of seizing the day and living a full life by seeking constant improvement and progress. But he also acknowledged that the road is not without struggle, and one must practice patience. As I head into the house, I notice a yellow object on the table. Alana's watch. Without thinking, I walk to the closet and retrieve my eyeglass kit. Sitting at my desk, I turn on my headlight, set the watch down, and begin removing the tiny screws.

SARA

———

JACOB DOESN'T COME BACK the next day. With every opening of the bookstore door, the charming bells now a crashing alarm system, I swallow and hold my breath, expecting to hear him or his mother, demanding to see Alana. He doesn't come back the day after that either. By the morning of the third day, I am assuming the delay is a strategic one, that they are seeking legal advice on how to proceed.

When Alana was a baby, the thought of Daniel's family knowing about her existence would break me out in hives. I'd go over my contingency lists. The feeling of helplessness and fear would wash over me in waves, spreading across my body, rendering me useless for hours. But, today, with my worst fears realized, I feel stuck. Alana is still in danger, and this time it's real, it's credible, it's present. And yet, someone in Daniel's family knows. The secret is no longer one-sided.

After Jacob doesn't return for a week, I finally act, my fog of confusion lifting and propelling me forward with determination. I call several Atlanta lawyers who all confirm what I already know: in the United States, no federal law explicitly restricts the parental rights of men who father a child through rape. In Georgia, in order to terminate or limit parental rights, victims must show clear and convincing evidence that termination of rapist parental rights is in the best interest of the child, meaning, despite his conviction, Daniel or his family can petition for visitation or, God forbid, custody, which they could possibly receive with their long standing as pillars of the community.

"Being convicted of a violent felony can often be grounds for revoking parental rights, especially if the parent in question goes to prison for the crime," one lawyer tells me over the phone. "Georgia law does establish a presumption about aggravated circumstances and the conception of a child through rape does qualify, but judges have wide discretion to weigh the circumstances of each family that appears before them."

Another lawyer tries to comfort me by reminding me that laws are changing, that before Alana's birth, more than two-thirds of states had no rape custody laws in place whatsoever. Today, exactly half of the state requires a criminal conviction for the rapist's parental rights to be severed.

"You would be hard pressed to find a judge who would award custody or even visitation in these cases," he says. "But it's not unprecedented." *Especially in Georgia, especially involving the Wyler family* are the unspoken words I hear.

His confirmation is all I need.

I have to leave Georgia.

"Where will you go?" Sylvia asks as I yank our suitcase down from the closet shelf.

"Back to Maine. Their laws specifically state no custody, no visitation for convicted rapists. You know that's why I moved there. As residents, we're protected under the law."

"So, you're just going to keep running, hiding?"

"Excuse me?" I say, and even I realize my voice sounds breathless and wild from pinballing around the room from the suitcase on the bed to the dresser to the closet and back to the suitcase again.

"You heard me," Sylvia says, twisting and turning toward the direction of my moving body. "You have to stop running. You can't run. They know about her."

"They are probably lining up a defense right now. I gotta get out of here. I should have left weeks ago."

"Maybe he hasn't told them yet."

"Of course he has," I say, opening a drawer, scooping up its contents in one swoop and dumping it in a suitcase.

"Why don't you try talking to Jacob?"

"Why would I do that? Daniel is his twin brother."

"He testified against him," she says, grabbing my wrist as I breeze by. "Sara…Jacob seems different."

"He's a Wyler, and he'll do anything to protect his brother. I can't believe you guys didn't know."

"Hosea knew, and if he tried to tell me I didn't understand

him. I didn't recognize Jacob. He was a teenager when he left. He changed his name."

I snatch my hand away from her but remain next to her, my chest heaving.

"What about your father?"

"He'll understand," I say. "We'll say our goodbyes now. I'll make sure we Skype every day."

"What about Alana? She loves it here."

"She knows this was never supposed to be permanent. When we get back to Lubec—"

"*No!*" Alana yells from the doorway, the word a frame around her tiny mouth.

Sylvia and I trade looks, both searching for what to say next.

"I don't want to go back to Lubec! I wanna stay here!"

I approach her, slowly, defensively. "I know. I don't want to leave either. But we have to."

"Why?"

"Because it's time. Remember that I told you we were only coming for a few weeks. To help Grandpa."

"But Grandpa's not better. He's dying."

"I know, sweetie. And I know that's hard for you. It's hard for me, too. But we can't stay here. It's time for us to leave."

"*No!*" She runs from the room. The pictures on my wall vibrate a second later as she slams her bedroom door.

I collapse on my bed, the weight of it all unbearable. "What am I supposed to do?" I say as sobs roll through me.

Sylvia sits next to me and gently pulls my head to her chest. For a week, I have not been able to rest, my mind churning with possibilities during waking hours, fear haunting me at night. Sylvia doesn't answer my question. She doesn't know what to do either. Instead, she calms me with her motherly touch until elusive sleep grabs hold, pulling me downward.

———

I blink my eyes open to a dark room; an afghan covers me. A quick glance at my cell phone reveals it is just after midnight. I slept for just a few hours, and yet it seems like an eternity since my day began. Feeling lethargic and groggy, I stand, the effort wobbly and cumbersome. A half-full suitcase sits on the floor, clothes spilling out. That's right. I had been spiraling in a frenzy of packing, just as I had been almost nine years ago.

On a mid-April day, what seems like a lifetime ago, I discovered I was pregnant. The sun shone. The leaves grew. The pregnancy stick sat, its faint pink line illuminated, on my bathroom counter, as did the other three I had used. I had just turned eighteen years old.

Faced with the unthinkable, it came down to making choices, and I had one available to me: leave. In court—a rushed trial to accommodate Daniel's fall admission to Harvard—I was vilified and judged as a lovestruck, obsessive teenager. I took advantage of Daniel while he grieved for his sister. He never raped me or even had consensual sex with me.

That was his choice of defense. What he told the world. Birdie Wyler believed that, lived with that, presumably quite easily. And that was her choice.

But facts matter. All the witnesses and therapists speaking the foolish, slutty ways of teenage girls couldn't erase the facts of the case. They found his DNA on me and in me. I had met Daniel at a party. I never knew him before that day. We both drank too much. He raped me. A jury found him guilty and sentenced him to a decade in prison. And now, I was pregnant.

Before leaving, I did try the other one option I had. Sylvia and Dad drove me to Atlanta, to a nondescript clinic located on the outskirts of town. But I couldn't have the abortion. It didn't seem fair to take a life for the sins of the father. Dad and Sylvia both understood, and by the time we drove the two hours back to Savannah, we had a plan. I would move to Providence, Rhode Island, soon after graduation and live with a friend of Sylvia's. I would never come home. Not even to visit. To everyone else in Savannah, I would simply disappear.

A creak from downstairs breaks my thoughts. A stranger to the house wouldn't have noticed it, but my ears, tuned to the sounds of this place, pick it up, and I descend the stairs to discover the light on in Dad's study and him sitting at his desk. Dad's study is small and tidy, enough square footage for a wall of bookshelves, a desk and chair, and his reading chair, once polished brown leather, now aged with cracks and indentations.

Leaning into the doorway undetected, I watch as he unfolds a Hershey's Kiss and pops it in his mouth.

"I wonder what Sylvia would say about you eating that," I say.

He smiles, holding up his forefinger to his lips, and holds a Kiss out to me, a bribe for my silence. We both know Sylvia knows, even quietly restocking his stash when he runs low. I peel away the silver foil in layers like a banana and allow the chocolate to melt for a moment in my mouth.

Dad and I had yet to speak about Jacob's discovery of Alana, and as I watch him study the pages of the book he holds, I think about how we have yet to discuss anything regarding what happened—then and now. It's a topic we both know we need to discuss. Never always seems to be the right time.

"Dad, did you know it was him?" I ask. "Did you know Jacob was David?"

He holds an inhale for what seems like forever but doesn't stop reading, his broad fingers turning one more page.

"Why?" I ask. "Why didn't you tell me? Why did you talk to him?"

He stops reading and closes the book, his thumb serving as a bookmark.

"God gives his child upon his slate a sum—
To find eternity in hours and years;
With both sides covered, back the child doth come,
His dim eyes swollen with shed and unshed tears;
God smiles, wipes clean the upper side and nether,
And says, 'Now, dear, we'll do the sum together!"

"Forgiveness? He wanted your forgiveness?"

Dad nods his head and moves his hand between me and him.

"Why? Why now? After all this time?"

"That you are here—that life exists and identity,
That the powerful play goes on, and you may contribute a verse."

Whitman believed that the worth of life lies *in* life and suggested that in our brief time on earth, we should contribute to the greater good. We decide what happens. Dad implies that Jacob is choosing to make the best use of his life, contributing his verse. Maybe that included forgiveness.

I'm not like my brother. Jacob's last words to me ring in my mind. He isn't like his brother, I know. Not at the trial, at least. When Jacob took the stand, he didn't look at the defense table; he raised his right hand and swore to tell the truth, the whole truth, and nothing but the truth. So help him God, he did. Unbeknownst to Daniel, his lawyers, and Birdie, his testimony damaged Daniel's case. Jacob testified that he saw us go into that room together and that he heard me say no. I appreciate him for that, but he hasn't earned my praise. He told the truth. What anyone should have done.

But what does "I'm not like my brother" translate to today? Does that mean he can be trusted with my secret? He looked genuinely remorseful after the pieces of the puzzle came together. Not the face of someone angry upon learning about a long-lost relative but of someone sorrowful. Someone full of regret.

"Dav—Jacob doesn't owe us anything," I say finally. The two names I know him by keep jumbling. "And I want nothing to do with that family."

Dad finally closes the book and looks at the floor. He knows that. Remembers what happened. But he offers no rebuke or confirmation of my statement.

"Do you trust him?"

"Then be not coy, but use your time,
And while ye may, go marry;
For having lost but once your prime,
You may forever tarry."

"You're telling me it's time to move on?"

His dark-brown eyes hold mine.

"How can you say that? You know what his brother did to me!"

"That you are here—that life exists and identity,
That the powerful play goes on, and you may contribute a verse."

"I know! You said that already." It comes out louder than I mean, my frustration ruling over me.

"Let us, then, be up and doing,
With a heart for any fate;
Still achieving, still pursuing,
Learn to labor and to wait."

I take a deep breath, willing away tears that fall anyway. "Tell me what to do, Dad. What do I do?"

"Forgive these wild and wandering cries,
Confusions of a wasted youth;
Forgive them where they fail in truth,
And in thy wisdom make me wise."

Dad stands, canceling an opportunity for a rebuttal. He has spoken very clearly and intentionally without saying much at all. *Forgive these wild and wandering cries, confusions of a wasted youth.*

This conversation is over. He kisses me on the top of my head, lingering, a kiss that means a parent is feeling protective of their child. As a father, he understands my plight and desire to protect Alana at all costs.

My first promise to Alana was not of love but of protection. In the delivery room, pale from exhaustion with wide eyes, holding her tiny, five-pound, three-ounce body in my arms, I made a sole promise to protect her. I didn't love her yet. I would grow to love her, the way she brushed her nose when she was tired. The way she said *saw you* instead of *sorry*.

The way she smiled in her sleep. But, at first, protection. That was all I had to give. And that now seems threatened. If David hasn't yet told his twin and mother, he will soon. Because families, like Dad and Sylvia, who took turns holding me as I cried to and from Atlanta, stick together.

Now nine years after that horrible day, and a long way from the promises I made, the secret is out. In the end, I think as I walk upstairs and slide back into bed, I bought myself eight years of a life not exactly free from what I ran away from. What I have been holding dear is really not so great an existence. I am not happy thinking about fleeing back to our home at the end of the world. I have to once again be proactive to buy myself time.

Let us, then, be up and doing,
With a heart for any fate;
Still achieving, still pursuing,
Learn to labor and to wait.

Then, I know. I know what I have to do.

———

The knock comes in the middle of the night. The clock reads 2:05 a.m. I know it's him, feel it in my spirit between the second and third knocks. Why did he come so late?

The house is quiet, except for a rhythmic crinkle of paper

on the bureau lifting with every twirl of my oscillating fan. I tiptoe past Dad's and Alana's rooms, both doors partially open, and I see their chests rising and falling in steady rhythms.

The knock comes again, harder and louder. As I descend the stairs into the dark foyer, lit only by a sliver of moonlight, I see a distorted body through the glass door window.

Reaching for the handle, my hand shaking, I can feel the beat of my heart pulsing like a second hand on a watch. *Thump. Thump. Thump. Thump.* I blink and brace myself, in my decision, into what I hold true. Nothing will be the same after this.

Opening the door slowly, I look past him, a silhouette outlined by the moonlight, and out into the dark night. Outside, there are new sounds. The chorus of cicadas and crickets chirp and sing their songs to a quiet world. A humid breeze rustles the leathery leaves of two magnolia trees.

He is alone.

I step aside and open the door wider, silently inviting him in.

I close the door behind him and cross my arms tightly, hugging myself. The space between us is claustrophobic, the static air snaps of stored energy, the wrong two ends of a magnet repelling each other.

A lump forms in my throat, nearly choking me, but I push the words out.

"Thank you for coming."

JACOB

———

THE CALL CAME JUST after midnight. "Jacob?" a quiet voice asked. "It's Sara. Did I wake you?" A dull buzz hummed from the lamp above me, its light casting a dim spotlight on Alana's watch. I turned off my headlight and rose from my desk. "No." I walked out on the porch, pinching the bridge of my nose, my eyes adjusting to the darkness. She wanted to talk, she said; could I come by tomorrow morning?

Now, at her father's front door, she's polite, thanking me for coming when it is I who should be apologizing for intruding so late. She invited me to talk, but I'm sure she did not mean at this hour. I didn't expect to come now either. After her phone call, I sat down in one of the Adirondack chairs and stared down at the water. A memory of Naomi diving off the dock blurred into focus. She loved that dock for the sole purpose of jumping off it. My heart ached over that memory, a pain eased only with the notion that she lives on through Alana. I couldn't wait until the morning. I would apologize to Locke for breaking quiet hours.

As Sara leads me into the living room, a warm and cozy space, she seems every bit as anxious as I expected her to be, fidgeting and, I imagine, willing herself, and failing, to relax as if it is the most logical thing for us to be here in this place at this time. But as she turns to me, she gathers up her confidence, stretching her body tall and elongating her neck. She doesn't sit. I don't either. The space between us is wide.

Two realizations crash over me as I scan the room, my attention landing on Alana's green backpack on the floor next to the couch. One is that Sara really is still here in Savannah. She didn't leave, even with her secret finally realized. She has something to say, and I need to listen with the understanding that this conversation could split into myriad directions. The second is that there is no other place I'd rather be. I don't want to lose sight of her again.

"How's Hosea?" I ask. Between working on the house, going to the doctor, and wrapping my head around everything, I realize I have not visited Hosea in a few weeks. I miss his counsel, his friendship.

Sara draws back at the mention of her father, her expression stony.

"He's a friend," I offer.

"Is he a friend so you can spy on me and Alana? Is that why you've been visiting him?"

The sweetness of her tone on the phone earlier has been replaced with a curt one, biting, smothered with anger. It hides a sadness as well. It seems she wanted to project that rage out at the first available person, and I am prepared to let her.

"Is that what you think I am?" I say in a soft tone. "A spy?"

"I don't know what to think about you."

"I'm no spy."

"So, who are you?"

I shrug. "I'm Jacob."

While her eyes search for a focal point, darting around the room and failing to land on anything, I find that I cannot take mine off her. Trauma changes you, hardens you, leaves its scars. On Sara, it does not show. She looks entirely the same and completely different at the same time. With every blink, my mind updates the memory of the girl I last saw eight years ago. In one, her short, cropped hair grows and coils into a long, fat braid resting on her left shoulder. In another, her legs and arms sprout, long and lean, and in others, her lips bow and her breasts plump, her skin glows. Another, her youthful, meek eyes transform into bright, full, and unassuming ones. Until the innocent girl from eight years ago has been replaced by this lovely woman before me.

"Did he ever mention us?" Sara says, bringing me back to myself.

I look down and back up at her. "Just you."

Exhaling, she glances at a framed picture of a younger Sara with Hosea. "He's sick," she says, looking at the ceiling, her eyes filling with tears, the pain fresh and raw. "He's dying."

With a shaky voice, she tells me of Hosea's brain aneurysm and the countdown to his inevitable death.

Sadness wells in my throat. "I'm sorry. I didn't know. He never—"

"Mentioned it? Yeah. I know," she says shortly, crossing her arms again. "Not that you would understand him."

"I understand him."

She furrows her brow, the act pulling her features downward.

"Well…we understand each other," I say. "Neither of us is known for our loquaciousness. I guess we bonded over the silence."

"Have you told anyone about Alana?" Sara asks in a rush, holding her breath, its release seemingly dependent on my answer.

"No."

Her chest collapses as she exhales. It's almost a sob. "Why not?" For the first time tonight, her tone is not curt.

"It's complicated."

She nods once as if she understands. Maybe she does.

"How is Birdie?" Her tone is again not pleasant.

Guilt, now familiar, surges through me, threatening to buckle my resolve. Despite my presence here, Sara still harbors ill will toward my family. And I don't blame her. For so long, I did too.

"Also complicated," I say, my voice thick with remorse.

She snickers, a short mirthless laugh, and hugs herself tighter.

"Complicated, huh?" She mimics me. "That's not an answer. Why haven't you told *them* about Alana?" She says *them* as if flicking something off her tongue.

"That's the best answer I can give you."

"They're your family."

"And that implies…?"

"It implies you stick together. Tell each other things. Share secrets."

"I've been away for a while. My relationship with them is not what you think."

"What do I think?"

"I'm not in the habit of thinking for others."

"You just said your relationship is not what others think; that implies a presumption."

"I make no presumptions for others," I say. "My relationship with my brother and mother is complicated. That's the best answer I can give you."

She pauses and rephrases. "Will you tell them about Alana?"

"Do you want me to tell them?" I know the answer to that question before I ask.

"No." Two simple letters. A complete sentence. Nothing more.

"Then I won't."

"I don't ever want them to know about her."

"That's not rational. You can't continue to keep this a secret." For eight years, from what I can glean, Sara has kept Alana hidden from the world, raising a brilliant daughter

who could very possibly solve one of the world's most difficult math problems. I have no doubt that she could disappear
again. I cannot allow that.

"Why not?"

"Because she has another family. A family who would love
to know that she exists."

"Are you implying that your family deserves to know
about her?"

"Yes." I add quickly, "But it's not about them deserving.
It's not for them—it's...for Alana."

Her breath catches, her chest opening as if coming up
for air. Something I said struck a nerve. She blinks at me,
wanting, waiting, for more. "You can't change my mind. Your
family doesn't deserve to have Alana in their lives."

"I don't doubt that," I say.

She opens her mouth to speak, but she can't seem to find
her voice.

"You knew I hadn't told them when you called me.
Didn't you?"

"I suspected it."

"How?"

"Because *we* are having this conversation. And not *us*."

I know exactly what she is implying. Birdie. Her domineer-
ing presence. Her inclusion into matters pertaining to her family.

She casts her gaze to the floor, and then her eyes rise to
meet mine. Past the brightness, there's a sadness along the
edges. "I want to make an arrangement with you," Sara says.

"An arrangement?"

"In exchange for your silence." She pauses, swallowing. "You can see her. Talk to her. You and you only."

I didn't expect this, and I hold still, expecting more details, conditions, as my mind contemplates and sorts through various responses. "Why? Why would you allow me to see her?"

"I can't go home yet. I figured we could come up with a compromise."

"Until?"

"Until—" she says softly, her voice fading away like the wind.

I look again at Hosea's picture. "And then?"

"And then we're gone."

"You don't think my mother could find you?"

She shakes her head. "Of course. But it won't matter. I'll be back home."

"Where's home?"

She doesn't answer at first. Then: "Maine."

I pause to consider why she would tell me where she lived. Then I know: custody laws are more anti-perpetrator in Maine than in Georgia. And she wants me to know that.

"Why do you trust me?" I ask.

"I don't," she says, "but everyone else, Alana, Dad, Sylvia, does. They say you are different. Are you? Different?"

"I am."

"You told me that you're not like your brother. Is that true?"

I step forward slowly, lightly, like walking on eggshells. "I'm nothing like my brother," I say. "I think you know that."

"I know that he's your twin, and I know Alana is the most important person to me on this earth."

It took courage for Sara to reach out to me, a muster of strength that usually exists dormant and deep in a person's soul until summoned. If I've learned anything about her and nothing else, I know that she is brave. This, my presence here, her arrangement, all examples of that. She owes me nothing. And yet, she's giving, willing. I can meet her halfway.

"Until recently, I hadn't spoken to my brother since the trial."

Her mouth opens slightly, her lips parting into a soft word. "Why?"

Sara's gentle tone indicates that if she and I were friends, a sympathetic gesture would follow. A hug, a pat on the shoulder, a hand clutch. But she refrains.

I allow her question to hang in the air between us unanswered, comfortable with the silence that follows. We are not in a place for transparency.

"She's a great kid. Alana," I say, gesturing to Alana's backpack and to Sara my desire for a subject change.

Sara follows my change of conversation, presumably understanding our unique predicament. "I know," she says. "She is."

I have a deal and presentation of my own to make. I motion to the couch, and after registering Sara's approval, I sink onto it. Sara does not sit. She remains standing and watches as I pull a manila envelope out of my knapsack.

"This is for Alana's care," I say, pushing the fat envelope

toward her, its form warping to the shape of its contents. "This"—I fan the envelope up and down—"is just the start… to make up for what you've already done. There's more, a lot more, for her present and future needs."

"Is that what you think?" Sara's posture falters as if pulled down. "Why I'm doing this? That I want money?"

"No, not at all. I just—"

Sara turns her head with the hardest shake. "No, I don't want or need your family's charity."

"Sara…this is not charity. Alana is"—I hesitate—"family. Please…take it."

"We get by. Alana has always had what she needed," she says. And I believe her. Alana looks healthy and happy. But as I listen to Sara breathe and with each deliberate intake and outtake of breath, I know there have been lean times, and I cringe thinking about what it's been like for her financially. "Accepting that money gives your family an invitation into her life."

"It doesn't. They don't know about her, about this," I say, still gripping the envelope. "It can be our secret. But I want to make sure Alana is taken care of for the rest of her life. If… you choose to never tell them about her."

I'm providing her with a window to accept the money without obligating herself to my family or telling them about Alana. But, from her crossed arms tucked tightly against her chest, I know she's not prepared to trust me yet.

"No…I'm sorry. I just can't. This arrangement has nothing to do with money."

I know that. In Savannah, the accumulation and extent of my family's wealth are well-known. The Wyler name evident across buildings, on vast donor lists, and among charity organizations. At any time, Sara could have reached out and had access to whatever she wanted. But she didn't. Not once. And not now.

I want to keep pressing Sara on this, give her an explanation to the truth and significance of the money, but I don't want to scare her away from her arrangement or for her to believe my motivations are untoward. More importantly, that I'm trying to buy my family's presence into Alana's life.

I concede and slide the envelope back into my bag and pull out Alana's notebook. Sara's eyes jump, pulling all her features upward.

"Where did you get that?" She takes it from me and presses it to her chest.

"Alana. She gave it to me," I say. "Indirectly."

"How?"

"I told you I met her at Fernbank a few weeks ago." I smile. "I was standing in front of the *Mathematica* exhibit, and she came up to me and told me that the exhibit is wrong."

"I've told her about doing that. Talking to strangers."

"Well...she was right. The exhibit was wrong."

Her expression falters, just a fraction.

"We need to talk about Alana," I say. "She's—"

"I know she's smart," she interrupts.

"Smart?"

"Yes, very intelligent."

It is my turn to laugh. "A high school valedictorian is smart. Alana is a genius."

Sara blinks, my comment landing and failing to make an impact. In that moment, I know Sara is already aware of Alana's abilities.

I open Alana's notebook and show a page to Sara. "This is the Navier-Stokes equation, one of the seven most challenging mathematical problems in the world. She's solving it."

"Alana is always solving math equations."

"This isn't a simple math equation. This equation has baffled mathematicians for decades. No one has ever solved it."

"And neither will Alana."

"You don't know that."

"I know that she's eight. I know an eight-year-old can't solve a problem that even the smartest people in the world can't."

"Sara," I say, attempting to center her in the moment. "She has the proficiency to solve it someday."

I reposition myself on the couch as if by doing so I can reposition Sara's obtuseness. "This is bigger than you could possibly understand. This is bigger than I can understand. This is the invention of the wheel, electricity, the airplane. Solving this problem could help us understand time. And once you understand something..." I trail off, daydreaming the possibilities. With this answer, could we make more time? "Once you understand, you can change things." I present my request. "Let me work with her."

"Absolutely not."

I stand. "It could be part of our arrangement. During my visits with Alana, I would tutor her. With a little help—" I stop. "What am I saying? With encouragement and guidance, she could solve it."

"How long would this take?" she asks, revealing a tiny crack in her armor of doubt.

"Tomorrow. Six months. Five years. I don't know. Great achievements have no timetable."

"If you're going to tutor her, why can't you just solve it?"

I smile wide. "I have a PhD in astrophysics, and I'm not smart enough to solve that equation. But she can."

"That's a lot of pressure for a little girl."

"Not to her. This is easy to her. Like tying a shoe and blinking. Like breathing."

"If it's so easy, then why do you need to work with her?"

"Because there are things, equations, fractions, that she's never been taught. Because public school teachers follow a curriculum based on grade and age. The equations she needs to learn won't be taught to her until high school, maybe even college." I think of Daniel's quip about a public school education. "But she's ready now. And once these principles are introduced to her, her brain will click, and she'll be able to continue to solve the equation."

Sara and I stare at each other for a moment before she says, "I can't decide this right now. I need more..." She stops short of saying the word.

"Say it."

"Time."

———

The smell of cinnamon wafts through the air as I walk into Birdie's kitchen to find Marsha standing at the island, several trays of cookies in front of her, mixing up another batch. A bowl of peeled and quartered apples awaits her apple cinnamon oatmeal cookies. I pop one into my mouth, savoring the sweetness.

"You look more and more like your father every day," Marsha says, wiping her hands on her apron then extending them, ushering me in for an embrace. Marsha has been my mother's housekeeper turned friend for as long as I can remember. It was Marsha who cleaned wounds and applied Band-Aids. Marsha who added the extra whipped cream to our ice cream sundaes. Marsha whose lap we fell asleep on. A stand-in mother, who gave us the affection lacking from our real mother. My father left instructions, among other demands, with his attorney that provided monetary compensation for Marsha for the rest of her life. He financially liberated her from Birdie. But she stayed anyway. For us, I like to think.

"Have you been here long?" she asks.

"I just got here."

She stops stirring, the bowl locked in her arm. "It's so good to have you home. I missed you. She did too."

I wave a dismissive hand and with it grab a warm cookie from the plate. Marsha gently slaps my hand but allows it.

"Those are for the new neighbors," she says. "I seem to be making a lot of these lately. So many of the original families have moved or sold their homes. Their children don't want these big houses anymore. They want open floor plans and outdoor kitchens. You know the Whatley house down the street? Their son gutted it. Ripped out all that beautiful hardwood."

"Why doesn't Birdie sell this place?" I say with my mouth full.

"She's had a few real estate agents come out over the years. They were all practically salivating. But she just can't bring herself to put it on the market."

"It's too big for her. Too big for you to keep clean."

"I get by. I do a little every day. Not a lot of people looking to hire an old woman."

In her late fifties with brown hair without a strand of gray, Marsha isn't an old woman.

"I think she's waiting for something," Marsha continues, rolling the dough in small balls.

"For what?"

"I think she wants to see her family in here again."

I lean back and cross my arms. "Our family? That will never happen."

Marsha laughs. "It's not too late," she says, scooping more cookie dough into her hand. "All that time away...when you were in those places, Alaska, Greenland, chasing your Aurora, you didn't get lonely?"

"I don't mind being alone."

"Being comfortable being single is one thing. You haven't met anyone?"

"There weren't a lot of available women in Greenland."

"What about here? You've been back a few months now. Please tell me you've ventured off that island a little." She winks.

"Not for that reason," I say. "Where is she?"

Marsha motions toward the back door with her head. "Where she always is these days. Out in that garden. I swear she lives there. Or at Bonaventure." The cemetery.

"I better go say hello," I say, kissing her once more and swiping a final cookie from the display.

The backyard looks like spring, with rows of multicolored flowers of all shapes and sizes. It would be enough to make any master gardener proud. Not Birdie, whom I spot on her knees flattening the dirt around a freshly planted annual with the heel of her hand. She looks the part of the gardener, a straw hat, a dirt-stained apron, and a look of escape.

Birdie catches me out of the corner of her eye as I approach and does a double take. "I was wondering if you were going to come see me or if you were going to make me trudge all the way back out there."

"I've been busy."

I walk over to her and kneel beside her. I know better than to repeat the awkward hug on the dock. Instead, I rub her shoulder, my hand lingering. She stops knocking the dirt off a zinnia and looks at my hand, touching it with her gloved one. It is all she offers, but it is enough, a start.

With a spade, she stabs at the ground repeatedly, loosening the soil, unearthing deep-brown chunks of dirt, and mixing in an inch of Miracle-Gro. I sit on the ground next to her.

"What are you doing?"

"I'm sitting."

"In the dirt?"

"Why not? You are."

She deadheads an annual. "I'm working."

"So am I," I say, following her lead and snapping off the dead flower heads.

"I didn't raise you to work with your hands."

I remember the muddy yellow nicotine stains on Daniel's fingers of his right hand, dirt permanently embedded in his pores and around his splintered nails, his hands calloused from working in the prison garden. My own hands, once unscarred, now displayed their own star-shaped scabs and scrapes from renovating the cottage and clearing the land.

"I'm actually enjoying working with my hands. Daniel too. You should be proud that we both like playing in the dirt."

"He told me you've been to see him several times."

I nod.

"Dr. Bennett says he has an infection. He can't do the evaluation until the infection is gone."

"I know."

"He'll never admit it, but he's pretty happy that you're back. He's never looked as good. Stopped smoking and everything."

I gesture toward the house, desperate not to make the focus of every conversation about Daniel. "Marsha said you sometimes think about selling the house. Why are you holding on to it?"

"Daniel is going to need a place to live after he's released."

"He doesn't need a mansion."

"He may want to have a family one day," she says. "Or you. It would be nice to have some grandkids."

"Is that what you want?" I ask, sliding a tray of annuals in front of me. "Grandchildren? To be a grandmother?" Knowing what I know, her comment hits too close, and I'm relieved when she changes the subject.

"I heard that girl's back in town," she says. "Have you seen her?"

I don't answer. Birdie reads my silence as a denial.

"I hear her father is sick," she says, her arms moving as much as her tongue. "Wasted all that money renovating his little bookstore. He's going to leave all that debt to her. I doubt she made anything of herself."

"That's presumptuous. Even for you, Birdie. You know nothing about her life, what she's done, what she's been through."

She emits a guttural huff. "Girls like that don't grow up to make a difference in the world. And all these years later, I see that I'm right. She's back working at that store, doing nothing of importance with her life."

I clutch a handful of dirt tight in my fist and watch as it oozes out from both sides of my hand and patters back to the ground.

Birdie sits back on her heels, wiping the sweat from her brow with her forearm. "Daniel would have cured cancer. You would not have moved to Alaska. There are no suitable women in Alaska," she says, stopping. "There would be laughter here if it weren't for her. Children playing. His children. Yours. The next generation of Wylers."

"You blame Sara for why you don't have any grand-children?"

"Absolutely," she says, lucid in her irrationality.

Just a few short hours ago Sara asked about Birdie, and I wish I could have told her she was different, that she had changed and morphed into a compassionate person Sara didn't have to fear. But her misguided anger remains locked and steady, if not elevated by time.

I settle, silent in the moment, ignoring the urge to defend Sara. There will be a time and place for such defense. Another time to tell her about Alana's existence. But not now. I have promises to keep.

"I spoke with Kelly Ferrer at Fernbank a few weeks ago about our family's annual donation," Birdie says. "Said someone anonymously corrected one of the exhibits. They think it was a kid. Can you imagine?"

I shake my head and glance up at the ominously dark sky with shifting steel-blue and gray clouds, my mood reflected in it, unsettled and roaring. "It's about to storm."

Birdie doesn't follow my glance, rather, keeps her eyes transfixed on the space in front of her. "I want to get this soil turned over and these flowers planted before it does. There's nothing better than rainwater."

"We had a record rainfall last month. Looks like we're on track for another this month."

"Looks that way."

I should be telling her that she already has a grandchild, her next generation. A genius granddaughter who corrected the *Mathematica* exhibit. A beautiful little girl who embodies everything she wanted for us and everything she lost. That Naomi's laughter lives on just fifteen minutes down the road.

I stand, brushing the dirt off my shorts. "I better head home before the rain, or I'll be stuck here."

She stops planting. "Would it be such a bad thing to be stuck in the house with your mother?"

We are divided, but we don't have to be. From here, we have somewhere to go. No option but to start over. If she wants. If I want.

"I could stay. If you don't mind."

"You know where everything is. I'm not sure what Marsha is cooking for dinner."

Birdie doesn't ask anybody for anything. Her declaratives are a watered-down version of asking me to stay, the closest I will get to her actually expressing a desire for my company. I accept it.

"Can I help you finish?"

She keeps digging and moving, working fast. I watch before kneeling beside her and picking up a container of zinnias. She stops digging. Surveying her as sweat beads down her face, her chest heaving slightly, I expect an answer of measured sarcasm, and for a brief second, I regret asking. The status of our relationship may be in limbo, but hope remains that the worst is behind us.

"Start here," she says without looking at me.

We work in tandem, in the silence, turning over the earth and, I hope, the past, planting a colorful display of flowers, a new future, until the sky opens and the first raindrops fall.

SARA

———

IT'S SUNDAY. OUR DAY off from the bookstore, and Alana and I are alone together for the first time in what seems like forever. It's always been the two of us, but now Alana splits her time between hanging out with Dad, attending Sylvia's trips to museums, and working on equations from Brixton. She's thriving here, blossoming into a brighter, well-balanced child, and I wonder if Alana will find her own way, being a genius and having friends her own age, as long as I don't stifle her and if I can give her space to find the right friends for her. With my agreement with Jacob, I may have given her both opportunities—and time for me to tell her the truth.

I watch her now working through another series of equations that Brixton looked up on the internet. Her long hair, once tucked behind her ears, cascades to the table in long, sandy locks. Her green eyes focus on the paper in front of her. Dad and Sylvia are napping upstairs.

"Mom," she says, not looking up at me. "Can we go swimming

soon? Brixton says the beach is only thirty minutes away. I need to practice holding my breath. I'm getting rusty."

"Sure," I say, the idea of relaxing at the beach a comforting thought. "It has been awhile. A fish needs water, huh?"

"Yeah...I'm drying out," she says, forming fish lips and sucking them. "Will you swim this time? You promised."

"We'll see," we say in unison.

"You always say that. But you never do."

I walk over and ruffle her hair. "Maybe. Maybe Grandpa and Sylvia will come with us. That will be fun. Let them see how long you can hold your breath."

She perks up like a flower in the sun. "Yeah. Grandpa is going to be so impressed," she says. "Can Jacob come with us?"

Her question flies out with no warning, no preparation, no filter.

"Why do you ask?" I say, my voice an octave higher. My response is a reflex triggered by fear, a placeholder as I take time to process.

"I like Jacob."

"You do?"

"Yeah...he gave me his watch."

"His watch?"

"Yeah..."

Alana lifts her arm from under the table, revealing a thick black watch strapped across her tiny wrist, the heavy face pointing downward.

I dry my hands on the dishcloth and take her wrist into my hands. How did I not notice it before? Removing the watch, I see its sleek black ceramic face inscribed with "Dark Side of the Moon" around the dial. It wouldn't take an expert to identify that this is no mere watch. It is a watch that does not belong to a child.

"We are giving that back to him. It's too expensive."

"But he gave it to me! He said I could keep it."

"Why would he give you his watch?"

She shrugs. "It's a trade," she says. "Until he can fix mine."

"Until he fixes yours? You gave him your watch? Which one?"

"The yellow one that stopped on the plane."

There have been so many watches over the years. I remember the yellow one because it is the most recent and the most expensive one. She saw it in a local store and fell in love. I knew better than to purchase a watch that expensive, considering. At an early age, Alana revealed that she belonged to a rare category of people who, for reasons unknown, cannot wear watches. Her fascination with time aids her obsession with them.

"When did he give you his watch?"

"At the museum."

I ease into one of the kitchen chairs. "Tell me about meeting him at the museum. Did he approach you?"

She looks away, guilty. "I just told him that it was wrong," she says. "I know I'm not supposed to talk to strangers, but he was looking at the exhibit, and I wanted him to know that it was wrong."

"I know, baby," I say, smoothing out wisps of her hair and tucking them behind ears slightly disproportionately large. Engaging with people on that level was who she was, the fabric of her character. She can't control it any more than a star can dim its light.

"He was the only person who believed me when I told them the exhibit was wrong. I told Sylvia, even Brixton, but they didn't believe me."

"Alana," I say, "how did you know the exhibit was wrong?"

"There were plus signs when there should have been minus signs." She says it so matter-of-factly. It is suddenly clear how subpar my guidance of her math education would be, how inferior a public school education would be.

It is difficult to pinpoint the moment I recognized Alana's genius. Maybe it was when her math proficiency revealed itself at five, and without being formally taught, she solved algebra and calculus problems in her head, earning her the nickname "human calculator." Or when by the time she was six years old, Spanish and Italian rolled off her tongue—she had, after all, first learned Latin in roughly twenty lessons. Or when she remembered chapters of the books I read to her, reciting them back to me word for word. Each was a moment when I knew *smart* wasn't the correct word, signaling that *normal* doesn't apply to Alana, and together, they remind me that she will never have an ordinary life.

"Would you like to see Jacob again?" I ask. "Maybe help you with some of your math?"

Her eyes hold mine. Teachers fail to impress Alana. Her attitude toward them, and school, borders between judgment and boredom.

"Jacob is different. He's an astrophysicist. Do you know what that is?"

"A person who studies the universe."

"That's right. Astrophysicists study a lot of math and science. I bet Jacob could help you."

"I know, Mom. He knew the exhibit was wrong. You have to be smart to be an astrophysicist. Is my dad smart like Jacob?"

This time, her question floats in the air above us, like an escaped balloon. I can no longer hide this anymore. I no longer want to.

"I think so," I say as she doodles, her tongue poking out from the side of her mouth. She deserves better in all ways.

"Do you think Jacob could help me with my Google Science Fair idea?"

My mouth forms an *O*. The Google Science Fair. I forgot.

"Would you rather work on the Google Science Fair idea or the Navier-Stokes equation?" I say, remembering Jacob's enthusiasm from a few nights before.

She stops writing. "What's the Navier-Stokes equation?"

"The equation in your LT notebook."

"That *is* my Google Science Fair idea."

"The Navier-Stokes equation is your Google Science Fair idea?" I ask, finally understanding. "Jacob thinks he can help you with it. Would you like that?"

She nods big and adds *Help from Jacob on Google Science Fair idea* to her LT notebook under her page before writing Jacob's name at the top of a new page. Like Dad, Sylvia, and Brixton in the weeks before him, Jacob officially has his own page, and just like that, he has become another person in her life.

"And then can we all go to the fair together?" She beams a hundred-watt smile.

"We'll see," I say, closing her LT notebook.

————

Jacob arrives at the bookstore just before closing. There is no mistaking him this time. Daylight introduces a whole new perspective to his family's striking features. Underneath a navy button-down shirt and khaki shorts, his skin, like Alana's, glows a burnt orange like he has spent some time in the sun. When she was a baby, people stared at Alana, finding her looks to be rare. And one too many people commented on her bold green eyes or her beauty. I imagine he encounters the same. To look at him doesn't hurt your eyes.

"Hi," he says, as though unsure pleasantries are allowed.

"Hi," I say with almost the same hesitation. "Thank you for coming. Again."

"Of course."

"If you don't mind, I'd like to wait until the last of the customers leave before we talk."

He reflexively raises his arm as if to look at his watch.

He's met by a pale band of skin, where his watch once sat. I wonder if most people still do that, instinctively look for a watch, even though we have cell phones. Based on nothing but instinct, Jacob seems like an old soul, the kind of man who probably, in the beginning, balked at cell phones.

The last of the customers migrate out minutes before closing time. I turn the front door's dead bolt.

Jacob leans against the front desk. His mood is one of unrushed expectance. He has all the time in the world.

"There's a couch in the back where we can sit and talk," I say, gesturing.

He follows me, waiting for me to sit first before he joins me on the love seat. He runs his hands across the royal-blue velvet, fanning the fabric with each sweep of his hand.

"Thank you for coming," I say, adjusting my position, moving my hands in and out of my lap, clasping and unclasping my fingers.

He smiles, staring at my hands. "You said that already. Sara, you don't have to be nervous," he says. "Your secret is safe. You can trust me."

Once again, I'm unsure how to decipher Jacob's tone, and it threatens to knock me off-balance. Much like during his first visit, his tone borders on caring. Is it a ruse? Why isn't he angry with me? Doesn't he care that I kept Alana from him and his family?

I take a deep breath, feeling my limbs loosen and the knot under my chest relax. Last time, to balance my uncertainty, I relied on snatches of anger and frustration, neither of which suited me, neither of which roused Jacob. This time, I decide honesty will be a better route. I decide to be myself.

"This has always been my favorite place. Right here. This spot," I say. "Well, it was a different couch then, but I'd sit here and watch my father work. I'd nap here. Do my homework. Or just watch the customers come and go. I remember this one time a man came in, and he knew one line of a poem his grandmother from Ireland used to read to him. So, he came in and asked my father if he knew this poem. He told him the line: '*on a horse with bridle of findrinny.*' This was before the internet, before you could Google everything. If you didn't know something, you had to research it in books. Dad just looked at him and sighed. So, the man thought he didn't know. Then Dad said, '*On a horse with bridle of findrinny / And like a sunset were her lips / A stormy sunset on doomed ships.*' I don't remember the rest of the poem, but I remember the look on the man's face, the tears in his eyes. He had been trying to find that poem for decades."

"What's the name of the poem?"

"'The Wanderings of Oisin,' by Yeats."

I feel Jacob's eyes on me. I avert mine, embarrassed at the duration and intensity of his stare. "I don't know what made me remember that. With all that's going on...these memories of Dad keep coming up."

"They have a way of doing that, don't they?" His voice is downy. "Memories. They just sneak up on you."

"Yeah."

He clears his throat and shifts on the couch. "That poem. 'love is more thicker than forget.' The Cummings poem I recited that night. It reminds me of my sister. The many forms of love, its shapes and sizes. It can be thick. It can be thin. It's normal. It's sane. *'it is most sane and sunly / and more it cannot die / than all the sky which only / is higher than the sky.'* Love doesn't die. Neither do memories. She's been gone almost twelve years now, and these memories just keep popping up, keeping her alive, almost."

I vaguely remember his sister, Naomi, dying in a car accident. The news report said she, a friend, and the friend's mother were coming home from an early breakfast when a drunk driver swerved across the road and hit them. The friend and her mother lived. Naomi did not. Her death captured the attention of Savannah for weeks and again during the sentencing of the drunk driver, who, I heard, was strong-armed into pleading guilty after no lawyer in town would take his case.

I am not sure why he shares that. Maybe it is to put me at ease. Or maybe he truly can relate to being captive to unprovoked memories.

"I think we got off on the wrong foot," I say after a while. "The other night at my father's house. My attitude, tone. That's not who I am."

"I know."

"But I don't know you enough to trust you, Jacob. Everything in me tells me not to. I hope you can understand my hesitation."

He nods, his elbows on his knees.

"I would do anything to protect Alana. I don't make this decision lightly."

"I know. I understand, and I appreciate what you're doing."

"Alana really likes you. You gave her your watch, and you are fixing hers. You just don't know what that means to her. No one has ever offered to do that."

His face quirks into a smile. It's a smile of pride and happiness rolled into one. And I know Alana, her existence, has already begun rooting deep within him.

I produce his watch from my apron pocket and attempt to hand it to him. He shakes his head.

"No," he says. "Not until I fix hers. I made a promise."

"This watch is too expensive for an eight-year-old."

"That doesn't matter. I don't make a habit of breaking promises. It's hers."

My breathing slows. Maybe I can trust him.

I thrust the watch in his direction again, the band swinging with the force. "She can't wear watches. If she wears this, it will probably stop working."

He smiles again. "I can't wear a watch either. I discovered that when I was a little older than her," he says, taking the watch in his hand and flipping it over, revealing the back to me. "The battery is solar powered. It will never stop ticking." He sets the watch on the couch and slides it over to me.

"That's pretty amazing," I say, circling the dial with my forefinger. "I can't believe she didn't know that. She would love that."

"You've done a great job with her," he says. He wants to say more. I can almost feel it, but he doesn't.

His tone, more than his words, conveys his sincerity.

"She wants you to help her with her Google Science Fair idea."

"Google Science Fair?"

"It's a worldwide science competition for kids. Turns out her idea is that equation you found in her notebook."

"'Learn the "Thriller" routine,'" he says, recalling an entry.

"Yeah… She calls that her LT notebook. Lost Time."

"So, she wants to enter this Google Science Fair?"

"I'll let her explain it to you, but it's something she's been bugging me about for years. And now she's finally old enough to participate. I'm not sure what her idea is, but it involves that equation."

"And you're okay with this? Allowing me to work with her?"

"I am," I say, wishing I felt as confident as I sound. "But I have some conditions."

His green eyes burn into mine, signaling for me to continue.

"You may work with Alana for two hours a day every other day. No work on the weekends, and I can interrupt at any time, especially if I feel she's being pressured."

"Okay."

"I understand evenings will probably be ideal to accommodate your work schedule so…"

"I don't have a work schedule. Mornings or afternoons are fine."

"You don't work?"

"There's not much work for astrophysicists in Savannah."

He looks down to the hardwood floors. I remember whom I'm talking with. A Wyler. His family's mansion in Ardsley Park. The unlimited resources they exhibited during Daniel's trial. That fat envelope he tried to present to me. Old money. From birth, he never had to work a day in his life.

He responds to my silence by saying, "My last project ended, so I'm taking a break. I've been offered a few professorships that I'm considering."

"A professor?"

"That's where I find my heart wants to go."

"That's honorable, but I would rather Alana grow up to be a decent human being than a mathematical prodigy. She needs to understand from someone like you that there's more to life than math."

"A balance."

"Yes, a balance. You have to teach her something else besides math. Something that's going to help her fit into a society that won't understand her."

He nods again. "I can do that."

"You can work with her either at my father's house or here. Nothing outside of that."

"Okay."

Too embarrassed to meet his eyes, I look down to my lap, fidgeting yet again. "I want to tell her who you are. That you are her uncle," I say, peeking up at him quickly. "But I need your help. She's going to have all of these questions about him and your family. I need your help answering them."

Jacob's Adam's apple rises and falls as he digests this information. "What would you like for me to say?"

"I don't know. She's been asking about him for the last few years, and I'm tired of lying to her."

"What have you told her?"

"Nothing."

"What sorts of questions does she ask?"

"Yesterday, she asked me if her father was smart like you are," I say, watching a slight smile push at the corner of his lips and then quickly disappear.

"How would you like me to address these questions? With the truth?"

"Yes and no. I don't want you to be truthful about his whereabouts or why he's not in her life, but I want you to be honest if she asks if he can wear a watch or if he likes to swim," I say. "I can't answer those questions, but she reasonably should know about her background."

He nods his understanding. "Circumvent the difficult questions and truthfully answer the easy ones. I can do that."

"But I don't want you to tell her too much about him. I want to satisfy her enough to stop asking questions until..." My voice falters. Even after all this time, the reality of what happened stops me.

"Until *you* tell her the truth."

I nod, the merest tilt of the head, willing myself not to cry.

He hesitates. "I'm sorry, Sara," he says, pausing, the words tight in his throat. "I'm so sorry."

There's so much for him to be sorry about that I don't know where to apply this apology. About what his brother did? His mother's relentless fight against me to save her son? Having to tell Alana the truth about her conception? But the directness of his stare gives nothing away. I decide to apply his apology to all of it and silently accept.

"Will you help me?" I ask, my voice brittle as thin glass ready to snap.

"Whatever you need."

"I will tell her in my own time," I offer, completely unprovoked, but I feel an urge to explain myself.

"When do you want to tell her? About who I am?"

"I was thinking just after the first tutoring session. I know Alana, and if we do it before, she'll be too distracted to concentrate. I want to be fair to you and uphold my end of the arrangement."

"Okay," he says. "Is that all?"

"Despite all of this, you cannot tell anyone in your family about her, especially him, and definitely not your mother. I still don't want them to know about her, not until we leave."

"Sara—"

I interrupt. "Either you agree to all of my conditions or no deal." I feel a pang of guilt for presenting him with such an ultimatum considering his unwavering support, but I need to make this point clear.

He sighs, exhibiting an expression of great patience and fortitude. "Okay."

I stand and extend my hand. He joins me upright, his head just above mine, and takes my hand into his, cupping it with his other hand.

JACOB

———

THE DOOR TO SARA'S house opens before I knock, my hand hovering in a fist inches away. Alana greets me with a huge smile. Looking at her, every time, I'm startled by our resemblance, and a tinge of sadness and joy fills me. A tiny miracle.

"Jacob!" she says, with youthful enthusiasm while wrapping her arms around my legs in a tight bear hug.

I wonder if my racing heart will explode. Unprepared for such a burst of affection, I awkwardly wrap my arms around her shoulders in a semblance of a hug just as Sara emerges.

"Hi," she says as Alana releases my legs and moves in front of Sara. At eight, she stands just taller than Sara's stomach.

"Hi," I say, shifting my weight from side to side and adjusting the leather knapsack on my shoulder. Sara is wearing a navy maxi dress, her hair swept to the side in a fat braid that ends just below her collarbone, her bangs sweeping above her eyes, brown and steady. If she is nervous about today, I can't tell. She displays no signs of her usual tells. I admire her courage.

"She's been waiting for you all morning."

Alana burrows her head in Sara's thighs, embarrassed.

"Please come in," Sara says. "Dad and Sylvia are at the bookstore. We have the evening shift," Sara says, looking at Alana and making a face.

"Mom says that we can work at the kitchen table," Alana says, grabbing my hand. "Let's go."

I allow myself to be led into a small kitchen with a rectangular table. Alana's open LT notebook, two sharpened pencils, and several sheets of loose-leaf paper lie on the table. The sweet aromas of syrup and coffee hang in the air.

"Is this okay?" Sara asks, trailing behind us. "I wasn't sure how much space you need."

"It's fine," I say. "Thank you."

"We just had breakfast," Sara says. "Would you like something?"

"No," I say, pulling the strap of my bag off my shoulder. "Thank you."

Alana climbs onto a chair and reaches for her notebook. I sit and pull out my own. Sara takes a red kettle off the stove, fills it with water, and returns it to the burner, turning it on. She opens the refrigerator, examining its contents, even though she just told me they had finished breakfast. She closes the door, empty-handed, and stands at the stove with her back to us watching for the water to boil.

"Are you going to give me equations off the internet?" Alana asks.

"From the internet?"

"Brixton says that you're just going to give me equations off the internet that he's already given me."

"Who's Brixton?"

Sara, opening one cabinet to retrieve a mug and another for a tea bag, answers for her. "He's a boy who attends Sylvia's camps. He's pretty smart too."

"He's my friend."

"Well…you can tell Brixton that I'm not going to give you equations off the internet," I say, pulling out a piece of paper. "Actually, I want to test you on some basic algebra and geometry first."

I slide the sheet over to her along with a calculator that I don't expect her to need.

Sure enough, when she sees it, she says, "I stopped using a calculator when I was four."

The kettle on the stove begins to rumble. Sara pours the hot water into the mug, then adds the tea bag, dunking it several times. She studies her mug before lifting it.

"I'm going to leave you two to it," Sara says, wrapping her fingers through the handle. "I'll be around if you need anything."

She disappears around the corner, and I wait for her quick return. I expected Sara to join us during our lesson, never imagining that she would leave me alone with Alana. She may be gone, but her acts of purposeless ceremony tell me that she doesn't fully trust me yet.

I start Alana with simple algebra and watch as she works through the problems with ease. I slide another sheet of more advanced algebra across the table and watch her frown. She sighs heavily but begins working through the problems. "Done," she says, less than a minute later, slamming her pencil down.

"I know this is boring to you…"

"Very boring," she says, breathing out the words instead of speaking them.

"But I want to gauge your abilities. It is not all about solving problems. I'm trying to study your methods and processes so I will know where I need to start."

"Differential equations. That's what I'm learning now."

Alana's abilities are more advanced than I thought. Her notebook only revealed a fraction of her capabilities. I had no idea about the foreign language proficiency or that she possessed a photographic memory. After an hour, she has worked through all of the basic skills test I crafted for her, and I am not prepared for anything else. I make a mental note to not be unprepared again, and I improvise by teaching her a few calculus formulas.

She works through the equations with ease, like an adult counting to ten. Her capacity to soak up information enthralls me, and I lose track of time, watching the speed with which she processes and commits to memory while drafting somewhat of a long-term lesson plan for her, until Sara comes into the kitchen.

"Time's up," Sara says with a look as if it pains her to stop us.

Even though we are just breaking the surface on some advanced calculus equations, I stand immediately.

"Come on, Mom," Alana pleads, her head lowered in disappointment.

"I think we're off to a good start, Alana," I say, gathering the tests and closing my own notebook. "We can pick back up in a couple of days."

Alana pouts and plants her chin on the table, doodling on the paper in front of her, the pencil perfectly erect.

Sara eases into one of the kitchen chairs. I remain standing, leaning against the wall. We trade looks.

"Alana, honey," Sara starts, the words fumbling for space. "There's something I want to tell you about Jacob."

Alana lifts her head and looks at me. Sara closes her eyes, takes a deep breath, and says, "He's your uncle."

I imagine there is no easy way to tell Alana. No simple lead-up. In my mind, it happens in the slowest of terms, but Sara doesn't believe in slowly removing bandages. Or maybe this was easier for her.

"My…uncle?"

"Yes, honey." Sara forces a smile.

"He is?" Alana says, processing. She knows her mom doesn't have any siblings. "Really?"

Sara nods.

"You know my dad?" she says, turning to me.

"Yes, he's my brother."

"Cool!" she says, basking in the knowledge.

Still looking at me, Alana asks, "Where is he?"

I slip into another one of the kitchen chairs. "He's away at the moment, but did you know that he was born four minutes before me?"

"You're twins?" Her eyes are wide, full of questions.

"Identical twins, except he has a tiny scar right here," I say, running a straight line across her eyebrow to illustrate the spot.

"How did he get it?"

I laugh. "Our sister."

"Your sister?" She thinks again. "I have an aunt too?"

I inhale with a feeling that stings. "No, she died." I say, watching the way Alana's face accepts the information. "But she looked just like you. You remind me of her so much."

"I do?"

"Oh yeah…you have the same color hair, the same eyes. She was left-handed like you," I say, touching her nose with one quick dab. Alana giggles, her nose twitching ever so slightly. "You even wiggle your nose like her."

"I don't," she says, slapping her hand on her nose.

"You do," I say. "How do you do that?"

"I don't know," she says through laughter, the sound muffled by her hand.

"Oh…I almost forgot. I have something for you." I reach into my bag and pull out an object. The yellow color is reflected in her eyes as they light up.

"My watch," she says, taking it in her hands, inspecting it. "You fixed it!"

She turns to Sara, holding the watch up proudly. "Mom! Look! Jacob fixed my watch!"

Sara smiles. "What do we say?"

If she thanks me, the words are buried in my shoulder as she hugs me tight. This time, I'm prepared and close my eyes and hug her back, enveloping the warmth and inhaling the sweet and powdery scent of my niece. My niece. The thought is comforting and exciting.

"Now...do you have another one of your watches that stopped working?"

Alana considers this, pushes her lips to the side of her mouth. "I think."

"Go get it."

She takes off so fast the pages of the notebooks fan in the breeze. Sara turns to me.

"You don't have to do this. You've done enough already."

"I do," I say. "A balance, right?"

Upstairs, Alana's quick footsteps bang the ceiling above us. A door slams. A drawer opens and closes before her footsteps stomp on the stairs and she's back in the kitchen.

"Found one," she says, triumphantly holding up a red watch with blue flowers running the length of the band.

"Now," I say, reaching back into my bag. I pull out a child-size pair of magnifier glasses and place them on Alana, adjusting accordingly. She beams. I glance quickly at Sara for her approval. "Your mom said no more math, but she didn't say we couldn't fix this watch."

———

An hour later, I say goodbye to Alana and leave the house with the realization that I formally gained a niece and, I hope, the beginnings of Sara's trust. One equally important as the other. Outside, flecks of rain patter the asphalt like an increasing round of applause. I raise my head and allow the steady rain to drip on it, opening my eyes and watching the falling drops cascade down.

A few seconds later, a door slams and hurried footsteps drum behind me.

"Jacob."

Sara hurries toward me, reaching me just as I grasp the door handle of my truck.

"I wanted to thank you," she says, ignoring the way the rain streams through her hair and down her face. "For that. For everything. I didn't...I didn't think that this may be hard for you too."

Her sincerity warms me, and my heart fills with an unexplained emotion. The rain creates a sheen on the smooth skin on her face and along her chest and collarbone. Sara wears her beauty as though she doesn't know she possesses it, but the drizzling rain casts a brighter light on it.

"It was my pleasure," I say. "The least I could do."

The water thrums against the steel of my truck as I open the door, sending a loud yawn echoing down the street, and I throw my knapsack into the cab.

"I'm sorry about your sister."

I release a shuddering sigh that relieves the pressure in my chest. It is getting easier, talking about her, therapeutic almost. "I appreciate that," I say, giving her a quick backward glance.

"No, really," she says, stepping forward and touching my forearm just above the crook of my elbow, her fingertips grazing my skin. Her unexpected touch sends a jolt surging through me. Her eyes find mine, holding them there. "Thank you."

I place my hand on top of hers, shielding the rain needling it. She is smiling, a smile I haven't seen since the first night we met when she joked about her poetry book about mermaids. I resist the urge to run my finger down her cheek, astounded that I want to, amazed by the unexpected burst of emotion.

Instead, I reaffirm my grip on hers and say, "You are a brave woman, Sara."

———

"Spanish, Italian, and Latin?" Daniel says. "All three? Fluent? At eight years old?"

"I've never seen anything like it. She stopped at three because 'she got bored with it.' She said learning languages didn't 'pose enough of a challenge' for her."

Daniel laughs. "Are you sure she's not a Wyler?"

My face freezes in a smile, hoping the truth isn't evident there.

But Daniel has moved on to perusing the basic skills test I gave Alana, thumbing through the pages and skimming her work.

"Impressive," he says. "There's still a lot of work to be done, but..." His voice trails off. "I can't believe she's familiar with most of these equations."

"Or I had only just introduced them to her. I walked her through one equation, and she could solve the next one without my help. She has a photographic memory. It's just as you said. She just needs to be introduced and her brain does the rest. It's extraordinary."

"Make sure she reads *A Transition to Advanced Algebra*. She needs to begin transitioning from calculus to proof-oriented mathematics."

I make a mental note. I know that consulting with Daniel about Alana has some risks, but his zeal to help has allowed us to partner on a project. It feels like old times. Good times.

"She displays this level of math proficiency and not one teacher in her school recognized it? What about her parents? They had to have known. Did no one realize the consequences of boredom in a gifted child?"

"Her father..." I frantically search for my next words. "He's not in the picture. She went to public school for a little while. Her mother knew she was smart, so she began homeschooling her but just wants her to have a normal life."

"Parents of mentally abled children don't know how to

interact with their children. Does the girl exhibit any abnormal social challenges?"

"Some, but not like you think," I say, remembering the first time I met Alana and the ease with which she approached me. "Because of her abilities and her lack of social interaction, she tends to not understand personal boundaries."

"That's normal with gifted children. People are too guarded anyway."

"That's not normal behavior for an eight-year-old."

"Normal? She's not normal. She never will be."

I flinch, remembering Daniel's reminding me on my first visit, and wonder what *not normal* will mean for Alana.

"Her mother understands that. But she doesn't want her to miss out on being a kid. I know you can understand that."

He leans back in his chair. "Do you think we missed out on a childhood?"

"Not at the time. Now...I think it would have been nice to play football or be on the debate team."

"Football? You wanted to play football?"

"I don't know. I never got the chance. It would have been nice to have had a choice."

My mind drifts to Sara when he says, "I've been thinking about Sara, especially of late. What happened to her. If what happened altered her life."

Once, when we were seven, I experienced a sharp pain in my arm. Miles away, at the cottage with Dad, I had no idea that Daniel had broken his arm at our home in Savannah.

As a scientist, I'm supposed to consider hard proof, but as an identical twin with more than one incident of intuition, I trust what I've experienced to be real.

It is the first time Daniel has ever even casually admitted something did "happen to her." I wait for him to continue.

At the trial, a young Sara placed her hand on the Bible and painstakingly detailed the events of that night. Daniel never took the stand in his defense. Birdie and his lawyers decided against it, claiming that the prosecutor could and would trip him up into admitting he had raped Sara. Instead, they focused on Daniel's intelligence and Naomi's death. Individuals with high IQs are often depressed, finding it difficult to adapt to a society less intelligent than them, one of his lawyers said. Another: Grief for his sister sent him spiraling down a dark path. Highly intelligent individuals often turn to alcohol or chemical stimulations as a way to dull pain. He has never offered his own account for that night, an explanation that I need to know, its truth critical to forgiving him.

I testified against Daniel, my own brother. I need to understand why he committed this act. "What happened that night?" I ask when the silence stretches like a spring.

"Do you think she still hates me?" His eyes, focused on the front of the room, do not meet mine.

"I don't know," I say. "But if she does, that's her choice." It's the best answer I can give. I will never dare to speak for Sara.

He squirms as if it's possible to make the metal chair more comfortable. "I don't want her to hate me."

This is a stark contrast from my first visit when he displayed a cavalier attitude about Sara. A raw and honest opinion from a man who never expresses such deep emotions.

"I think people react and adjust to the hand they are dealt," I say, willing him to continue.

"Yeah…" His voice trails off, and I know the moment is gone, but not forever.

"Maybe you should have studied psychology in here instead of botany," I say to lighten the mood. I don't want him to shut down completely.

He snickers. "Look at us. Talking about feelings. Birdie would hate this."

"Not as much as you think. She's not selling the house in case you want to raise a family there."

He coughs, which turns into a laugh, a small one at first that intensifies. "Excuse me?"

"I know. I couldn't believe it myself."

"Birdie? Our mother? Birdie who never changed a diaper or wiped a runny nose. Wants a house full of grandchildren?"

He laughs again, and I join him. We laugh for a bit longer at Birdie's expense, recalling memories of her lack of maternal instincts, like the time she asked Marsha to hug Naomi when she fell off her bike. It feels good to laugh with him again.

Finally, I say, "People evolve. They become different people. Everyone is capable of it."

"Yeah… Do you know what I want?" He shakes his head. "Never mind. You're going to laugh."

"What? Tell me."

He pauses. "I want to fall in love."

I draw back in my chair. "You? Want to fall in love?"

"Sounds crazy, right?"

"No...not at all. I'm just surprised. Coming from the man who wrote a paper on why love is an illusion and does not exist. That love can be"—I pause and clear my throat—"'replicated by eating large quantities of sugar.'"

He laughs. "That was a long time ago. You just said that people change. I've changed my position on love."

"That's fair. So...what are we looking for? Women? Men?"

He shoots me a bird. "A woman."

I hold my hands up. "I'm just making sure. What kind of woman?"

"I'm not sure."

"Tall? Short? Petite? Curvy? IQ?"

"I don't know." He looks around the room filled with various types of women as if trying to size them up. "What about you? What kind of woman is your Aurora?"

"My Aurora is outwardly beautiful. But she's more than that. She's quiet, understated, and it shows. She just exists."

Daniel laughs. "I'm the one locked up in here, and it looks like I'll be falling in love before you."

"You have plenty of time. You'll get out. Meet someone. You'll know what love feels like."

"I hope so. So...how about it? Are you going to fill Birdie's house with children? I always thought you would be the one to have a family. You were always the more sensible one."

"You mean sensitive?"

"No, I mean sensible in all variations of the word, including sensitive. You were more like Dad, caring and loving. I'm like Birdie. I don't know what kind of a father I would have been."

"Would have been? It's not too late."

He waves a dismissive hand. "Like I said, I'm too much like Birdie. But not you. Your life has always been shaped and planned. This perfect circular life. I see you with a family. A beautiful wife. One, no, two girls."

Against my will, my mind casts to images of Sara and Alana earlier today. Or maybe I will it to.

"Maybe," I offer him. "Someday."

"No," he says. "What are you waiting for? I appreciate these visits," he says, holding up Alana's test. "I appreciate you showing me this and letting me help. It's given me something to look forward to while this cancer eats away at me. A life outside of these walls. But you don't owe me anything."

I lean in. "You're getting the bone marrow transplant, and believe it or not, I have missed you. As long as you are in here, I'll be here. I missed so much time already. I don't want to miss any more."

He smiles. "Okay. Maybe I did mean sensitive."

SARA

———

TODAY, WE ARE ON the way to Dad's doctor's visit, another routine checkup. He isn't a willing participant on this visit or most. He is silent on the drive, his body language doing all the speaking for him, his upper torso turned away from me and angled toward the passenger window as if the scenery offers more than the usual fast food restaurants and grocery stores.

He's made his peace with his diagnosis. Not once has he expressed any sadness or anger about his impending death. And if you didn't know any better, you wouldn't know that his last days are upon him.

He exits the car, his cane tapping a steady rhythm on the asphalt with each step, the chain from his silver pocket watch sparkling in the sun. As we enter the hospital, he tips his hat to all in view, nurses and patients alike. Despite it all, he has lunged forward with an increasing momentum that is both inspiring and upsetting, logging a full day at the bookstore and making up for lost time with Alana. Not once in his life has my father ever expressed fear of any kind. Why would death be any different?

Two hours later, a nurse wheels Dad in from his CT scan. The oversize wheelchair swallows his medium-size frame, and he looks fragile, thinner than usual, tired too, but still with an expression of focus and determination. I flash him a smile that feels forced and fake as I hold it steady across my face.

"We'll have the results in a few days," Dr. Mundy says, scribbling something on Dad's chart. "But we are not expecting any changes. Just keep doing what you've been doing."

Back in the car, Dad has returned to his view out the passenger window. I do not want my last days with him to be spent wallowing in pity and sadness. I want to remember the good days and create new ones, focus on the moments in front of us. Time, in a way it has never been and may never be again, is ours.

"How about a poem?" I ask, remembering that on car rides, instead of listening to the radio, Dad regaled us with poetry. It's been awhile since we've done this, and I want nothing more than to remember the good times. "Whatever is in your heart."

He turns from the window and smiles. I wait for his deep voice, as he clears his throat and proceeds, as if the poem were on the tip of his tongue, waiting for its moment.

"When all is done, and my last word is said,
And ye who loved me murmur, "He is dead,"
Let no one weep, for fear that I should know,
And sorrow too that ye should sorrow so.

When all is done and in the oozing clay,
Ye lay this cast-off hull of mine away,
Pray not for me, for, after long despair,
The quiet of the grave will be a prayer."

I glance at Dad as he continues. By reciting, "When all is done," Dad is telling me that death cannot conquer his soul. I decide right then that I will attempt my own acceptance.

"When all is done, say not my day is o'er
And that thro' night I seek a dimmer shore:
Say rather that my morn has just begun,—
I greet the dawn and not a setting sun."

As sad as it makes me feel, I realize that this, without his telling me so, is his final wish. Focus on what you want to remember, Dr. Mundy had told me. And it occurs to me that these moments are what I want to remember. My proud father who, on what could be the eve of his death, recites a poem that welcomes death and reminds me that life doesn't end after it.

"I don't have much yet, but I'm starting a new collection."

He perks up at this. Though separated by miles, we worked

on my first collection together. His critiques were tough to decipher without words, but with every frown and curl of his nose, I knew he wanted me to dig deeper into myself.

"It's not flowing as freely as the first one. It's a bit raw, but I would love your advice as I work. Maybe you could take a look?"

He reaches over and takes my hand in his.

―――

At home, we meet Jacob as he arrives in his patchwork truck of different color metals. It seems odd that he would drive such a truck. Or maybe not. I don't know much about him.

He greets me first, a simple hello. I return the greeting. His presence is growing on me and isn't as jarring as it once was. Jacob shakes Dad's extended hand. I watch as Dad's face transforms. I know nothing of their relationship, why they connected, but I see the connection across Dad's face every time he sees Jacob.

Dad says:

"I will arise and go now, and go to Innisfree,
And a small cabin build there, of clay and wattles made;
Nine bean-rows will I have there, a hive for the honey-bee,
And live alone in the bee-loud glade,"

Jacob smiles and nods his head. "It's going pretty well. If the rain and humidity would loosen their grip, I would be able to get a lot more work done."

He has his own personal greeting. And it's one I do not know. Every time I witness an exchange between them, I realize just how close they are. It makes me wonder, *Who is Jacob?*

They continue talking, heading into Dad's house as Sylvia's front door across the street slams and Alana runs home. Inside, Alana greets Jacob and immediately pulls him into the kitchen, excited to begin her lesson. Sylvia follows us through the front door just as Dad heads upstairs.

"I'll be up in a minute," she calls to Dad, before turning to me. "How did it go?"

I shrug. "Same."

She nods, expecting that answer. "Jacob's here?" She moves past me just as I answer. "I better go say hello."

Jacob snaps to attention, standing immediately when we enter the kitchen. Alana, studiously bent over her notebook, doesn't notice.

"Jacob," Sylvia says. She walks over to him, standing too close, her gaze traveling down the length of him and back up again. "Good to see you again."

"Yes, ma'am," he says. "It's good to see you too."

"Hosea is laying down for a nap," she says, finally releasing him with her eyes but maintaining her proximity.

"How's he doing?"

Sylvia looks at me, then back at Jacob. "He's making his peace with everything," she says, her voice fading to a whisper. "It helps having our girls here. He's never been happier."

"Will you please let me know if there's anything I can

do?" Jacob says, reaching for her hand and squeezing it. "Anything."

Jacob's display surprises me. It had been an impulse, an act performed without thought or consideration, something comforting and thoughtful.

"I will," Sylvia says. "But I think you've already done enough. He has enjoyed your friendship these last few months. I'm just upset that he kept you all to himself."

"He's been a good friend," he says. "An unexpected perk to coming home."

"How's our little student?" Sylvia asks. "Are my girls giving you much trouble?"

He laughs. "Not at all. It's been very fascinating watching Alana. She's actually teaching me a few things," Jacob says, his face warming to a blush. "And Sara has been the most hospitable host."

Sylvia studies Jacob for a second then suddenly turns her head as if straining to hear something. "Did you hear that?" We all fall silent, tilting our heads, except for Alana, whose pencil continues scratching against a piece of paper.

"I don't hear anything," I say, looking at Sylvia, my eyes questioning. *What is she doing?*

She's silent for another beat. "I think Hosea is calling me," she says finally. "It was nice to see you again, Jacob. I'll be seeing you around."

"Yes, ma'am."

Dad doesn't call anyone. Not by name, anyway. What is she up to?

Sylvia leaves and I begin to follow, but Jacob stops me. "I have an appointment this afternoon, so I need to leave earlier than usual," he asks. "If that's okay with you."

For a few weeks now, Jacob has arrived before 10:00 a.m., just as Sylvia and Dad leave to open the bookstore. He spends a few hours tutoring Alana, and then he leaves. He's never disclosed any personal information. And I've never asked.

"Sure. We don't have to commit to a set schedule. We can be flexible."

"It should be just for today."

"Done," Alana says, slamming her pencil down and immediately picking up the thick math book Jacob brought.

Jacob looks down at Alana then back at me as if seeking confirmation that our conversation is over.

"Please don't let me interrupt," I say. I can tell that he's eager to resume his tutoring.

He sits and begins skimming Alana's work. I start to leave the kitchen when the door swings open and Sylvia returns, stopping in the doorway. Jacob, once again, stands abruptly, pushing the chair back, the metal legs shrieking against the tile floor.

"I forgot to ask how Marsha is doing," Sylvia says. "I haven't seen her in ages."

"She's good."

"Well…tell her I said hello."

"Yes, ma'am."

This time I follow Sylvia out of the kitchen and into Dad's

study. "What were you doing?" I say once I close the door and we are out of earshot. We sit on the couch in view of Dad's vintage books lining his bookcase. "Was Dad really calling you?"

She laughs, waving a dismissive hand. "He's asleep."

"So, what were you doing?"

"You didn't notice that every time I came into the room, Jacob stood?"

I think back and do remember him standing but fail to find the humor in that act. "Yeah, so?"

"That's old-school. They stopped teaching men that in the forties."

"Why does that matter?"

"It's called manners. Every southern boy is taught 'Yes, ma'am,' 'No, ma'am,' 'Yes, sir,' 'No, sir.' I know not one who stands when a woman enters the room. He's a true gentleman."

I think back to every conversation or interaction I've had with Jacob and remember that he never sat unless I sat or entered the house without being asked to do so. But I'm not sure of the implication.

"What are you saying?"

"I'm saying that he's more genuine than you think."

"And you came to this conclusion from him standing when you enter a room?"

"A person can't hide their true nature or mask their character for very long. I don't think it's a ruse with Jacob. I think that standing when a woman enters a room is who he really is. If he says that you can trust him, I believe you can."

"I don't know yet."

"How do you feel about him being here?"

"I'm okay with it. Dad trusts him. Alana really likes him. He's polite, as you've noticed. So far he's keeping up his end of the arrangement."

"And what if he doesn't?"

"I don't know. We go back to Maine."

She rolls her eyes. "You can't keep falling back on that. That's no longer an option. Jacob knows about her. There's no going back now."

"Sylvia, you know I have rights in Maine. I'm not protected here."

"So what?"

"You don't think I'm doing the right thing?"

"I'll answer that if you answer this question first. You think that Jacob tutoring Alana is enough?"

"Yeah. Maybe. Why can't it be?"

"To answer your question…I think Jacob is a placeholder for a conversation and a reality you're going to have to face."

"And what's that?" I know what it is; I know in every fiber of my being. But I want her to say it out loud, so she can hear the enormity of what she wants me to do. "That Alana deserves to know the truth and that they are going to find out about her anyway."

"Why can't this be enough?"

"Because it's not the truth."

"I'll tell you the truth. The truth is they don't deserve to know about her. I'm not leaving Dad. I can't do that again. And I know that I can't take back that Jacob now knows about Alana. But I can still control them having a presence in her life."

"Have you considered that they might not want to have a presence? Birdie has always proclaimed Daniel's innocence. Alana is proof of his guilt. Maybe she wouldn't or couldn't accept that idea that she was wrong."

I snicker, an ugly snort. "She would sue me for custody just to spite me. I ruined her precious son's life."

"Then we do what we didn't do the first time. We fight. We stand our ground and fight."

The shock of her words stings and collapses my entire body under its weight.

"You think I should have stayed?"

"I think we did what we did because it was the best solution at the time. The first trial was ending. They had just launched the appeal. Leaving was the best option," she says, clutching my hand and raising my chin with her forefinger. "But now? We fight. No more running."

There is strength in her words, a power, a call to action. The idea of being free from this burden calms me.

"That includes Alana," Sylvia continues. "You have to tell her the truth."

"She's eight. She can't possibly understand the magnitude of the situation."

"No, she can't. But that's where Jacob comes in. You've

already started by telling her who he is. Jacob's a bridge to her other family. It's a start."

"I still don't know if I can trust him."

"Has he given you any reason to believe that you can't? Let's recap. He accidentally runs into a little girl who could easily be his daughter at the museum. He comes to the bookstore's grand opening and runs into you. He still hasn't put the two incidents together. It's only when he sees Alana with you that he realizes who she really is. He disappears for a week, doesn't tell his family about her, and only materializes when you call him. He comes over in the middle of the night just to talk to you. He tries to give you an envelope full of Lord only knows how much money. He then agrees not to tell his family about her in exchange for tutoring her. He helps you tell Alana about her other family while circumventing questions about Daniel. I think that he deserves the benefit of the doubt. He doesn't have to be here, but he is. That counts for something."

"Well…according to you, all he needs to do is stand when a woman enters a room, so…"

We share a laugh that deflates the tension.

Her face relaxes. "Does it bother you, to look at him?"

"They're twins, but I see two different people. I look at him and see Jacob, not Daniel."

"He's not the David I remember. The David I remember was a tall, skinny kid, all knees and elbows. He's all grown up and has come into his own, especially that body."

"Sylvia!"

"Don't tell me you haven't noticed how beautiful he is."

"Beautiful?"

"A man can be beautiful."

"I'm not thinking about that."

"Smart too. Did you know he has a PhD in astronomy?"

"Astrophysics. He has a PhD in astrophysics."

"That sounds even fancier."

"I will admit that he's very smart." I pause, wondering if Jacob would be offended at being called just smart. "And nice looking." I think back to the curve of Jacob's jaw under his baseball hat and wide smile.

She concedes. "When this is all over, I'm going to find you a nice southern boy to settle down with. You have so much to offer someone. An internal strength that's severely lacking in women today."

Single life can be lonely, and my hands have been the only ones on my body since Todd. I do miss touch. A spark. That's why my relationship with Todd ended. He touched me softly and carefully, which I appreciated, but his touch lacked a jolt that even in my limited experience I knew should exist. We had reached the pinnacle of our relationship. There was no future there. But I didn't mourn the end; I felt, finally, normal, and confident of knowing what I wanted in a relationship.

There are too many distractions right now to ever think about being in a relationship with someone, but I appreciate Sylvia's efforts. "We'll see," I say.

"I just want you to be happy, Sara. Free yourself from this burden and really live. You have so much life left to live."

A soft rap on the door sends us both jumping.

"I just wanted to let you know I'm leaving," Jacob says from the doorway. "Alana is finishing up a few equations. I'll be back on Friday."

"Take care, Jacob," Sylvia says, her legs folded, the top one swinging. "You must join us for dinner soon."

"I would be honored," he says, looking at his newly returned watch. After fixing Alana's watch, he finally agreed to take his back.

Remembering his appointment, I decide to help him out before Sylvia monopolizes any more of his time.

"Sylvia," I say, "Jacob has an appointment he needs to get to."

"Don't let me keep you," she says. "We will see you later."

JACOB

———

THE CLINIC IS ALMOST empty, eight in the morning a bit too early for sprained ankles, broken bones, and lacerations. I'm the sole person huddled in the bank of navy chairs. A janitor pushes a cart across the stark-white floor, a squeaking noise from one rusted wheel trailing behind him. The Coke vending machine kicks on.

Yesterday, I received the first injection of filgrastim in Dr. Bennett's office in Atlanta. Before determining the best fatty spot for injection, my stomach, he reminded me that the filgrastim will increase my blood cells, so I should be ready for the actual collection in four days. I could possibly experience some minor side effects, he said, flu-like symptoms, fever, headache, and muscle aches. I asked if the remaining injections could be administered in Savannah. He wanted to administer the first injection but didn't see the harm in allowing a colleague in Savannah to administer the remaining four. I hated leaving my tutoring session with Alana early.

Sara didn't seem to mind, but I don't want to make a habit of changing our schedule or give the impression that I'm not taking our arrangement seriously. I need her to trust me.

I experienced no side effects from the first injection, but by the time I arrive in front of Hosea's house after the second injection, a dull headache has appeared, and my body begins to ache like I've run a marathon. I'm rubbing my arms when Alana pushes her paper to me.

"Does my grandmother live in Savannah?" Alana asks in our final hour of tutoring. As usual, she's impressive, accepting instruction and lessons, digesting everything I'm teaching her. Her question catches me off guard as I look over her latest work.

I clear my throat; the act vibrates and accentuates my headache. "She does," I say, offering nothing more. Unsure of what else to say.

"Can we go over to her house?"

I listen for Sara, who usually finds a reason to pop in about once an hour, but I hear nothing. "She's not at home," I say, remembering that Birdie is, in fact, visiting with Daniel today. With his pending release and bone marrow transplant rapidly approaching, our visits are increasing.

"Can we go over to her house when she gets back?" Alana asks, looking directly at me.

"We have to ask your mom," I say, hoping the ibuprofen I took works soon.

"She's going to say 'We'll see,' which means no," she says sadly. "She always says no."

"Hey now," I say. "That's not a fair thing to say."

"It's true," she says.

"It's your mom's job to protect you. She would never agree to something that could hurt you. Do you believe that?"

Alana lifts her shoulders and releases them with emphasis. "Why would going to my grandmother's house hurt me? Grandmothers are nice. Brixton's grandmother knits colored socks and watches *Judge Judy*."

Despite Birdie's treatment of Sara, Sara has never spoken ill of her to Alana. Alana has no reason to believe that Birdie isn't like Brixton's grandmother. In Alana's eyes, Birdie has a clean slate, a starting place for a relationship. I wonder if that's by Sara's design. Sara's bravery continues to impress me.

"What's my grandmother like?"

"Well...she loves to garden. Her backyard is full of flowers. I even helped her plant some."

"Can I help?"

"Sure," I say, too quickly. "But you know what we could do? We could start our own garden here."

"We could?"

"Absolutely. We have to ask your mom though."

Alana sulks again. "She's going to say 'We'll see.'"

"I don't think so. Let's ask her."

As if on cue, Sara walks into the kitchen. Alana launches out of her chair to her.

"Mom, can we start a garden? Please!"

Sara looks at me for help. I nod my head, modeling Sara's behavior.

"I think that's a great idea," Sara says, following my cue.

"Jacob, she said yes!" Alana exclaims as if Sara were not in the room.

"See. I told you."

Sara turns to Alana. "Pack up your stuff and take it to your room. I want you to straighten up before dinner."

Alana leaves, practically bouncing.

"A garden? You let her talk you into starting a garden?" she asks with a hint of a smirk, leaning against the kitchen sink. "I know it's tough to say no to her when she stretches those big green eyes at you, but you're going to have to find a way. Or she's going to have you building a rocket ship to the moon." Her mood is playful and friendly.

Stretches is a funny word for eyes, but Sara is right in her description. At times, Alana seems to make her eyes even bigger just through the intention behind her gaze. "She doesn't get that from us. The way she stretches her eyes. She gets it from you."

Sara's smile fades as she opens her mouth to speak, words at first failing to materialize, but then: "I don't see very much of myself in her."

"Are you kidding me? She has your bravery, your strength. She may have our eye color, but the way she uses them is all you." I find myself staring into Sara's brown eyes now, open and inviting, lovely, like seeing into her soul. I look away before she notices.

"You're just saying that because she tricked you into starting a garden," she says, her smile returning. And I regret that her elusive smile, our casual banter, will fade when I tell her the reason for the garden.

"She asked about Birdie. If she lived in town and if I could take her to her house."

Sara grimaces and her breath catches, snatching with it her good mood, which evaporates like water in the desert. "What did you say?"

"That she was out of town for a while, but I pivoted to the garden. I hope you don't mind."

"Is she badgering you with questions? Has she asked you anything else?" Her questions come quickly.

I shake my head. "Just this, today. Nothing else. Not yet."

Sara studies her fingers, as if newly growing familiar with them. "I'm afraid this is just the tip of the iceberg. She's going to ask you more. Much more. Trust me."

"I'll be ready."

Sara looks at me with bewilderment. "How do you do that? Be that confident? Know what to say?"

I shrug. "I don't always know what to say, but there's no situation I can't think my way out of."

"I wish I had your confidence."

"There's strength in you. More than you know."

"You keep saving me," she says. "Thank you. I hope to return the favor one day."

"It's really the least I can do. But you don't owe me

anything. I think I got the best part of the deal." I don't elaborate on what the best part of the deal entails.

"But now we have to start a garden," she says, a small grin reappearing.

I wave a dismissive hand. "Gardens are easy. It will be fun. I'll help. If you like."

"That would be nice. First, watches. Now, gardens. I think that's the balance she needs. What she's always needed. She's really thriving here, more than I thought she would."

"And what about you? How does it feel to be..." I pause to consider the correct word. *Home* doesn't seem to fit the context of the question if she doesn't consider Savannah to be her home anymore. "Here," I finally say.

"Me? I'm fine," she says, in a way that I know she's not fine. How can she be? "I love being with Dad and Sylvia. I love this house, the bookstore. I love watching Alana come into her own here. I try not to think about anything else. I take each day as it comes."

I don't know if I've ever admired someone more.

"May I ask you a question?"

She lifts her eyebrows.

"'We'll see'?"

Sara slides into a chair and runs her hands through her hair. She closes her eyes, drained from the effort of keeping her composure, her hands clasped in prayer atop her head. "I feel as if I'm always saying no. 'We'll see' became another way of saying it."

I join her in sitting. "You don't have to protect her from the truth. When you're ready, it's okay to paint an accurate picture of Birdie and Daniel. I appreciate you sparing them, but they certainly don't deserve it."

She opens her eyes. "How can you say that? They're your family. Your mother. Your brother."

"They also hurt you. We all must be held accountable for our actions."

"You don't think I should give them a clean slate?"

"Absolutely not. But Alana deserves to know the truth. Providing them with a clean slate is not the full truth. Alana knows nothing, so she's filling in the holes herself, like with information about grandmothers that she gets from Brixton."

"What?"

"Brixton's grandmother knits."

"Does Birdie knit?"

"No, she gardens."

Sara nods, understanding with each nod how and why we arrived at starting a garden.

"She's going to get banged up in this life. Sometimes by her own family." I'm thinking of Birdie and Daniel when I say this. "You must prepare her for that. It starts with you. Don't let her idolize them." I regret my choice of words, of speaking at all, offering unsolicited advice.

"I didn't realize that's what I've been doing."

"You don't want to keep her from discovering their good

points on her own, but they shouldn't be granted a pass for all the bad. My dad used to say that good comes with the bad."

"Thank you. I mean it. Thank you for being here. For helping me with Alana." She pauses, her voice quivering. "For not hating me."

My tone collapses with the force of her honesty. "Hate you? Why would I ever hate you?"

"Because I kept Alana a secret. For not letting you tell your family about her. How you found out about her. I know you have your own healing to do."

Her acknowledgment sends a rock plummeting into my gut. Her eyes are soft and open like a book begging to be read. Her modesty, unassuming and caring, accentuates her obvious beauty. In this moment, more than any other, she is so strikingly beautiful, inside and out, that it physically hurts me.

"You did what you had to do. What you felt was right. You don't owe me anything, especially an explanation," I say, suppressing the urge to touch her, to comfort her. "I'm glad I can help, Sara. You don't have to carry this around alone anymore. I will help you any way I can. You can stop thanking me."

"Thank—" She smiles, and the force of it electrifies my soul. We share a laugh. "I appreciate that."

Sara stands and opens the refrigerator door, examining its contents. Shielded by the open door, I exhale for a second, slow and deliberate, willing my pulse to slow before closing my notebook and tucking it into my knapsack. I stand and hoist it on my shoulder.

"Jacob?" Sara calls after me as I turn to leave, peering over from the refrigerator. "Would you like to stay for dinner?"

I stare into her brown eyes, thinking that it's not just Alana I have trouble saying no to, and I don't think twice about what she's asked. "I would love to."

"It's Friday. We eat pizza on Fridays. A family tradition from when I was a kid. Sometimes we order out, but most of the time we make our own."

Her invitation signals a loosening of the distance Sara fashioned between us. There's no way I can say no to this. Even if I wanted to. "I love pizza."

"Sylvia is headed to the store for a few ingredients. If you want to hang around. Or…"

"Do I have time to take a shower and change?" I omit that this would take place a few miles away at Birdie's house. It has become my routine to visit with Birdie and Marsha after Alana's tutoring sessions. I don't want to saw at Sara's olive branch with any more Birdie talk.

Sara's eyebrows jump. "It's just pizza."

"I know, but I'd like to change."

"Okay…we get started around six. I'll leave the door open for you. Just come on in."

I check the time. Five until two. "Should I bring anything?"

"Just an appetite."

The kitchen door creaks open, and Alana returns with her LT notebook, climbing into a chair, her face serious and stern. "I've been thinking about this garden," she says. "Do we need a tractor?"

———

It's a few minutes before six, but it might as well be midnight to my body. After my shower at Birdie's, I fight the urge to rest my eyes for a bit. The filgrastim, from this morning's injection, no doubt working. But, for now, my headache is gone as are the muscle aches.

The last bits of daylight cast a reddish glow across the sky as I pull in front of Hosea's house. The house is already illuminated with lights, and I can see Sara's and Alana's silhouettes in the kitchen. Alana is standing on a chair emptying a bag of cheese into a large bowl. Sara is busy cutting something. Hosea stands at the stove while Sylvia sits at the kitchen table.

I knock once and the door swings open. Inside, the mood is jovial with laughter echoing around the foyer. I smile at the togetherness and love, even without seeing it.

"Come on in, Jacob," Sylvia calls. "We're in the kitchen."

I open the kitchen door to a thunderous "Jacob!" from Alana.

I greet everyone while surveying the kitchen. Small bowls of onions, tomatoes, cheese, green peppers, and more dot the kitchen table. Five balls of pizza dough line the counter. On the stove sits an assortment of pepperoni, sausage, and other meats. When Sara said they make their own pizza, I assumed it was of the frozen variety, not that they created and baked their own from scratch.

"Settle an argument for us," Sylvia asks, handing me a bottle of beer.

"If I can," I say, taking a swig. I'm already more energized, more awake than when I pulled into the driveway.

"Would you rather be able to reverse one decision you make every day or be able to stop time for ten seconds every day?" Sylvia asks.

"Wow," I say, the question snaking through me. I hover in the corner away from everyone. "I need a second to consider. What does everyone else say?"

"I would reverse a decision," Alana says, still standing on a chair, bending down for another bag of shredded cheese to open.

"And what decision would you have reversed today?" Sara asks her.

Alana twists her lips. "I would...I would have asked Grandpa for French toast instead of pancakes. Sorry, Grandpa."

Hosea shrugs and nods his approval.

"I agree with Alana. I wouldn't reverse the pancake decision this morning, but I would definitely like to reverse one decision I make every day. There's not a day goes by that I don't put my foot in my mouth. Like today, with Miss Celeste and Miss Emma." Sylvia turns to me. "Miss Celeste and Miss Emma are these two old women from church who both have a little crush on Mr. Porter." I nod as Sylvia turns her attention to kneading the dough in front of her. "Anyway, I saw Mr. Porter at the store today in the produce section. Not five minutes later I saw Miss Celeste by herself, and she asked if I had seen Mr. Porter. I said yes—he was in the produce section. Why did I say that? I look up and Miss Emma is standing next to Mr. Porter helping him pick out a watermelon." Sylvia turns back to me. "Now, Miss Celeste and Miss Emma can't stand each other because of Mr. Porter. So when Miss Celeste sees Miss Emma with Mr. Porter, she hits her cart into Miss Emma's cart. Next thing you know, these two old biddies are deliberately ramming their carts together."

Everyone, including me, laughs, as much for the story as Sylvia's dramatic retelling of it.

"Finally, I step in and separate them. Miss Celeste's wig is turned. Miss Emma is out of breath. All while Mr. Porter is still looking at watermelons."

"You're kidding." Sara chuckles, finishing the onion she was dicing.

"What's a biddy?" Alana asks, now eating cheese directly from the bowl.

"An old woman," Sara answers, moving the bowl of cheese from Alana's reach.

Sylvia continues. "So, if I could reverse one decision today, I would not tell Miss Celeste I saw Mr. Porter in the produce section."

Everyone laughs again, except for Alana, who uses the opportunity to snag a green pepper cube that fell out of the bowl.

"What about you?" I ask Sara, who is now washing her hands in the sink. "What would you choose?"

"That's easy. I would stop time."

"Why?"

She dries her hands on a kitchen towel. "I think there's something to being present in a moment. To be frozen there. To think. To prolong a moment." She looks embarrassed. "I don't know."

Hosea kisses Sara on the cheek, marking his approval of her choice.

"I agree, Hosea," I say. "Time doesn't work backward, so what's done is done. Time is a measure of change, and change can only happen in forward motion. I like the idea of playing with time. Giving a moment or moments more time."

"Well…we're sticking by our decision, huh, Alana," Sylvia says, giving Alana a high five. "If y'all had seen Miss Celeste and Miss Emma ramming them carts together, you would have chosen differently."

The kitchen erupts again in laughter before settling down and the business of creating pizzas begins.

"Since this is Jacob's first Pizza Friday, we need to explain the rules to him," Sylvia says. "Rule number one. No judging another person's pizza. To each their own."

"Rule number two. You can't make the same pizza twice," Sara says, hugging Alana's shoulders. "You have to make a different combination every week."

"Rule number three," Alana says. "Rule number three… What's rule number three?"

"If you make it, you eat it. Even if you don't end up liking the combination," Sylvia answers.

"Rule number four. The most inventive pizza wins an extra scoop of ice cream for dessert," Sara says.

"Now, Dr. Wyler," Sara says teasingly, holding a pizza crust out to me. It is refreshing to see this side of Sara, lively and free. "If you agree with our rules, you may begin."

"I accept your rules," I say playfully, taking the crust from her hands.

"The meats are on the stove, all of the toppings on the table, sauces are on the other counter," Sylvia says. "We bake two pizzas at a time. First two finished go in first."

I watch as they all grab a crust and begin spooning and spreading various sauces. Sara and Hosea go for the tomato sauce, while Sylvia and Alana choose a white sauce. They move together around the kitchen adding toppings and talking. My heart eases at the sight of a family, and I think back to the last time my entire family was together. A few nights before Naomi died.

"Jacob?" Sara asks. The vision of my family disappears. "You okay?"

"Yeah," I say too quickly. "I've never made a homemade pizza before."

It's a strange thing to admit, and the room stops with my realization.

"You've never made a homemade pizza before?" Alana asks.

"No," I say. "I'm just considering all of my options. I want that extra scoop of ice cream."

"Bless your heart," Sylvia says. "Take your time."

"Any anchovies?" I ask, surveying the ingredients again to ensure I have not overlooked them.

Four sets of eyes shoot in my direction.

"Eww…" Alana sings.

"He's kidding," Sara says, sprinkling cheese on her pizza.

"I'm not."

"Eww…" Alana says again.

"What…no one likes anchovies?"

Suddenly, everyone's pizza in front of them becomes more interesting.

"No one?"

"Anchovies are nasty," Alana says.

"Do you really like anchovies?" Sara asks, her face crooked in contemplation.

"Absolutely. I live on an island. I eat a lot of fish."

"You live on an island?" Alana asks. "That's so cool."

"I do. It's about a forty-minute drive from here."

Hosea says forcefully:

"What islands marvellous are these,
That gem the sunset's tides of light—
Opals aglow in saffron seas?
How beautiful they lie, and bright,
Like some new-found Hesperides!"

"He *loves* islands," Sara whispers mockingly.

Hosea grabs a piece of sausage from Sara's pizza and pops it in his mouth. She responds by taking a green pepper from his pizza.

"That's quite a ways from Savannah. Why so far out?" Sylvia asks.

"It's quiet and peaceful," I say, selecting bacon in lieu of anchovies. "There's not much light pollution out there. I can see the stars."

"What's light pollution?" Alana asks.

"It's the presence of anthropogenic—" I stop and refocus my answer. "It's when the sky is flooded with artificial light from buildings. It obstructs the stars."

I smile approvingly as Hosea, the first to finish his pizza, chimes in with William Cullen Bryant.

"The sad and solemn night
Has yet her multitude of cheerful fires;
The glorious host of light
Walk the dark hemisphere till she retires;
All through her silent watches, gliding slow,
Her constellations come, and climb the heavens, and go."

"Is your house close to water? Our house in Lubec is close to water, and we go swimming. Do you go swimming?" Alana asks.

"Sure," I say. "All the time. I look out my front door, and all I see is water."

"Cool," Alana says, arranging chunks of tomatoes on her

pizza in the form of a smiley face. "Mom says that maybe one day we can go to North Beach and I can go swimming so I can show Grandpa how long I can hold my breath under water."

Sara looks away, and I know that due to the crowds on North Beach, going there would not be an option. No way she would risk running into someone who could possibly recognize Sara and identify Alana.

"North Beach is nice, but I know a much better beach. Private and less crowded."

"Can we go?" She asks me first, then Sara. "Can we go?"

"Sure," I answer for Sara, remembering the "We'll see" conversations from earlier today. "Soon, okay?" For this, I am gifted with a smile of appreciation from Sara.

"Do you promise? Pinkie promise?" She holds her tiny pinkie to me, and I loop mine in hers.

My pinkie promise placates Alana, and she returns to arranging her tomatoes. Sylvia comes over to inspect my pizza as I make my way to the toppings. "Next Friday, I'll get you some anchovies."

No one seems to notice Sylvia's invitation or oppose it. "I appreciate that," I say, grinning at her, a warmth crawling over my skin. "How about some pineapples too?"

"Eww…" Alana says.

Hosea pats me firmly on the back and tugs on my shoulder tight, an embrace of acceptance.

"Not this again," Sara says, topping her pizza off with sprinkles of onions and green peppers.

"What?" I ask.

"There's been much debate in this household about pineapple on pizza," Sylvia says.

"I'm guessing only Hosea likes pineapple on pizza?" I ask.

I look around the room. Only Hosea meets my eyes.

"Pineapple balances out salty toppings," I say.

"No," Sylvia says. "Nope. Nice try."

"Pineapple has no business on a pizza," Sara says.

"Amen," Sylvia says.

I laugh. "Wait a minute. What was rule number one again?"

"No judging pizzas," Alana yells.

"Thank you, Alana. I hear a lot of judging right now."

Hosea laughs first. Sara follows before everyone else joins in.

Sylvia raises her hands in defeat. "Okay, okay. Next Friday, I'll get you some anchovies and pineapple."

As we eat our pizzas, Sara and Alana snuggle on the couch, and we listen to Sylvia regale us with more Miss Celeste and Miss Emma stories; a buzz spreads in my muscles, and the beer Sylvia gave me earlier and the one in my hand keep me steady. I have felt this way before. A long time ago. It is the feeling of the love of a family.

A few hours later, pizzas have been eaten, and as the winner of the most unique pizza, I swallow the last spoonful of ice cream from my extra scoop. My winning combination was tomato sauce, bacon, onions, and no cheese; the lack of that, I believe, cemented my win.

Honestly, I'm not sure my pizza warranted a win as much as they wanted me to win as a way to help me feel accepted and welcomed. And I do.

"This was nice," I say an hour later as I watch as Hosea walks Sylvia across the street to her house, serenading her with a poem that I don't recognize and following her inside. "It's a nice family tradition."

"Did you have any family traditions like that—" Sara stops. "I'm sorry. I shouldn't have asked you that. You don't have to answer."

"It's okay. I want to," I say. "My family's togetherness was always wrapped in learning. We were rarely fun and silly as a family. Rarely let our guard down. I think we weren't built that way."

"Not all families are the same."

"Yeah...but there has to be something that holds the family together. A foundation. Those memories we talked about."

"Is love not enough?" Sara asks.

I sigh. "It wasn't for us."

The wind rustles a cup across the sidewalk. Somewhere in the distance a dog barks, the sound echoing around the block as I descend the front porch stairs and walk to my truck. Sara and Alana join me.

"Mom, can Jacob watch the movie with us tomorrow night?" Alana asks.

"I think we've intruded on Jacob enough."

Alana turns to me. "Have we intruded on you?"

I laugh.

"It's Saturday, honey," Sara says, attempting to save me. "Jacob may have other plans."

"Do you have other plans?" Alana asks me.

Sara and I both laugh. "No, I don't," I say.

Alana looks at Sara. "See, he doesn't have other plans. Can he come over?"

Sara looks at me for confirmation. I nod slightly, a move invisible to Alana's eye. "You have to ask Jacob."

"Jacob, would you like to watch a movie with us tomorrow night?"

"What time?"

———

At home, the energy, the rush of togetherness is gone. I'm barely inside, barely in bed, before the pull of exhaustion overwhelms me. But my mind, operating independently from my body, refuses to embrace sleep. It replays the events of this evening and the participants in it, the anchovies and pineapple discussion, Sylvia's sense of humor, Hosea's quiet but forceful presence, Sara and Alana's connection. There are some things more powerful than the mind. Just before my thoughts whir to a stop, Sara's beautiful, smiling face is the last image I see as my eyes blink closed and a deep sleep comes for me.

SARA

—————

JACOB DID NOT COME back for the movie. Alana sat on the front stoop, her elbows planted on her knees, her tiny fists dug into her cheeks, and waited. A bloodred sun moved lower in the sky while I busied myself by making popcorn and a pitcher of sweet tea. Jacob had never broken his word and I had no reason to believe that he would fail this time. But, after the darkness swallowed us in shadow, I finally conceded that he was not coming and convinced a disappointed Alana to come inside.

He did not come back the next day either. I assured Alana that Jacob's absence from the movie was the result of a miscommunication, but I struggled to explain his absence from her tutoring. After the second day, a combination of anger and disappointment began to fill me. We had a deal. In between customers at the bookstore, I pulled out the business card he gave me and dialed the number. Voicemail. Today, the third day of his absence, my anger eclipses into worry. Something is wrong. I notice the address on the card and ask Sylvia to fill in for me at the bookstore while I satisfy my curiosity.

My GPS navigates me to a marina approximately forty minutes outside of Savannah. I pull in and see boats aligned in front of me. *This can't be it.* I look at the card again. I get out of the car and walk along the docks looking for an address. There is a clang of lines, and halyards tap against sailboat masts as a soothing tide rocks the boats.

"May I help you?" asks a short man with thinning gray hair pulled into a ponytail.

"I'm looking for Jacob Wyler."

The man smiles wide. "He doesn't live on the pier, ma'am."

I fidget with Jacob's card in my hand, turning it several times. "Do you know him?"

"Yes," the man says.

"I was wondering how I could get to his house. I seem to be lost. Can you tell me the way?"

"Sure," the man says, walking over to me. He points. "You go north about five nautical miles, turn right at the marker and straight for another seven."

"You mean, by boat?"

The man laughs. "You could swim, but I wouldn't recommend it."

Jacob said he lived on an island. He never said that the island was not accessible by car.

"Or single-engine airplane," the man continues, "but it's been impossible to fly with all the rain we've had."

I twist my lips at the unexpected obstacles in front of me. "How can I get out there?"

The man's smile fades as he inspects me. "What did you say your name was?"

"Sara," I say hesitantly, wondering if providing my name will make any difference.

"Is he expecting you?"

Based on this sudden interrogation, I know this man not only knows Jacob but also is a friend.

"Not exactly." I pause. "He's tutoring my daughter, and he hasn't shown up in a few days."

It is the man's turn to contemplate, twisting his lips, before a perking up, as if remembering something. "You're *Sara*."

My brow rises. "He's mentioned me?"

"Of course," the man says dryly, offering nothing more, and I wonder what else Jacob has shared with this man.

"I tried to call, but his phone goes straight to voicemail."

"Now that you mention it, I haven't seen Doc in a few days myself."

"Doc?"

"Yeah...Doc. You know...because he's a doctor of astrology. He told me about entanglement. I told my wife, and she loved it."

I smile, not correcting him on the astrology/astronomy mix-up. "She did, huh?" Jacob does have a way of doing that, making science sound intriguing. I'm remembering our first meeting and his explanation of magnetic attraction.

"Doc is as smart as they come. And can make that science stuff sound good enough to win me some points with my wife."

I scan the pier. "So, how can I get there?" I say, mostly to myself.

We stand in silence as a small boat eases alongside a sixty-foot vessel on the other side of the pier. The man appears to have an internal conversation with himself, shifting his head from side to side, weighing thoughts and options, dismissing some, accepting others, and finally nodding once.

"Come on," he says, gesturing toward a boat. "I'll take you out there."

I don't have time to contemplate before the man steps onto a boat and extends his hand to me. "The name's Locke."

"Sara," I say again, taking his hand and help onto the boat. "Nice to meet you."

"You are as pretty as he says you are."

"He said that?"

"Well…" he says, gesturing toward a seat along the bow, "in his own way. He doesn't talk much, but I've come to know that what Doc doesn't say tells me what I need to know."

I understand exactly what he means.

Locke scurries about the boat, pulling in the anchor, adjusting things, and after a few minutes, we are pulling away from the dock.

"In the 1800s, Hird Island was used for harvesting lumber,"

Locke says, his accent having its way with the words. "Today it's just a handful of private homes, mostly second houses and fishing cottages."

"Have you lived out here long?"

"My whole life," he says. "This land has been in my family for centuries. I can't imagine living anywhere else."

The expansive sky, dense with pending rain, is cloaked in low-hanging gunmetal-colored clouds. Despite the threatening storm, the view offers an impressive landscape of oak trees and salt marsh.

"It's beautiful," I say as the wind catches my hair, and I take a deliberate breath.

"It has that effect on people," he shouts over the noise. "Jacob has always loved it out here, even when he was a boy."

I perk up at this new information. "You've known him that long?"

"Yes, ma'am. The Wylers owned most of Hird Island at one point. Jacob's father, Tom, and I were good friends. When he wasn't at the hospital, he was out here. The kids were always with him."

Locke bends the boat around a curve, and a gray house hoisted on rickety stilts comes into view. A boat, much like Locke's, is docked on a pier.

Locke slows the boat. "His boat is here."

He extends his hand again and helps me disembark. I ascend the stairs, observing the neatly cut grass.

"You go on up," Locke says, opening a secret compartment

under the boat and producing a boat hook. "I think there's some kelp on the hull. I'll be up right behind you."

At the door, I notice that it's ajar. When you live on an island, I imagine the practice of locking doors to be unnecessary, but open seems strange. I push the door open. "Jacob?" I call.

No response. Just a slight breeze clanging tree branches against the steel roof.

Now I'm really worried. What if Jacob is unconscious? Or worse?

Inside, the cottage is more expansive than it looks from the outside. Walls of beige wood paneling greet me. A small kitchen with a square table huddles in the far corner, a wooden desk flanked by several bookcases is in the other, and there is a cozy living area with a navy couch and coffee table. This space suits him. I take another step inside.

"Jacob?" I call again, listening.

A stirring of some kind sounds from a room out of view. Bed springs complain, and a few seconds later, Jacob shuffles into view. He is barefoot, dressed in a pair of navy striped pajama pants. His shirtless chest glistens with perspiration, and a wool blanket covers his shoulders.

"Sara?" he says, his voice just above a whisper. His bleary, weak eyes meet mine, drooping with every blink as if they could close into sleep at any moment. "What are you doing here?" He stumbles; the blanket falls from his shoulders.

"Are you okay?" I ask, walking over to him, grabbing his

arm to steady him. My hand warms at the heat radiating from his body.

"Yeah…" he says. "I'm just tired."

I lay my hand across his forehead; it's damp and hot to the touch. "You are burning up."

He turns around as if looking for something, then looks at me again. "I missed the movie, didn't I? I'm sorry."

"Jacob…it's been three days."

Confusion whips across his pale face, jerking his head back. "What? It's Saturday."

"It's Tuesday," I say.

He staggers like a man on stilts, and I catch him, settle him on the couch. In the kitchen, I find a towel, wet it, and on my way back to Jacob also grab the blanket where it fell on the floor. His closed eyes slit open as I press the cool towel across his forehead.

"How did you get out here?"

"Your friend Locke," I say. "Who is also concerned about you. He's probably on his way up here right now."

"No," he says, swatting at air in slow motion. "I'm fine. I just need to rest."

"I don't think you are. I think we need to take you to the hospital. I'm worried about your fever. Have you taken anything for it?"

Jacob's eyes blink closed as his body relaxes; a quiet stuttering snore follows.

"Jacob?" I say softly, my eyes studying his body for movement. "Jacob?"

He jerks awake as the towel slides off his forehead.

"You fell asleep," I say, repositioning the towel. "Jacob, you don't look very well. I want to take you to the hospital."

"I'm fine," he says again. "This is a normal side effect."

"Of what?"

"A bone marrow transplant."

I bristle. "You had a bone marrow transplant?"

"No, not me," he mumbles. "Daniel."

His high fever must have loosened his inhibitions, and I freeze with the intake of unexpected information. Jacob doesn't move, fails to realize his admission. His head rests on the back of the couch as I quickly put it all together. Daniel must be sick, and Jacob donated his bone marrow to Daniel. This sickness, his weakened state, is a side effect of his donation.

A soft rap comes from the front door. Hat in hand, Locke stands in the doorway. He seems content with keeping his distance, so I meet him at the door.

"He's sick," I say, unsure of how much Jacob has shared with him.

Locke lowers his voice and leans in. "He had a procedure a few days ago," he says. "For his brother."

He doesn't mention bone marrow transplant, cancer, or Daniel by name, selecting his words carefully.

I do not press Locke for more, choosing to respect his role as Jacob's friend. "He doesn't want to go to the hospital."

Locke looks past me. "Hey, Doc. You got us all a little worried."

Jacob lifts his hand as if to wave, but the gesture is weak.

"I'm fine. Just a little under the weather."

Locke looks at me for help then back at Jacob.

"This is a side effect from the procedure," I offer. "He told me just before you came in."

Locke nods, not removing his eyes from Jacob. The confidence he exhibited on the dock vanishes, replaced with genuine worry.

"Doc," he says, maintaining his distance, "why don't you let us take you to the hospital?"

Jacob doesn't answer. Instead, he moves his head back and forth across the back of the couch as if it were too heavy to lift. Locke searches me again for answers.

"I think he just needs some rest," I say. "I'll stay with him."

"I'll stay too."

"There's no need for both of us to stay. I think he'll be fine. They wouldn't have let him leave the hospital if the side effects could be that serious," I say. "You go. I'll take care of him."

Locke looks at Jacob again. His eyes dance in contemplation.

"Jacob," Locke says, his voice slightly louder, "this pretty lady is going to stay and take care of you, but if you need anything, you call me."

Jacob's chest rises and falls with every breath.

"Take my number down," Locke whispers to me. "If you need anything, you call me. I live on the other side of the island. I can be here in five minutes."

I type his number into my cell phone. Locke looks at Jacob

again before sidestepping to the door, as if prepared to change his mind. "I mean it. Call me if you need anything."

"I will," I say as I close the door and watch him descend the stairs. A few minutes later, a boat engine roars and fades into the distance.

I turn back to Jacob. Despite his awkward position, he looks peaceful, and I almost hate to move him but conclude comfort will not be found on this couch.

"Let's get you back in bed," I say, sliding my arm across his back and cradling his head. Despite it all, he smells good, clean, warm, and woodsy. His eyes slit open again. "Can you stand?" With a little effort, he does.

"You don't have to do this," he says, wrapping his arm across my neck for balance. "I don't want to be something else you have to take care of."

His statement is sincere and honest, an admission he would have never made in a lucid state.

"Don't you worry about that," I say, guiding him out of the living room and into his bedroom. "Just feel better, okay?"

I ease him back into bed, tucking a pillow behind his head and pulling the sheet over him. Within seconds, he's asleep.

In the living room, I survey my surroundings. On the counter, three orange prescription bottles stand at attention. A phone number for a Dr. Bennett along with the proper dosage wraps around them. Jacob may not want to go to the hospital, but I want to at least get an opinion on his condition. I call the number and ask for Dr. Bennett, expecting to hit a wall of doctor patient confidentiality. When the person asks what I'm calling about and I say Jacob's name, she responds with, "Are you Birdie?" I murmur something that isn't a yes but that could be taken as confirmation, and a few minutes later Dr. Bennett is on the line. I tell him about Jacob, and he tells me that Jacob's fatigue is not a side effect of the bone marrow transplant but of filgrastim, a drug used for preparing Jacob's body for the eventual transplant.

"Has he eaten anything?"

"I don't know," I say, looking around the kitchen for signs of food or cooking. One single glass sits in the sink. "I don't think so."

"Let him sleep it off, but make sure he eats and drinks plenty of fluids," Dr. Bennett says. "He's probably dehydrated, which is making him weaker. He needs to eat something filling, nutritious. Vegetables and protein, preferably."

"What about his fever?"

"Give him Tylenol. If his fever doesn't break by tomorrow, take him to the emergency room and call me."

"I will."

"I'm sorry that we can't continue with the donation," Dr. Bennett offers, unprompted. "Daniel's infection is not subsiding. I'm going to increase his dosage of antibiotics. It's my hope that we can resume Jacob's pre-op in a few weeks."

"Thank you for the update."

I collapse on the navy couch where Jacob just sat, my cell phone still faceup in my hand. I search my heart to consider my feeling about this news. I spent so much of my life not thinking about Daniel and yet subconsciously thinking about him all the time. He was a dark secret locked in a box. This realization breathes fresh life into him again, another layer to the convoluted story.

Daniel has spent almost eight years in prison. And now he has cancer. His potential savior? Jacob. Is this why Jacob deems his relationship with Daniel and Birdie complicated? He said that he hasn't spoken to Daniel since he left Savannah. Is this why he came home? To give him his bone marrow?

I ignore these questions and think of Jacob instead. Faced with incredible circumstances, Jacob kept my secret from Daniel and Birdie. He is helping me, and I will help him. I will be a shoulder for him like he's been one for me.

I end the call with Dr. Bennett and call Sylvia. It rings several times before her voicemail answers.

"Hi. I'm at Jacob's cottage. He's sick," I say, pacing the front porch. "I'm going to stay and take care of him. It's a long story, and I'll explain later, but can you stay with Dad and Alana tonight?"

I walk back into the cabin and curse to myself for allowing Locke to leave before checking the refrigerator for food or medicine. Luckily, I find a bottle of Tylenol in the bathroom. I shake out two and fill a glass of water in the kitchen before taking them to Jacob, who is still asleep. He's moved since I lay him down, one of his arms stretched above his head, the sheet pushed off him, revealing his bare chest. His body is long and lean like an athlete's. I watch him, longer than I expect to, before waking him. If only he weren't so sick—it is refreshing to see him this way, open, unguarded, and relaxed.

I sit on the side of the bed, placing the Tylenol and water on the nightstand. "Jacob," I whisper, my head just above his. "Jacob. Wake up."

I don't touch him at first, but when he doesn't respond to me calling his name, I gently place my hand on his forearm and shake. His eyes blink open slowly.

"Hi," he says, as if he's forgotten everything, as if he's surprised to see me. A shadow of a smile appears as he takes my hand from his forearm and places it over his heart.

"Hi," I say.

"I must be dreaming," he says, his voice full of sleep and tenderness. His hand cradles the side of my face. Disarmed by his gentleness, I relax into it before pulling my head away.

"You are not dreaming," I say, reaching for the Tylenol and water with my free hand. "I need you to take these."

He doesn't question the request, swallowing both Tylenol with one gulp of water before downing the rest, keeping my hand on his chest.

I take the glass from his hand. "Get some sleep. I'll be here when you wake up."

He closes his eyes, not releasing my hand but tucking in with it, like a child sleeping with their favorite stuffed animal. The innocent gesture tightens my chest and tugs at something within me.

After a few seconds, I extract my hand from his and pull the sheet up to his chest. In the kitchen, I open the cabinet doors, searching for something to cook, finding onions, cans of green beans, corn, and peas along with bags of flour and sugar among various spices, and a box of saltine crackers. I pop one of the saltines in my mouth. It's stale. The contents of the refrigerator are just as sparse: a carton of eggs, a few carrots, cheese, a half-gallon of milk, butter, and condiments. The freezer holds packages of round steak, ice trays, and white paper-wrapped packages that I'm guessing are fish. On the counter, I see a bottle of red wine, potatoes, oranges, and apples.

I try to make sense of the hodgepodge of ingredients before me. Dr. Bennett said Jacob needed something filling. I consider the contents of the cabinets and refrigerator again. Jacob has most of the ingredients for a beef stew, except for beef broth, which I can make from scratch using a package of round steak.

Searching the cabinets once more, I discover a huge pot and several utensils. I pile all the ingredients on the counter and get started. I'm finishing browning the last of the round steak when Sylvia returns my call.

"What's wrong? The flu?"

"No," I say in a loud whisper, instinctively looking in the direction of the bedroom. I don't know how to tell her what's wrong.

"I can't imagine a cold would keep him from Alana," she grunts.

I add the red wine and water, which sizzle with heat.

"What's that noise? Are you frying something?"

"I'm making beef stew."

"Why are you cooking?"

"Because he's weak, and his doctor says he needs to eat."

"Sara, what's going on?"

The pot roars to a boil, and I reduce the heat to allow the steak to simmer. I retreat outside for privacy, sitting in one of the Adirondack chairs on the porch. The rain falls steady now.

"Sylvia...Daniel has cancer," I say, leveling my voice. "Jacob is donating his bone marrow to him. The drugs he's taking to prepare his body for the donation are making him sick."

A long silence follows. Sylvia is rarely rendered speechless. "Oh my."

"Locke and I found him in his cottage."

"Who's Locke?"

"A friend of Jacob's."

"Does he need to go to the hospital?"

"No, he doesn't want to go. I called his doctor, and he told me what to do."

"Do you need me to come help you?"

I snicker and take in the rippling water as a flock of birds take flight against the clouds. "You can't. Remember that island he said he lives on? It's only accessible by boat or airplane."

"What?"

"I know," I say, shaking my head. "I'll explain it all tomorrow."

"You better," she says. "In the meantime, Alana and Hosea are fine. Just take care of Jacob."

Inside, I chop the onions and carrots and add them to the pot. Next, I peel the potatoes and add them. I lower the temperature. I wash all the dishes and return them to their spots before wiping down the cabinets and sweeping the floor as the stew bubbles on the stove.

I look in on Jacob. His chest rises and falls under the blanket. I take a coffee cup from the living room to the sink and fold old editions of the *New York Times*. Underneath one, I see Whitman's *Leaves of Grass*, *The Complete Works of W. B. Yeats*, and *The Complete Poems of Paul Laurence Dunbar*. All Dad's books. Among them are also Maya Angelou's *The Complete Poetry* and E. E. Cummings's *100 Selected Poems*. Next to them are stacks of notebooks, one open. I smile at the sight of a student's notes and run my hands across it. No wonder Dad likes him so much; they share a connection that Jacob didn't know he had in him till he met Dad. The thought unravels a new level of appreciation and admiration for Jacob.

Wedged between two books lies an overturned picture frame. I lift it to reposition it and see a young, lanky Jacob staring back at me. From when he was David. He's sitting on a dock, the very dock now less than a thousand feet from me. A man who I assume is his father, Tom, is between Daniel and Jacob, his arms draped across both of them. Naomi—I know immediately she's their sister—sits on Jacob's lap, her legs extended. I gasp at Alana's resemblance to Naomi. Birdie's head appears between Tom and Daniel. She's smiling. They all are, five rows of white teeth grinning at me. A big, happy family.

I stare at the picture, studying each person carefully, including Daniel. He and Jacob were barely teenagers when this picture was taken, years before they grew into their bodies, before their limbs filled out with muscle and they shot up several inches. Years before the rape. Before Naomi's death and Tom's suicide. Before the smiles in this picture faded. I place the picture back as I found it, suddenly feeling like an intruder.

In this moment, I realize, like me, Jacob is a victim of his own family. He has weathered some unspeakable traumas. None by his own hands. And I believe the sincerity he has exhibited toward me; his reaction and actions have been real because he can relate to being hurt and confused. I know now there's more that combines us than separates us. The weight of this realization makes me lighter.

I flip on two lamps. They cast an intimate golden glow across the room. The stew cools on the stove, the smell wafting around the cottage. I pour a glass of wine and settle back into one of the chairs on the porch, stretching my feet on a nearby stool. The rain has stopped, leaving everything dripping wet. Two breaths and a sip later, I see it. Why Jacob lives here. The moon, round and full, radiates its beauty on the motionless water. I call Locke and give him an update. He tells me he'll swing by in the morning to take me back to the dock if I like. I hang up and wrap both hands tighter around the wineglass.

"Something smells great."

I turn quickly and see Jacob leaning in the doorway. He rubs his hand over his head.

"How are you feeling?" I ask, walking over to him and placing my hand, once more, across his forehead. "Your fever is gone."

He watches me carefully. "How long was I asleep?"

"A few hours," I say, ushering him out on the porch. "Come. Sit. You're probably still a little weak."

He eases into a chair, unsteady. "I thought I dreamed you were here."

I smile. "No, you weren't dreaming."

"I see," he says with a hint of a smile, keeping his eyes on me.

Suddenly uncomfortable, I stand. "I hope you don't mind; I made a beef stew with what I could find in the kitchen. You must be starving. Stay here. I'll bring you a bowl."

I'm standing over the stove, lifting the pot lid when Jacob appears behind me.

"Mmm," he mumbles, his voice over my shoulder. "That smells so good. I can't wait to try it."

The word *good* arrives slow and airy, sending a slight wind through the hairs on my earlobe.

"I want to take a quick shower first," he says, heading toward the bathroom. "Do I have time?"

I nod as he disappears. Seconds later, I hear the shower turn on.

I taste the stew one final time, adding just a pinch more salt and a dash of pepper, before turning the heat up. A few minutes later, the stew bubbles on the stove. I'm ladling it into two bowls when Jacob reappears. He's wearing a gray shirt that hugs his arms and chest and a crisper-looking pair of navy bottoms.

"I feel like a new man," he says, standing next to me. He smells even better than before.

"Wait until you eat and drink," I say, handing him a bowl of stew and a glass of water. "You will feel even better."

"Let's eat on the porch."

I take my bowl and follow him. He sits in what I assume is his usual chair. I sit opposite him.

"You really didn't have to go through all this trouble," he says, blowing on the stew to cool it. "A peanut butter and jelly sandwich would have been fine."

I smile. "That's what I wanted to make, but you didn't have any peanut butter or jelly or bread. So…"

I watch as he chews and swallows, his Adam's apple rising and falling.

"Wow," he says between bites. "This is great."

"Thank you," I say, following his lead and eating. "Not the best I've ever made. I didn't have all of the ingredients."

Jacob barely hears me as he downs spoonfuls of stew in a constant motion. The spoon scratches the bottom and pings in the empty bowl a few minutes later.

"Would you like more?" I ask, standing and reaching for his bowl.

"You don't have to serve me," he says. "You've done enough already."

"I don't mind. You need to rest," I say, taking the bowl from his hands. "Drink your water."

Jacob finishes the glass of water when I return with another bowl and hand it to him.

"Do you cook much?" he asks.

"Not since I've been here," I say in between bites. "Sylvia has been waiting on us. But Lubec doesn't have very many restaurants and no fast food. It can get expensive if you eat out regularly. So, I cook, especially in the winter."

"That doesn't sound too bad."

"It wasn't. Not for me. I understood that it came with living there," I say, finishing my stew. "But now Alana's fascinated with McDonald's, Burger King, and Chick-fil-A since being in Savannah."

"Most kids are."

I laugh. "You try convincing her why she can't eat it every day."

Jacob finishes his second bowl and sets it on the table. He leans back, settling in as if the position is routine as I notice a tinge of color returning to his face. Dr. Bennett was right. I debate whether to tell him that I called Dr. Bennett. I decide against it. For now.

He sighs, stretching to loosen his limbs. "You're right. I feel much better."

"Don't push yourself," I say, standing again. "Let me get you some more water."

I take one step toward the door, but Jacob grabs my wrist, standing. His touch is electric. "Sara," he says, staring into my eyes as my pulse quickens. "Please. Sit with me."

I comply, but he does not release my hand right away, and when he finally does, a bereft feeling floods me. He turns his attention out onto the water. I do the same.

"It's beautiful out here," I say.

"I sit out here almost every night, just watching the grass and the water. The sun sets; the stars appear. Sometimes I read. Mostly think."

A sticky breeze reveals itself, the air muggy and light, but it's not enough to send us retreating into the cottage.

"Thank you for today," he says after several heartbeats of silence.

"It's no problem," I say dismissively.

"No," he says, his stare unadulterated. "I know these last few months have been hard. It must have taken a lot out of you."

"You don't have to—"

Jacob doesn't wait for me to finish. "You are strong for everyone else. Take care of everyone else. Even with your own turmoil. It's inspiring."

I look away, embarrassed by his sincerity, his relaxed demeanor speaking for him.

Jacob sighs, a deep trembling, as if he's letting go of

something heavy. "I don't blame you for leaving. When I left here, I swore I would never come back. My dad and my sister were dead, and I was left with two people I didn't know anymore. I wanted nothing to do with this place, my family. I just wanted it all to go away."

I knew that mix of feelings: dejection, guilt, sadness.

"I put my head down and powered my way through college, grad school, and when I finished my PhD, I went to work at NASA. I chose assignments in these far-flung places like Alaska, Greenland, and Antarctica." He props his elbows on his knees. "Birdie told Daniel about my whereabouts, what I was up to. And she kept me updated on Daniel. She sent me letters and emails. But I never reached out to him. Not once. And he didn't either. He respected my wishes."

I open my mouth and close it without a word. I want him to keep talking. I want it probably more than I realize.

"When you are on these assignments, you work in pretty close proximity to other astrophysicists, doctors, and researchers. You learn about their families and hear stories about birthdays, Christmas, and Thanksgiving mishaps. When the assignment ended, they all went home to their families. Eventually, I wanted that. To go home to a family. In Alaska, I decided the best thing I could do was to come home and piece together the family I had left."

"How's that going?" I ask. "Being home?"

Jacob lets his gaze fall again to the salt marsh. "Daniel has cancer."

I expected an answer, but not the truth.

"I know."

Jacob raises his brows in surprise. "How—"

"When you didn't let us take you to the hospital, I called Dr. Bennett. His number was on the prescription bottles."

He nods as the pleat of skin over his eyes wrinkles as if he's in deep thought, as if he's gathering his next words.

"You don't have to talk about it," I say. "We don't have to ever talk about it. Or him."

"Do you mind that I told you any of that?"

"Not at all. I don't know anything about you. It's nice getting to know you. All parts of you."

He turns to me, his eyes burning through me. "We don't have to be strangers, Sara."

His words lodge deep into my chest and loosen something there. "No, we don't."

We hold each other's eyes, long enough to understand that we can never be strangers. Like particles, we are connected.

"I mean...we are definitely not strangers after what you said earlier."

Jacob's face deflates like a pricked balloon. "I..."

I laugh gently. "I'm kidding."

He stares at my face for confirmation, but he's still unsure. "Are you sure I didn't...?" He doesn't finish his sentence.

"I'll never tell," I tease. "But I thought you were very sweet."

Jacob grins. I return his smile. He quiets again, his

expression peaceful as if he has unloaded his mind. Seconds later, he stifles a yawn.

"You better go back to bed. You need to restore your strength," I say. "I'll clean up out here."

"You don't want to go home?"

"I called Sylvia and asked her to stay with Dad and Alana tonight. I assumed...I would stay. I didn't know if you would feel up to taking me home. I called Locke, and he's going to take me to the dock in the morning. I hope that's not a problem."

"It's no problem. You are more than welcome. I'll take the couch. You can have the bed."

He should keep the bed, but I know I won't convince him that I can take the couch. "I'm not tired yet," I say, pulling my knees into my chest.

His eyes meet mine. "Me neither."

JACOB

———

I BLINK MY EYES open to a pair of legs tiptoeing past me on the couch. Sara. She's wearing the gray V-neck T-shirt I gave her and, from the looks of it, nothing else. Of course, she's wearing something else, shorts, perhaps. Sara's a lady, but the thought of just a thin piece of cloth shielding her body from view sends blood to all sorts of interesting places. Through slitted eyes, I watch her turn the doorknob and gently pull the front door open. It yells, and she shoots her forefinger to her lips to shush the door as if it could obey such a command. Her eyes dart in my direction to see if the noise disturbed me. I lie still, watching her. She pulls the door open slowly, just enough to slide through, careful to keep the sunlight out.

We stayed up longer than expected, sometimes talking, sometimes resting in the silence. I introduced her to Reggie and pointed out Venus, the brightest star in the summer sky. She pulled back from the eye of the telescope when Venus came into focus, her beautiful eyes stretched in surprise, before going back in for more. She touched her fingertips to her lips and smiled underneath them. "Wow," she whispered.

First-time observers of the stars or planets through a telescope sometimes experience a visceral reaction. But it's Sara's presence that's causing one in me. She looks good here; she fits, like a piece of a puzzle. She seems to like it here too.

A few minutes after she has gone outside, I find her on the porch in the same chair, in the same spot, as last night, her knees tucked into her chest. Naomi did that, wake before anyone else and watch the day begin. I watch as Sara inhales deeply, savoring the fresh air, soothing to her lungs. The sight pleases my soul.

"I'm sorry. Did I wake you?" she asks, already apologetic and thinking of others, and it's not even daybreak yet. Even early in the morning, her beauty shines. Her usual braid is slightly scruffy and disoriented, but her makeup-free face is flawless. "How are you feeling?"

I ease into the chair next to her, moaning once I'm off my feet. I'm a new man today, better than yesterday, but some residual muscle aches remain. "Much better."

She returns her attention to the horizon, now golden and red with the rise of the sun. The light catches the soft curve of Sara's jaw, almost illuminating it. "I love watching the sunrise. Sunsets too."

"Ah, a sunchaser."

"A sunchaser?"

"A person who loves sunrises and sunsets. The real term

is *solist*, but *sunchaser* sounds better. Like you are chasing the sun on both sides."

"Lubec is the easternmost town in the continental U.S., home to the first sunrise in America. Being out here reminds me of that."

"Do you miss it?"

"Sometimes, but when I see how much Alana has taken to Savannah, it's hard to miss it," she says. "But I miss the quiet. I miss the anonymity. I miss what had become my normal life."

"Do you think you'll go back?" I ask with a mix of hope and longing. I realize that, until now, I stopped considering they would ever not be here.

Sara exhales slowly, and in the silence that follows I know she is letting me in on how much she's considered this answer, since well before I asked. "Nothing here will be the same without my dad. But there's Alana. She has needs, and it's not fair to keep her there, so locked up, in a sense. Then again, this arrangement is not fair to you. You can't tutor her forever."

I stare at her and blink.

"What?" she says, aware of herself.

"How do you do that? Consider everyone else's needs before your own?"

She looks away. "I don't know. I wasn't aware I do."

"You're not, are you? It's just who you are."

She smiles. "I'm a mother. It's what we do. What any mother would do."

"Most mothers aren't faced with the same set of circumstances you have."

"I appreciate that. But I love her, and I'll do anything for her."

"I can and will tutor Alana as long as you allow. And once I've exhausted what I can teach her, I'll see to it that she has the best tutors. No matter where you are. Here, Maine, wherever."

"You would do that?"

"Absolutely," I say with a lump in my throat and remind myself that I should be grateful that I have had this time with Sara and Alana. "Whatever you want." This, of course, is not the full truth. But I have no right to voice my opinion.

It's only a matter of time, I realize, before they leave. The knowledge of that presses down on me harder than I expected. My thoughts are interrupted by the roar of a motor. In the distance, Locke's boat moves into view.

"He's early," Sara says, standing and moving toward the door.

"He's a fisherman. He's probably been up for hours."

Sara opens the door just as I stand and call her name, stopping her. "I just wanted to thank you again for coming out here to check on me, for nursing me back to health, and for that excellent beef stew."

"It's the least I can do for all that you've done for me."

"I told you. You don't owe me anything. I want to help."

"And I appreciate that so much," she says, moving in,

arms outstretched. She wraps her arms around me, my chin brushing the top of her head, and settles into the crook of my neck. Disarmed by her gentleness, I pull her against me, into my chest, holding her there, imparting gentle pressure at the small of her back. I take a deep inhalation of her, the moment, and close my eyes. She smells as she always does—of wildflowers and spring. She doesn't let go right away. Neither do I. Our chests rise and fall in rhythm with each other as my heart beats against hers and the world falls away.

"Hey, Doc!" Locke yells from the water, breaking the trance. Time seemingly stopped for us but not for Locke, who has pulled to the dock and is now walking up to the porch.

We separate. Sara opens the door and goes into the cottage. I watch her with a look of possibility, of what if. Before I can look away, I see her thinking is the same: her eyes search for and find me one more time before she disappears behind the door.

I wave at Locke and move toward the stairs, my body rigid with frustration, confusion, and want. As I descend the stairs to greet Locke, I wish the scenario posed at Pizza Friday were real. That I could stop time, hold a moment, for ten seconds.

———

Dr. Bennett presses the cool, round piece of his stethoscope to my chest and listens. He moves it several inches to the left, up, and then to the right, instructing me to take several deep breaths in and out. I'm in his office for a follow-up after my adverse reaction to the filgrastim.

"I'm sorry to hear about your side effects. I can assure you that they were normal," Dr. Bennett says, pressing his fingers to my abdomen. "How are you feeling now?"

"I'm fine. Just a little achy."

"That should subside in a few days as the filgrastim leaves your body."

A voice clears. "Will he have to start the injection again when the transplant is rescheduled?" Birdie asks, making her presence known from a chair in the corner. She insisted on coming today after learning about the bone marrow transplant delay and my reaction to the filgrastim. "He was bedridden for three days. Thankfully, a family friend thought enough to check on him."

The trip to Atlanta is the farthest that Birdie has traveled in years. As Daniel's release and transplant approach, she's full of agitation and angst. The first couple hours, we drove in alternating silence and discussion pertaining to Daniel. Other times, she was on the phone, calling in old favors, lining up potential job interviews and other possibilities for Daniel. Mostly, she fidgeted, moving her purse in and out of her lap, removing and cleaning her sunglasses, a ball of nervous energy.

But as we drew closer to Atlanta, I began asking her questions about gardening. About certain plants. Low-light plants. Full-sun plants. Fertilizer. She knows I've never taken much of an interest in gardening before and questioned me on the sudden interest. I know she hated to see the dirt collecting under my fingernails as I helped her, working without gloves. Some of my questions were research for Alana's garden, but also for her, my attempt at getting to know her again. I suspect she knew this and played along. When I asked her about plant placement and the best place to buy plants outside of Savannah, she was happy to share her knowledge with me.

When we weren't talking, my thoughts were trapped on the porch of my cottage, my mind drifting to Sara, the hug. I can't stop thinking about her. She's everywhere. In my truck on the way to Atlanta. In Dr. Bennett's office. I replay the hug, the way her body felt pressed against mine, the ease with which she fit against me. Thoughts of her liven my mood, and I'm not bothered by anything. Not Birdie's attempts to help Daniel rejoin society or the four-hour ride. Not the side effects of the filgrastim or the transplant delay. Nothing can spoil my mood.

"Unfortunately, yes, we will need to start the filgrastim injection again before the transplant," Dr. Bennett says, answering Birdie's question and bringing me back to the present.

"What about Daniel?" Birdie presses. "When do you think he'll be healthy enough for the transplant?"

Dr. Bennett adjusts his stethoscope around his neck. "His labs report that he has a pretty nasty infection right now. It's just too risky to proceed," he says, scribbling something on my chart and tucking the pen into his breast pocket. "But I'm hopeful that the increased antibiotics will help."

"We should have gone with Dr. Downey for the transplant," Birdie says on the drive home. "He was a good friend of your father's. How did they not see Daniel's infection? Sloppy, sloppy, sloppy."

She makes it seem easy, replacing Dr. Bennett on such short notice, as if time isn't a factor. "Dr. Bennett is close and he's the best in the South," I say.

"How did they not catch Daniel's infection sooner? Before you almost die for nothing."

"I didn't almost die."

"Thank God Locke was around."

And Sara, I resist the urge to say, letting my mind drift to her face hovering above mine as she woke me.

"Dr. Bennett is doing the best he can," I say. "It's going to work out. Let's just be patient."

I feel Birdie's stare burning into the side of my face. "Since when did you become such an optimist?"

"Was I ever a pessimist? I just think you're overthinking this. Daniel is going to be fine. He just needs to kick that infection—which he will—and Dr. Bennett will do the transplant," I say as I pull onto the interstate. "Would you like to stop somewhere for lunch?"

She continues to study me. "What's gotten into you?"

"What do you mean?"

"You didn't push back when I asked to come along today.

You are inviting me to lunch. You've been visiting frequently and staying at the house."

I laugh. "And these actions imply that something is wrong with me?"

"No, but something is going on with you."

"We have a four-hour drive back to Savannah, and I'm hungry. I thought you would like to stop and have lunch."

"I know my son," she says, pressing her lips together. "I may not have been..." I wonder what she was about to say—*I may not have been much of a mother?* "A woman knows these things. A mother knows these things. You've met someone."

My heart pounds in my ears. "Because I ask you to lunch and let you come to Atlanta with me?" I am not aware that my buoyant mood opened the door to such a conversation.

"Because you've been staying over more, almost four days a week, staying out late and leaving early in the morning. It has to be because of a woman. You're different."

"Different? What do you mean?"

"The way you look, sound, everything," she says, and I can tell she wants to say more, but Simple Minds' "Don't You (Forget About Me)" plays on the radio, stopping her train of thought. It was one of Naomi's favorite songs, one she would play repeatedly. I grip the steering wheel as the song's chorus serenades the car.

I look at Birdie, her oversize sunglasses shielding the whole top half of her face. She turns toward the window, and I can tell that she remembers the song.

It is a sign, I think, an opening to talk about Naomi. Birdie has never been able to speak at any length about her. She sees Naomi's death as the first in a short string of personal losses—in one way or another—with her daughter, husband, and then son, all within a year. In mourning she had become, more than before, a stubborn, bitter woman.

"The twelve-year anniversary of her death is next month."

The Birdie I have come to know could have let the song play without mention, but she doesn't. I realize that I'm not the only different person in the car.

"I know."

"I can cut two bouquets if you would like to visit her grave with me."

"I'd like that."

The song continues.

"What was the name of this movie?" Birdie asks.

"*The Breakfast Club*."

To my surprise, and hers too, I think, she smiles. "I hated that movie. I didn't understand the appeal. What was so influential about a bunch of delinquent teenagers in detention ignoring instruction and discipline?"

I laugh. "That's why she liked it so much."

Birdie sighs. "She was the rebel of the family."

"That she was."

How is it possible that a song, Naomi's favorite song, encapsulates so much about her? After all this time, I still can't say her name. For a brief second, I consider opening up to

Birdie about this, have a normal conversation between mother and son, but I know that's not possible. She will think I'm blaming her for why I can't say her name, because she didn't want to go to therapy and talk about her. She'll probably just tell me that I'm being emotional. I can almost hear her say, "Just open your mouth and say it. It's just a name."

But, to my astonishment, she's still talking about Naomi. "Remember when she staged a sit-in with her friend Mae when the homeowner's association wouldn't let the Gruens paint Mae's tree house yellow?"

"Dad was convinced that she would stay in the tree just a few hours. But she stayed there for three days." I laugh at the memory, at Naomi's courage. "I threw some candy up to her at night. Whoppers."

"It was a silly little protest, but that's when I knew that she was something. Bigger than us. Destined for something great."

"You expected us each to be extraordinary. Nothing less. Not even just good but extraordinary."

"Your father and I always wanted the best for our children. But it was also important to us that you all were happy. If that meant taking a different path than what we imagined for you, so be it."

"You would have accepted that?"

"Yes," she says, not convincingly. After a few beats, she says, "Eventually. Maybe."

We share a laugh, and I do not recall another time when

we've done so. She recognizes this too. I consider leaning into more Naomi talk but decide to allow her to guide the conversation. Maybe this crack, one day, will split open further and we can discuss Naomi and the truth about Daniel without holding anything back.

"I see the way you laugh and kid around with Marsha." She stops abruptly. "You know…you can talk to me about her, the woman you're seeing."

"It's new," I say, feeling the words tumble out of my mouth, inspired, perhaps, by Birdie's openness. Am I speaking the truth or an impossible wish? "I doubt that anything will come of it."

"Why?"

"It's complicated."

Birdie twists her lips. "I ran into Priscilla and William last week. They told me that Brit is a partner at a law firm in Atlanta. Maybe you could give her a call sometime?"

"If I were seeing someone, and I'm not officially, how have you already decided that she is unacceptable?"

"I haven't. It's just…Brit is from a fine family. There's no way this other woman is a proper match for you in terms of intelligence, career, and finances. Not like Brit. I just want to see you with someone more of your caliber. Someone without complications."

I am not naïve enough to believe that there could ever be anything between me and Sara. I regret saying anything at all, but Birdie surprises me. "Or…you could uncomplicate it," she says, completely changing her position, her tone so clear, so matter-of-fact, an accurate representation of how Birdie tackles life. She doesn't believe in weakness. In the word no. She doesn't accept the concept of failure. There are no obstacles she cannot overcome or reverse. She has no idea the layers of complication a potential relationship with Sara would spawn, but I appreciate her trying, offering some motherly advice. That's all I ever wanted from her.

"Your father was a rich white boy from Savannah who fell in love with a poor Black girl from Atlanta. It was never supposed to work. It was the definition of complicated. Your grandfather wasn't too happy with it. But we loved each other, and that's all that mattered."

Never the romantic, Mom rarely spoke of her courtship with Dad. Not that as kids we wanted to hear about it, but as an adult, I find the story intrigues me. "How did Dad tell his family?"

She smiles at the memory, before she's even shared it, a prideful smile. Even after all these years, her love for my father is still evident. "He said he marched into his father's study and told him that he was in love with me and that he didn't care what they thought."

"How did they take it?"

"They needed time. But he was prepared to walk away from them if they didn't accept me," she says. "Love is never complicated. The circumstances are but never the love."

"I wish it were that easy."

Her face softens. "You are so much like your father, in looks, in temperament. Quiet and caring. That's what drove me to him. He was genuine and real and honest. I didn't stand a chance. She won't either. You'll find a way to uncomplicate it."

No sound emerges as I try to agree with her. Instead, I listen, sobered by her openness and support. It is the longest dialogue we have ever had without mentioning Daniel, and I'm reeling in the idea that we can have such a conversation when she says, "But no respectable woman is going to want to live on that island. What your father saw, and what you now see, in that god-awful cottage is beyond me. All those gnats and flies. Please consider purchasing something a bit more suitable."

SARA

———

WE SUCCESSFULLY PUT OFF talk of the garden for a few weeks, but Alana's pursuit is relentless. I finally concede, and we clear a small patch in the backyard. Jacob offers to drive us to the store and help us select everything we will need. I start to object, but before I can, he announces that he knows of the perfect place—and it's outside of Savannah.

There's a mood of repose in Jacob's truck as we drive outside of the city limits with windows rolled down, the wind rushing through our hair and ushering in the smell of the open road. Classic soul blares from the radio's speakers, clear at times, scratching and full of static in others. Alana takes a position on the passenger side of the front seat next to the window, watching the scenery change from city roads and electric poles to the open countryside of rolling trees and hills. Jacob is quiet, mouthing the words to Otis Redding's "These Arms of Mine," sliding a glance with a lazy smile at me, his elbow bent out the driver's window.

When in public, the rules for Alana are simple: Don't talk to strangers. No telling them stuff you know, which includes calculating problems in your head. No speaking in foreign languages. These were the rules I adopted for Alana as a hindrance. But they've always been suggestions for her. She's drawn to strangers. Like now, once we've arrived at the nursery and I listen to her explain to a customer that the low-light plants in her cart will not work for the front of her house because it gets full sun.

"Alana!"

She jumps, immediately recognizing her mistake, and freezes.

"You know you're not supposed to be talking to strangers," I say, my voice stern.

The woman whispers a sympathetic apology before pushing her cart away from us toward the register, the rickety wheels screeching.

Alana lowers her head in shame, then looks to Jacob for help. He squats, eye to eye with her, and whispers something in her ear. She nods and casts her gaze to the floor again, but Jacob lifts it, his forefinger to her chin. She listens, her expression brightening just before he dabs her nose once and she wraps her small arms around his neck. He lifts her and carries her to me.

"I'm sorry, Mom," she says, sorrow radiating from her eyes. She reaches for me and I take her into my arms, hugging her tight, breathing in her sweet scent.

"I know, baby. You scare me when you walk off and talk to strangers."

"I'm sorry."

We ride back to Savannah, the bed of Jacob's truck a bloom of colorful annuals and perennials, bags of dirt, and all the equipment we need. He backs the truck into the backyard, and the sun beats down on us as we unload our haul and outline our garden.

Jacob's calm nature, speaking only when spoken to, relaxed face, continues to unnerve me. Not even the incident at the store rattled him. His patience with Alana is boundless even when she knocks over a tray of annuals and accidentally bangs his truck with the shovel; none are met with a disapproving look or change in tone. He's accepting of all of it, all of her.

He's exhibiting no signs of the filgrastim that slowed him down a few weeks ago. He hasn't mentioned the bone marrow transplant either. I imagine he doesn't talk about it because it involves Daniel, a topic of conversation we have successfully avoided, by design for both of us, I think.

Now, he's perched on the back of his truck, the tailgate sprinkled with an array of fallen petals, finishing the last of the sandwich and sweet tea Sylvia made for us. Citing her infinite distrust for dirt, sweat, and sun, making lunch was how she said she'd help. His eyes sweep across our work and Alana's pursuit of a butterfly. The intense heat and the work haven't seemed to bother Jacob at all. His white shirt is soaked in sweat and covered in splatches of brown dirt, but he seems to be enjoying it all with an amused look on his face.

"You do realize it's hot out here, right?" I ask, approaching him from where I'd retreated to the one tiny patch of shade, wiping my forehead with the back of my hand while holding a glass of sweet tea with the other. My arms feel heavy, like they may split from my shoulders, from raising the hoe and bringing it down hard against the earth.

He pats the truck bed twice, and I accept his invitation and climb gingerly up and settle next to him, our thighs pressing against each other. Suddenly, I no longer notice that my muscles were screaming from too much time bent at forty-five degrees.

"I like being outside."

"Me too, but not at the threshold of Mordor."

He smiles. "It's not so bad. I'll take this to a summer in Greenland."

"They have actual summers there?"

"Sure...if you consider it summer if you have to wear jackets and wool socks."

"That's not a summer."

"I agree," Jacob says. "It reminds me of,

Give me the splendid silent sun, with all his beams full-dazzling;
Give me juicy autumnal fruit, ripe and red from the orchard;
Give me a field where the unmow'd grass grows;
Give me an arbor, give me the trellis'd grape..."

My mind cartwheels back to his cottage, Dad's poetry books, including this one by Whitman, and Jacob's notes. I knew he had become a student of Dad's. A pretty good one. But he had really taken to poetry, given it life inside of him.

He stops, but I continue.

"Give me fresh corn and wheat—give me serene-moving
*   animals, teaching content;*
Give me nights perfectly quiet, as on high plateaus west of the
*   Mississippi, and I looking up at the stars;*
Give me odorous at sunrise a garden of beautiful flowers, where
*   I can walk undisturb'd…"*

When I finish, I say, "Not you too. Another Whitman convert?"

"You're not?"

"Yes, but not like Dad. I'm not sure I have a favorite. I'm partial to Yeats and Angelou if I had to choose. Whitman is Dad's influence on you. On everybody. He makes you think there's no one else."

"He's great. Wise. He's helped me open this other side of myself and not be afraid of it."

"What side is that?" I ask before I've even realized, the words tumbling out, and I wonder if he's comfortable answering such a personal question.

"An emotional side. Feelings. Whitman believed in connections with nature and self. To the simpler pleasure of life. To what really matters.

*Give me for marriage a sweet-breath'd woman, of whom I
should never tire;*
*Give me a perfect child—give me, away, aside from the noise of
the world, a rural domestic life…"*

"Does that poem illustrate everything that you want?"

"Perfectly."

It is then that I understand who he is. Quiet and astute
and possessed with the ability to see the grand in simplicity.
He knows exactly who he is and is entirely comfortable with
it. The thought brings an overwhelming trace of admiration.

"I have to ask…where did you get this truck?"

"It was my dad's work truck." He rubs his hand back and
forth across the bed slowly, affectionately. "For hauling lumber
and equipment from Savannah to the dock. It's not aestheti-
cally pleasing, but I've always loved it."

I nudge him with my shoulder playfully. "It's nice. It fits you."

"How so?"

"It's unassuming."

He emits an appreciative *hmm.*

"Can I ask you another question?"

"Always."

I twist my glass in my hand, the condensation wetting my
fingers. "What did you say to Alana? At the store. To get her
to understand?"

"I told her that it makes us uncomfortable when she talks
to strangers."

"She's never followed the rules."

"Rules?"

I recite the rules. "I came up with those rules as a way of preventing anyone from recognizing her genius and, now that she's here, from recognizing who she is. My way of protecting her from those who may hurt her. Nothing I've ever said has made her understand them the way you did."

Jacob nods, understanding. "Don't be so hard on yourself. She doesn't register much fear, so playing off a fear she doesn't have is not going to resonate with her, but expressing your fears to her does because she doesn't want to hurt you."

"I had never considered that. How did you know to do that?"

Jacob doesn't answer. Instead, he watches Alana, his eyes dancing, as she carefully lines up the flowers. "Alana reminds me of her so much."

I resist the urge to ask who *her* is. Mainly because I want him to keep talking. I want to know more about him, all that he feels comfortable sharing with me. But then, suddenly, I know. I know how he knew what to say to Alana. Because he used to have a baby sister.

"Was Naomi going to be a scientist too?" I say, uttering the name he doesn't say, has never said in my presence.

"A mathematician. She was studying advanced physics and equations in middle school," he says. "But at times I wondered if she would run away and join the circus. She had that kind of spirit, the proclivity to change her mind. And she didn't care about the consequences. She could have done anything and been great at it."

He chuckles to himself. "Her first love was not math but dinosaurs. She wanted to be a paleontologist, but paleontology was not an accepted science in the Wyler household." He clears his throat. "'Paleontology is a made-up profession for those too lazy to study a real science.'" He mimics in a woman's voice.

I widen my eyes. "She said that?" Without knowing Birdie all that well, I know it's absolutely something she would be capable of saying. "How devastating that must have been for Naomi."

"Not at all. She would get under Birdie's skin. She wasn't afraid of her. She was encouraged by Birdie's negativity. In her spare time, she continued studying dinosaurs. Until, one day, we were waiting for my dad outside of his office at the hospital. She walked off, as she often did. I looked up, and she's talking to this man and a woman. A few minutes later, she's yelling and running down the hall. 'She's a paleontologist! She's a paleontologist! A real one. And she's not lazy!'" Jacob's shoulders shake with the outpouring of laughter. I join him, the truck shaking with us.

"How did Birdie react to that?"

"There wasn't much she could do," he says, still smiling. "She was so embarrassed."

"Did she finally accept Naomi's wish to be a paleontologist?"

"No, because after that, she didn't want to be one anymore. She had moved on. She fell in love with math."

"Did Naomi talk to a lot of strangers?"

"All the time. She was the social butterfly of the Wyler family."

"How did your dad and Birdie handle that?" It felt weird speaking about Birdie in a different context than I normally did. As a mother, not an evil woman capable of a relentless attack on a teenage girl.

"Emotionally, my parents did a lot of things wrong, but they always encouraged our abilities. They knew how to do that. They let her be who she was. They understood the importance of exposing her to different experiences."

"By talking to strangers?"

"Sure. I know this may sound crazy, but there's nothing wrong with talking to strangers."

I laugh. "Yes, that sounds crazy. I don't like the idea of Alana talking to people we don't know, telling them stuff about her, asking them questions. Seems intrusive."

"Most people don't mind at all. They laugh. They think it's cute. Wished their children weren't as shy. You don't have to buy in to the idea. Just understand that this is part of her character and her intellectual and emotional needs. Raising a gifted child is not easy."

I turn and face him, pulling my knee into my chest and holding it, with the comfort and ease of snuggling up with an old friend.

"When I had Alana, I read all of the books and articles. I bought all the essentials. None of that preparation trans-lated into love for my daughter. It was hard to see her without remembering how she got here. Nothing prepared me for becoming a mother, *her* mother, the mother of a daughter conceived from rape."

Jacob breathes heavily as if pained, but his eyes remain open and kind, softening me further.

"I focused on Alana and her needs, her protection and safety, falling into my daily routine, always moving forward. Then it happened. One day—I can't remember when—I looked into her eyes, and just like that, I was hooked. And for eight years, I kept my promise by protecting and growing to love her. And yet, now, I'm in awe of her and all that she is. I can honestly say that no one has helped me understand love and all its fullness like she has."

"*it is most sane and sunly / and more it cannot die / than all the sky which only / is higher than the sky*," Jacob says, quoting Cummings, the same one he recited the first time I met him at the bookstore. We trade smiles at the memory, which presses on me like a hand to the chest.

"I've always imagined this scenario where I'm holding her hand and then I just let go. Let go of all of it." I peek at Jacob. He's watching me. "Does that sound crazy?"

"Not at all. It's a symbolic gesture. You're not letting go so much as you're moving forward. The closing of one chapter and the starting of another. Sometimes our dreams are manifestations of what our heart wants."

"This has been a long chapter. And being here makes me want to close it. But I don't know how. If I'm ready."

Jacob covers my hand with his own, the gesture sweet and unassuming, his eyes grayed in the sunlight. There is barely any wind at all as we sit enclosed within the comfort of silence. He doesn't try to maneuver or manipulate the conversation. I know he prefers his family to know about Alana, but he doesn't push that agenda. Nor does he try to offer a solution to fix the problem. For which I'm grateful. He understands that words aren't always a necessary comfort, that silence can have the same benefit as the simple touch of a hand, that it can be all the support someone needs. Tension from earlier drains from my shoulders, aided by his company, his calm.

My mind turns once more to Naomi. "Were you and Naomi close?"

Jacob adjusts his position on the truck. "We had a rather unconventional upbringing, as you can imagine. We were homeschooled, so we had very few friends, and it was difficult to relate to the ones we did have. She understood me, and I understood her."

I nod.

"The chair you sat in at the cottage," he says, staring ahead. "That's her chair."

He tells me about Naomi's appearing to him in Alaska and his promise to her, why he came home.

"It's not logical for a scientist to believe in ghosts," he says, continuing. "We believe in facts. What can be deduced and proven. And yet, she's there. Most nights. Sitting in that chair," he says through a soft sigh.

"Does she ever speak to you?"

He shakes his head. "She's only said two words to me. *Home* and"—he pauses—"*Sara.*"

"Me?" I ask, drawing back. "What was she trying to tell you about me?"

He doesn't look at me as much as he looks through me. "I don't know. But I think she knew about you and Alana. She wanted to bring us all together."

"It's funny," I say. "Alana has always been this puzzle that I struggled to understand. Her fascination with time and watches. Her love for math. All of her abilities. But since I've been back, I'm learning so much about her from you and Naomi. Maybe that was the plan all along."

The skin between his eyes wrinkles. "How's that?"

"You're giving me context about her. Alana talks to strangers. Naomi talked to strangers. Alana loves math. Naomi loved math. Now I know where she gets it from. I look at her and see him. You look at her and see Naomi."

"Alana is more like her than him." He follows my lead and does not say Daniel's name. "It's eerie how much they have in common. It's almost like they are the same person."

"All this time I've watched her grow up and wondered if some of the things she did were because of him. She would ask so many questions about him. Questions I couldn't answer. But I had my own questions. It bothered me that it seemed she was all of him and none of me. She's all Naomi, and from the sound of it, that's not a bad thing."

He smiles at me with the warmth of a thousand suns. "Thanks for saying that."

"Why won't you say her name?"

He looks away at Alana shoveling dirt. "I don't know," he says, his face wounded when he turns back to me. He rubs his head. "I just stopped. There's no logical reason why."

"How do you feel about talking about her?"

"I didn't for so long. It was almost easier to pretend she didn't exist. But I felt like I wasn't honoring her, her existence, by doing that. When I came home, I promised myself that I would talk about her. Remember her. And it has felt good talking about her, giving her life, outside of my own memories."

Just then, Alana runs over, winded, flushed from digging. She takes each of our hands and pulls us off the truck. There is plenty of work to be done, and she seems determined to do it all in one day.

"Come on, guys!" she says, pulling us with all her might. "We have a garden to plant."

JACOB

———

I CAN'T RECALL THE last time I watched a movie. Or TV for that matter. The Wyler household didn't have one, a habit that I carried into adulthood. Nor did I ever have the desire to watch a movie, especially one called *Beetlejuice*. But when Alana once again invited me to attend their family Saturday movie, and since I missed the first one, I said yes.

Not that I need to be convinced to spend time with her or the rest of them. As I watch Beetlejuice attempt to frighten the Deetzes, I can't help but gawk at another main attraction, this one playing out right in real life. Like at Pizza Friday, the energy of the love and acceptance Alana, Sara, Hosea, and Sylvia exhibit toward one another is palpable, a transference of affection shifting from person to person. They laugh. Tease each other. And they can never be too close to one another, at times sharing the same blanket or resting their head in someone's lap. Alana, having made her way from Hosea's, Sylvia's, and Sara's laps, is now lying between me and Sara on the couch as her eyes droop heavily with every blink, and by the time Beetlejuice is summoned back to the afterlife, she is asleep.

After the movie, Sylvia pats Hosea on his knee, and they stand, announcing that they are calling it a night, but when I hear the front door close and don't hear Hosea's footsteps climbing the stairs, I smile.

I tilt my head toward the front door. "Yeah?"

Sara reads my playful expression. "Yeah." She smiles, her hand covering her lips. "Does that seem weird to you?"

"Not at all," I say. "I think it's great. Very inspiring."

"They've been companions for quite a while now. They're happy. We don't know how much time is left."

I think of Daniel and his lingering infection and wonder if I need to question the same thing. "I admire the way you guys are handling that."

Sara props her elbow on the back of the couch and rests her head on her hand. The amber of her eyes glows in the light. "It hasn't been easy. The beginning was hard. But we decided that instead of watching him die, we would help him live."

Here's a family staring mortality in the face and instead of ignoring it, they are embracing it. They've discussed it. Sure, death is a scary thing, but they are facing it together. What if we had done that after Naomi's death? "That's very wise."

"Do you think it's weird that he doesn't speak traditionally?"

"I don't. Actually, I'm relieved. It makes it easier. Spares the small talk. Which I've never been good at."

Sara picks at an errant thin thread on the pillow in her lap.

She is full of tells. She fidgets, her fingers twinning together, mostly when she's nervous, but at times, she averts her eyes. Something about Hosea's untraditional way of speaking has struck a nerve with her.

"What was it like to be raised with a father who essentially didn't speak? I can't imagine that was easy."

She lifts her eyes to me. "It's always been who he was. But sometimes you just need to hear the words, you know? Without having to decipher the meaning or search through a book or the internet. Take out the trash. Hand me that piece of paper. Turn off the light."

"What did you want to hear the most?"

Her eyes burrow into mine. "I love you."

My heart aches at this. It hits too close to home like déjà vu, a piece of a remembered dream. I've never heard those words myself.

"Birdie was never inclined to show any of her personal feelings with her children or my father," I say. "I have never seen her cry—not when Naomi died or my father—and I don't recall her ever telling us she loved us. You know...not through action but in saying the actual words. *I love you.*"

"How did that make you feel?" She leans into me, her lips parted slightly. Hungry for my response, and I want to feed it to her, push this out to the one person who understands.

"I didn't realize it then. That she had never said the actual words," I say. "But later, after my sister died, and the trial...I realized how emotionally empty we all were."

"Why?"

"We weren't built that way. We didn't know how to express emotion. We weren't in touch with that side of ourselves. Weren't used to battling or conquering something we didn't naturally know how to fight."

"Is that why your dad..." Sara pauses, but I hear the words in my head, loud, as if she had said them.

"Killed himself? Yeah."

Sara retreats as if burned by an ember. "We don't have to talk about this if you don't want to."

I look away at the television and it rolls along, muted, flashing, changing the light of the dim room with each change of scene. Sara notices and turns it off, immediately smothering us in a pale light, a warm glow from a single lamp.

We have been carefully dancing around the topic of Daniel and the trial for some time now, and I imagine we could go on forever not talking about it. But I want to clear the air. There is something that needs to be said: the truth.

"I want you to know something. Celestial mechanics is a branch of astronomy that deals with the motion of objects in outer space and dictates that when two objects collide, there's always collateral damage."

"Are you saying that..." She swallows the words, but she forces them back to the surface and out. "I was collateral damage?"

I take a deep breath. "I'm sorry for what my family did to you. How Daniel's lawyers and Birdie treated you. You didn't deserve what happened."

"I appreciate your saying that." Her countenance is light, considering. "I've had a lot of time and therapy to come to terms with what happened. I'm still dealing with it. In my own way. But I don't blame *you*."

"We're not bad people, Sara," I say, noting the distinction in her *you*. "Just damaged. Hurt people hurt people. That's not an excuse. But it's true."

"They hurt you too." She moves closer to me on the couch, her knee brushing mine. "But why do you include yourself with them?"

I rest my head on the back of the couch. "They're my family," I say to the ceiling. "My life here has allowed me plenty of time to come to terms with what happened, what I lost, how I wish I could change the past." I look back at her. "But I'm learning that the way to do that is through forgiveness. And eventually, when we're ready, we need to let go and forgive."

She smiles wide, a shy grin. "You go first."

I feel myself smiling back, but her face turns serious.

"I never thanked you for testifying on my behalf. I know that must have been difficult for you." She takes my hand into hers, and the act, the tenderness of it, calms my soul. "Thank you."

"You don't owe me that. It was the right thing to do."

"Is that why you're helping me now?" she asks, her voice soft like petals. "Keeping my secret? Out of obligation? Or guilt?"

Maybe it is all three. Or maybe it isn't. How do I explain to her that I've felt more at home with her family than I ever have with mine? Like an invisible thread bound me to them.

I cover her hand with mine and find her eyes. "I'm here because I can't *not* be. For all of the reasons you said and for others I can't explain." I stop. "I know that probably doesn't make sense."

I don't want to scare her away with my potent honesty. She has, slowly, begun opening up to me, like a book. Introducing anything else could throw us off-balance. But Sara's feeling the same. "It does, actually," she says too quickly, without missing a beat.

"We're not strangers, remember?"

"We're too connected to be strangers."

"We're like photons, particles of light. They always travel at the speed of light. A photon emitted by the sun will be absorbed by your skin when it touches you." I take her arm into my hand and dab it in various spots from her wrist to her elbow, then drag my finger the length of it, before tracing circles up and down it. "But to the photon, no time will have passed from when it was emitted to when you absorbed it. From the point of view of the photon, the time of its emission and the time of its absorption is the same. They happen simultaneously."

Sara listens intently, so I continue. "To the photon released during the big bang until just now, no time has passed. To the photon, the big bang *is* now. In a sense, since time and space are inextricably intertwined, if all times are the same time, then all places are the same place. Time and space and distance and separation are some sort of illusion that we are in the midst of but can't quite understand. That means"—I clasp her fingers into mine and hold them up—"you and I, right now, are in the same place, at the same time, occupying the same mind. I am in you, touching you, being you, quite literally."

Such an intimate thing, the clasp of hands, the linking of a chain, and Sara doesn't immediately withdraw her hand. The absorption of our warm touch remains, and I find the sensation I derive from it exhilarating.

"Wow," she says, trying to sound collected through a stunning smile, which she tries to hide with her other hand. And whatever I said, whatever I did, I immediately want to do it again, just for such a reward. "Locke was right."

"Locke?"

"He said you had a way of making science sound... interesting."

"He said that. Interesting?"

"Actually, he said you told him about entanglement, and it 'won him some points'"—which she frames with air quotes— "with his wife."

I laugh. "Well...that wasn't my intent, but science can be very sexy."

"Yes, it can," she says, holding my stare. Sara twirls her braid through her fingers.

Alana stirs on the couch between us, murmuring something incoherent in her sleep. Her movement severs our eye contact and hands. Sara clears her throat and straightens up. And the magic that passed between us, the moment, is gone, snuffed out like a flame.

"I can carry her upstairs, if you like."

Sara nods, and I lift Alana in my arms. She stirs, her eyes fluttering, and wraps her legs around my waist and rests her head on my shoulder. I carry her gently up the stairs, wondering how something so small could have such a huge presence within my heart in such a short period of time. I lay her down on the bed; she sprawls out flat, one arm hooked above her head—the same way Naomi used to sleep—and I look at her once more. She is smiling in her sleep, and the sight, like so many before, catches me off guard, the miracle of her.

Downstairs, Sara is folding the blanket.

"She's still out," I say.

"It doesn't take much. She's always been a hard and fast sleeper."

The air pricks with energy, a mood, hovering in the space above us, and I don't want to leave. I want to stay right here in it, be present, feel its vitality. The night is still young. It is the kind of night for a stiff drink, intimate conversation, for exploration into the unknown, into each other. But I don't want to intrude further or allow myself to hope. The night has to end sometime. I start to say this, but Sara speaks first.

"I was going to have a glass of wine and sit on the porch if you would like to join me." Sara feels the same way, feels the pull to explore whatever gripped us both. She fidgets again, in anticipation of my answer or in regret over her proposal, I am not sure. But then, she stops, her nerves vanishing like smoke.

"I'd like that," I say.

Outside, the night air is filled with the sound of the rustling leaves. The sky is a stained black save for the static gray clouds that blot out the stars in preparation for the storm that's brewing. I instinctively look up and fill my lungs with fresh air.

"Do you always look up?" Sara asks, watching me and not hiding it. I settle next to her on the bench, our thighs having no choice but to touch. We are closer than before, and the thought is not lost on me.

"Yeah…but it's a habit I'm trying to break. I'm learning to keep my eyes here on Earth, on what's in front of me."

"Why is that?"

"I'm learning to be more present. Looking at the sky is like looking back in time. I've spent so much time looking into the past, I can forget to be in the present."

"Does being present on Earth make it your favorite planet?"

"Oh, absolutely. Most people say Saturn because of its rings or Jupiter due to its size. But Earth…" I sigh. "This is where the dreamers are, the adventurers. There isn't another planet that we've discovered yet that sustains life. That makes it pretty special. Plus," I say, looking at her, "everyone I love is here."

She takes a sip of wine and continues looking at the sky, her black lashes curled upward. "I guess that would make Earth my favorite planet as well."

"An old psychology professor once told me that a person's personality can be likened to a planet."

She considers this and turns to me, drawing her knees into her chest. "Which planet am I?"

"Uranus."

She laughs. "Really? Uranus? Very funny."

"No, really." I laugh with her. "Name aside, Uranus is a pretty cool planet."

"How's that?"

"Thousands of years ago, when Uranus was forming, something, and we're not sure what, smashed into it. The impact was so forceful that its axis tilted by ninety-eight degrees. It still spins but on its side. There's no other planet in our solar system that's tilted that much." I look at her. "That's you, Sara. You took a hit, it knocked you off your axis, but you keep spinning no matter what."

She looks away shyly, blushing, and I wonder if I'm coming on too strong, if it is the wine or the intoxication of the chemistry between us that is now speaking.

"Did I say something wrong? When I start talking about the universe I can rattle off. I don't even know I'm doing it."

"I like that about you," she says, sounding genuine. "That you do that."

"Did I offend you? Because—"

"No, no." She interrupts. "It was so right it scares me."

"Why?" I press, my voice low. "Why does that scare you?"

"I feel unveiled." She twists her fingers. "And seen."

She doesn't say any more, but I know what she means. Understood. The knowing of a person, the knowledge going both ways.

"I see you, Sara."

A look of unease creeps across her face. In her expression I sense that she feels conflicted by this, being naked and bare to unexpected and conflicting emotions.

Then, a crack of thunder rolls across the darkness. Next comes the rain, in sheets that pepper the ground in a chorus of a thousand claps.

Sara combs her fingers through her braid, loosening the hair that billowed on her shoulder, and runs off the porch into the rain.

"Come on!" she yells. She spins and twirls in the street. "It feels amazing!"

I walk to the edge of the porch and watch her. She rarely indulges in laughter, in fun. But now, a fissure in her forced reserve. She is wild, free. Her laughter infectious, wrapping around me. She calls to me again, but when I don't move, she runs to the edge of the porch and stands below.

"Don't tell me, Dr. Wyler, that you are afraid of a little rain?" Sara smooths her hair back, which accentuates her features, the sharp ends of her cheekbones, full lips, and smooth skin.

In an alternate universe, a galaxy light-years away, I pull her in my arms. I kiss her with a force so necessary, so right, the logical conclusion (or beginning) of the obvious chemistry we share. But we are not in an alternate universe, we are here, the place where we are governed by the rules of this planet, where the force of reality reigns. Here, I'm Daniel's brother. A man who shares the same blood, same face as the one who hurt her. Of all the connections we share, this is one we cannot ignore.

The rain hits me like a wall when I step into it. Instead of kissing Sara, I tip my chin to the heavens and kiss the rain, its drops puckering on my lips, eyes, and cheeks, and don't think about what could be. I think of my place, my role in her life. I am Alana's uncle, her tutor. And to Sara, I am conscripted to the service of her secret. Nothing more. The rise of a promise not worth the fall of reality.

———

"No update from our genius?" Daniel asks after surveying the table and finding it devoid of the usual papers I bring for his perusal.

"We've taken a break," I say. For the first time since its inception, the Google Science Fair was canceled. They didn't cite why. The news hit Alana only slightly before she shrugged her shoulders and asked to go play in the garden with Brixton. Honestly, Sara and I were both relieved. With her work on the Navier-Stokes equation incomplete, I didn't feel comfortable sharing any parts of it with the world. Not yet. The cancel-ation of the fair provided us with an opportunity to take a mini break, which, I think, has been helpful for Alana, who is easily absorbed into mathematics.

"That's not a bad idea. Kids need that. It's summer. She needs to play. Ride bikes. Run around."

"How are you feeling?" I ask. During my checkup, Dr. Bennett told me that Daniel's infection has not subsided, making the bone marrow transplant almost impossible for the next month. Studying him now, I estimate he's dropped a few pounds. His collarbone protrudes more prominently over his V-neck shirt.

"Never better." He looks away.

"Don't tell me that. I know your infection has worsened."

"Tell me about this woman you've been seeing," Daniel says.

"What?" His abrupt change of subject sucks the air out of my lungs.

"Birdie told me you've been seeing someone."

"Do you and Birdie sit around and talk about me?"

"Are you kidding? You are all she talks about."

"No way."

"'Jacob is in Alaska. Jacob launched his probes. Jacob moved back home. Jacob stays over.' She loves that you do that, by the way."

I laugh. "You are all she talks about to me."

"She's proud of you."

"Nah."

"She is."

"I wasn't the one who was supposed to be something. That was you and…"

"Naomi," he finishes for me, understanding, still, my hesitation. "Birdie wants you to be happy. She's happy that you're involved with someone."

"I'm not involved with anyone," I say. It is the truth, but it feels like a lie. Or, possibly, the beginning of a truth. Especially after the night on Hosea's porch. There was something there. A presence as palpable as a steady heartbeat. Just as I had, I know Sara felt it too.

"Anyone we know?" He searches my face for an answer.

I blanch. "Not anyone Birdie would approve of."

"Because of her family, education, money?"

"All of the above."

"What is she like?" Daniel presses. Simple, generic answers will not satisfy his curiosity. Without Alana's work to discuss and his reluctance to talk about his condition, we have nothing to hold us together.

As I stare at the green metal table between my brother and me, Sara's face appears in my mind, and before I know it, I'm talking about her. "She has these amazing eyes. Big, brown, and beautiful. She opens them wide, and it takes my breath away. Every time. It's like I can see the whole world in them. She's graceful. She doesn't move; she floats. She's brave. Not in the way you may think, though. It's a quiet bravery. It churns and churns and churns under the surface. She's kind and thoughtful. Always thinking of others. She touches my cheek, just as *she* did. She just knew to do that. Like she knew that's what I wanted, needed. Sa—" I stop myself just in time. Daniel doesn't notice.

I look up, and Daniel is staring at me. "What?" I say, aware of myself now. My face flushes in embarrassment.

"Remember that girl," Daniel says, snapping his fingers. "What was her name? Rose. Rose Halverson."

Rose Halverson was my first everything. First kiss. First love. First time.

"Do you remember when you told me you lost your virginity to her? That's how you look right now."

I wave a dismissive hand against his accusation. "I was sixteen. All boys have that look after their first time."

Daniel smiles. "You're right. This is different than Rose. Much different," he says, studying me, searchingly. "Monumental like that but even more. You found her. Your earthly Aurora."

I cannot hide my smile or the truth from the one person who knew me best. I think of Sara, the carefree way she twirled in the rain. Suddenly, I'm filled with a deep longing for her, to feel her warmth against me once again, to shield her from everything.

"How does it feel?"

Until this moment, I haven't given my feelings for Sara space and life outside of my own head. Thinking about all of this now, my body lightens and loosens like an unknotting rope. "Good." I hesitate, rubbing the nape of my neck. "Very good."

"Does she feel the same way?"

"I don't know. I think so. It's complicated."

"Why?"

You, I fight the urge to say. Instead, I say, "She's been hurt before. I don't know how open she would be to a relationship."

I am not a fool. There were limits to whatever piece of impossible luck I somehow lucked into, and I'm not naïve to think that it extends to an actual relationship with Sara. No matter how much I want it to.

"You know. Women don't hide their emotions well."

"Not if there are barriers that prevent it." My hope thins.

"She will tear them down when she's ready. When Rose was ready, she came to you, didn't she? Just wait for her. You've been waiting your whole life for her. What's a little longer?"

"Did you know that Grandma and Grandpa Wyler didn't approve of Birdie? That Dad was prepared to walk away from them if they didn't accept their relationship?"

"It was a different time. I can imagine such a relationship would have been difficult for them to accept, especially within their social circles."

"Do you think love is worth walking away from your family?"

"Love?" he says, tilting his head.

"I'm speaking in general terms. If you found your soul mate, would you sacrifice your family for them?"

"That question implies a belief in soul mates, which I don't have," he says. "But in the case of Dad and Birdie, I think so. If the love is real and pure. If they are each other's Aurora."

Daniel settles back in his chair and runs his hands along the tops of his thighs. His features shift into serious downturns. "Birdie told me that Sara is back in town."

I should have known this was coming. Of course Birdie would tell Daniel about Sara. I can't believe it never crossed my mind that she would. If so, I would have been prepared for this. Instead, the mention of her name, especially after thinking and talking about her right in front of him, renders me silent.

"Why didn't you tell me?" Daniel asks, his voice steady, his face like a board.

I look away and rub the back of my neck again. "I don't know. I just...thought..."

"You could have told me," he says. "You didn't have to keep that from me."

If only he understood the complications of telling him about Sara.

"Have you seen her?"

I take a deep breath and decide giving him colorless answers would be the best course of action for the barrage of questions ahead. "Yes," I say, adjusting my position in my chair, the room suddenly growing warmer.

"Where?"

"The bookstore."

"How is she?"

"Her father has an inoperable brain aneurysm."

"The man who doesn't speak, right?"

I nod. Daniel's stoic expression doesn't change.

"Is that why she came home?"

"Yes."

"Did she say where she's been all this time?"

"Not exactly."

"How does she look?"

I narrow my eyes at him.

"Not like that. Like...does she look"—he gestures as if trying to conjure the word—"happy?"

"Her father is dying."

"Not happy. But...you know. Is she married?"

"No," I answer and wonder if he'll ask if she has any children.

"Have you talked to her?"

"Yes."

"And?"

"And what?"

"Does she still hate me?"

"We haven't—" I catch myself. *Haven't* implies continuous conversations. I don't want to give Daniel the impression that my interactions with Sara are anything more than a onetime occurrence. "We didn't talk about it."

"What did you talk about?"

"Her father. The bookstore."

"And she was okay talking to you?"

"Yeah."

"Did she ask about me?"

"No."

"Well…maybe she doesn't hate me."

I shrug. "I don't know."

Daniel takes a deep breath and straightens his posture, and the moment is gone.

SARA

———

JACOB BECOMES AN ACCEPTED presence in our house like a summer shower slowly moving in on a clear day. Nothing at first; then, out of nowhere, the clouds descend, their first drops falling tentatively in a whoosh. Finally, as suddenly as they appeared, the clouds vanish, revealing a clear sky again, but evidence of the rain remains.

At first, he knocked and waited for permission to enter. Then, the knock came simultaneously with the opening of the door. Later, the knock stopped all together, and he just entered, announcing himself from the foyer. No one, not even myself, opposed or questioned Jacob's increasing presence. We welcomed it, encouraged it. A place automatically set at dinner. Anchovies and pineapples purchased for Pizza Fridays. An assumption of his presence at the Saturday night family movie. When he wasn't tutoring Alana, he came by anyway, fixing whatever needed to be fixed, at the house or bookstore. When he automatically handed me tea in my favorite mug, I knew that he had become part of the fabric of our family. We liked it. I think he did too.

So, it came as no surprise when he showed up early one Saturday morning and announced he had secretly arranged for coverage at the bookstore and was taking all of us to a beach on a private island. No one opposed. Not even Dad, who rarely takes an unscheduled day off. Excited for a change from our normal routine, we packed our things and met him in the foyer.

I'm the last one to descend the stairs, hoisting our beach bag on my shoulder. Jacob steps hurriedly forward as I do so.

"Wait a minute," Jacob says. He's wearing a smile as bright as his white short-sleeve button-down, which I notice he's paired with an equally crisp pair of navy-and-green swim trunks. "What do you have in there?"

"Just a few things," I say, securing my and Alana's heavy bag on my shoulder with both hands.

"What *do* you have in there?" Sylvia asks, adjusting her own much smaller bag up on her arm. She is wearing a black-and-white polka-dot swimsuit and a long, white cover-up. "Is there a weight limit on your boat, Jacob?"

I shoot Sylvia a look. "What? I packed for two," I say defensively.

Jacob smiles wider. "I'm sorry, but I have to inspect your bag, ma'am. Captain's orders."

"Cool! Jacob's a captain," Alana says. "Can we call you Captain Jacob?"

"*O Captain! my Captain!*" Dad chimes, from Whitman's *Leaves of Grass*.

"*O Captain! my Captain!*" Alana repeats.

"This is crazy. I packed a few things we may need," I say. "Let's just go."

"Sorry. But there really is a weight limit on the boat so…"

I allow the bag to plop on the floor. It makes a thud that rattles several hanging picture frames.

Jacob rummages through the bag and hands to me, one by one, two beach towels, a container of sunscreen, my notebook. "This is all you need."

I quickly inventory the remaining contents: three more beach towels, two pairs of goggles, a hairbrush, a fully stocked first-aid kit, one book for Alana and two for me, a safety whistle, an umbrella, Alana's pink life jacket, a second swimsuit, and a snack bag that contains several bags of chips, granola bars, and bottles of water. "What about the goggles?"

"She doesn't need them."

"I don't need them, Mom," Alana agrees. "I don't like them. They squeeze my head."

"What about the life jacket?" I ask, looking to Sylvia and Dad for reassurance. Surely, they agree with me on the importance of a life jacket.

"I have several on the boat," Jacob says, rubbing his hands together. "Are we ready to go?"

"What about snacks? Will there be someplace to get food and water?"

"Yes," Jacob says, offering nothing more.

I open my mouth to protest again but decide that it won't be fruitful, conceding that I have no allies here.

"Oh, wait," Jacob says, returning to the abandoned bag, plucking out a bag of chips, opening it, and popping one in his mouth. "Now we can go."

———

Alana and I ride with Jacob in his truck; Sylvia and Dad follow along in her car. Less than an hour later, we arrive at the marina. Puffy clouds dot the sky, changing shape as they inch along.

"What's the name of the island you're taking us to?" Sylvia asks.

"It really doesn't have an official name," Jacob says, closing my door behind me.

"Have we heard of it?" Sylvia asks. "What's the unofficial name?"

"Wyler Island," Jacob says, his voice low. He immediately moves to unload our bags and a cooler from the bed of his truck, avoiding our gaping mouths and frozen postures.

"You have your own island?" Alana asks, the first to snap back into reality.

"Well…it was my Dad's and his father's before," Jacob says. "I inherited it."

"But…it's…yours?" Sylvia asks slowly. "So…when you

said that you were taking us to a private island…you were talking about your own island?"

I look at Sylvia and shake my head out of view of Jacob, hoping she can read my mind, willing her not to press him about this. She throws me a bug-eyed look back that tells me she's going to ask all of the questions she wants.

"Yeah…but I guess I don't consider it mine. I mean, it is, but I hardly ever go there," Jacob says plainly, and I can tell the topic makes him uncomfortable. "But it's private and great for swimming. And sunsets." He winks at me.

"That sounds perfect," I say, thinking about watching the sunrise with him at his cottage.

A few minutes later, Jacob taps his forefingers on the silver steering wheel as he pulls out from the marina. Alana, his copilot, stands in front of him, just tall enough to see over the wheel, giddy with excitement that she's allowed to steer the boat. Behind them, Dad and Sylvia sit close, their arms linked, taking in the scenery and pointing out various hawks and migratory songbirds taking flight. From the bow of the boat, I breathe in the salty air, savoring its freshness and admiring the cerulean sky, my eyes squinting against the sun's reflection off the water.

It's hard to believe it's been three months since I came home, the passage of time marked by the end of spring and the burst into summer. For those months, we have confined ourselves to Dad's house and the bookstore, the days blending into a sameness that provided a comfort. But it feels good to be out, on the water again, loose from rules and restrictions I placed on myself.

There have been moments when I hardly recognize who I am. Week by week, I feel myself laughing more. Smiling more. Worrying less. I have started to become a figment of the person I used to be, like a flower opening to bloom. I've written some more poems, showing them to Dad, who nods or scowls. Either way, I usually end up revising. I feel myself changing and force myself to examine why. It is simple. Dad doesn't seem sick. Alana doesn't seem unsafe.

And then, there is Jacob.

We are getting close, too close, I know. Ever since his cottage, I have found myself opening up to him, telling him about the first years of Alana's childhood, our life in Maine, and my poetry. He has offered me the comfort of his ear, his presence. He listens more than he speaks, hears more than what I tell him. It is what I need most. From the unknowing attraction I felt when we first met at the bookstore, I have steadily and intensely felt myself drawn to him and have become more aware and attuned to the way he patiently explains an equation to Alana, how he listens to Dad even if he can't decipher his meaning, and the way he always knows what or what not to say to me. We are not strangers. We have moved from strangers and eased into familiar. Or, maybe, something else, something deeper yet undefined. He has crept under my defenses, becoming less of a possibility and more of the question of what next?

I look at Jacob whispering instructions to Alana. I take stock of him, the way the sun frames the curve of his square jaw, the lightness of his face, the arrangement of his features in beautiful placement. He is striking. Even more unnerving, none of Jacob's actions seem calculated. Not even the next one, which, as though he knows I'm admiring him, seems too intentionally placed. We're on a straightaway, so he lets Alana hold the wheel by herself as he straightens up and removes his shirt. Scientists aren't known for their physiques, but Jacob is clearly the exception. I turn away. Focus on…his words. He has a genuine way with words, and his prolonged eye contact reaches deep within me. And his touch. His hand over mine, an unassuming hand on my waist in passing, the brush of his fingers across my shoulders. All pricks on my skin that remind me that I'm still alive, that I'm allowed to feel. His quiet energy provides a confidence that is unbelievably alluring.

But I'm often conflicted about Jacob. I find it difficult to see the full context of him clearly. Sometimes it's like I'm looking at him through someone else's glasses. He's opened up to me about his dad, Naomi and Birdie, his assignments, sporadic snatches of his childhood, even the constant flooding of his boat. But he doesn't talk about Daniel, his cancer, or his relationship with his brother. In that, I feel that Jacob hides a sadness, a truth untold.

The boat completes several half turns, winding through salt marsh until a long beach, expanding for miles, comes into view. It's empty save for a rotation of crashing waves against the sand. Once again, we stand, mouths agape, as Jacob pulls the boat alongside a dock that points to a taupe house with long white columns. Jacob turns the motor off, and the world falls silent to the sounds of nature and wind and water. It is impossible not to feel a wave of relaxation wash over me.

"Wow." I am the first to speak as Jacob helps everyone off the boat.

"Jacob, this is beautiful," Sylvia says. "All of this belongs to you?"

"It's mostly salt marsh, except for the house."

Jacob ushers us toward a set of stairs that lead down to the beach. We load up our few bags and follow him. On the way, he tells us that there are beach chairs and umbrellas at the house that he will retrieve once we've identified a spot to set up and that the refrigerator is fully stocked with all of our favorite foods for when we grow hungry.

"So, when I asked about a place to get food, you meant your kitchen?" I say.

Jacob's smile melts away as his eyes focus on something across the water. "You know, actually let's get back in the boat."

"No!" Alana yells. "We just got here."

"What's wrong?" I ask, following his gaze to a second dock, visible if you know where to look around a jut of land, where another boat sits.

"Marsha's here," he says, just above a whisper, just loud enough for Sylvia, Dad, and me.

He says Marsha, but his tone has chilled me from the inside out as I think: Birdie.

"Marsha? Marsha Pendleton?" Sylvia asks.

"You know her?" I ask Sylvia, feeling slightly less edgy. Marsha clearly is not Birdie, though Jacob has restarted the engine, so I know they are connected.

"We graduated from high school together."

"I rent out the property as a vacation rental. Marsha manages it for me," he says. "I asked her to prepare the house and stock the refrigerator. I thought she would have been gone by now." Jacob moves around the boat, preparing for departure again. "I can circle around the island a few times until she leaves. She won't even know we were here."

I've imagined this moment a million times. Someone recognizing Alana. While Jacob and Sylvia contemplate the next move, I pinch my eyes shut, knowing what's about to ensue. I wait for the panic to rise in me. Wait for the hives, the sweat, the heart palpitations. Wait for the flood of thoughts choking my ability to reason. The fear for Alana will come next, and all the consequences that come along with someone else finding out.

I wait.

Then:

"It's okay," I hear myself say, surprising them and me. They stop talking, their lips parted mid-sentence, words failing to materialize. I look at Dad who nods and move inches from Jacob's chest, my head just below his, with the ease and comfortability of a lover angling for a kiss. None of what I feared welled up inside me. If there is one person I can trust, it's me.

I stare up into his eyes, a paler shade of green, his forehead wrinkling in worry. "It's okay, right?" I ask, knowing that Jacob would never allow this if he didn't believe Marsha would keep my secret.

"Sara," Jacob says, his forefinger lifting my chin to him, centering my face to his, "Marsha is like a mother to me. A true mother. I trust her. But if you tell me you want to go, we will go. Just tell me what you want."

I search his eyes and see the trust that has been building, and a peace surrounds me. "Then it's okay," I say to him, touching his cheek. I repeat this to Sylvia.

She steps to us. "I'm proud of you. So proud."

Dad whispers in my ear,

"Let us, then, be up and doing,
With a heart for any fate;
Still achieving, still pursuing,
Learn to labor and to wait."

I nod, at peace with my decision.

"I'll go up to the house and get the chairs and umbrellas," Jacob says, heading toward the house. "If I know Marsha, she'll want to come down and say hello. I'll bring her back down with me."

Alana, seeing there's at least a crack in our resolve to get back on the boat, peels off her shorts and flings her shirt into the sand.

"Can I go, Mom? Can I go?" Alana asks, bouncing, wound up like a toy ready to be set free.

"Go ahead," I say as I spread the beach towels across the sand.

She shoots off toward the ocean like a missile programmed for a target, her hair blowing behind her.

Ten minutes later, Jacob and Marsha make their way down from the house to the beach. Jacob is holding four chairs, two in each arm. Marsha carries two large green umbrellas. They talk as they walk, and I wonder what they are discussing. More than once, her eyes cast over to me.

"What are you doing out here?" Marsha asks Sylvia, as though they've run into each other at the same remote holiday resort.

Next, to me: "Hi, Sara. How long have you been back?"

"A few months."

She processes the information, smiling kindly in a way that tells me her mind is whirring in confusion.

"Jacob!" Alana calls, running out from the water at full speed. Everyone turns their attention to her. "Did you see me? Did you see me?"

Even with wet hair, Alana's resemblance to the Wylers is obvious to Marsha, whose face freezes in shock.

"I did," Jacob says, just as he finishes installing the umbrellas and wiping his hands free of sand.

"Alana, there's someone I would like you to meet," I say. "Alana, this is Marsha. Marsha, this is Alana."

Alana utters hello and begins digging her toes in the sand as Marsha's eyes well with tears.

"I can hold my breath for almost a minute," Alana says to her. "You just missed it."

Marsha bends down to Alana just as a tear falls. "Oh yeah? That's a long time. You must be a good swimmer."

"Yes, she is," Jacob says, flipping Alana backward and up on his shoulders. Alana giggles in flight. "Come on, Alana. Let me show you how long I can hold my breath," he says up to her.

We all watch as Jacob, with Alana still on his shoulders, walks toward the ocean. Alana releases a string of laughter just before Jacob plunges, face first, into the water, carrying her with him.

Marsha holds her hand to her heart once they are in the water. "I can't believe it. She's the spitting image of..." She pauses for a moment, and I wait for her to say Daniel. Instead, she says, "Naomi."

I never considered that Naomi would be what people who knew about Daniel and me would see first.

"Marsha," I say, "I'm sorry that you found out this way, but I hope you can understand that I don't want Birdie or Daniel to know."

She nods, but her eyes are full of questions. "How did Jacob find out?"

While Jacob and Alana swim, I tell Marsha the story. I tell her about my decision to have Alana, Dad's illness, Jacob's accidental meeting of Alana at Fernbank, and his tutoring. Marsha's reaction alternates between sadness and disbelief. I am shocked that I feel a layer of tension dissipate. Afterward, she stands, and I join her, and she hugs me tight.

"I'm so sorry, Sara. So sorry."

"So, we can trust you not to tell Birdie or Daniel?" Sylvia says. "I've held you as a good person since childhood, but we need you to give us your word."

"I've been keeping the Wylers' secrets for decades." Marsha turns to me. "I hate how she treated you during the trial. I love Daniel like he is my own son, but I never believed he was innocent. I'm sorry they put you through that." She pauses again and peers at Alana in the water. "And mostly, I'm sorry you had to hide her."

I note her tone and eyes and believe her. We sit and talk until Jacob and Alana return. I smother Alana in a towel until she wiggles away, grasping at a shell she spied, and then another, until she runs off looking for more. Jacob stands behind me and places his hand on my shoulder, silently inquiring about my welfare. "Are you okay?" he whispers, his lips grazing my ear. I pat his hand and hold mine on top of his. Marsha notices.

"I better get back to Savannah," Marsha says to us after a while. "It was nice to see you again, Sara." She tells Sylvia that she will call her soon. Jacob walks her back to the house but not before she steals one more look at Alana.

"You are growing quite comfortable around Jacob," Sylvia says as we watch Alana back in the water, this time with Dad.

I think back to touching his cheek earlier, his hand on my shoulder. I'm not bothered by either action. Or Jacob in general.

"It's okay if…"

"If what?" I know what she's implying, but I want her to try out the words for size, see how they fit.

"If you like him. These things happen when you least expect it."

"I'm not sure it will ever be anything more than what we are now."

"Why?"

I shoot her an annoyed look, but Sylvia holds my stare. "Who cares?" Sylvia says finally. "You can think of Jacob separately from them."

"That's impossible."

"No, it's not. Just give yourself permission. You guys have a connection. There's no denying that."

A huge smile grows on my face. "We are in the same place, at the same time, occupying the same mind. I am in you, touching you, being you, quite literally." He had touched me that night, running his finger up and around my wrist. His admittance that he saw me, truly, also touched something, producing a yearning down in me. In that moment, more than ever before, I wanted him. The realization shocked me and filled me with pleasure.

"What?"

I tell her about Jacob's explanation of photons, the gentle

way he held my hand and touched me. Our conversation on the porch, the rain, and the moment that held us both.

"If you have that kind of connection, can you imagine what the sex is like?"

I laugh so sharply that Dad and Alana turn their attention to us. "Sylvia!"

"Tell me you haven't thought about it."

I have. That night on the porch, in the rain, ends differently. So many do, in my daydreams, my imaginings.

Now, I look away, back at the house, and see Jacob walking toward us, and I hope my face doesn't betray me. As if on cue, Jacob flashes a bright smile at us that cuts right through me.

"That's what I thought," Sylvia says, biting her lip. "I had a lover like that once."

"Like what?"

"Deliberate. Calculated. When he touches you. *Really* touches you..." She shudders from what I assume is a vivid memory. "He's a feast, and he'll treat your body as one."

It is my turn to shudder. The thought of Jacob touching me like that sends a thrill through me. "He's never given any indication or said anything."

"That's out of compassion and respect for you because of what happened, and he's not going to risk not being in Alana's life."

"There's no way of knowing if what's happening between us is genuine or circumstance."

"Genuine is real. It's true and easy. Circumstance is obligation. It's stiff and hard. You'll know the difference."

———

The hours slip away as Sylvia, Dad, Jacob, and Alana play in the water. The waves laugh with them as the sun moves toward the horizon. A line of clouds hunch and settle low in the sky. I brush silvery sand from my legs and open my notebook. *Your hand in mine. Our search for light.* Several lines of a poem tumble out and I jot them, and others, down. Every so often Alana or Sylvia tries to coax me into the ocean. Unsuccessful each time, they return to the water.

Eventually, Jacob tells us about the lunch Marsha prepared at the house, and we all exclaim how hungry we are. Sylvia and Dad, wanting to stretch their legs, offer to bring it down to the beach. Jacob and I watch as they walk along the ocean, hand in hand, overturning stones with their feet or stopping to pick up a shell. Alana, taking a break from the water, plays nearby building a sandcastle.

"It's a beautiful island, house, beach, all of it," I say as Jacob settles into the chair next to me, digging his long toes in the sand, a thick biography of Benjamin Franklin in his lap.

"Thank you," he says as the uncomfortable grimace from earlier returns.

"Why are you so uncomfortable talking about your family's wealth?"

He takes a deep breath and sighs. "Mainly because the accumulation of it began decades before my birth and I contributed nothing to it," he says. "And because I would

310

trade it all, in a second, for one more day with my dad or my sister."

I realize he, like me, returned home to grief. He keeps mentioning my bravery, but it is he who is brave. I came home by obligation. He came home by choice to face the past. I'm still hiding behind it.

"Your father sounds like a good man."

"He was. He was the balance in us. A very smart man. Not just book smart. He traveled the world and had all of these great experiences he would tell us about. He knew things like where to stay in a tree house in Laos or how to get to Greece from Bari, Italy."

"Did you travel with him much?"

"His work at the hospital and our tutoring schedules kept us all busy, but we always took a summer and winter vacation as a family. Europe in the summer. Asia and Africa in the winter."

"I like that he strived for balance. That he understood it. That's what I want for Alana."

"We all could have enrolled in college early, but Dad wanted us to have a normal childhood and matriculate with the rest of our peers. Birdie vowed that none of her children would step foot in a public school. So, they compromised. Birdie homeschooled us because she didn't trust our educations to anyone but her, but we could not start college until we reached the appropriate age."

"Do you recommend that for Alana? With Dad…" I stop.

"I'm going to need to make a decision. Enrollment will start before I know it."

"Absolutely. She needs to be in school. She needs social interaction with children her own age. But we can't stifle her genius. She'll need constant tutoring. Public school teachers are not equipped to handle her intelligence."

Jacob's use of *we* instead of *you* tugs at my heart. He doesn't notice the slip, and I don't comment on it.

"Jacob," I say, softened by his face. "I can't enroll Alana in school here, and I don't want to homeschool her."

A look of unease flashes across Jacob's face. "I don't want you to go back to Maine."

"What do you suggest I do?"

He considers my question for a bit. "There's a private school just outside of Savannah. The one that Brixton attends. We can enroll her there with him."

"I can't afford that."

"I will pay."

"I can't ask you to do that."

"You didn't. I'm offering."

"We don't need your family's charity." As soon as the words leave my mouth, I wish I could suck them back in. But they've already reached Jacob's ears.

His expression clouds, a shadow falling across his face as he turns away from me.

"I'm so sorry for saying that."

He's still hurt, looking down at the trampled sand, and

this wounds me so unexpectedly and completely, as if I were cut by those words.

"We appreciate everything you have done for us. We love your company."

His attention finally drags toward me. "We?" he asks, choosing not to ignore my own use of the word. His eyes burn into mine and I don't look away. Instead, I take his hand, lacing my fingers with his. "Me. I like being with you."

Jacob affirms our grip. "I like being with you too."

Neither of us speaks. Words would have crowded such a moment. Because in that moment, we both stop pretending.

"We can enroll her in a public school a few towns over," Jacob says, sometime later. "No one will know who you are or who she is."

"*We* will figure it out," I say as the word *we* writhes between us. I tug on his hand in mine before brushing my lips across his knuckles. Jacob moans.

Alana returns, ending our conversation and our hand holding. "Can I go back in the water until Sylvia and Grandpa come back?"

"Sure," I say, extending my fingers to capture the remaining sensation of Jacob's warm hand, the feel of his skin on my lips.

She turns to Jacob, smiling before she speaks. "I'll race you," she says. "Ready. Set. Go." Alana takes off without notice, her ever-growing legs moving as fast as possible.

"I'll be back," he says, giving her a head start to let her win.

I laugh as I watch Jacob close the distance between them

in just a few strides. A few minutes later, Jacob returns, standing over me, his wet body glistening in the sun, and extends a hand. "If I may."

I regard his hand coolly and look back at him. "What?"

"Accompany you to the water. It's perfect."

I shake my head. "I don't swim anymore."

"But you spin in the rain? Come on."

"No," I say playfully but firmly, smiling.

A flicker of something flashes in his eyes. He opens his mouth to speak but squats in front of me instead. Beads of water roll off him and plop into the sand.

"What?" I ask.

"I love your smile."

My heart lurches into a new rhythm. He extends his hand again, this time with an accompanying smile that is as warm as the summer sun. "It'll be fun. Trust me."

And I do. Trust him. With all of it. Alana. And whatever else comes next.

I take his hand and run into the ocean.

JACOB

———

EVERYTHING ABOUT THE VISIT with Daniel feels different. The roads to the prison seem too narrow. The air thicker. The drive longer and more tedious. Even Daniel's unchaining, normally seamless, appears cumbersome and clumsy as the latest guard, Barry, struggles to unwrap the pattern of chains from Daniel's wrists and ankles. The air-conditioning offers no respite to all our misery. The lukewarm air vibrates through the vents and buzzes throughout the room.

A woman with two small children, a boy and a girl, walks by, all of them holding hands, to the table next to ours. The little boy, the younger of the two, jumps into the lap of the prisoner there.

I spread out the latest of Alana's work for Daniel's review, but Daniel doesn't look at it. Instead, he studies me, and I think I notice a hint of a smile appear and disappear. Then he rubs both hands across his head and draws in a deep, long breath, holding it before releasing it in a rush.

"Do you think if Naomi hadn't died, our lives would have been different?"

"I don't know. Sometimes," I say.

"Dad would not have killed himself."

"Do we really know that? In that context, for that reason, no. But we don't know for sure. It's the grandfather paradox."

"Are you saying that I would have...you know...anyway?"

"I don't know. It's a comforting thought to think that if we can go back in time and prevent one thing from happening our lives would be better off. But the honest truth is that we just don't know. There's no crystal ball."

Daniel considers this.

"There's a poem by Robert Frost called 'The Road Not Taken.'" I think of Hosea, his tutelage, the ease with which poetry pertaining to life rolls off his tongue, as I recite the poem to Daniel. All those late nights at the bookstore and on my porch with Naomi, studying, have led me here, to using poetry to evoke an emotional response, to helping me decipher and explain the world around me. The knowledge that I am learning, have learned, wrapping around me like a weighted blanket.

Daniel stares at me, unblinking. "Poetry?"

My face warms. "It has really helped me understand life and love in ways I never expected."

"You're reciting it from memory," he says, his expression registering between shock and amazement.

"It's no different than learning an equation or mathematical formula or scripture."

He crosses his arms and relaxes his face. "You really did it. You really are Jacob now. No more David."

"He's still here. He just evolved. Like I said before, everyone is capable of it."

My statement triggers something in him because he says, "I need you to talk to Sara."

His expression changes, loosens, into a relaxed state. I study him as uneasiness worms through my body. All these years later, despite his good deeds and restitution, it's clear his criminal act against Sara plagues him more than he admits. I decide to press him on this.

"What do you want to know? What do you hope to gain? Will it even matter now?"

He inspects his hands and holds them out in front of him. They shake ever so slightly.

He has something he wants to say. And I want to hear it. I lean in and place my forearms on the table, my hands clasped in front of me. "Daniel," I say, "what happened that night?" I ask, not just for Sara but for me. I was there, at the end. I have my own guilt to seek forgiveness for, and my own forgiveness to dole out.

"A friend, if that's what you would call her, left her and went home with that kid Tommy, who lived down the street from us. She was drunk. I was drunk." He stops. "I didn't invite her into the room with the intentions of... I thought she was pretty. I was in so much pain from losing Naomi, and I didn't want to hurt anymore. I would have done anything to not hurt anymore. It was like I was outside of myself."

"Do you regret it?" I ask, my voice cracking as I fight the sudden dryness in my mouth. I think of eighteen-year-old Sara, innocent, free, a whole world ahead of her, at the wrong place at the wrong time with the wrong man. "And don't quote scripture from the Bible or justify your actions in any way. Yes or no. Do you regret it?" My voice rises with reserved anger.

"Yes," he says, so simply, final, that I believe him. "I do."

They say the truth hurts. This truth knifes my heart and bleeds for my family, for Sara and Alana. One mistake. How one bad decision can alter the course of so many lives. Set us all on a course we never planned or imagined. But no matter how painful this truth is, it needs to be free. And we all have to let it be. True freedom comes from the truth, and this truth has held so many hostages for so long.

"I think about Sara every day," he says, compassion registering in his face. "What I did. The person I was back then. Cocky. Arrogant. Angry. Sad. She got in the way. That's not her fault."

My fingers are balled into a tight fist, the nails cutting into my palms. My heart hammers in my chest. "Why did you let Birdie defend you when you knew you were guilty? Let her tear Sara apart?" I have never asked these questions before, but I've thought about them since his trial.

All of my questions land like punches from a bully, but Daniel absorbs them as if he expected them. "Do you know I've never seen Birdie cry?"

"Don't change the subject. Why did you let Birdie defend you when you knew you were guilty?"

"Think about it. Have you ever seen Birdie cry?"

I know such a time doesn't exist. But I'm baffled at the question.

"You can't remember a time, can you? Not at Naomi's funeral. When Dad died. Never."

"Are you saying—"

Daniel interrupts. "You asked why I let Birdie defend me. Why I allowed her to tear Sara apart." He swallows hard before saying, "I didn't know this then, but I think I wanted someone else to suffer." He swallows hard again, a thickness building in his throat. "To hurt the way I hurt. Birdie taught us not to let anyone know we can cry."

"You could have told me. We could have faced it together."

"We're not built the same. Castor and Pollux. Remember?"

"That's bullshit. I'm your brother. We were a family. We could have weathered it. Beat it back together."

He sighs. "You are a good brother."

"Why are you telling me this now? Why admit it now? Because Sara's home? Because of the interview? Is this what you plan on saying?"

"Because you're falling in love with Sara."

The words choke me as if they have hands. Daniel stares, lips pursed as the sting vibrates through me.

"It's okay."

"What's okay?"

"For you to be with Sara."

I reach across the table and grab his shirt and pull him into the table. My metal chair screeches against the concrete floor as it is pushed backward with the force. It crashes to the floor. "Fuck you!" The bass of my voice echoes across the room. Within seconds, three guards are at our table. I'm still leaning over the table, holding his shirt tight, my other hand knotted into a tight fist.

"We're fine," Daniel says, wincing. He holds his hands up defensively. "We're fine. Just a misunderstanding."

Two of the guards straighten me up in one swift motion, but I keep hold of Daniel's shirt, and Daniel jerks forward. "Let him go!" one of the guards says to me. "Let him go now!" Daniel begins coughing wetly, the effort racking his body, his eyes reddening. I release his shirt, and he falls back into his chair, his shirt wrinkled and limp at his chest.

"You two going to play nice?" the other guard says, his eyes sending a warning. "Or do we need to end this visit?"

If Daniel were any other prisoner, I'm sure I would have been removed, visitation privileges revoked, but his status allows for such grace, which he immediately reminds them of. "Thanks, guys. Stop by my cell later." Daniel smooths out his shirt. "We're fine now. Right, Jacob?"

I shake the guard's hands from my shoulders in one motion and stare him down as I turn my chair upright and ease back into it. The other people in the room return to their conversations.

"I'm sorry," Daniel says, producing a handkerchief from his shirt pocket. His forehead is scored with sweat as he dabs it, once, twice, then around his mouth.

I'm a man of controlled, reserved emotions. I can't recall the last time I lost my temper. My chest pumps up and down as my breathing slows. I wipe the back of my hand across my own forehead.

"For implying that you needed my permission to see Sara," he continues, handing me his handkerchief.

I hold my hand up, refusing. "She doesn't belong to you."

"That's not what I meant."

"What did you mean?" I ask, my jaw rigid.

He returns the handkerchief to his pocket and squares his shoulders. "I need your forgiveness, and it's hard to ask for that. I offered mine, misplaced instead."

"Your forgiveness? Why now?"

"Because…" He coughs, cutting off his words.

"Because of what?"

He looks away and coughs into his handkerchief.

My anger dissipates like a flash of lightning. There's a moment of stillness before either of us speaks again.

"How did you know? About Sara?"

"I didn't. Not at first. But when Birdie told me that Sara was back in town and you didn't, I wondered why. Then you told me that you've met someone. I put them together. I didn't know you were falling in love with her. That, I guessed."

The first time he said it, the word *love* didn't quite fit.

Like a key in the wrong door. His second mention of it, and it slides in like a shadow. I was capable of love and being loved. Open to the possibility of it and accepting of it. For the first time in years, the unease stirring in my stomach stills.

"I didn't know either. I didn't expect this."

"I know."

"Does Birdie know?" I hold my breath, nauseated by the notion.

"She doesn't have any reason to suspect. I'm assuming she doesn't know."

"Birdie can never know. She blames Sara for you, for Dad's death."

"That's nonsense."

"You have to tell Birdie the truth about that night."

"She knows the truth."

"She has convinced herself of your innocence."

"Why?"

"It's one of the few things she has left. Us."

He takes a deep breath and then says, "You want to know why I want your forgiveness now? I need it because...the cancer has spread."

———

I'm sitting at Birdie's kitchen counter drinking a beer when Marsha enters from the other room. It was a long drive back from the prison, and I need the potency of the beer to relax me from the tension bunched across my shoulders. The kitchen is cast in faint darkness, just a dull glow of a single light on the stove.

"I didn't hear you come in," Marsha says, her purse pulled up on her shoulder. "Are you hungry? There's some leftover meatloaf in the refrigerator I can heat up for you before I go."

I shake my head and run my fingers up and down the bottle while pumping my leg.

"How's he doing?"

"I almost punched him," I say, downing the last of my beer, the bitterness sliding down my tongue. The sound of the glass bottle touching the marble countertop creates a ringing wail.

"What? Why?"

I blink as she approaches me.

"Sara." She sighs a long, careful sigh. "Jacob, what are you doing?"

I rub my eyes. "I'm tired. I don't want to talk about this tonight. I'm going to bed." I kiss her on the forehead and move past her, heading toward the stairs.

"Jacob," she says, "you have to tell Birdie and Daniel about Alana."

I keep walking, ignoring her.

"You cannot continue to keep this from them."

I finally stop but don't turn around, the act requiring more strength than I currently have. "You met Alana. You talked to Sara. You know I can't do that. I promised."

"He's dying," she says to my back. "The cancer has spread to his lungs."

"There's still time. He just needs time for the infection to subside. Then we'll do the bone marrow transplant."

"What about Birdie?" Marsha asks, her voice a raised whisper. "She has a granddaughter ten miles away. You don't think she needs to know?"

I turn around. "That's not my choice."

"Talk to Sara. She trusts you."

"And that wasn't easy. It has taken months for her to trust me. I won't pressure her into doing something she doesn't want to do. Something I'm not even convinced she should do."

"I know you two have grown close."

I throw my hands in the air and release them hard. "What does it matter? Sara and I have an arrangement. She is allowing me to spend time with Alana in exchange for my silence."

"I saw you on the beach. Playing with Alana. Your body language with Sara. It's more than an arrangement."

"Would that be wrong?" I ask, expecting an answer, a confirmation or rebuke, but it reaches Marsha as a rhetorical question.

"I'd hate to see you disappointed."

"I'll be fine."

"But you're fighting with your cancer-stricken brother in prison."

"He deserved it."

"Jacob, I don't need to tell you how complicated this is."

"Complicated? You don't think I know that? I'm trying. I'm trying to be there for him, for Birdie. And keep my promise to Sara."

"You are going to have to come to grips with the idea that you can't save him."

SARA

———

THE LETTER ARRIVES WITH as much fanfare as a credit card offer or the power bill. Except it's been slapped with black letters spelling out "State Board of Pardons and Parole" prominently across the white envelope. A sharp chill runs down my spine as I stare at it. I tuck the envelope in my purse, unopened, place the rest of the mail in its usual spot on the front table, and head to the bookstore.

Throughout the morning rush, I am acutely conscious of the letter sitting in my purse, its presence a silent beacon calling to me. No matter the task, how demanding the customer, how misshelved the book, once it's completed, my mind pinwheels back to the letter.

Just before noon, Dennis, our weekend employee, arrives. For once, I'm glad Alana is not near; Sylvia and Dad have taken her on a mini-adventure to Atlanta.

I take a bite of my chicken salad sandwich and swallow, the flavor bland as if my taste buds are as distracted as I am. I repack the sandwich, retrieve the letter from my purse, rip it open, and read.

Re: DANIEL JOSEPH WYLER
DOC# 220460

Dear Ms. SARA LANCASTER:
  This letter is to inform you that DANIEL JOSEPH WYLER has an upcoming parole hearing scheduled for the September 2nd docket. As a victim or survivor of this crime, you may complete and submit a Victim Impact Statement form (enclosed) by mailing it to the address found at the bottom of this page.
  The Georgia Crime Victims Bill of Rights, O.C.G.A. 17-17-1, et seq., provides individuals who are victims of certain crimes specific rights. These rights are constitutionally protected and enforced (Georgia Constitution Art. I, Sect. I, Paragraph XXX).
  These rights include:
- *The right to file a written objection in any parole proceedings involving the accused;*
- *The right to be treated fairly and with dignity by all criminal justice agencies involved in the case.*
- *The Parole Board is firmly committed to working with victims and all private citizens to establish a more responsive, accountable, and effective criminal justice system. For additional information, call or email the*

Georgia Office of Victim Services. If you or a victim's family member wishes to meet with a Board represen-tative about a case, you can come to the Board's central office on any work day between 8:15 a.m. and 4:00 p.m. No appointment is necessary.

I have had plenty of time to think about Daniel. About what happened, what I lost, where I would be if that night had never occurred. My pregnancy prevented me from falling into complete denial about the magnitude the rape would have in my life. It has been impossible to simply throw those skeleton bones in a closet and slam the door. There have been constantly flashing neon lights at every turn, reminding me that Daniel will have a major role in my life forever.

I only vaguely remember the conception. On sleepless nights early in my therapy, I would clamp my eyes shut and try to see past the fog, wipe away the haze, and push him off me or decline one of the many drinks I had that night, or not attend the party altogether.

Once I knew I was pregnant, the questions from other people came. Doctors didn't just want to know *my* medical history. My unborn daughter's father's family, people I swore would have no active role in her life, had medical histories that were important to Alana's health. *Have you, your partner, or anyone in your family or in your partner's family had: diabetes, hypertension, heart disease, autoimmune disorders? Are there any genetic conditions in your family or your partner's such as Down syndrome, neurological disorders, muscular dystrophy?*

Has there been a history of violence, trauma, physical, sexual, or emotional abuse in your family, or in your relationship?

Therapy helped. Repeating mantras—*I did nothing wrong. I told the truth*—helped. Stating and believing my truth helped. As the years wore on, I tried not to dwell on the crime against me, knowing that some rape victims never recover enough to live any semblance of a normal life. I didn't want it to destroy me forever and allow it to affect other parts of my life. Or so I thought. Only later did I understand that the assault had become the center of my world. Those early and frequent therapy sessions healed my emotional wounds, but with scars.

And I might need to pick those wounds back open. Over the years, as I watched Alana grow, celebrate birthday after birthday, I was knowingly aware that Daniel's sentence was drawing to a close. But it didn't matter. He would never know about Alana's existence. And as long as I stayed away, his release from prison had no bearing on my life. Informed right away of my victim's rights, I long ago decided against ever submitting a Victim Impact Statement. While I hated what he did to me, I do believe that a person should be tried and convicted only once. I have been content living my life, not knowing about his.

But things have changed. I'm back in Georgia now. Jacob, and now Marsha, knows of Alana's existence. All the protections I put in place are gone. Daniel will be released soon and will live ten miles from us, if we both decide to stay in Savannah.

I need to know what kind of man Daniel is today. Is he the same arrogant, rich kid who sat smugly at the defense table, hiding behind Birdie and his team of lawyers? Does he regret his crime? Is he rehabilitated? Will he seek visitation, or even custody, once he learns about Alana?

There is only one person who can answer my questions.

"Jacob," I say into the phone. I picture him sitting on his porch, watching the water.

"Sara?"

"Are you in town?"

"I can be."

"Don't worry about it. It can wait until Monday."

"Sara…what's wrong?" Jacob asks, the words sputtering through the concern in his voice.

"I wanted to talk to you about something."

"Where are you?"

"The bookstore. But—"

"I'll be there before you close."

I call his name once more, but he's already gone.

———

Jacob arrives just before closing, and after he says hello and asks about Alana, he's immediately fixing things, replacing the burned-out light bulb over the front desk, tightening the loose latch on the bathroom stall, helping Dennis before he leaves for the night to carry out flattened boxes from the shipment we just received.

I turn the dead bolt on the door a few minutes after closing, but I'm still a ball of nervous energy. I grab a stack of books to be shelved and notice Jacob, having finished his self-appointed tasks, on the love seat where I first presented our arrangement. So much has changed since then. He is relaxed, his right leg crossed over his left knee, his elbow on the back of the love seat, watching me approach. As much as it did the first time we met, despite the knot pitted in my stomach, Jacob's gaze on me excites and relaxes me.

"Busy day?"

"Don't ever let anyone tell you that people don't buy books anymore."

"What, even with the internet? Can't people just look everything up online? Aren't people reading on their phones?" Jacob mocks, repeating several annoying phrases Sylvia and I have shared with him that would normally conjure a chuckle between us. Instead, I flash him a placid smile, one that's meant to pacify him, but it reaches him as strained.

He stands and moves quickly toward me. "What's wrong?"

I start to move again, but he centers himself in front of me and takes the books from my hands, laying them on a nearby table. He takes my hand and guides me to the love seat. My fingers feel delicate in his strong grasp. We sit, settled next to each other, our legs touching. He doesn't release my hand.

"What's wrong?" he asks again, his eyes fixated on me.

"This came today," I say, staring at the big front pocket of the gold, charcoal, and graphite work apron I wear. I produce the letter, sans envelope, from my apron and hand it to him.

He reads the first sentence, and then his eyes meet mine. "Sara." He doesn't finish reading, lowering the letter. He knows what it says. He refolds it along the seams and rests his elbows on his knees.

"Did you know?"

"Yes," he says, looking straight ahead. "I didn't know how to bring it up. I know you don't want to talk about him."

"I didn't," I say. "But I do now."

He looks at me again, his brow peaked.

I reposition myself on the couch, tucking my feet under my legs. "I don't think I've ever admitted this out loud, but when Alana was born, I questioned my love for her. I couldn't see past her conception in those early years. It didn't help that she was none of me. That I didn't see myself in her. I didn't have one thing"—I hold up my forefinger—"not one characteristic I could hold on to that made her mine. But I swore I would protect her. No matter what. I threw myself into mothering. And I guess that's what's helped me not think about Daniel. I had a job to do."

I take the letter from him, returning it to my apron. I turn and face Jacob. He says nothing, barely moves, just listening, not with pity but, I think, with admiration. "I want to know about him. What's he been doing? How's he lived these last eight years? Everything. I'm ready to know."

"Are you sure?"

"He's being released soon. I need to know if he's changed. If I have any reason to fear for my safety, or Alana's."

He affirms his grip on my hand. "I will never let him hurt you again." He will protect me, us. I know this as surely as I know oxygen flows in my lungs.

"I know, but I need to know." I squeeze his hand.

Jacob settles on the love seat and starts at the beginning. He tells me about Daniel's prison projects, the name he has made for himself, and his addiction to helping others. His good fight. He tells me about the program Daniel created that teaches inmates how to read and write at a college level and produce SAT scores that will get them into college. He tells me about Daniel's Sustainability in Prisons Project, a program that brings science and nature into prison while reducing the environmental, economic, and human costs of them. He even tells me about the female prison guard Daniel saved from another inmate's attack.

I absorb all of this, and I feel numb. I'm slightly relieved that he has spent his prison sentence atoning for his criminal act. But I didn't know much about Daniel before that night. Is it all an act? Does he regret his crime? What does Jacob think about all of this?

"You once told me that your relationship with him was complicated. Is it still?"

"Daniel has always been a complicated person. Even when we were kids. You have to understand him to know him, and even then, you don't."

"When you were sick, I saw a picture of your family at your place. The picture was taken at the cottage." Jacob's eyes flicker warmly. "You and Daniel were teenagers. You all looked so happy. Such a complete family."

"That's my favorite picture of us. It's amazing how much things change, how people change."

"Do you think he regrets it?"

"Yes," Jacob says, the word falling like the first sprinkle of an eventual storm, with confidence and purpose.

"How do you know?"

"He told me."

It stuns me that I have been a topic of conversation between the two of them. Even briefly. As if they were discussing the weather or the score of a football game, as if it were normal to dip a foot into the waters of the murky past.

"Does he talk about me much?"

"Occasionally."

"What does he say?"

Jacob rubs his neck. I realize the awkward situation I have asked him to plant himself in the middle of, to speak on Daniel's behalf, but over these last few months, we have shared things we've never told another soul.

"He asked if you hate him."

"He actually cares about that?"

"He's not an evil person."

"He knows that I'm back in Savannah?"

"Yes, Birdie told him."

"She knows?" I ask, my voice rising.

Jacob looks at me. "Small town."

I take a deep breath to refocus my thoughts. Finally, after a few moments: "Have you…kept your promise?"

"Yes," he says. Final. Exact. "But there's something else you need to know." I watch him gather his thoughts. "NBC wants to do an interview with Daniel about his Sustainability in Prisons Project. The interview is scheduled to air live in a few weeks."

I stare at him, blinking; my thoughts scatter like autumn leaves in the wind. Of everything I expected Jacob to tell me, this is unexpected. "Are they going to bring up the assault?"

"I don't know, but he may."

"What's he going to say?"

"That he regrets what happened."

"But not that it *did* happen."

I stand abruptly and begin pacing the space in front of the love seat. Jacob remains seated.

"I can't hide a television interview from Alana. I don't know what I'm going to do."

Jacob casts his gaze around the dark bookstore, to rows of stacked books, book covers with frozen smiles, and when he returns his gaze, it's pained. "You could tell him. Tell her."

I shake my head. "No."

"Sara…this could all be over." He stands, taking my wrists into his hands and finding my eyes. "I'll be right there with you. We can do it together."

"I can't."

"You can. You told Marsha."

"That's different. She's not going to try to take Alana from me."

"He's not going to do that."

"How do you know? Birdie never accepted that Daniel raped me. How is she going to feel knowing the truth? That she has a granddaughter I kept from her?"

"It happened. She can't deny it anymore."

"What do I say to Alana? How do I tell her?"

"You tell her the truth. That her father hurt you. That you love her so much, and you wanted to make sure that he would never hurt you two again. That she is nothing like him."

He makes it sound easy. All my fears and concerns addressed and wrapped up so nicely like a Christmas present.

"Have you forgiven him?"

He looks away, releasing my wrists.

"Why not?"

"I was so angry with him for such a long time. I hated what he did. What you've been through these last eight years. The effects of his crime on my family. But I believe in atonement. A person should be allowed to start over. Maybe I believe that because he's my brother. I haven't forgiven him, but I believe I can."

I stare up at the ceiling as my breathing increases. "I can't lose her. I can't go through another trial."

"That won't happen."

"Promise me, no matter what happens, that you will never tell them about Alana."

He turns his whole body away from me. "Sara...he's dying."

The shock throws me off-balance as if I have been pushed. Then I refocus on Jacob, standing frozen in the shadows. I lift my hand to touch his back. Invisible pain crashes off him in waves almost palpable under my touch. I pause, understanding that this touch is one not just of comfort but of affection. His shoulder blades flinch at my unexpected touch.

"What happened with the bone marrow transplant?" I say to his back.

"His infection worsened. While they were treating that, they discovered that the cancer has spread to his lungs and other places."

"I'm so sorry, Jacob," I say as he turns to face me. It feels strange to apologize for his pain when the source is Daniel. But I want to be there for him.

He takes in a deep breath and blinks his face into a smile. But it's forced, controlled. He takes both of my hands in his. "I appreciate that, but you don't have to comfort me. I'm here for you. I didn't come here to talk about that."

"Jacob," I say, searching for his focus. "Talk to me."

"It's okay. I'm fine."

"You're not fine."

"I can't talk to you about him. It's not fair to you."

We aren't that different, I realize, when he looks away from me, concealing the pain that I know he feels. Two people stung by the same person: Daniel. Me hurt by him. Jacob hurt for him. Our pain different but relevant to one another. We have given each other a flashlight and invited the other to shine a light on the darkness that has plagued us for years, making it a little less frightening.

The silence between us is unlike any other before, full of conflicting emotions tugging at each other. We hold each other in the dark, our chests rising and falling together, the bookstore steeped in shadows and illuminated by moonlight. We don't have any answers. Just questions in a sea of unknowns. I don't know who is holding whom, who is comforting whom. It doesn't matter. We are two people bound by common circumstance, comforted by the fact that we are not alone.

JACOB

———

I WASH MY HANDS, the dirt retreating in a cyclone of brown as I watch Alana and Sara turn over dirt for our next planting. I'm not bold enough nor could I have expected that when I returned home I would be here exactly. I had no idea that my path would lead me to discover that I had a niece and to fall in love with an amazing woman.

And to feel a tug of betrayal against my family.

Hosea and Sylvia shuffle into the kitchen just as I reach for a towel.

"How's it going?" she asks, opening the refrigerator and grabbing a bottle of water.

"Pretty good."

"Alana has been so excited about that garden. It's all she's been talking about. I told her I wouldn't mind us trying our hand at planting some greens."

She continues talking and I try to look attentive, but out of the corner of my eye, I see Alana and Sara playing in the garden. They are spraying each other with water. Sara is smiling, laughing as Alana chases her with the water hose. They are lost in their own world of love. The innocence of it all makes me lighter.

Or maybe it is something deeper, more unknown than love. Sara has gotten to the heart of me, and I'm not sure what I feel isn't more than love. Last night I held her against me under the light of the moon. Her body pressed against mine made the pain of Daniel's prognosis easier to comprehend. Equal to the power of that is that she let me hold her at all. Watching her now, I wonder if my heart will ever be large enough to handle what I feel for her. She let me in, into her life, into her heart. She trusts me with Alana. She has given it all to me, free and clear.

It isn't until Hosea puts his hand on my shoulder that I realize I have been staring. He gives Sylvia a look, and she leaves the room.

Hosea follows my gaze outside to Sara and Alana and then looks back at me. A grin grows across on his face, and he chuckles to himself as he walks away from the window and sits at a kitchen chair and starts spreading mayonnaise on two pieces of bread. I turn back to the window and begin reciting a poem that has popped into my head.

"in the rain—
darkness, the sunset
being sheathed i sit and

think of you
the holy
city which is your face
your little cheeks the streets
of smiles…"

I stop, forgetting the next line.
Hosea's voice booms around the room.

"your eyes half-
thrush
half-angel and your drowsy
lips where float flowers of kiss
and…"

He stops and looks at me, urging me to continue.

"there is the sweet shy pirouette
your hair
and then
your dancesong
soul. rarely-beloved
a single star is
uttered, and i
think of you."

I move away from the window and over to Hosea.

"I'm falling in love with your daughter."

He nods in a way that's both knowing and accepting.

"I don't know if she'll have me because of my family, the circumstances. But my intentions are honorable. I hope to have your blessing."

It feels old-fashioned. Asking the father for permission to date his daughter. But these are no ordinary circumstances. I know the care and well-being of Sara and Alana are important to him. He will be gone soon enough—I know he knows this—and I want him to have peace that they will still know unconditional love.

He places several slices of roast beef and cheese on his bread.

"I whispered, 'I am too young,'
And then, 'I am old enough';
Wherefore I threw a penny
To find out if I might love.
'Go and love, go and love, young man,
If the lady be young and fair,'
Ah, penny, brown penny, brown penny,
I am looped in the loops of her hair.

Oh, love is the crooked thing,
There is nobody wise enough
To find out all that is in it,
For he would be thinking of love

Till the stars had run away,
And the shadows eaten the moon.
Ah, penny, brown penny, brown penny,
One cannot begin it too soon."

He pats my hand and inclines his head toward the window.

"No, I can't," I say.

He smiles again, not looking at me, his eyes on the sandwich in front of him.

Even as I confess my love for her, a sharp pang that goes through me, sudden.

"I'm torn. I don't know if I'm doing the right thing by Daniel, my family, if I'm betraying them somehow."

"If you can dream—and not make dreams your master;
If you can think—and not make thoughts your aim;
If you can meet with Triumph and Disaster
And treat those imposters just the same;
If you can bear to hear the truth you've spoken
Twisted by knaves to make a trap for fools,
Or watch the things you gave your life to, broken,
And stoop and build 'em up with wornout tools..."

He stops, his eyes searching for more.

"And—which is more—you'll be a Man, my son," I say, remembering the end of Kipling's poem. This stanza of Kipling's gives advice on not allowing our thoughts and dreams to

343

control us or being too influenced by success or failure. Hosea is telling me anything of value that's broken is worth fixing.

I stand to leave but turn back to him. "Thank you for not throwing me out on the curb when I first came to visit you." He laughs. "Thank you for allowing me into your family. I will take care of them."

He stands and pats me on the shoulder.

———

Birdie kneels, pulling weeds from a row of annuals that flanks Naomi's grave. There is no sound except the late-summer wind rustling the Spanish moss dripping from the live oak trees. By late August, most of Bonaventure Cemetery is devoid of color, stripped by the summer sun. But not Naomi's and my father's graves, which explode in color unusual for the end of the summer, Naomi's is a sea of yellow, her favorite color, and Dad's is a kaleidoscope of red, blue, and purple.

Birdie sprinkles water on the newly planted annuals and pats down the soil where she pulled weeds. I stand behind her, watching her work. She's a frequent visitor here, removing dead flowers and planting new ones a few times a month. This is my first visit in eight years.

She finishes and stands, folding the gardening kneeler. I close my eyes and bow my head.

I don't know why it took me so long to come here. Now I know why you wanted me to come home. You knew. She looks just like you. She is you. But I guess you knew that too. She's going to change the world. Just like you wanted to. It used to hurt when I thought about you. But lately, it doesn't hurt as much anymore. It doesn't hurt to remember you. I've been telling them about you, how you gave Daniel the scar over his eye, how I always thought you would run off and join the circus. Birdie and I heard your favorite song on the radio, and she actually asked me about it. Can you believe that? You were always the best of us, and we will never forget you. Say hi to Dad for me. Tell him I found my earthly Aurora. I love you.

I open my eyes, and Birdie's are still closed, her lips moving without sound. When she opens them, she sighs.

"I want to see her," she says. "Sara."

The mention of Sara's name takes me aback. "Why?"

"Why? How can you ask me that? Because she took everything from me, from us."

"Birdie…" I don't finish. I don't have the words.

"Your brother should be here. Your father. We should be here together as a family. She took that away from us."

I pinch the bridge of my nose between my thumb and forefinger and breathe loudly. "Sara is not to blame for what happened to our family."

"Well, who is?"

"We are."

She unfolds her garden kneeler and returns to pulling weeds like a maniac. I kneel beside her and place my hand on hers. "Birdie…he did it."

She jerks her hand away from me in disgust. The scowl

from her eyes could cut through a rock. "How can you say that? Your own brother." She stands abruptly and walks toward my truck, haphazardly refolding the kneeler. "You never believed him. You wanted him to be guilty. That's why you testified against him."

I follow behind her. "He's going to admit it during the interview."

She stops suddenly but doesn't turn around. I take another step closer to her. "He told me what happened. He told me he did it."

She turns slowly. "Is this why you came back? Is this why you've been going to see him? To get him to admit to something he didn't do?"

Her words sting. "I came home to put my family back together."

"Family?" she says, squinting her eyes into slits. "Family?" Each time she says it, the word changes in tone. "You left your family. Left us. Left your brother to die."

"I was wrong to leave. I regret that. I regret the time I lost with you, with him. I should have stayed. I should have been there for you. For Daniel. But I'm here now."

"You're not here for us. You're here to feed your conscience," she says, her words biting with every syllable. "I will never forgive you for what you did. Never!"

I've heard these words before when she hurled them at me all those years ago. They hurt then but not now. "You may never forgive me for what I did. But I forgive you."

"Excuse me? You forgive me? Forgive me for what?"

"Daniel raped Sara. He did. And that's what he is going to say during the interview. He's going to tell the whole world what really happened. What you never wanted to believe happened." She turns and walks away, but I keep talking. "You didn't want to believe it because you were grieving for Naomi."

Her name falls out of my mouth naturally and unforced like it had been wedged there and finally worked itself loose. "We all loved Naomi. Me. Daniel. Dad. We were all grieving for her. He was hurting, Birdie. Sara just happened to be in the wrong place at the wrong time. She didn't deserve that or what we put her through after."

"I don't want to listen to any more of this." She pulls on the truck handle, but the door doesn't open.

"He's dying. Let him absolve himself of this. Before he dies. Let him accept this."

"Why are you driving this piece of junk?" she says, yanking harder and harder, her hair freeing itself from her updo with each pull. "Your father leaves you millions, and this is what you drive? Hundreds of thousands of dollars spent on your Ivy League education, and you have scarred hands and live in a shack."

"I am my father's son."

"Don't you speak of him. Not here. Not now."

"Someone has to. Someone has to talk about them."

Birdie slaps my face before I even know she's done it. A quick smack that pops like a clap. "How dare you? I loved your father and your sister."

I don't touch my cheek, ease the sting, despite the urgency to do so. I sit in the pain and accept it for myself and her.

"I wish it were you instead of Daniel. He would have made something of himself."

Instead of feeling hurt, I consider her sorrow. Perhaps she needed to say that. Maybe I even owed her that for leaving. "I know you don't mean that. I know it's coming from a place of pain and grief. I love you anyway, Birdie. I forgive you. I forgive you for everything you have said and done, then and now."

"Forgive me? Forgive *me*?" Again, every time she repeats, the tone changes, her voice rising in anger as if someone is turning up the dial notch by notch. "For what?" She doesn't wait for an answer but huffs and begins walking down the highway, her heels scuffing the asphalt.

"Daniel is going to die," I yell to her. This stops her in her tracks. "And we have to face it. We can't ignore it like we did with Naomi or Dad. We only have each other."

I know my words, the reality, reach her. It tilts her head downward for a second, before she continues stomping down the street.

———

It's past midnight, and I can't sleep. I sink into my chair on the porch. The sky is black, a sea of vastness before me. The salt air is thick and still. Naomi is no longer with me, guiding my thoughts, her chair empty.

I try not to dwell on it, the incident at the cemetery or the fight with Daniel, but the memory of them floats into my awareness, the thought leading me into a darkness as gloomy as the sky. I have no name, no solution for the emotions flowing through me. I've always needed space around my head to think, to mull things over and test conclusions. Particularly challenging problems, especially those that I cannot deduce, produce anxiety in me, creating a crippling paralysis in my mind. As a scientist, I believe every problem has a solution. Everything can be reasoned and solved. But making decisions in a pressured environment when things are beyond my control overwhelms me and shuts down my ability to think.

Let us, then, be up and doing,
With a heart for any fate;
Still achieving, still pursuing,
Learn to labor and to wait.

I need time.

I reach for my cell phone and dial Sara's number, aware of the hour and not caring. I want to hear her voice. She answers on the second ring.

"Hello." Her voice is low, muted.

"Did I wake you?"

"No, I'm up, writing. I finished another poem." There's a pause. "Jacob…what's wrong?"

"Tell me about the poem. Please."

Another beat of silence lapses after my appeal. Then: "Yeah…they've been pouring out of me. I don't have enough for a collection yet, and some of them are pretty rough, but it's a start."

"That's great. So great."

"We were just talking about you earlier," she says. She tells me that they were making their shopping list for Pizza Friday and wanted to introduce some new toppings. They wanted to see if I had any ideas.

"I'm not going to be able to make it to Pizza Friday this week."

Her tone changes into a concerned one. "Are you okay? What's wrong?"

"Nothing," I lie, my tone escalating on the last syllable. "There are a few things I need to work out."

"Would you like some company? I could come out there. Make a better beef stew."

My heart warms at her offer. "It's not that. I just need to be alone for a while."

Her voice catches. "You've been spending so much time with us. Are we crowding you?"

"Oh no," I say. The implication that she could be the source of what pains me causes my stomach to knot. "Sara…I love spending time with you." I allow that statement to linger before continuing. I want it to expand and settle inside her. "And Alana, Hosea, and Sylvia. These last few months have been some of the happiest days of my life. I just need to deal with a few family issues. I hope you understand."

"Of course," she says. From her tone, I can tell she does. "I'll tell Sylvia not to buy any anchovies or pineapples this week."

I smile at her joke and wish she could see it. "I'll call you in a few days."

I place the phone on the arm of my chair and reach for the book at my fingertips.

If you can bear to hear the truth you've spoken
Twisted by knaves to make a trap for fools,
Or watch the things you gave your life to, broken,
And stoop and build 'em up with worn-out tools.

Movement catches my eye. I stand and look down at the dock to see a bright-yellow light. It's Naomi. She turns to me and smiles before diving off the dock and, something tells me, out of my life forever.

SARA

———

ON THE DAY OF Daniel's televised interview, I wake up smiling. I dreamed of Jacob. His green eyes, his lips, his bright smile. He has been away for a week, his presence leaving a noticeable void in the house and within me.

"I miss Jacob," Alana announces at breakfast. Dad and Sylvia trade looks that convey their agreement. I try to play it coy, but I miss him too.

I don't plan to watch the interview. As I have over the past eight years of my life, I want to carry on, keep moving forward. Instead, I plan on conducting an end-of-summer inventory that will keep me at the bookstore late into the night, missing the interview and keeping Alana with me so she won't see it either.

The day proceeds well enough with the steady traffic of students and other customers. With school starting soon, we have been fielding orders for textbooks and classic novels. Finally, by the late afternoon, we have a break to breathe and restock and straighten shelves. Dennis has just returned from the back room when the doorbell chimes.

It has been years since I have seen her, but I recognize her immediately as she stands rod straight by the front desk.

Birdie.

Crow's-feet flank the corners of her eyes, her face fuller and round, but she is still as gray as she was eight years ago. Her stark-white suit with a navy paisley scarf draping her shoulder casts a bright glow around her, almost illuminating her.

A twist of anxiety turns in my gut, but I take a deep breath, and I whisper to Dennis to go next door and ask Ms. Cookson at the stationery store to keep Alana there until I come get her.

I point my chin upward to exude confidence just as Birdie reaches me. Her perfume, floral, finds me first. She inspects me from head to toe, taking in all of me, but she doesn't speak; instead, she smiles, a forced smile that she drops too quickly.

"May I help you?" I say, swallowing hard to stabilize my voice.

Her eyes sweep across the bookstore before returning to me. "Do you remember me?"

I cackle, a hideous sound. "Are you kidding me?"

A memory surfaces then, of Birdie in the courtroom, Daniel sitting slouched in his chair while one of his lawyers sought to discredit me. He approached me as if we were friends catching up. *Ms. Lancaster, I know this is difficult for you,* he said without a southern drawl, *but I want to ask you about the night in question. You can understand how important it is for the jury to understand exactly what happened? Did you know the defendant before that night? How many drinks would you say you consumed?* Throughout the questioning, Daniel sank lower in his chair as if hoping it would swallow him, but Birdie held a perfect posture.

Now, Birdie adjusts her purse on her arm, tucking it in the crook of her elbow. "I heard you were back."

"Yes," I say, waiting for more and sliding a quick glance at the door.

"I heard about your father." She pauses. "How is he?"

Her feigned politeness bothers me, and I find strength in that. "Is there something I can help you with?"

"You've done enough already."

Her abrupt statement whips me back into focus. "Excuse me?"

"Don't stand there and pretend you don't know what I'm talking about."

She knows. She knows about Alana. "I don't." Inwardly, I'm trembling, but I keep my expression taut.

She takes a tiny step toward me, her heeled shoes clicking in step. "The interview?"

My entire body relaxes, my chest opening in relief. She notices, though my reason for relaxing is not the reason she imagines. "Of course you're glad he's planning to lie on live television. Don't think for a minute I don't know what you are. *You* are the liar."

Her words bite, even now, across space and time. And yet, it fades; the venom of her words is no longer a death sentence.

My turn to step forward, and I stretch my body as tall as it will extend. "I told the truth."

She waves her hand. "That's all behind him now. He's being released soon." She narrows her eyes at me, her face taut, her forehead puckered. "Stay away from my boys."

Her words reverberate through me but fail to do damage. So many years ago, her stare, unwavering and resolute, scared the eighteen-year-old I was. I remember I ran into Birdie in the courthouse hall on my way into the first day of the trial. I averted my eyes, too afraid to meet hers, as we walked past each other. But not anymore. She seems different, weaker, her voice thin and weary. Her once-fierce eyes are now bruised with pain and exhaustion. Or maybe I am stronger, immune to her ways. I know her better now, understand her. And I am done running and hiding from her.

"Do your *boys* know that you are here defending them?" I ask. Does Jacob know? No way he does, or he would have warned me first. I trust him, but I want her to have to face what she's doing.

"No, but that's what a mother does. She protects her children."

I smile. "I couldn't agree more."

My statement and grin catch her off guard, and her eyes widen as she considers it.

"Is that all?" I ask, looking pointedly at the door and moving back around the desk. "I have work to do."

She walks to the door. "Send my regards to your father."

I watch her leave, the door clanging as it closes.

Birdie took nothing from me when she left and yet I feel lighter, free. As if the foot that pressed on my throat has been lifted. The anger, which I had expected, is slight. Instead, sorrow floods me. For Jacob and, surprisingly, for her. She dedicated her life to defending Daniel. And in the process, she has missed out on a life, something I understand all too well.

And yet, I have done the impossible. I faced her, head on, and came out unscathed. That means something.

———

The first crash comes while I am in the back room scanning the last of the books. I am not sure what to make of the sound. I turn the music down and listen intently before walking out to the front. Outside sounds, tires driving over fresh puddles, are now inside. One of the large front windows is gone, a million diamonds now sparkling on the floor. Before I can finish processing the severity of the situation, a second crash shrieks in my ears. Instinctively, I duck behind the counter, my heart racing. Then there is a third crash of glass, and a blunt object skips off the front table display, taking with it several books and rolling across the floor. A rock.

In the distance, I hear sirens moving closer. I run next door to retrieve Alana. I find Ms. Cookson and Alana hunkered down behind her front desk. All her windows are broken too. Alana launches herself in my arms.

"What's going on?" Ms. Cookson asks.

"I'm not sure," I say, holding Alana close to me. She's quiet, trembling. "I heard sirens. I think someone has already called the police."

As soon as the words leave my lips, we hear another crash followed by laughter and the quick patter of feet fading in the distance.

"That sounds like Mr. Whitehead's store," Ms. Cookson whispers.

We cower down behind Ms. Cookson's counter until we hear the crunch of glass, and a beam of light skates across the dark store.

"Anyone in here?" a deep voice says. "It's the police."

Thirty minutes later, I'm back at the bookstore, assessing the damage. All three of the large front windows are gone as well as the glass in the door. Two officers are behind me and begin their own investigation, including asking me questions. The adrenaline from before subsides as I sit on the couch.

Outside, a loud bang, metal hitting something, then the screech of tires, followed by the sudden slam of a door, grabs everyone's attention.

Alana sees him first. "Jacob!"

He doesn't bother opening the door. He contorts his long

body through the shard-edged frame. A young officer attempts to stop him, but he blows past him. Jacob doesn't see the officer, his focus latched on to me and Alana. Locke is a couple of steps behind him; he stops and speaks to the officer. Jacob reaches us in three large strides, shattered glass crunching underneath his feet. But to my eye, it happens through slowed time. As Jacob walks toward me, sounds wind down into a blur so that the only thing I hear is the rapid cadence of my heart.

"Are you okay?" he asks, his face inches from mine. I hear him speak, but the sound is muffled as if said underwater. There are so many things I want to say to him. But a torrent of gratitude, relief, and passion surges to a flash point and bottle-necks in my throat. Before I can answer, his hands brace the sides of my face, studying it. His green eyes burn into mine. I can only nod, rendered speechless by his display of emotion and awash with my own. He kneels and scoops Alana up in his arm. He turns back to me and takes my chin in his hand, lifting my face to his.

"Look at me," he says, his eyes searching. "Are you okay?"

"We're fine," I finally say, my head clearing.

His face relaxes. "What about you?" he says to Alana, rubbing her back in small circles. "Are you okay?"

Alana tells him that she was playing with Smokey the cat next door when the first rock came in through the bookstore's window. Jacob grimaces, curses under his breath, and pulls me closer, his arm around my waist, just as the officer he ignored walks toward us.

"How did you know?"

"I was at the marina when the first call came over the radio. Locke heard it."

"I can't believe you're here," I say.

He stares down at me and says, "I will always be here for you."

The officer says to me, "It looks like some kids just playing around. They got almost every shop's windows on this street. But we got one of them. We'll have the rest by morning."

I nod, calmed by Jacob's hand lingering on my back.

"Is there anything else you need, Officer?" Jacob asks briskly but politely.

The officer flips open his notepad. "I'd like to ask Ms. Lancaster a few more questions." I sigh. "What time—?"

"Listen," Jacob says, interrupting him. "Can this wait until the morning? They're both pretty tired and shaken up. I want to get them out of here."

"Absolutely," the officer says, closing his notepad as quickly as he opened it. "Take your family home. If we need anything else, we'll contact you."

Jacob doesn't bother correcting the officer. Neither do I. I guess it didn't matter as much that we weren't a family as much as we looked like one. Jacob's and Alana's skin tone the same tanned brown, their eyes matching, their resemblance obvious to all. Jacob holding me close to him. To the officer, we look and act like a family. We are a family.

Locke signals to Jacob, and he lowers a sleepy Alana to the ground. "You guys get your stuff. I'll take you home."

Alana complies. I watch Locke and Jacob talk at the door before grabbing my purse from behind the counter.

"We'll get this fixed for you, don't worry, Sara," Locke says.

I thank him and Jacob leads us to his truck. I enter first and then Alana, who immediately plants her head in my lap and falls asleep. Jacob closes the door behind us. He enters on the driver's side and the dimensions of the small cab put us together, our legs touching, shoulder to shoulder. Next to him, feeling the warmth of his body and the rhythmic rise and fall of his chest, I feel completely safe. I lean my head on his shoulder and relax against him, the scent of him fresh and masculine. He slides his arm around me as I settle deeper into his chest, his heart throbbing strongly under my ear.

We ride like that, in the darkness and silence, to my father's house. At a stoplight, the blanched light from a streetlight illuminates Jacob's face. He is focused on the road ahead, the truck idling, rocking gently. The way the light frames his face, I can see him fully now, finally, with such clarity and focus. In it, I find solace and a sense of calmness, and I know with an absolute certainty what I want. I want Jacob in my life, and all that comes with him. The bad with the good.

"Thank you," I say to him, looking up at him, my head still on his shoulder. He looks at me, a spark lit in his eyes, and sweeps the hair from my forehead, kisses it. One single kiss. He doesn't advance his affections beyond that. Like he is waiting for permission. I take my hand to his cheek, lean up, and touch my lips against his. We kiss slowly and softly, tasting, until a honk from a car behind alerts us that the light has changed.

At home, he carries Alana from the truck up to her bedroom. I follow and watch as he lovingly places her on her bed. I remove her shoes and pull the comforter over her before leaving her room.

Downstairs, I see Jacob in the foyer on his cell phone, pacing. The foyer is dimly lit by the streetlight out front and the moonlight. As I descend the stairs, I hear him say, "I'll be right there," before hanging up.

"You're leaving?" I ask, stopping two steps from the bottom.

Jacob slips his phone into his pocket. "I'm going to help Locke and a few others board up the bookstore and the other shops."

I want him to stay, but I appreciate the fact that Locke and he are thinking about the windows, and his selfless act only makes me admire him more; my passion for him swells like a balloon.

He walks over to me and stops, his head level with mine. I search for his face in the shadow of the foyer. In the faint glow, his face begins to take shape. I cradle his cheek, and he settles into it, his eyes closing. I watch his face relax and the slow intake of breath.

"We…I missed you," I say, caressing his cheek. "Are you okay?"

He opens his eyes and takes my hands into his, bringing our entwined fingers to his lips and kissing them. The act pushes waves of energy through my body. "I am now."

He studies my face, his eyes first searching, then his fingertips, running them down my cheek, his thumb across my lips. His gaze falls to my mouth. Every move is gentle and deliberate, the explanation of something communicated beyond words, evidence of something deep and pure and real.

"I love looking at you," he whispers against the darkness.

I lean in and touch my lips against his. We kiss, slow at first, our lips exploring, locking together, and then, suddenly, the kiss grows, unfolding in layers and expanding. He pulls me into him, his arms tightening around my waist. I wrap my arms around his neck, my fingers curving around the nape, and I allow myself to fall into him.

The kiss ends, but we stay together, our foreheads touching, our breathing rapid. I'm clothed, but I feel completely naked, vulnerable to him, to the opening of my heart to him.

"Jacob," I whisper, my body buzzing with electricity. There is no need on the other side of calling his name. I want to say his name in a new context with new meaning and understanding. I want to call this feeling by its name.

He knows.

He is gentle yet intentional to my vulnerability, arching me, tilting my head back, his hand palmed in my hair until I'm stretched out on the stairs. He drags his fingertips around my neck, across my collarbone, and down to the top of my breasts. My skin prickles at his touch, rising to meet him. His mouth retraces the route of his fingers, his lips hovering, brushing, and trailing kisses down my throat. The straps of my dress slide down my shoulders, and he buries his face in my breasts, moaning into my skin and grazing my nipples. I feel the heat rising on my skin and between my legs.

Low, soft groans escape my lips, and my body bends and bows, accepting and absorbing every kiss, every touch. It surprises me. This feeling, a feeling unlike anything I've felt before. And yet, my body knows what to do, how to move, what sounds to make.

And so does Jacob. He's read my body's every thought and knows, knows how to touch me, where to touch me. He always knows.

"Yes," I whisper to nothing. It's a plea and a prayer, permission, really, to the question I hear, though he doesn't ask with words but with his hands and mouth desperately, hungrily devouring my body.

One word is all he needs.

He kneels between my legs and slides my dress up my thighs. It's a halo around me as he pulls off my panties. He moans deep. "Open for me." And my knees splay open like butterfly wings. My mind spins off on waves and waves of pleasure as the heat of Jacob's tongue finds and works the heart of me. It's like wildfire, consuming and hot, spreading. My body tightens around him, coiling tighter and tighter. I cry out, my back arching off the stairs, as I come undone, as pleasure washes over me, deep and rolling, and my body ripples around him.

Then, I'm floating, moving up the stairs, and Jacob's there, looking at me, his eyes soft and wanting, holding me. He places me on the bed and removes my dress, my entire body on display, exposed. And I like it, like being in control of my body and yet surrendering to it, to its sounds, its urges, its movements. I open my eyes, and Jacob's watching as I move against the sheets, still transfixed in the aftermath of his pleasure. He's fully clothed, an unnecessary boundary because I trust him with my body, with all of me. He's the reason for this freedom, this pleasure. I moan and reach for him, removing his shirt.

We kiss again, lost in each other, searching, satisfying a longing. The kiss punctuating everything that had been slowly building between us and marking both the end and the beginning of something we have not yet defined.

His cell phone pings, and reality slams back into sharp focus. He forgot. So did I. The windows. He curses under his breath and sighs, a breathless sound full of regret. He sits up.

"You have to go," I say, feeling bereft, wanting more, so much more.

Jacob looks down at me, desire and adoration flooding his eyes as he takes in every exposed inch of me. "I promised."

I touch his face again. "A man of unbroken promises."

"That's not easy when you're in bed with a beautiful woman," he says, lowering his head and kissing my shoulder, my neck. His lips brush my collarbone, and his hand moves to the curve of my breast before he stops and stands with a groan. I chuckle as he pulls a blanket over me.

As he slips back on his shirt and heads toward the door, I try not to wonder when he will come back. He is a man of many promises, I know, and one of them is probably a promise to his family. "Will you come back?" I ask, sitting up, my voice cracking unexpectedly.

He stops abruptly and walks back to me, sitting on the bed, his brows peaked in a question. "Of course. Why would you ask that?"

I let my gaze fall to my lap and twist my fingers. He notices and takes them into his hands. "You do this when you're nervous. What's wrong?"

"You've been gone. I didn't know if—"

"That has nothing to do with you."

It is the barest version of the truth. I smile through it, but for the first time since I met him, I don't believe him.

He brushes my cheek with his forefinger and looks at me with an intense longing.

> *"I will find out where she has gone,*
> *And kiss her lips and take her hands;*
> *And walk among long dappled grass,*
> *And pluck till time and times are done,*
> *The silver apples of the moon,*
> *The golden apples of the sun."*

Staring at me steadily and taking my hands into his once more, he says, "I've finally found you. I'm never letting you go. I need you."

I smile as Yeats's words invade my soul. And Jacob's own words are so pure, so honest, the expression in his green eyes so unadulterated and raw. I press my forehead against his. "I need you too."

I feel no fear in saying those words. No doubt. No shame. Just a complete and absolute sense of rightness.

Jacob tells me to get some sleep and that he'll be back first thing in the morning. He doesn't kiss me again. Instead, he touches my nose and leaves, a move by design, I think. Had he kissed me one more time, he would not have left and I would not have let him go.

JACOB

———

IT TAKES US MOST of the night to board up the bookstore and the five other shops. Only when the sun breaks the horizon do we drill the last screw. I thank the men who came to help and press a few bills in their hands for their time. Locke's twisted lips and folded arms tells me it's too much before glaring at the even larger wad of bills I have for him. He tells me he'll call his nephew about replacing the glass at the bookstore and then walks away, leaving the money in my hands.

I check the time. It's 6:32 a.m. I contemplate driving to Birdie's house to sleep, but Sara's face, her body, floats into my awareness, the softness of her lips, the taste of her skin. I replay the conversation just before I left, our admittance that we needed each other. It is all out now. We walked into a spiderweb, and there is no way to fully lose it, or the feeling of it. I told her I would be there first thing in the morning, and I yearn to see her face, touch her again. I recall the way she whispered my name last night, breathlessly, the way she moved against the bed, wringing out every ounce of pleasure from her orgasm, and that's all it takes for me to start driving toward her.

I pull my truck in front of Hosea's house and kill the motor. The house is still, bathed in a cast of fog. It's early. Too early to knock on the door, to wake the house. I settle into the front seat, crossing my arms across my chest, and decide to wait in the truck for at least another hour or two.

It isn't until I hear several soft taps on the window that I realize I fell asleep.

It's Sylvia, holding the morning newspaper and clutching her lavender robe closed. I rub my eyes with the heel of my hand and roll the window down.

"Did you sleep in your truck last night?" she asks, casting her inquisitive eyes over the front seat of the truck.

"No," I say, stifling a yawn. "I got here"—I check my watch and see it's 7:55—"about an hour and a half ago."

"What's going on?"

I tell her about the kids and the windows. She shakes her head in disbelief.

"Damn kids," she says, ushering me out of the truck. "Come inside. You can take a shower and have a nap before breakfast."

An hour later, I'm inside Hosea's house and at the kitchen table. He's making pancakes while Sylvia starts the coffee. As he waits for the air bubbles to appear and the edges to brown, I recall the story of last night to him and watch his face register from anger to sadness to appreciation. He pats me on the back.

"The nephew of a friend of mine owns the company that replaced all of the glass during the renovation. They have all of the measurements on file, so the glass should be replaced by the end of the day," I say to Hosea. "Don't worry about anything."

"I didn't know you two discussed the renovations," Sylvia says.

Hosea turns his back to us, which seems to stop Sylvia from saying anything else, and pours the batter for another pancake on the griddle. I open a cabinet door and retrieve a mug before easing into a chair.

"Thank you, Jacob. For your help," Sylvia says, planting her hand on my shoulder. For a minute, I wonder if she's guessed something, but then she says, "It's good to see you. We missed you."

A sleepy Alana hobbles into the kitchen carrying her LT notebook and mumbles an apathetic good morning. She's wearing the same clothes from yesterday, her face still tender and puffy from sleep. She walks over to me and climbs into my lap without thought, facing the table, and rests the back of her head against my shoulder. My chest swells, and I kiss her head and hold her tight. Even after all this time, her existence still conjures an instinctive reaction in me, a stirring of love, of protection. It's a feeling, I'm learning, that never subsides.

"Hey, ladybug," Sylvia says. "I heard you had a long night."

"Mom let me go to Ms. Cookson's store and play with Smokey. And then a rock came through the window. Poor Smokey. He was so scared. He ran under the desk and wouldn't come out."

"Were you scared?" Sylvia asks, listening intently with Hosea to the harrowing tale.

Alana shakes her head. "Mom ran in, and she looked really scared, and then I got really scared, but then Jacob busted through the door and got us."

Hosea and Sylvia turn to me. "You didn't mention that," Sylvia says with a crooked grin. "You busted through the door?"

"Not exactly. The glass was already broken."

"He drove his truck on the sidewalk."

Hosea and Sylvia look at me again. "The police had sectioned off the street. It was the only way I could get there."

"What else did Jacob do?" Sylvia asks.

"He pushed the police out of the way and picked me up."

"I brushed, gently, past him."

Alana continues, "And then the police started asking Mom all of these questions, and then Jacob told the police that we were tired and he was taking us home."

"Sounds like we missed quite the event," Sylvia says to Hosea before standing and picking up the coffee pot.

Hosea says to me:

"And, while the mortal mist is gathering, draws
His breath in confidence of Heaven's applause:

This is the happy Warrior; this is he
That every man in arms should wish to be."

I wave a dismissive hand. "Thank you, but there's nothing I wouldn't do for them, all of you."

"How's Sara?" Sylvia says, pouring coffee into our mugs.

A flash of Sara's naked body fills my mind, and I close my eyes to trap the vision. She wears nothing so well.

A smile pushes at the corner of my lips before I answer, a response that Sylvia notices. She looks at me over the top of her mug as she takes a sip. There's a smirk in her eyes. "A little startled by it all, but she was fine when I left her."

"I bet," Sylvia says, smiling wide, eyeing my reaction.

Hosea finishes the pancakes and slides two on a plate for Alana, who crawls out of my lap and into her own chair.

I'm buttering my pancakes when Sara walks into the kitchen. I abruptly stand, the chair dragging across the hardwood floor.

"Hi," she says, her face brightening when she notices me.

"Hi."

A moment of stillness, but not silence. Bathed under the morning light, her hair flowing, free from its usual braid, she is stunning. I clutch the back of the chair and resist the urge to cross the kitchen and scoop her up in my arms.

Last night, I countered every move she made first, allowing her to dictate what she wanted and how far she wanted to go. She whispered my name, and I knew. She said yes, and I knew. Then, she opened her world to me. What a world.

Now, for a moment, I think she may have changed her mind. That as she drifted toward sleep last night, the spell ended. But then, she smiles, and all is right.

"You're here."

"I'm here."

She grins and another awkward pause follows.

"He's been here since six o'clock," Sylvia says. "I found him sleeping in his truck." Hosea glares at Sylvia, who hunches her shoulders and mouths a silent *What?* to him.

Sara's facial features collapse in a frown. "You slept in your truck? You didn't have to do that. You could have come inside."

"We didn't finish until early this morning. There were a lot of windows."

I hear Sylvia curse the damn kids again under her breath.

"You boarded up the whole street?"

"Yeah."

"The shop owners will pay the people who helped."

"I took care of it."

"You didn't have to do that."

"I wanted to."

"Thank you."

"My pleasure."

"Did you sleep okay?"

She smiles big. "Yeah."

Another long pause follows. Sara is still on the other side of the kitchen. Hosea's and Sylvia's gaze volleys back and forth from me to Sara, like watching a tennis match. Alana, oblivious to what's happening, finishes shoveling her last pancake square into her mouth.

There's too much distance between us. Too much stored energy pushing us together. Too many people in this kitchen.

"I think we need to go assess the damage and call the insurance company," Sylvia says. "Sounds like we have quite a bit of cleanup to do, so we're not going to be able to open today. It's probably going to take us *hours* to clean up everything." She says the last sentence louder and with emphasis on hours.

"Hours?" Alana asks.

"Yes, *hours*," Sylvia says, drawing out the word again and shooting a look at Sara, who shakes her head in embarrassment. "Let's go, baby."

Hosea heads out first, followed by Alana, and finally Sylvia, who winks at me as she leaves.

We reach each other in a second, knocking over a chair, our bodies colliding in a crush. When Sara reaches my arms, I lift her and press my mouth on hers. Like two magnets, we cling to each other, unwilling to move. Our kisses are desperate at first, as if we need each other to breathe, then long and unraveling, as we reach deeper and deeper, drawing into each other. The delicate care and self-restraint we exhibited last night have been cut loose, replaced by unbridled passion and intense desire.

Sara is the one suspended, but I also feel weightless. I ease into a chair to steady myself, pulling her down on top of me. I want to touch her everywhere, kiss her everywhere, meld our bodies together as one. No matter how hard I press her against me, it isn't close enough; the attraction is too great. Finally, we separate, winded like we sprinted a mile, our chests heaving, but our foreheads remain pressed against each other.

"I have an idea," she says as I kiss her neck and work up to the hollow behind her ear.

"Yes," I whisper, the word laced with pleasure. The touch of my breath and lips to her neck causes a quiet moan to escape her lips.

"Why don't we—"

"Yes," I say again, pulling down the strap of her tank top and kissing her collarbone, my hands traveling up her spine.

She giggles. "Let's—"

"Yes."

"You don't even know what I'm going to say."

She could have asked me anything in that moment and I would have agreed, my mind moving in and out of focus, my thoughts eroding. I am so full of her, I can hardly stand it. "I'll do whatever you want."

She curves her fingers over the nape of my neck and plants soft kisses across it as she speaks. "Can we go to your cottage for some privacy?" she says. "I would *really, really* like to know more about photons. I was a bit confused about the, 'I am in you, touching you, being you, quite literally,' part. I think I need a more in-depth explanation."

My breath catches. Sara smiles, in a way that's focused, intense, and sexy all at the same time. I know what she is implying, and it sends an ache of desire low in my body. A hard kiss acts as my response.

Then, in a moment of awareness, a forgotten commitment punches through. I have to go see Daniel today, the last visit before his release. I pull back.

"What is it? Are we moving too fast?"

"No. Hell no," I say, too quickly at the slow burn of our attraction finally being extinguished. "Unless you think we are. Unless you are uncomfortable..."

"You don't have to be cautious with me. I want you," she says, her voice low and sexy.

My hands move to her hips. "I want you too."

"So, what is it?" she asks. "You can tell me."

"There's something I have to do."

I refuse to say his name. He has no business here, in this kitchen, in this moment. But she knows it has something to do with Daniel, and I prepare for her to slide out of my arms, ending the moment, as she is reminded of the consequences of being with me, my familial baggage.

Instead, she considers this, and her eyes search and find mine. "It's okay," she says, placing her hand on the side of my face. "Go. I'll be here when you're done. I'm not going anywhere."

There's no accounting for love when it materializes for

another. I have no frame of reference. No experience to recall. The intense feeling surging through me is nothing short of a miracle. She sees me. She trusts me, wants me, and accepts me. Despite Daniel and Birdie. Despite it all. She pushes all her chips to the center of the table. She is all in. In that moment, I know that I love her.

I take her wrist into my hand and pull her fingers softly over my lips, kissing them. "Tonight, when I get back, let's go away for a few days. I'll take you anywhere in the world you want to go."

She grins and nuzzles at my ear. "I want to go to the cottage. I love it out there."

"Whatever you want," I say, sliding my hands to her thighs. "But how about a physical example of photons right now?" I move a hand to the space between her legs and rub for a few seconds.

"Yes, please." Sara moans to the ceiling as I slip a finger inside.

I kiss the skin just below her neck and whisper, "I'm in you, touching you." I press my finger in deeper. "Can you feel me?"

———

Daniel shuffles into the visitor's room, handcuffed and shackled, a surgical mask dangling around his neck. The guard unchains him, his hands first and then his ankles. As he stands erect, his prison uniform hangs loosely from his frame; his neck is slim, his collarbone prominent. Staring back at him now is no longer like looking into a mirror, as it once was. He's a different version of me, of himself, from just a few months ago. His face: sullen cheeks, with eyes, faint purplish circles, frozen in an offset stare.

He is dying, has been dying, right before my eyes.

The sight unravels something within me, a truth I have yet to face, a reality I rejected.

"You look like you've seen a ghost," he says, easing into the metal chair across from me. He clasps his hands in front of him. He doesn't look at me, his eyes on the table, the scab on his hands, anything but me. "I'll be a ghost soon enough."

It wasn't enough that Dr. Bennett had reached this conclusion weeks ago or that Marsha believed it or that I had even uttered the words myself, but for Daniel to believe it shreds my insides. For so long I refused to believe the words—there's no way Daniel can die. I'll donate my bone marrow; he'll kick the infection, I told myself. We didn't see Naomi's death coming. Had no time to react or plan, just accept. With Daniel, we've had a detailed road map that I saw coming. And yet, I'm not ready.

I rub my hands together and smile, a feeble attempt to mask the pain. "What are we going to do first? Count cards in Vegas? I'm afraid I'm out of practice, but it won't take me long to get back into the swing. Or a poker tournament?"

He snickers, his expression sober, like a young child's. "Vegas, right."

"We had always talked about going to Vegas when we turned twenty-one. Let's go do it."

"I told you." His voice drops an octave. "I want to fall in love."

"And I told you I can't help you with that, but if we go to Vegas, I'm sure you can be in love by the end of the night."

"What I want can't be achieved in a night. I don't have enough time left."

"No Vegas then. Where? What would you like to do?" I say, my tone upbeat.

He looks up at me but past me, which tells me his physical body is here but his mind is elsewhere. "I want to go to the cottage."

"Okay," I say. "It still needs a lot of work, but maybe you could help me with that."

"Jacob…" He looks away, and when he looks back his eyes are heavy and red-rimmed. "I won't be alive that long."

I take a deep breath and swallow, nauseated by the thought of losing him, of losing another sibling, of being the only one left. I shake my head. "Don't say that."

"For a scientist, you've become very optimistic."

"And for a Christian, you've lost your faith."

He smiles, but it soon fades. "I'm going to die. I've accepted that. I've made my peace with it. Asked God for forgiveness. But…" He doesn't finish, allowing the word to linger in the air.

"But what?"

"Did she watch the interview?"

"What?" I ask. "What does that matter?"

"Do you know if she watched it?"

I shake my head.

"How do you know?"

I look at the table and back up at him. "Because she was with me."

Daniel withdraws his forearms from the table, sitting up straight. "Ah, okay." He shakes his head.

"I…"

"You don't have to explain. I get it. She was a pretty girl then. I'm sure she's a beautiful woman now."

"Don't talk about her like that," I say, my voice a warning.

"So…we are not falling but have fallen, huh?"

I narrow my eyes at him. "This is not about her."

"It is about her. I have accomplished nothing. Invented nothing. Created nothing. And the world will soon forget me."

"What are you talking about? You have spent the last eight years making a difference here. Look at what you've done."

"No one is going to remember any of those things. They are only going to remember what got me here in the first place."

"That's not true. You have done something. Helped people. That will account for something. The people you helped. They will remember you."

"I may seem strong, but not a day goes by that I'm not reminded of the fact that my arrogance put me in here. When I could have been doing so much more out there."

He shakes his head just as a tear falls, then another. He doesn't wipe them away; they linger and run down his face.

"Your life matters," I say, my own eyes filling with tears.

"I wanted to make a mark on this world," he says, his voice full of sadness. "I've failed Dad. I've failed Naomi."

Tears spill down his cheeks. I close my eyes and wish for some fresh air, the atmosphere in the cramped space stagnant, pressing on my heart, distorting the beat of it, which pulses like a watch's tick. I breathe deeply, feeling the rise and fall of my chest, with every deliberate inhale and exhale, actions I can control. I can't save Daniel, his life, but I can focus on the cadence of my breath and can relieve the torment and the sense of powerlessness coursing through my veins that has settled at the bottom of my stomach like a cement brick. I can give him a reprieve.

"You have a daughter."

"What?" he asks, blinking.

I take a deep breath and continue. "I told you that Sara was back. What I didn't tell you was that she has a daughter. Your daughter."

He stares at me for a moment, his hands trembling with the slightest shake. I can't read his reaction; his body is tense, just a crease of skin bunched between his eyes in confusion. "I can't believe it."

"There's something else," I say, realizing there's no going back now. "She's the genius I've been tutoring."

"The one solving the Navier-Stokes equation? The one whose work we've been discussing?"

I let my shoulders slump, feeling lighter at the unloading of the secret I've held for months.

He presses both hands on the chair and eases himself

upright. He paces the area around the table, shaking his head in disbelief. He doesn't speak.

"How long have you known?" He's still pacing, his eyes volleying from left to right as if searching for something not there. "Did you know the first time you came to see me?"

"Not the first time. The second time, when I showed you Alana's notebook."

He stops and eases into his chair again. "Alana. That's her name?"

"Yeah…Alana."

He mouths her name again, the sound too hushed for me to hear. "How did you find out?"

"It was an accident. I ran into her at Fernbank." I smile. "Remember the *Mathematica* exhibit? She correctly identified that the plus signs should be minus signs. All that time we looked at it, Naomi looked at it, and we didn't catch it. She did."

He blinks, allowing the realization that he has a daughter to settle within him, his eyes wild with disbelief. I watch as the knowledge snakes through him.

"See…" I say. "Your life wasn't for nothing. She's going to change the world. Your daughter."

"Why didn't Sara tell me?"

"She was scared."

"Of what?"

"You. Birdie. Us," I say. "You know how your lawyers and Birdie treated her during the trial. She didn't want to go through that again."

He clasps his hands in front of him in prayer. "All this time, you knew I had a daughter, and you didn't tell me?"

"I promised Sara I wouldn't."

"You promised *her*?" he says, his voice rising. "You promised her? What about me? Your brother."

"She was going to disappear again. I didn't want that. In exchange for my silence, she promised to let me see Alana. I figured one of us should know her."

He laughs to himself. "That's why you didn't tell me about Sara coming home. Because you wanted her. You wanted them all to yourself."

"No," I say. "My feelings for her came later. I told you. I didn't expect it to happen."

"Bullshit!" he says, his anger crossing over to rage. "I'm agonizing over my legacy, my place in this world, and you knew I had a daughter. All this time." He slams his palm on the table hard. "Sara comes home and fucks you, and you forget where your loyalties lie. That you are a Wyler!"

"Fuck you, Daniel! Everything I've done has been because I'm a Wyler!"

"Tell me, Jacob…" His eyes narrow. "Is she as good as I remember?"

I launch myself across the table before I even know I've done it, my mind, my emotions detached from reality. I collide with him with enough force that it knocks him backward. We collapse in a flailing heap and wrestle on the floor, pummeling each other over and over. Every punch I throw, every blow, bent on inflicting harm, retribution for Sara, for destroying our family, for the pain and frustration I've endured for eight years, until three guards pull me off him, but not before Daniel lands one final punch to my face.

SARA

—

I KNEW HE WAS going to see Daniel. According to the letter I received, his release date was approaching. I don't care. I missed the interview and had no desire to watch it. Daniel is my past. Jacob is my future. They are twins, but not the same. And I can see Jacob for what he is. A man who unexpectedly came into my life and enhanced it. A man who had returned home, crawled back into the midst of chaos and fought.

I'm smiling when I walk into the bookstore in the late afternoon to help with the cleanup. Alana is next door, and Dad is typing on the computer, his face pinched in concentration. Sylvia beams when she sees me. She stops sweeping and looks at the clock on the wall, nodding approvingly.

"Feast?" she asks when I'm in earshot.

My face warms. "Oh yes," I say, biting my lip. "Like…a feast spread out on the stairs last night and the kitchen table this morning."

We look at each other, shudder, and burst into laughter.

"That Jacob," Sylvia says, shaking her head. "He definitely pulled some strings for us. Our glass should be replaced by the end of the day. Ms. Cookson said it's going to take a few days for hers to be replaced. Where is he, by the way? I hope he's somewhere getting some sleep."

"He went to see Daniel."

"Oh." Her eyebrows jump. "And what about that? Now that you and Jacob are officially an item. You can't continue to hold him to that promise. It's time to tell them."

"Daniel's dying," I say, kneeling and picking up the larger shards of glass and putting them into the trash can. "He doesn't have long."

"How's Jacob handling that?"

"He doesn't talk about it, especially with me. But I know he's hurting."

"So…is that the solution? Let Daniel die. If he dies no custody issues, right? It will all be over?"

"You say that as if that's not fine."

"It feels sticky. Too easy." She slides a full dustpan of glass into the trash can, the sound like nails on a chalkboard.

"Good. I'd like some easy," I say, my voice dripping with sarcasm.

"Nothing in life is." She gives me a sympathetic look. "There are no easy roads, Sara."

"He doesn't deserve it. He doesn't deserve to know that he created a brilliant daughter who is going to one day change the world. He doesn't get to die with that knowledge, with that pride."

"No arguments there. But do you really still believe that? Sometimes we get what we don't deserve. What about Alana? Think of her. With Jacob here, she's not asking about him much anymore. Doesn't she deserve to meet her father at least once? Even if he wasn't a nice person?"

I shrug in a question and sigh, holding firm to my earlier proclamation.

"And what about Birdie?"

"She won't have much of a case without Daniel. Plus, I can deal with Birdie. She's not as intimidating as she was eight years ago."

"I still can't believe she had the nerve to show up here," Sylvia says. "'Stay away from my boys,'" she mocks. "You should have said, 'One of your boys is in love with me.'"

I give Sylvia a questioning glance. "Love?"

She curses under her breath.

"What?"

She looks over at Dad, who is restacking a pile of books that fell during the commotion last night, and lowers her voice. "A few weeks ago, Hosea and I walked in on Jacob staring at you and Alana playing in the garden. He had this look in his eye. He was there, but he wasn't, you know? Hosea signaled for me to leave so they could talk, but I heard him tell Hosea that he was falling in love with you."

"He did? He told Dad?"

"Sara...there's something else. I think I know who paid for the renovation." She presses her lips together before speaking again. "Jacob."

I stare at her as I process the possibility. I think back to the grand opening and the way Jacob perused the bookstore, running his hands over the shelves, looking at the light fixtures. He didn't come in to shop. He was admiring and appreciating something he'd had a hand in creating.

"How do you know?"

"When I asked for a quote for the windows, the man said that it had already been handled. That's exactly what happened during the renovations. I looked and asked for invoices, and there were none. Everything had been paid for."

"Do you think Dad asked him for the money?"

"You know better than that. Absolutely not."

"Why would he do that? Just decide to renovate the bookstore."

"I don't know, but it is very generous."

"Did you ask Dad?"

She shakes her head. "No, and I'm not going to. And you shouldn't either. Neither of them wanted us to know. It's something Jacob wanted to do. Something they worked out between the two of them. Let's leave it alone and be grateful. Sometimes we don't need to question everything. We just need to let it be."

———

I feel Jacob's presence, instantly, even before I look up from my work, where I'm kneeling on the floor. Much like the first time I saw him here at the bookstore, dark shadows obscure his face, but unlike last time, I know who he is. A rush of love inundates me, and I've never felt so much at once, raw emotion exploding with every breath and every blink.

"Hi," I say.

"Hi," he says, his voice penetrating the darkness of the bookstore.

"I was just thinking about the first time I saw you. Remember the E. E. Cummings poem?" I rise up on my knees. "But after last night and this morning, I'm thinking of a different Cummings poem:

"i like my body when it is with your
body. It is so quite new a thing."

He moans a drawn-out breath that moves from deep in his throat. I continue:

"Muscles better and nerves more.
i like your body. i like what it does,
i like its hows. i like to feel the spine
of your body and its bones, and the trembling—"

"Sara…"

I stop, smiling. "You don't know that one? That's

surprising, coming from a so-called E. E. Cummings fan," I say teasingly. Jacob's position remains enveloped in the shadows. Too far from me. My skin prickles at the anticipation of his touch.

"Why are you all the way over there?" I ask, extending my hand to him. "Come here."

He steps out of the shadow, his head lowered. He is wearing a white V-neck T-shirt with three quarter-size circles of blood splattered across the chest and a small hole along the collar. A deep purple bruise looms under his right eye.

"Oh my god! What happened?" In an instant I'm at him, examining his discolored face lightly with my fingers and searching his chest for the source of the blood. He grimaces at the pain then turns his head away from me.

"Where are you bleeding?"

"It's not my blood."

"What happened?" I ask. He won't meet my eyes.

He moves past me, sitting on the couch and clasping his hands in front of him. "I got into a fight with Daniel."

"Why?"

He's silent for a long moment, his face unreadable until he sees my overnight bag next to the couch. The corner of his mouth twitches, and his expression softens before hardening again. "Are you ready to go?"

"Tell me what happened with Daniel. Why do you have his blood on you?"

"I don't want to talk to you about Daniel."

I kneel in front of him, between his legs, and hold his face in my hands. "I want to know."

He pulls away, grabbing my wrists and moving them away from his face. "You don't want to hear about this." His tone is gnawing and sharp, shocking me, but I immediately understand that he walked into the pain he has been avoiding, planted himself in the middle of it, and it is now doing the talking.

"I do."

He stands again. "He's a complicated man, Sara. I don't say that as circumvention. It's hard to explain the depths of him. You won't understand. Not you."

"I can try."

"He's dying, Sara. Dying. I've been watching my brother die all this time. But I thought I could save him. That it wouldn't happen to him. That I had no reason to feel guilty about all of the time I spent away because we would have plenty of time. But he's dying. And I hate that." He glares at me, his green eyes piercing mine. "But do you know what I hate more? What he did to you is all anyone will ever remember about him. And I hate that. I hate it." He clinches his fists into two tight balls and emits a raucous growl.

I hold my breath to bite back the tears that spring to my eyes as I watch Jacob fight an interior battle within himself, conflicting emotions at war within the depths of his heart and mind. I resist the urge to reach out and touch him.

"You can say a lot about Daniel…" He sneers to himself,

half laughing, half groaning. "But you couldn't say he wasn't brilliant. The smartest man I will ever know."

Jacob sits on the couch again and wraps himself in a hug, his eyes glassing over as if he's remembering something. "When we were kids, while we were at the cottage, we would wait until Dad fell asleep and we would sneak out to go fishing or look at the stars or swim. It was just the three of us. Out there, it was like we were the only people in the world. Nothing else and no one else existed." He squirms back and forth as if sitting on something uncomfortable. "And they both left me. She died. He's dying."

I ease in the tight space next to him, taking his hand into mine, but he moves it away and hugs himself tighter as if holding something close to his chest.

"And I can't even mourn for him. My own brother." His voice cracks as the tears pool into his eyes. "I can't mourn for him. Because I love him, but don't like him very much right now. Because he hurt you. And I don't know if I can ever forgive him for hurting you. For destroying the family we had left."

I collapse to my knees between his legs again. He lowers his head just as the tears cascade down his cheeks, his shoulders shaking through sobs.

"I don't have a family anymore," he says, his voice fading away.

"We can be your family. Alana, me, Dad, and Sylvia, we will be your family. We can start our own." I wrap my arms around his neck and press my body hard against his chest, feeling the choppy rhythm of his breath. "Did you hear me? We can start our own family." It is true, and I know it when I say it, the thought of it spreading through me like wildfire. I want to be a family with him, raise Alana with him.

"Sometimes the worst thing that happens to us turns out to be the best thing." The words are heavy, pressing the air out of my lungs, but needing to be released. There is more room for them on the outside. It is the realization that I waited eight years to discover, what I had never said out loud. Inside Jacob's pain, I discovered the truth about my own.

Jacob's taut body slumps, losing its shape in my arms. "I told him about Alana."

"What?" I say, slipping out of his embrace.

"He was so broken." Jacob looks straight ahead. "He thought he didn't have anything. That he would be forgotten. I wanted to make him feel better. To know that his life wasn't a waste."

I lean back as the news sinks into me. When it does, there is no buzz of panic, just a gushing of sadness. A feeling of betrayal. "How could you do that?"

He lowers his chin. "I'm sorry." His voice has fallen to almost a whisper.

"You promised."

Jacob jerks himself upright again. "I know! A man of unbroken promises!" He scoffs. "But I can't continue to split myself in two. I can't be what they need and what you need."

"You don't have to. You can be who you want to be."

"I'm being who I have to be."

"And what's that?"

"A brother. A son."

"No room for anything else?" I ask, my voice quivers.

He knows what I am implying the second I say it. "I'm not saying…"

"It's pretty clear to me where your loyalties lie. I thought you were different. I thought you understood. But it was all a lie. I never should have trusted you." I blink, swallowing back tears before standing and walking to the front door.

"Sara…wait." He follows me, repeating the entire way: "I'm sorry."

I reach the door and swing it open. He steps toward the door but does not break the threshold. He turns back to me.

I take a breath and straighten my posture. "Please go."

"Sara—"

"Just go." I swallow, suddenly feeling depleted and exhausted, my eyelids leaden, my breathing slowing. "Please."

He takes a step toward me. Just a few short hours ago, I ran into his arms, the warmth of the memory still exhilarating and comforting, but now I withdraw like a shadow and turn my head away from him. I can't look at him. Can't let him see the tears in my eyes. I trusted him. Now I feel as if something has been taken from me.

"Doubt thou the stars are fire,
Doubt that the sun doth move,
Doubt truth to be a liar,
But never doubt I love."

And I don't doubt that he loves me. I know that he does. He helped ease the blow of being home after so much time away. He helped me give Alana something I could never do on my own. He became a shoulder to lean on. He helped me understand that love has no face even if it looks like the one that hurt you.

None of that matters now. He betrayed me. I need to find my own way forward.

Faced with my silence, Jacob steps outside. The street is eerily quiet, the air unmoving and still. I wipe a tear that escapes my eye as I close the door behind him.

JACOB

————

THE LATE-SUMMER SUN BEARS down on the pavement as
the metal gate slides open, the rattling of chains shrieking
across the dense field. Daniel appears from behind a blue
steel door. I move off my truck, parked across the street,
and walk to meet him. He shakes hands with each of the
guards who escort him before taking two steps outside of
the prison walls. He's standing on the other side of the
fence, for the first time in almost eight years, as the gate
once again rattles closed.

We stand, facing each other, on the edge of yet another
precipice. The last time, when he walked into prison, the last
time I would speak to him, see him until a few months ago.
Now, we face each other. Unsure of the future, our past still
present between us.

"I didn't think you would show," Daniel says, his posture
square, his white button-down shirt starched and pressed, his
jeans high and loose on his waist.

"I told you…I would keep coming back. I meant it." I stand, head tilted, with my hands clasped in front of me.

Daniel slides one hand into his pocket, looks down at his feet, swiping his shoe at a rock, then back up at me. "We should have just fought it out during that first meeting." He takes his forefinger and thumb to his chin and moves it. A grimace invades his face.

"Yeah," I say, my tongue finding and pressing a soreness from his blow across my cheek.

Daniel moves his lips into a straight line. "I'm sorry."

"I know," I say, almost too quickly.

"No, I'm sorry. About all of it. I want you to know that."

I close the distance between us in two steps, and we hug, two firm pats on the back and an embrace that neither of us relinquishes right away. I can feel the smallness across his shoulders, the once firm muscles now soft, and the bones pointy and sharp. I still don't let go.

In the truck, Daniel's attention is focused out the window, taking in the scenery he hasn't laid eyes on in years. The sun is barely visible from behind the clouds, holding the rain at bay. Fall is coming; the greens of the fields will soon make way for yellows, golds, and browns. The world is as it has always been, but I imagine it feels altered to him after all of these years. Colors a little brighter. Smells a little stronger. I respect his reorientation and allow the only noise to come from the rumbling of the engine and the wind cutting against our ears.

"Where are you taking me?" he asks sometime later when

I pass all the exits for Savannah, with fast food restaurants and gas stations once again changing back to rolling fields of trees and grass.

He knows. All of the time away can't erase memories. I know that now. He does too.

"Birdie is going to kill you," he says, snickering.

"I know." I peer at him, then back at the road. "It's just for a few days. I need you to help me with a little project."

He agrees and looks out the window. "No more tutoring?"

The question stabs me like a thousand needles. "She's not exactly talking to me," I say, thinking back to the last time I saw her several nights ago, her trust cracked into pieces.

"Because of me?"

I shrug. "Because I'm a Wyler."

My comment wounds him as he remembers what he accused me of, and his features pull south. "Look...I didn't mean—"

"It's okay. She has every right to be upset with me. She trusted me. We had a deal, and I broke my promise to her."

"To not tell me or Birdie about..." He stops as if her name is caught in the back of his throat.

"Alana." I finish for him, like he did for me with Naomi.

He mouths her name, silently, several times, turning it over and over. Each time his face lights up as it moves through him. "She had every right to keep Alana a secret. I wasn't in the space to accept the idea that I had a child. God only knows how Birdie would have reacted. I don't blame her for not telling us. This was for the best."

"I'm glad to hear you admit that. But I need to admit something too. I'm not sorry for falling in love with Sara or for keeping Alana from you."

"You shouldn't be. You did what was best for them. And for you."

"I'm not sure about that. I keep replaying it in my mind. What if I had told you earlier, or Birdie? What if I had tried harder to convince Sara to do so? I keep wrestling with all of these different scenarios, but none of them put us in a different situation than where we are now."

"I'm not going to try to meet or see her."

I look at him skeptically.

"Knowing she exists is enough for me. I lost the right to be in her life, but you're going to have a harder time convincing Birdie."

The time for honesty between the remaining Wylers has finally come. "You can help me with that."

"Whatever I need to do."

"They're probably gone now," I say, my voice faltering at the end of a conclusion I did not want to accept. I stare at the road ahead, watching but dazedly, longingly, and grip the steering wheel tighter.

Daniel notices my distant look. "Yeah…that's definitely love, huh?"

My heart flutters at the idea of loving Sara, my Aurora. Even now, the word *love* feels new and exciting against my heart, in my mind. I miss her deeply, her soft voice, her calm reassuring way, the feel of her body in my arms, the smooth-ness of her skin, and I can't imagine my life without her. A life without losing myself in her beautiful eyes. A life without Alana. Makes me wonder how I survived without them before. How I functioned at all.

"I'm jealous," Daniel says, interrupting my train of thought.

"Of what?"

"Not of you and Sara," he says, aware of himself. "That you're in love. Have experienced love. Know what it feels like."

"You still can. It's not too late to fly to Vegas."

He laughs before turning serious again. "No, real love. What you're feeling right now."

I reach into my bag and pull out my cell phone and scroll a bit before finding what I'm looking for and holding the phone out to Daniel. He looks at me for a moment, his body frozen, and blinks his eyes down at the picture without moving his head. He glares at it, wordless. Finally, he looks up. "She looks like…" I can hear him, but only faintly, the words fading.

"Naomi," I finish for him. He looks at me. "I can say it now. She," I say, pointing to the phone, "helped me with that. Naomi's not gone, she's here. In her."

He finally moves, taking my phone into his hands; it moves with a slight shake. I can't read his reaction. "I can't believe it. She's beautiful."

"And smart and funny."

I watch as his eyes focus on the picture of Alana and take

in every pixel of her features: our eyes, her button nose, her slightly crooked teeth.

"Do you have any more?" Daniel asks, his voice hopeful, not looking at me.

"I'll do you one better." I open my phone and play a video I only recently discovered. Alana's high-pitched voice reverberates and ricochets around the truck like a boomerang.

"Hi...Jacob. It's me, Alana. You left your phone on the table, and I finished all of the equations you gave me, so I'm killing time while you go to your truck. Oh...I hear you coming back into the house. Bye!"

The tears that were welled in his eyes now fall freely down his sunken cheeks as he replays the video repeatedly. Each time, his face lights up as if it's the first time. And I know he knows, just as I knew, the first time I saw her, that love at first sight is possible.

"How's that for falling in love?" I ask. "There are many variations of love. You never said which kind."

He wipes his eyes, still clutching the phone tight. "Thank you. Thank you for what you did. For taking care of her. Because of you, I have this." He shakes the phone. "I know that I have a daughter. I can never repay you for that."

"No thanks necessary."

He nods before saying, "Tell me about my daughter."

———

Daniel and I spend the day at the cottage, just as we did as kids. The color in his face returns the moment the boat rounds the bend and the cottage eases into view. Dad's cottage is for him a respite, as it was for me when I returned to Georgia. Under the dark sky illuminated with the same stars of our childhood, I tell him all about my summer with Alana, from the first time I met her at Fernbank to starting the garden to our tutoring. He mostly listens, captivated by a daughter he knows he'll never meet. And yet, the pride radiating from his face is akin to that of a father watching a child win first place at a science fair. I show Daniel Alana's latest work on the Navier-Stokes equation. He shakes his head in amazement at her abilities and proficiencies.

"With proper study and constant tutoring, she'll solve it by the time she's eighteen."

I too, not long ago, realized not *if* Alana could solve the equation but when.

"But that's the conundrum," Daniel continues. "Are we doing her a disservice by prioritizing her math proficiency over her just being a kid?"

"Sara doesn't want to subject her to constant tutoring."

"Then let her be a kid. There are no rules or time limits to solving it. She can start and stop whenever she likes. I hope she solves it. But if not, that's fine too."

"Even if she attends public school?"

Daniel's jaw is rigid. "Of course," he says, which produces a cough that he can't control, one that reddens his eyes, one that causes him to gasp for breath.

There's nothing worse than watching someone die, to know that their life, their days, are truly numbered. But I force myself to watch him, to see him through labored breaths and all. For months, Sara, Sylvia, and Alana have watched Hosea live, never knowing if that day, that breath, will be his last. I will do the same. I will watch Daniel live now and grieve for him later. I take him a towel and a glass of water and push away the sadness that threatens to surround me.

The hours slip away as we talk. I tell him about Sara, Sylvia, and Hosea. He laughs when I tell him about Pizza Friday and my attempts to make a homemade pizza and to watch a movie. I show him the notes and observations from NASA's Ground-to-Rocket Electrodynamics-Electrons Correlative Experiment on Poker Flat. He points out several possible conclusions and observations that I had not yet discovered. Every so often, Daniel will cough or wince in pain, his eyes glassy and weak, a reminder of a reality that will soon come to pass. Despite this harsh truth, it feels good to be like this again, in these conversations, in the way we were before our world was turned upside down.

The next day, Birdie threatens to come to the cottage if I don't bring Daniel back to Savannah. I tell Daniel this as he shuffles slowly from the kitchen and settles on the couch, his lungs releasing a long breath as he rests. He smiles a weak grin.

"She wouldn't."

I laugh, remembering Birdie's first and only visit out here months ago. "She would."

"Well…we better go."

"One more day, if you're up to it," I say. "We haven't gone fishing yet, and there's something I need you to help me with."

Daniel has always been the artist of the family, and I ask him to outline a new name on my boat. *Ocean Breeze* no more. I watch as he wills his hand to be steady enough to freehand the letters. He finishes, and I take the paintbrush and slowly fill in the letters with paint.

"Has Alana been out here?" he asks as I move to the letter *A*. He's sitting on the edge of the dock, the effort to stand for long periods of time too much for his fragile body.

Like the fishing rod at our feet, my mind casts back and snags on Sara's visit here. For a moment I curl into the memories of her. Her level of comfortability and ease at being out here. The tasty beef stew she made that she repeatedly apologized for. The way she touched her lips when observing the stars for the first time. I would see Sara again. I had one final promise to keep, the first of many I would make after I returned home.

But I shake my head and the ache the memory produces goes away, and I'm jolted back to the dock, to Daniel looking at me, awaiting an answer to his question. "Just Sara."

"Promise me that you'll bring her out here." He stares out on the water. "Let her dive off this dock. Just like Naomi."

"I will."

"And I want you to tell her the truth about me. When she's old enough. The whole hard truth. Make sure she's a good person who doesn't turn out to be like me."

I nod.

"Make sure she has a happy, balanced life that we didn't have. Teach her there's no weakness in crying or grief. There's nothing wrong with showing affection. And there's no shame in being a paleontologist."

We both laugh as the memory clings to us, no longer tripping us up. I join Daniel on the dock and look back at our work as the bright-yellow paint dries and Naomi's name stands out against the white boat, here in the place she loved the most.

The shadows grow thick in the setting sun as the rustling of cicadas ticks as frequent as a clock's second hand. As I cast my gaze out into the water, murky in color, my heart grows heavier, not yet eased, but something else continues to pull at me. Then I know.

I look at my brother, his face barely visible in the increasing darkness. He isn't perfect. He's made mistakes and then some.

"Daniel," I say as he turns to look at me, "I forgive you."

"Thank you," he says, taking in the deepest breath he can hold without spurring a coughing fit. "I haven't been the brother to you like you've been for me."

"I got the brother I needed."

I drape my arm around Daniel's shoulders and feel the shallow rise and fall of his chest, each breath he takes labored and pained, and try not to think about a future without him. A future I know that will be soon. As an astrophysicist, I understand time and its demands better than anyone. Instead, I remind myself to be here, present. To just be here with him, with Naomi, encapsulate them, the memories of them, in our favorite place, where there's nothing but light and water and stars and time. That will have to be enough for now. Forever.

————

The next day, as Daniel and I pull into Birdie's driveway, my phone rings and I answer.

A voice that I wish were Sara's but is not says, "Jacob?"

"Sylvia? Is everything okay?" I ask, knowing the answer, knowing there is only one reason why she is calling.

"It's Hosea."

As soon as I end the call with Sylvia, I turn and see Daniel slumping against the passenger door. I touch his arm to shake him awake, calling his name. He blinks his eyes open. Just as I help him out of the car, Birdie and Marsha descend from the house with smiles that disintegrate when a weak Daniel slips out of my hold and collapses in front of them.

SARA

——

"IT WASN'T THE BIG one," Dr. Mundy says, inspecting Dad's chart and parroting to us what he's been telling us since the seizure that brought me home. There's nothing he can do, that after monitoring him for seventy-two hours, we can take him home. "Your father is a fighter."

"Are we…are we…you know…getting close?" I ask, hating the implications of the question. "You gave him months to live. It's been five."

Dr. Mundy tucks his pen back into his breast pocket. "We just don't know. It could be today, tomorrow, or months from now."

By the second day, Dad is his usual self, weak but up reciting his morning poems to Alana over hospital oatmeal. The sight is unfathomable. How can this be? How can he be back to his old self so quickly? As if the last forty-eight hours never happened. By midmorning, he clears his throat and dutifully points to his watch, three sharp ticks against the face, an indication that it is time to open the bookstore. But Sylvia doesn't relent, turning her head in the opposite direction, before leaving the room entirely. He turns to me and lifts his brows. I shake my head and take his hand into mine. He points to his watch and glares at the clock on the wall. He wants the bookstore open. But why? He knows that if I go, I'll take Alana with me, and if anything is to happen, it will happen so quickly that we would miss it. Or maybe that is his intention all along.

"We're not leaving," I say, the tears forming in the back of my eyes.

On the third day, Sylvia, Alana, and I are sitting in Dad's room when Sylvia asks if I want to call Jacob. A nurse has just wheeled Dad out of the room for more tests. Alana's eyes are glued to the Weather Channel tracking a potential hurricane's track up the Gulf, her and Brixton's latest obsession.

"He loves Hosea," she says when I don't answer her question. "He would want to be here."

"Jacob is where he needs to be. Where he chose to be."

"He did choose. From the first day he met Alana, he chose her, and you. For months he kept your secret from his mother and twin brother. He chose."

I drag my hand through my hair, greasy and in need of washing. "He broke his promise."

"A promise that he should never have been asked to make. He was placed in a very hard position, but he tried. He tried for you because he's a good man. He continued to try because he loves Alana like she is his own."

"He lied to me," I say weakly, sounding unconvincing to my own ears.

"Bad man, that Jacob." Her face is stern, an expression I've rarely seen. "He only kept your secret while tutoring your daughter. Helped you introduce Alana to her other family. Paid for the bookstore's renovations and god knows what else. Oh, and he's in love with you. Yeah…what an awful man."

"Can we not talk about this right now?" It seems surreal to be talking about Jacob in the midst of Dad's illness. I do not want to disengage and pretend this isn't happening. "It's not the right time."

"Hosea would want him here." Sylvia stands, grabs her cell phone, and heads toward the door. Alana jumps up to go with her. "And I think you do too."

An hour later, Dad stirs awake, his eyes fluttering open and around the room as if looking for something or someone. He turns to me with a look of peace and relaxation, not the face of a man who may be nearing the end of his life.

I move away from the seat by the window and into the one next to his bed.

"Sylvia took Alana to the cafeteria. She should be back soon." I take his hand into mine, the frigid cold startling, and press my other hand on top to warm it.

He nods.

Dad says:

"I will arise and go now, and go to Innisfree,
And a small cabin build there, of clay and wattles made;
Nine bean-rows will I have there, a hive for the honey-bee,
And live alone in the bee-loud glade,"

It is Jacob's greeting. He is asking about Jacob.

"He's not here," I say, now rubbing his hand. "I'm not speaking to him. He told Daniel about Alana."

Dad turns his head toward the ceiling.

"That you are here—that life exists and identity,
That the powerful play goes on, and you may contribute a
verse."

"I know, Dad, but it's over now. Let's focus on you. What can I do for you? Can I get you anything?" I ask, hopeful that it will be enough to turn the conversation.

Dad says again:

"I will arise and go now, and go to Innisfree,
And a small cabin build there, of clay and wattles made;
Nine bean-rows will I have there, a hive for the honey-bee,
And live alone in the bee-loud glade,"

"Dad…I don't want to talk about Jacob. I want to be with you. How are you feeling?"

His face softens.

"I thought of you and how you love this beauty,
And walking up the long beach all alone
I heard the waves breaking in measured thunder
As you and I once heard their monotone."

I grip his hand tighter and press it to my cheek. "I'm glad to have spent this time with you. I have loved every minute. And I'm especially happy that you got to really know Alana."

Dad says:

"Tripping along with impetuous grace,
Joy of her life beaming out of her face,
Tresses all truant-like, curl upon curl,
Wind-blown and rosy, my little March girl."

I move from the chair to the side of his bed. "Dad...I'm sorry for leaving. For leaving you. I should have stayed. We would have had more time."

It needed to be said. If I am going to say goodbye, I want him to know all of it. I want to feel all of it, the pain, the guilt, the regret.

Dad looks at me, eyes full of words he won't say. Instead, he says,

"in the rain-
darkness, the sunset
being sheathed i sit and
think of you."

I scrunch my brow at the poem. It's E. E. Cummings. But Dad rarely quotes Cummings. Then I know. "Jacob said that to you about me?"

He touches my cheek, and I try to smile. He wants to talk about Jacob, and I have to oblige him. Sylvia was right. Jacob has come to mean something to him. And I can listen.

"I don't know it. Can you recite it to me?"

Instead, Dad reaches over and grabs one of the many books we brought for him.

"I know you gave Jacob some of your favorite books. He's cherished them."

Dad smiles proudly as he hands me a book opened to the poem. I read silently. I touch my hand to my mouth to cover the smile that has grown across my face as I take in comprehension of the poem.

He places his hand over mine.

"And you're okay with this?" I ask.

He holds his eyes tight on me, raising his brows.

I know what he wants me to do, to admit. And I realize I have not said it out loud. That I love Jacob, have been in love with him for months.

"Yes, I feel the same way. I really like him."

He looks over the top of his glasses at me. His glare questioning.

"No, you're right," I say sheepishly. "I'm in love with him."

He nods, smiling.

"Gather ye rose-buds while ye may,
Old Time is still a-flying;
And this same flower that smiles today
Tomorrow will be dying."

He pulls me into a hug, and after a moment, I pull back.
"I know, Dad. I know. But…"
He places a finger gently against my lips.

"Be still, be still, what can be said?
My father sang that song,
But time amends old wrong,
And all that is finished, let it fade."

"Dad," I say, his name once more a plea against what he is asking.

"Stop this day and night with me and you shall possess the origin
of all poems,
You shall possess the good of the earth and sun, (there are
millions of suns left,)
You shall no longer take things at second or third hand, nor
look through the eyes of the dead, nor feed on the spectres
in books,
You shall not look through my eyes either, nor take things from me,
You shall listen to all sides and filter them from your self."

———

The nurses politely yet sternly tell us to go home for a few hours. It has taken all of our strength to get through these days, our bones sore from too many hours perched on uncomfortable furniture, so we don't fight.

Hours later and after a long nap and a shower, we return to the hospital. As we approach Dad's room, Alana releases my hand and takes off running. Jacob moves into my line of vision and scoops her up in his arms.

Once again, and as always, he has come for us.

I watch him hold Alana tight against him with one arm and reach out to Sylvia with the other one, pulling her into him, all while never taking his eyes off me. Alana's head is planted on his shoulder, her arms wrapped around his neck as he whispers something into Sylvia's ear. She kisses him on the cheek before turning to look at me. Jacob eases Alana back to the ground, and Sylvia takes her into Dad's room.

I don't ask how he knew to come. Sylvia. She knows what I need and makes no apologies for the forcing of her will. All summer she prevented me from capsizing, balancing me when I listed hard in one direction or the other, or was too afraid to row across the difficult waters. She knows what I need, and I need Jacob.

I look up at him and instantly forget why I am angry with him. It doesn't matter anymore. Here is the man I love. Whom I am in love with. The breaking of a promise he should have never had to make isn't going to change that. Nothing will. And I wonder how it's possible to feel such debilitating sadness and an explosion of love at the same time.

"You can still be mad at me and let me hold you," he says, holding his arms out to me, bracing himself against his own hope. He looks slightly disheveled, his clothes wrinkled and slouched after a long day of wear, his chin and jaw dusted with a day's worth of stubble.

I walk my head into his chest and cry. He envelops me and places his mouth in my hair while rubbing small circles around my back, the warmth of his whole hand comforting. In that instant, the deafening clamor quiets, and I am glad he came. So much has been collecting within me; a cloud of exhaustion gathers around me, pulling me into a daze as I melt deeper into his arms.

After a while, he asks, his voice as light and delicate as a cloud, "How is he?"

I shrug and tell him that the seizures have stopped, and they are monitoring him. I say it all to his chest through a series of sobs.

"What can I do?" he asks. "Tell me what to do."

"You're doing it."

We stand together for a full minute before Jacob moves us to a pair of seats by a window. Outside, dark shadows form as the sun begins its descent in the west. He pulls me close to him, his arm across my shoulders, my forehead pressing the skin of his neck, the delicate pulse of his vein jumping. He smells so good, feels so good, and I want to fold myself into him. In his arms, all is not lost.

"There are a few things I need to tell you," he whispers into my hair, pausing for a long moment, his chin brushing the top of my head. I feel him sigh softly before his tone turns serious. "Daniel is out. And he's here. Five floors up."

I nod. "Okay."

"Sara…did you hear me? Daniel is here. Birdie is here. In this hospital. Right now."

I look up at him beneath wet eyes and ask, "How is he? Daniel?"

Jacob's Adam's apple rises and falls as he swallows hard and shakes his head, the move slight.

"I'm sorry. I'm so sorry," I say as I watch a range of emotions dance across his features. "What can I do?"

He runs a finger down my damp cheek. "You're doing it."

"Are you okay?" I ask, remembering Jacob's denial, his brokenness from a few days ago.

"I'm dealing with it," he says, looking at me with a resolved sadness. "I've been watching him live."

"You don't have to be here. I don't want you to have to choose between us or them. They are your family."

"You, Alana, Sylvia, and Hosea are my family too."

We hold each other tighter as the rain splashes off the windows and thunder rumbles across the sky not yet dark as we both sit in the knowledge that two people we love may never leave this hospital. We are two halves, perfectly connected, who fit inside one another, our lives mirroring the other's. We are the same, share the same hurt, the same pain. We have given so much to each other these last few months, it was appropriate for us to be together at the end.

"Sara," Jacob says. "There's something else I need to tell you." He pulls away and takes two envelopes out of his bag. "My father left instructions in his will to financially provide for you and your father. I went into the bookstore when I came home not only to apologize on behalf of my family but to give him the money. This"—he holds up one envelope—"is the paperwork. We used some of it to renovate the bookstore, but there's quite a bit left. You'll never have to worry about money again. There will always be enough."

"What?" I take the envelope out of his hand and open it. My eyes scan through the wall of words, the legal jargon, and rest on a number with a series of commas and zeros that stretch the page, and Tom Wyler's signature on the bottom.

"I tried to tell you when I offered to help you financially with Alana. When you stopped me, I didn't want you to think that money was the only reason why I wanted to help."

"Why are you telling me now?" I ask. But I know the answer.

"You were underage when my dad made this will, so he put everything in Hosea's name. This all transfers to you when…"

"Why? Why did he do this for us?"

"I don't know, but it's absolutely something he would do."

"I can't take this," I say, attempting to refold the thick

group of papers and stuff them back into the envelope. "It's too much."

"Yes, you can. It's already done."

I shake my head and open my mouth to protest again, but Jacob interrupts me.

"It's not charity. It's money for private school for Alana, for a host of tutors she's going to need, for an Ivy League education, money for grad and post-graduate degrees. Whatever she needs. Whatever you need."

I sit silent, comprehending this generous gift, when Jacob begins to speak again. "There's something else." He hands me the other envelope. This one thinner. "This is from Hosea."

Taking a sharp breath, I look at him, his words barely registering as if they've lost meaning. "What?"

"He wanted you to have this."

I take the envelope and open it, one single piece of paper. At the top, I see my name and at the bottom Dad's signature. In between, there are words, sentences, a letter. Not poetry.

I shake my head. "My father did not write this. He doesn't write."

"He didn't. I did."

I blink. "I don't understand."

"When I first started meeting with him, he told me that he wanted to find a way to talk to you. It took a while for me to understand what he wanted. He recited the poems, and I deciphered them, studying the meaning and forming them into this letter. It took a few drafts before he approved, but this is what he wants to say to you."

"You did that? This must have taken you months."

"I had time, and Hosea was an excellent teacher."

I try to swallow, but the back of my throat is dry. "I don't know what to say. I can't believe you did this."

"I assumed he would mail it to you, but you came home. Now...I know he wants you to have this before he..." He stops. "And I promised him I would give it to you."

I look at the letter again and think of Dad lying in his hospital bed, the end sooner than later, and now know why Dad wanted Jacob at the hospital. The tears rise up again, the pain sharp and real, the scowl of a deep burn.

"Sara...I need to..." Jacob gestures his head toward the elevator. "But, I want to apologize for breaking my promise. I'm so sorry."

"There's nothing for you to be sorry about. I should have never asked you to choose between me and your family."

"In the process of writing that letter, I learned so much about poetry, love, and you. I often asked myself why I didn't leave when I first saw you working in the bookstore. Now I know it's because I had already started to fall in love with you before I even knew you."

There is so much I want to say to him, need to say, but all at once, I feel overwhelmed by Tom's gift, Dad's letter heavy in my hands, and Jacob's face, vulnerable and beautiful. I brush tears from my cheeks and sniff. "Jacob...can we talk about this later?"

He nods his understanding, but it's forced, his features strained, his eyes brimming with words he can't say. A tinge of sadness gathers around him like a cloud that pains me. I hear him say that he'll be back in a few hours before he stands and takes my hands into his, kissing them before walking toward the elevator.

I turn Dad's letter in my hands as Jacob walks away from me, the distance between us expanding, and my self-pity-induced haze lifts just a bit, enough for me to realize what I hold and what is walking away from me. For so long, I wanted my father to speak to me, to use a voice he lost years ago. Now, in my hands, I hold everything I wanted, the words I've longed to hear. Jacob gave me that.

"Jacob...wait." When he turns, I'm already at him, in his arms, kissing him, thanking him for these gifts, for his presence these last few months. His arms close around me, tight, his mouth smothering my words.

"I love you," I say, pulling back to look at him, touching his face as if he were not there, as if he could disappear at any moment. It isn't the right moment for such words. But they are important. They need to be said and heard. I want to feel them, for him to feel them, the heaviness of them, right then, a momentary comfort to outweigh and lessen the pain we both face.

"I love you too," he says, lifting me off the ground and burying his face into the crook of my neck, our bodies swaying with movement.

He would stay if I asked, so I don't. Instead, I close my eyes for a moment, exhaling, willing my pulse to slow as I watch him press the "Up" elevator button and disappear behind the doors. I return to the quiet spot next to a large bay window and listen to the drum of raindrops tapping the window before opening the envelope and unfolding the letter. I run my hands across the page and begin to read.

JACOB

———

SEVERAL HOURS LATER, I'M staring out the window, my entire body still buzzing from holding Sara, from her admittance that she loves me, that no matter the heartaches we both immediately face, we would weather them together in a future that would completely belong to us. In Daniel's room, we continue our careful ballet, delicately moving around each other after receiving the news we all suspected from Dr. Bennett—there's nothing more he can do—until Daniel clears his throat. I look at him and something unspoken passes between us, an understanding, that pulls at my heart. There is nothing left but the truth. No way to avoid it. I watch him gather himself.

"Birdie," Daniel says, pausing. She's perched on the orange chair next to his bed. She's been quiet, absentmindedly watching the local news, her face locked in a trance.

Birdie is up and at him. "Do you need something? I can call a nurse." Daniel's prognosis has pushed her into a rare place. There's no one to call. No favors to ask. Death is the one thing money and influence cannot fix.

She reaches for the call button, but Daniel places his hand on her arm. "No, there's something I need to tell you."

Birdie eases back into her chair as Daniel continues. "I can't leave this earth without…without…" He stops, unable to finish his sentence, his jaw quivering.

Birdie's eyes squint. "What is it? What's wrong?"

"It's about Sara and what happened."

She blinks as Daniel continues. He draws in a deep breath that gets caught in the back of this throat and turns into a cough. Marsha hands him a tissue and adjusts the pillows behind his back, pushing him upright. I relax my forearms on my knees and lower my head.

He looks at me again and I give him a reassuring nod that Birdie notices.

"What's going on?"

"I did it, Birdie. I raped her."

Confusion registers across her face as she processes the words, the truth she has long denied. But she dismisses them, shaking her head as if it could shudder away the truth, like a fly. "No. I know you only said that for the interview. It's fine, honey. Don't you worry about that anymore. It's over. It's all over now."

Daniel looks at Birdie with an expression heavy with sorrow. "I did it, Birdie. I did. I was drunk. I was grieving Naomi. I didn't know how to do that. All of the things you taught us, you never taught us how to grieve."

Daniel didn't plan to say this, and as soon as he does, he realizes his mistake, but it's too late.

"Not you too." She looks at Daniel but points a finger at me. "First, your brother comes home and accuses me of being a horrible mother, and now you blame me for not teaching you how to grieve?"

"None of this is your fault," Daniel says. "The fault is all mine."

"Why are you doing this? Why are you saying this now?"

"Because…because…Sara got pregnant," Daniel says, pushing the words out with anguish and shame all over his face. "She had a baby, a daughter."

Birdie is silent for a second; then a hearty, manic laugh erupts from deep inside her. "A daughter? That girl has a daughter," she says, as if the notion is ridiculous. "Is this some kind of a joke?"

"Yes, a daughter," Daniel says, his voice tender, almost a whisper. "Your granddaughter."

Birdie continues to laugh, but it soon fades as she looks at Daniel and then to me for confirmation, even to Marsha, all of our heads bowed.

She walks over to me, her entire body tense. Until then, I have never seen Birdie look so lost, so uncertain, so unsure of herself, as comprehension washes over her. "Is it true?" she asks, her voice strained, her face shifting in emotions with every blink.

I nod, the slightest of movements. "She's eight."

"Eight?" Birdie says repeatedly, her mind calculating, doing the math. "Eight."

The room falls silent as the realization, the truth, wraps itself around Birdie. In the hallway, two people are talking as they pass Daniel's room. A few seconds later, a cart with a squeaking wheel echoes down the hall. Finally, Birdie breaks the quiet, asking Daniel, "How long have you known?"

"I found out a few weeks ago."

She then turns to me, her eyes silently asking the same question.

I sigh. "Four months."

"Have…have you met her?"

I nod as Marsha steps closer to Birdie. "I've met her too. She's wonderful."

Birdie crosses her arms, holding herself tight, shaking her head emphatically. "So you all have known the truth and no one thought to tell me?"

"I found out by accident," I say. "She…Sara never meant to ever tell any of us. We were never supposed to know."

"That little bitch," Birdie says.

I jerk upright. "Wait a minute."

She snickers to herself and shakes her head. "She just stood there and didn't say a word."

"What are you talking about?"

"I went to see her. After we visited Naomi's grave."

"You did what?" I ask, my voice rising. My mind flips back to the days after the anniversary of Naomi's death, the same day that the bookstore's windows were broken, the same day we kissed for the first time, the same day we admitted that we needed each other. Sara never said a word about Birdie's coming by.

Marsha stands, equally between Birdie and me, the palms of her hands flat to the ground as if pushing something down. "Let's all calm down."

But it's too late for calm. I want answers. "Why did you go see Sara?"

"I wanted to look her in the eye. Let her know the damage she's caused."

"Damage? The damage *she's* caused? What about the damage we've done to her?"

Birdie narrows her eyes at me. "She threw your brother in prison! She ruined this family!"

"He did it, Birdie! He did it! And there's proof. She got pregnant! She didn't ruin our family. She was a victim to it."

Birdie exhales sharply, straightens her shirt, and pats her hair in various places, rearranging herself back into the woman she's always been, the mother of my youth. It angered me to think of this woman being a grandmother to Alana. "I want to see her. I want to see my granddaughter."

"No," I say quickly. "Absolutely not."

"No?" Birdie repeats, her head drawn back. "Why not? Everyone else has. You all have kept her from me. Why can't I meet her?"

"Would it be so bad for her to meet Alana?" Marsha asks.

"Alana?" Birdie asks.

"That's her name," Marsha says. "Alana."

"Well...I would like to meet Alana."

"That's not our choice," I say.

"And whose choice is it? That girl's?" Birdie spits out the last word.

"Sara. Her name is Sara. Not 'that girl.' Sara. And yes. It's her choice. Not ours."

"What does *Sara*," she says, drawing out the syllables of her name, "know about good choices? She got drunk at a party. Excuse me while I question her choices."

"She managed to raise a genius child and hid her from the world all because she didn't want you in her life!"

Birdie opens her mouth to speak, but words fail to materialize. "Genius? My granddaughter is a genius?" She turns and looks at Daniel, who nods. "How do you know for sure?"

"She was the person who corrected the *Mathematica* exhibit a few months ago."

Birdie brightens as if a light bulb turned on over her head. "That was her?"

"Yes."

"Ever more the reason why I need to meet her. That girl is not equipped to handle a mentally brilliant child." Her words come quick. In Alana's existence, her genius, Birdie saw a new opportunity, a new purpose, and grabbed at a lifeline unexpectedly given to her. "She needs to be with us. Be in the best schools. Have access to the best tutors. She's the next generation of Wylers."

"Sara told me that we didn't deserve to have Alana in our lives. She was right. Not with our track record. We've taken so much from her," I say.

"Your brother is dying. Was that the plan? Let him die without him knowing that he had a daughter? Let me die without knowing I had a granddaughter?"

"I don't know. But that would have been her choice. And we would have had to accept it."

"Don't you understand…she could change the world."

"Maybe. Probably, but it's not for us to decide. She's going to have a normal life."

"A normal life? You of all people know that's not possible."

"It is for her. We are going to make that possible for her."

"We?"

"Me and Sara." I look at Marsha and then Daniel. "I'm in love with her."

Birdie releases a scornful laugh once again. "You're in love with her? Wait…she's the woman you've been seeing? Her?"

"Yes."

"Where did I go wrong with you? You hate me that much. You hate being in this family so much that you would shack up with that girl. After everything she's done to this family. I…"

"Stop it!" Daniel's weak voice booms around the room. "Just stop it."

The room falls silent except for the beeping of machines. Birdie and Marsha walk to Daniel's bed, one on each side.

"Daniel…honey…don't you want to see your daughter?"

"No," he says. "We lost the right to be in her life. We have to own that. Just as you have to own that I raped Sara. Alana is a consequence of my sin, my crime."

Birdie sits down in the chair next to Daniel's bed. "She's our blood."

"It's enough for me to know that Jacob knows her, loves her, and she loves him, that he will be there for her. She's going to be fine without us," Daniel says.

"I can't take back what I did to her," Birdie says. "It's done now."

"We can't take it back. But we can atone for it," I say. "We can let her go. We can let her choose."

Birdie grabs her purse and yanks open the door. I think of Sara and Alana a few floors below us and follow behind her. In the hallway, I almost run into the back of her.

She's frozen, her body locked, unmoving. I don't have time to wonder why she suddenly stopped. Why her stern face slowly dissipates as she kneels to the level of the person in front of her, her hand extended down to the floor for balance.

I know what Birdie sees, the glints of brown specks sparkling in her green eyes, the same ones she sees in mine, in Daniel's, as she pieces together what I already know.

The little girl standing before her could be her daughter.

Birdie grabs her chest as the air leaves her body.

SARA

———

THE ELEVATOR DOORS OPEN to a long hallway that stretches the length of the floor, its white tile floors shiny and reflective. It is the vision from my dream. And I knew I was doing the right thing. Every decision I have made has led me here, to the place where I would untether myself from a long and painful past.

Alana will never stop asking about Daniel. Just as I never stopped asking Dad to talk to me. She will have Jacob, an unexpected father figure literally the spitting image of her father, but he isn't Daniel. He has always been a puzzle to her, and until that puzzle is solved, she will never fully be satisfied. I don't want Daniel to become a ghost for her like he's been for me, a figment of her imagination that was once real and is now not, a being that would haunt her for the rest of her life. Dad placed Jacob in charge of my closure in the event of his death. In that, I realize, I am in charge of Alana's closure with Daniel. Before it's too late.

Alana is quiet as we navigate the hallway, gripping my hand tight, as I look at the patient names on the dry-erase boards on the walls next to the rooms. When I told her where we were going, she smiled wide, and an air of nervousness surrounded her. She has asked about Daniel and Birdie so much, and now the day she would meet them had arrived. I think about Alana's obsession with time as we walk. I've always been aware of it, as she has, its steady pace in our lives, the invisible force that moves us. There is no stopping time for an extra ten seconds. No matter how hard you try. But just like all of the watches Alana mysteriously breaks, there's something deep inside you that cannot be explained. It just is. To me, that's time.

We freeze as a door to a room we had not yet reached suddenly swings open, and Birdie storms out immediately followed by Jacob. Birdie freezes, the shock of us standing in front of her rendering her still, before her knees buckle and shake. She lowers herself to avoid falling, kneeling slowly, using her arm to balance herself, as if the floor would give way. Jacob's eyes travel to Birdie and back to me before stepping in front of Birdie, standing as a solid barrier, like a shield, between us.

"What are you doing here?" Jacob says. His face is a map of concern.

I touch his shoulder and look into his eyes and know that I made the perfect choice with my heart. That one day, I would marry this beautiful man and he would be a great father to our children, to Alana. That we would love each other for the rest of our lives. "It's okay."

"Are you sure?" he asks, his eyes scanning my face for an inkling of doubt. If I say no, I know he would burrow a hole through the floor for us to escape. But I've run too many miles for too long. I have reached my destination. I'm exactly where I want to be.

I look at Alana. Summoning the last ounce of courage, I release her hand, aware of the notion that in a moment's time, everything will change.

Life hurts. The truth about her, her father, one day, will hurt. That day will come. And when it does, I will acknowledge her pain. And we will sit in it together. Then I will tell her the most honest and powerful truth I have, that I now know, and have never doubted: that she is and has always been loved.

Alana walks toward Birdie but stops and looks at me. Jacob moves to my side and holds my hand tight. His palms are sweaty as are mine. I smile at Alana. She takes a tiny breath and continues walking.

Birdie is hypnotized by what I imagine seems like the ghost of her dead daughter standing before her. Her eyes travel the length of her, studying, cataloging, Alana's and by extension Naomi's features, her face neither a smile nor a frown but a straight line of concentration as she takes her in.

"Are you my grandmother?"

Birdie nods. "Yes, I'm your grandma Birdie."

Alana twists her full lips and shifts her bony hips. "Your name is Birdie?"

"It's short for Bernadette."

"Birdie is much cooler," Alana says with a giggle.

Birdie laughs. "I guess it is."

"Jacob says that you have a big garden. I have a garden too." Alana throws a shoulder before raising it and dropping it again. "Maybe...maybe you could come see it sometime."

Birdie hesitates for a moment before looking at me, then back at Alana. "I would love to," she says, raising a hand to Alana's hair, rubbing a golden strand between two fingers.

"Jacob says I have hair like my Aunt Naomi and that I look like her. He says that I wiggle my nose like her too, but I don't think I do."

Birdie laughs again, but then her face crumples, the corners of her mouth drooping, her lips quivering. It's not easy to cry. Especially when the act is as foreign to your body as poison. Birdie doesn't cry. Until she is faced with everything she lost. Until she is faced with something she can't run from, intimidate, or throw money at. Until she is faced with the innocence of a granddaughter she never knew existed, delighting in her grandmother's name. Birdie buries her face into her hands, the wailed sound of her cry muffled by her cupped fingers, the prolonged tears for her daughter and husband streaming down her face. The pain is visceral. She's remembering everything, releasing everything she held so tight for so long.

I look at Jacob, and he's mesmerized by the sight before

him. He releases my hand and starts to take a step toward them when Alana lifts Birdie's lowered gaze, her forefinger to her chin and says, "It's okay." She dabs her nose once, just as Jacob did to her, before she walks into her and wraps her small arms around Birdie's neck. Birdie's arms hang awkwardly, all elbows and angles, like an unmanned marionette, before finally enclosing around Alana.

Jacob helps Birdie to her feet, staring at her with a look of disbelief and love. He is a little boy again, the boy in the picture I saw at the cottage, before death and grief ripped him apart. He opens his arms and pulls Birdie into his chest. She lays her head on it and wraps her arms around his waist. "My baby," she says into his chest. And I know she isn't talking about the child holding her or the first child she lost, but the next one she will lose. It would be soon enough. The remaining Wylers. Jacob told me once that they were a broken family of five, divided by two, remainder of one. Now, plus one, Alana. They *were* once, he said. And would be again, as hope stands in front of them.

Birdie releases Jacob, and they both walk to me. Birdie's made-up face streaked with mascara and tears. "Thank you," she says, her eyes yet again filling. "I'm...I'm..." The words seem stuck inside her. Words that I'm sure she never thought she would say to me. "I'm sorry."

I have waited so long to hear those words. And now that I have, I realize I never needed to hear them. The war we have been fighting has been a long one, unnecessary, claiming too many victims. There are no winners. No losers. Just survivors left with raw wounds and scarred with the memory of battles we never wanted to fight.

"After you came and visited me, I realized something," I say. "We're not that different, you and me. Just two mothers who would go to any lengths to protect their children. Whether it's right or wrong."

I extend my hand. She looks at it, unsure. "We don't have to be enemies."

She looks at my hand again, then pulls me into a hug.

The groaning of a door sounds as Alana pushes open the door to Daniel's room. From the doorway, I see Daniel lying in the bed and Marsha sitting in a chair next to him. They both turn toward the door, their expressions wide as they register what is happening.

Jacob is behind Alana as she steps inside. I'm close behind but I do not enter the room. It is the furthest I go, the length of my forgiveness. Daniel and I find each other's eyes. He lowers his head, nodding once, a thank you and an apology equally. And it's enough for me. Forgiveness, I've learned, is like a door. You can open yourself up to it or close yourself off from it at any time. We can't rewrite history or change the outcome. Life is a series of choices. And we live in and with those choices we make.

Alana takes a few steps inside, her tiny body swallowed up by the vastness of the room, and says, "Are you my dad?"

"I am."

Without hesitation, she climbs up the side of the bed. Shocked by her bravery, Daniel quickly makes room for her, shifting his body to the side and smoothing the wrinkled sheets, as she settles in a space next to him.

They stare at each other for a moment, taking each other in. Matching green eyes and skin the color of wet sand. Father and daughter. The same but very much different.

She looks down at her wrist, then back at him, and asks, "Can you wear a watch?"

POEMS

"Song of the Open Road"—Walt Whitman

"The Tyger"—William Blake

"I Thought of You"—Sara Teasdale

"Sonnet 140"—William Shakespeare

"A Clear Midnight"—Walt Whitman

"Something Left Undone"—Henry Wadsworth Longfellow

"A Prayer for My Daughter"—William Butler Yeats

"My Little March Girl"—Paul Laurence Dunbar

"The Mountain Sat Upon the Plain"—Emily Dickinson

"The Song of Wandering Aengus"—William Butler Yeats

"Jabberwocky"—Lewis Carroll

"Stopping by Woods on a Snowy Evening"—Robert Frost

"Continent's End"—Robinson Jeffers

"Forgiveness"—George MacDonald

"O Me! O Life!"—Walt Whitman

"To the Virgins, to Make Much of Time"—Robert Herrick

"In Memoriam A.H.H."—Alfred Lord Tennyson

"i like my body when it is with your"—**E. E. Cummings**

"A Psalm of Life"—**Henry Wadsworth Longfellow**

"The Lake Isle of Innisfree"—**William Butler Yeats**

"Three Marching Songs"—**William Butler Yeats**

"Song of Myself"—**Walt Whitman**

"in the rain"—**E. E. Cummings**

"When All Is Done"—**Paul Laurence Dunbar**

"The Wanderings of Oisin"—**William Butler Yeats**

"The Cloud-Islands"—**Clark Ashton Smith**

"love is more thicker than forget"—**E. E. Cummings**

"Hymn to the North Star"—**William Cullen Bryant**

"Give Me the Splendid Silent Sun"—**Walt Whitman**

"The Young Man's Song"—**William Butler Yeats**

"If"—**Rudyard Kipling**

"Character of the Happy Warrior"—**William Wordsworth**

READING GROUP GUIDE

1. Poetry plays an important role throughout the book. Why do you think Sara's father only speaks in poetry? Do you think poetry has the ability to communicate more than simple words can?

2. Throughout the book, Jacob struggles to forgive his brother. Some say family should always be forgiven, no matter the transgression. Do you believe there are some things that cannot or should not be forgiven?

3. Do you believe you can still truly love someone even if you can't forgive them for their past actions?

4. Do you think Daniel deserved to know of Alana's existence? Did Sara have an obligation to tell him he had a daughter?

5. In the United States, no federal law explicitly restricts the parental rights of men who father a child through rape,

meaning, depending on the individual state's law, the man or his family could petition for visitation or even custody of the child. Do you think this is fair or just?

6. Why do you think Birdie cannot or will not accept what Daniel did, even after he explicitly admits to her that he raped Sara?

7. Do you agree with Jacob's decision to reveal Sara's secret to Daniel despite his having promised her he wouldn't?

8. The love of a mother for her child is often described as an impossible love. In what ways does this play out for Sara? For Birdie?

9. Homemade Pizza Fridays are an important tradition for Sara's family. What was your favorite family tradition as a child? Did that tradition carry through to the present?

10. In a conversation between Jacob and Daniel, Jacob asks if Daniel thinks love is worth walking away from family for if they're unaccepting of the relationship. Do you think it is?

11. On one Pizza Friday, Sylvia poses a question: "Would you rather be able to reverse one decision you make every day or be able to stop time for ten seconds every day?" What would your answer be?

A CONVERSATION WITH THE AUTHOR

What inspired you to write *One Summer in Savannah*?

Inspiration for *One Summer in Savannah* stems from the 2015 Emanuel African Methodist Episcopal Church shooting. Days after that terrible tragedy, some of the survivors and relatives of those killed walked into a South Carolina courtroom and forgave the shooter. At that moment, I realized I knew nothing about forgiveness. I assumed that there were crimes, acts, that were unforgivable. But when they forgave him, they challenged me to look inward and create my own definition of forgiveness, and I knew then that I wanted to explore that by writing a book that challenged readers on what they believe is or is not forgivable.

One Summer in Savannah is also inspired by the #MeToo movement and all of the brave women who have stepped forward after years, decades, and who spoke their truth and shared their stories with the world.

How did you come up with the characters Sara and Jacob? Did the characters come first? Or the plot?

The plot, always. I know what my story is about, the overall theme, and how it ends before I write one word. Once I have the plot, the characters start to come alive. *One Summer in Savannah* has always been Sara's story to tell, but as I began to write, I realized that I was missing an entire side of the story. That's where Jacob comes in. Jacob's perspective allows the reader to see and understand the complete picture.

Where did the idea for Hosea only speaking in poems come from? How did you go about finding the perfect poem every time to serve as Hosea's dialogue?

I love poetry, and I knew that I wanted to somehow incorporate it into this book. From the beginning, I wanted Hosea to communicate to the world differently. Hosea's character is loosely based on my grandfather, who suffered a stroke and lost his ability to speak. But that didn't stop him from finding a way to communicate with us and for us to learn how to understand him. In Hosea's case, why not use poetry as his way of communicating?

Originally, I had most of his dialogue as poems, but as I began to write, the poems took over entirely. I thought my early readers would have a problem with it or difficulties understanding him, but they didn't. In fact, they loved it! All the poems in Hosea's dialogue are in the public domain, so that played a huge part in the selection. But like Hosea, I'm a fan of Whitman, Yates, Angelou, Cummings, and Dunbar.

Why did you decide to place this story in Savannah? What do you love about Savannah?

The decision to place *One Summer in Savannah* in Savannah came from Jacob's cottage, based on a real cottage I saw for sale on Hird Island. I knew immediately that's where Jacob would live, and because of that, I based the entire story in Savannah.

I could live in Forsyth Park! I also love the antebellum architecture and cobblestone streets.

What do you think is next for Sara, Jacob, and Alana?

I wrote a somewhat happy epilogue (a letter Alana wrote to Birdie) but decided not to include it. I'm drawn to (and write) stories with bittersweet endings and didn't want to wrap *One Summer in Savannah* up in a cute bow. It just would not have been fair to the topic. As Sara says, life is hard and so will their life be moving forward. Unfortunately, their happy ending is not immediate. Yes, Sara and Jacob decided to be together, but they still face obstacles. First, they will mourn the deaths of Hosea and Daniel. Next, they will have to find a way to incorporate Birdie into their lives after so many years of strife between them while balancing how to handle Alana's genius.

Years later, they will find their footing and that eventual place of contentment. I envision Sara and Jacob having their own child, another girl, another genius. This time, pregnancy will be much more fulfilling for Sara. I also see Jacob finally embracing his desire to teach, but two of his students will be Alana and his daughter. As for Alana, she will solve the equation by the time she's sixteen. Solving it leads to the definition of time, a subject that has always captivated her. Fame doesn't change her because Sara and Jacob have allowed her to be a normal girl. Oh...and she still loves to swim!

What was your path to becoming a writer?

I knew early on that I wanted to be a writer. When I was younger, I had always written poems and stories, but my love for writing materialized in Julie Cook's sixth-grade class. Back then, we had a period called DEAR, Drop Everything and Read. But Mrs. Cook also allowed us to write. So, I did and wrote my first book, *The Class Party*. I wrote for my college newspaper and spent decades as a freelance writer. But it wasn't until a few years ago that I decided to try my hand at writing novels.

What is your writing process like?

I need absolute quiet so I can focus and turn inward. I spend a lot of time in my head, so I need to work without distractions—my characters demand it. Before I begin a new book, I need to know how it ends. Once I have that worked out, I write the beginning and go from there. I don't write linearly. I write whatever scene comes to me that day, then I put all the scenes together.

I handwrite most of my books. I can't explain it, but the

words flow better that way. I have stacks of notebooks, but I prefer to write on scrap pieces of paper with a dully sharpened pencil. I work full-time, so I try to handwrite about five hundred words a day during the week and a few thousand on the weekends. I write in my car on my lunch breaks or at stoplights.

What are some of the books that have influenced or inspired your own writing?

I consider *As I Lay Dying* by William Faulkner a literary masterpiece, and its influence is the basis for my next book, a family drama centered on the death of the patriarch. *Everything I Never Told You* by Celeste Ng is the perfect execution of third-person omniscient present and the blending of multiple POVs and also serves as inspiration for my next book.

I've been obsessed with reading my entire life, and when I'm not writing, I read approximately a hundred books per year. I enjoy reading widely across all genres and can honestly say I find inspiration in almost everything I read. Whether it's a character trait or word choice or sentence structure. Working as a librarian in charge of collection development, I'm responsible for selecting and purchasing all the adult material for my libraries. This job (which I absolutely LOVE!) keeps me apprised of new books and allows me access to them.

ACKNOWLEDGMENTS

I'm a simple girl. A girl who loves baseball, books, and writing. A girl from Tamms, Illinois, population 800. More than anything, I am a dreamer. This book is for the dreamers. For those who imagine something more. For those who look at the world and think why not? For the dreamers in small towns with one stoplight, with one school, kindergarten through twelfth grade.

This book is for my first friends at my own K–12 school, Egyptian. Riki, Terra, Farrah, Jean, Kara, Crystal, Trish, Julie, Christy, Kristen, Norlisha, and the late Jarod, you walked with me on those dirt roads, created dance routines with me at sleepovers, and laughed with me in class. For Rachel Wilson, Chad Vinson, and Anthony (Tank) Pruden, who filled my youth with laughter and fun. You helped craft a childhood that gave my mind the space to create stories and fill them with bold and bright characters. Though distance separates us now, I often turn back to our time and remember it fondly.

A special thank you to my second family, LaDonn, Michelle, Danece, and Tiffiny. Love you guys!

For Julie Cook, my sixth-grade teacher, who encouraged me to write all those years ago, who looked at the girl with big pink glasses and saw her future. This book would not be possible without you.

For Erin McClary, my editor, my angel, who shined a light on me during one of the darkest times of my life. You will never know how much that phone call lifted my spirits. Thank you for being a champion for this book, for seeing the beauty in such an emotional story, and for making my dreams come true. Thank you for changing my life. A huge thanks to the entire team at Sourcebooks for bringing this book into fruition.

For Abby Saul, my brilliant agent, who, after a few minutes, I knew was the perfect agent for me. Thank you for your unwavering endorsement of my work and for your keen insight into what I needed to make it better. Thank you for pulling me along and for never letting me fall. I am grateful for your energy and dedication and for your ability to always know what to say and your capability to return emails seconds after I send them. For Team Lark, my fellow agent siblings: Tony, Brianna, Elle, Kris, Meredith, Daisy, and Mindy. Thank you for accepting me into the club, for the encouragement, and for lively chats on WhatsApp! Thanks to Jason Powell for being an enthusiastic reader for my work and for being an overall awesome guy.

For Kristin Thiel, my editor, friend, and therapist, who makes my writing sing. Thank you for the tough edits and for never being afraid to challenge me to dig deeper. Thank you for listening to me whine after writing my first book and pushing me to write a second one. I am a better writer because of you, and I cannot imagine writing a book without you.

For three of my favorite writers who pushed me across the finish line. For David Howard, who has nurtured my writing career from the shadows and offered advice and friendship over the past decade. Thank you for always being an email away. For Mateo Askaripour, who encouraged me in the early days of querying and rejection. Thank you for being such an encouraging champion for writers. For Kim Michele Richardson, who urged me to stay true to myself and always fight for what I believe in. Thank you for that fun and insightful two-hour phone call and for the baculum bone. Ha!

For Jocelyn Bates and Jennifer Bohmueller who offered unwavering encouragement during the drafting and query phases. Thank you for listening to me vent and whine and for your overall support and guidance. A very special and heartfelt thank you to the Tor House Foundation for their assistance in the use of Robinson Jeffers's "Continent's End."

For the team at the Dothan Houston County Library System: Chris Warren, Kristin North, Derrick Tiller, and Kaitlyn McAnulty, thank you for being such a fantastic group of people to work with. Thank you for your dedication and passion to serve others. A special thank you to Richard Danley for his astronomy expertise and who generously and patiently answered every one of my questions. You will always be one of my people.

For all the fearless librarians all over the world, making good trouble and fighting the good fight. Thank you for all the work that you do on the front lines and behind the scenes. Your patrons salute you. I salute you.

Note: I used several true inventions, discoveries, and programs as inspiration for Daniel's, Alana's, and Jacob's achievements. Daniel's Sustainability in Prisons Project was inspired by the Evergreen State College and Washington State Department of Corrections's project, and the flashlight he invented as a teenager was inspired by this article: https://www.smithsonianmag.com/innovation/this-flashlight-is-powered-by-the-touch-of-your-hand-180950226/. Daniel's computer program that detected breast cancer was influenced by MIT's Computer Science and Artificial Intelligence Laboratory (CSAIL) and Massachusetts General Hospital's model. Jacob's aurora borealis work on Poker Flat Research Range in Alaska is based on a NASA-funded experiment to understand how energy is transferred and dissipated during auroral displays. Lastly, Alana's correction of the Mathematica exhibit is loosely based on this article: https://www.washingtonpost.com/news/local/wp/2015/07/10/did-this-teen-spot-an-error-in-a-34-year-old-math-exhibit-at-a-boston-museum-not-exactly-but-hes-enjoying-the-ride/. I have taken liberties regarding these discoveries and achievements, including moving the Mathematica exhibit from the Museum of Science in Boston to Fernbank Science Center in Atlanta.

For the people who made an impact on my life and don't know it. For Dr. Matthew Ragan who saved my life and gave me so much energy and focus. I'm a different person now because of you. For Rose Maddox, one of my first Alabama friends. Thank you for being a true constant for me after all these years. For David Page, trainer extraordinaire and my spiritual adviser, thank you for pushing me and keeping me in shape and healthy all these years. I'm in the best shape of my life because of you and your constant insistence on living a healthy life. Four o'clock in the morning comes early, but the words and knowledge you drop on me fuels me the rest of the day. This is an incomplete list. There are more of you who deserve acknowledgment and appreciation. For those I missed, I thank you too. Please forgive your absence here, on the page, but know your influence is forever present within my heart.

For my friends who have encouraged and supported me. For Everlie Bolton, my dear friend, who cheered me along the way. Thank you for being an early reader and for your encouraging words about the book. Thank you for your passion and enthusiasm for life, libraries, and the world around you. The world needs more Everlies! For the late Evelyn Screws, who cheered me on when I had a nugget of an idea and when I turned that nugget into a draft. Thank you for being the first reader of this story and for encouraging me to see it through. I wish you were here to see this, but I know you are still encouraging me from the heavens. For Jennifer Harmonson, who started as my boss and later became one of my best friends. Thank you for always being a text away and for allowing me to vent about my book and the world around me. Thank you for being not only *my* champion but a champion for all people, especially those who don't look like you. Thank you for your early vote of confidence in this book, for being my loudest cheerleader, and for being one of my favorite people. And for Keturah Williams, who has played so many roles in my life, thank you for your loyalty and love. I can feel it from here.

For my two best friends, Sheneka Ezell and Kaslina Love Mosley, who hold me up, catch me when I fall, and breathe life into me. Sheneka, I'm in awe of you and the person you are. Throughout our friendship, I've watched you make a way out of no way, dig deep inside yourself, and keep going. You are such an inspiration to me. Kaslina, your infectious attitude and positivity never cease to amaze me. You lift my soul and pour life into my bones. One call from you and I'm ready to conquer the world. I can't imagine my life without you guys.

For the Griffin/Harris (Eddie, Mary, Teasa, George, Jamal, Tiffany, Aunt Jean, and Tiffany) family, who welcomed me into your family all those years ago. Thank you for your love and support. There is never a dull day with you all, and I thank you for the laughter, color, and culture you've introduced into my life. And thank you for your understanding when I disappear for weeks and months to write. For Shelia, the sister I never had, thank you for being a shoulder to lean on. And a special thank you to Mamie for being the best mother-in-law a person could ask for.

For Alexis Shelton, my niece and sister, who has been with me every step of this long process, who requested her own paragraph on this acknowledgment page. Ha! Thank you for reading every word and for telling me what's working and what's not. Thank you for the insight on how to write dialogue for an eight-year-old girl. Thank you for your energy and passion for life. This book would not exist without you.

For my brothers, Adam and Ben Shelton, who have always been in my corner, even when I'm wrong, even though I can be stubborn. With Mom, it's always been the four of us, and I couldn't have wished for a better family, for two better brothers, for a better childhood. Thank you for always being there for me. Thank you for being my first best friends. Adam, thank you for being you, for your unwavering support and guidance, for your determination to be better to inspire others. Thanks Gayle for being such a great sister-in-law, for using your voice to call out all that's wrong in the world, and for being a passionate advocate for all people! Ben, thank you for your fierce protection, now and then. I know you would walk through fire for me. Thank you for being the father I never had. You are the best man I know.

For Jordan, my son and one of the best people I know. I have watched you grow from a vibrant three-year-old boy into a handsome, determined young man. Thank you for voting with me against your dad. We make a great team! I'm so proud of the man you have become. More.

For Leir Williams, my mother and best friend, the trailblazer in our long line of dreamers. Thank you for introducing me to God and His abundant love, for your unswerving faith in me and others, and for the abundance of love, wisdom, and knowledge you have infused in me. Thank you for teaching me the who behind the what and to always see the good in everything and everyone. You are the one who stops me from falling down and clean my knees when I do. Without you, there would be no me.

Lastly, for Jamel, who plays so many roles in my life. You are my protector, therapist, grill master, fellow adventurer, opener of things, keeper of secrets, but more importantly, my loving husband. But it's your love language for helping others that truly shows your character. Thank you for being the man who stops and helps people on the side of the road, who slings couches on his back, and who is always a phone call away from anyone who needs him. After eleven years of marriage, I am blessed to have such a handsome, supportive, and caring man. Thank you for knowing when I need to write and providing me with the space to do so. Thank you for listening to every book idea I have and for living with me and the characters while I write it. Thank you for never questioning my desire to travel to far-flung destinations and for always going with me. Your love makes me possible. More.

Finally, for the person who shall remain anonymous, who lived Sara's story and provided me with insight and knowledge, a heartfelt thank you for sharing your story with me. And for all the women who read this book and find pieces of themselves in Sara's story, thank you for your bravery, silent and loud, seen and unseen. I see you. The world sees you.

And now to the one without whom none of this would be possible. Thank you, God, for your light, wisdom, and understanding. Your grace powers me.

ABOUT THE AUTHOR

© Sarah Willis

Terah Shelton Harris is a collection development librarian and a freelance writer who now writes upmarket fiction with bittersweet endings. Her work has appeared in *Catapult*, *Women's Health*, *Every Day with Rachael Ray*, *Backpacker*, and more. Originally from Illinois, she now lives in Alabama with her husband, Jamel. Terah is a lover of life and spends most of her time reading or traveling. *One Summer in Savannah* is her first novel.